MELVILLE DAVISSON POST: MAN OF MANY MYSTERIES

Charles A. Norton

MELVILLE DAVISSON POST:
MAN OF MANY MYSTERIES

MELVILLE DAVISSON POST:
Man of Many Mysteries

Charles A. Norton

BOWLING GREEN UNIVERSITY POPULAR PRESS
BOWLING GREEN, OHIO 43403

*Barry College Library
Miami, Florida*

Copyright © 1973 by the Bowling Green University Popular Press, Ray B. Browne, Editor.

The Bowling Green University Popular Press is the publishing arm of the Center for the Study of Popular Culture, Ray B. Browne, Director.

Library of Congress Catalogue Card Number: 73-83359

ISBN: 0-87972-056-5 Cloth
       0-87972-060-3 Paperback

Printed in the United States of America.

Short quotations from the Post papers are used with the permission of the West Virginia University Library.

CONTENTS

ACKNOWLEDGMENTS   1

INTRODUCTION   3

I   BIOGRAPHY   7

II   THE RANDOLPH MASON STORIES   64

III   TWO NOVELS AND THE NAMELESS THING   87

IV   UNCLE ABNER   109

V   FOUR SHORT STORY COLLECTIONS   145

VI   THE NOVELETTES   175

VII   NONFICTION AND UNCOLLECTED WORK   195

VII   THE LAST STORIES   217

IX   A FINAL EVALUATION   229

NOTES   234

BIBLIOGRAPHY   246

INDEX OF TITLES   256

●●●●●●●●●

ACKNOWLEDGMENTS

Melville Davisson Post developed as the subject for this book because so little published information regarding him was generally available. Because of the cooperation and inspiration of a lengthy list of persons, many unfortunately not named below, that which seemed at first an almost impossible task proved not only possible but also a source of many pleasant encounters along the way to completion.

First, I should like to express my appreciation for the kind assistance allowed by Mr. Frank Atterholt, a nephew of Mr. Post, and Mrs. Robert Richie, a niece, both who graciously granted interviews and use of materials in their possession. Also, sincere thanks is due to Mr. John DuBois and his sister, Mrs. Caroline DuBois, likewise a nephew and niece of Mr. Post, for granting a pleasant interview and the sharing of valuable information. Other relatives and acquaintances of Mr. Post also provided much useful aid in putting together the biographical information, particularly those I was able to meet through the friendly assistance of Mr. Jack Sandy Anderson, whose article on Mr. Post published in *West Virginia History* is a most valuable source of facts. Particular thanks is due also to Mrs. Agnes Smith Parish for sharing her personal recollections of Mr. Post and to Mr. E. M. Taylor who provided rare information recalled by his mother. Assistance in the gathering of information and materials provided by several libraries and their staff members, especially the West Virginia University Library for excellent cooperation including their permitting use of the Post Family Papers for this work, needs to be recognized.

Wise and helpful editorial assistance during the final preparations of my manuscript for publication was provided by Mrs. Sandra Wright and Dr. Ray B. Browne of Bowling Green University. Valuable aid and encouragement during the early stages of composing parts of my manuscript was generously given by Dr. E. M. Branch, Research Professor in the English Department of Miami University, and by Mr. Robert Sinclair, Professor Emeritus. Mr. Leland S. Dutton together with many other members of the Miami University Library team also provided instances of aid to the work without which this book would have lacked much useful information. Words are inadequate to express the true value of the concern and understanding allowed me by my co-workers at Miami University Library during the many months I worked on my manuscript, with special thanks going to those with whom I have worked daily (Erin, Gwen, Violet, Roseann, and Mr. Mintz, along with Patty and others who have moved on) for their constant inspiration and enthusiasm made my efforts all the more enjoyable and worthwhile. I would also like to express gratitude to the author of *In Search of Dr. Thorndyke,* Norman Donaldson, and his daughter, Rosemary, for suggesting the publishers of this book.

Most certainly the constant support of my wife Harriet, who did not complain of the hours I spent in research and writing, and who gave freely of vacation days to accompany me in conducting interviews and research, helped make this book a reality. To her it is dedicated with love.

●●●●●●●●●

INTRODUCTION

Sinclair Lewis, writing a "Foreword" to a 1943 Readers Club edition of *The Golden Violet*[1], offered some strong opinions regarding crime-mystery-detective stories which deserve further and more serious consideration. This bit of prose was, of course, a sales effort for the book at hand, but the general ideas presented in the first two paragraphs are worth rereading in full:

> The dog that howled at midnight—the debonair chief inspector—the thing that crept about the woodshed behind a lonely Connecticut farmhouse—the tough private detective smashing into a stale hotel room—the whimsical criminological vicar in Devonshire—these charming incitements to fear have replaced the lissome young lady and the stalwart lover for popular fictional enjoyment, and the crime-mystery-detective school of fiction has become so portentous an escape from reality that some day, a hundred years hence, even the college professors and the critics will begin to notice it. A bishop or a burlesque queen who does not have a crime story on the bedside table is suspect and perhaps ruined.
>
> The quality of dreary trash in this school is not surprising. What is surprising is the quality of authentic

literature, shrewd and competent writing with the power of suggesting more than is said, of awakening the emotions and the imagination, that is the sign of literature. We should rejoice that not all inspired authors dwell on the vigorously placid backwoods or the psychological problems of the communistic Modern Woman. Like Dickens and Dostoevsky, a few are also willing to enliven us with the delightful shocks of murder, cruelty to children and the long hatred between man and woman.[2]

What Sinclair Lewis suggested here continues to be all too significantly true. The crime-mystery-detective school of fiction has been shamefully ignored by the more erudite critics who have repeatedly mined the more profitable nuggets of other fields of literature. Although numerous noted and educated persons, including Presidents from Theodore Roosevelt to John F. Kennedy, have read and enjoyed mystery and detective fiction, most critics agree with Edmund Wilson[3] that they are on firm ground in denying the alleged values of the major proportion of this class of writing. Only in recent years has there appeared signs that the prediction of Mr. Lewis will prove accurate and perhaps in much less than the hundred years cited.

The universal classification of the author Melville Davisson Post as a "mystery and detective writer" has undoubtedly contributed to the steady neglect he has received at the hands of persons writing our literary history and criticism. Ironically it was this aspect of his writing that gave him the limited fame he enjoyed for a time, and it is likely that he often thought of himself as a mystery and detective writer. Yet it would hardly be accurate to believe that this was the only factor that led to his undeserved and nearly complete obscurity since his death in 1930.

Melville Davisson Post is an author whose name few persons can now readily identify, although he is given some minor mention in nearly every standard reference claiming extensive coverage of American literature. He is usually noted as the creator of several original fictional characters and as a master technician of short story construction. In spite of a fame that once extended to one-and-a-half million readers of the *Saturday Evening Post* and other popular serial publications, he is today virtually forgotten except to true buffs of the American mystery and detective short story. His books are nearly unobtainable since almost all have been out of print for many years. Until recently only his best known collection of stories was available in an inexpensive paperback edition.

What are the reasons for this neglect of Post and his fellow mystery and detective authors? The "quantity of dreary trash of this school" which Mr. Lewis mentions is an obvious matter which has been noted many times over. Post was cognizant of this fact and dwelt on it when he composed the "Introduction" to his first volume of stories in 1896. Nor should it be overlooked here that over the years Post himself, certainly unwillingly and perhaps unknowingly, contributed his full share of weary and weak tales. The answer to our question is more complex and will not be found here.

If the whole truth regarding Post concluded at this point, there would hardly be reason for a book-length study and his obscurity would be deserved. But this is not the case. First of all, the classification of Post as a mystery writer has been as totally unfair as it has been damaging. Much of what he wrote, even when it bordered on the mystery and detective field of fiction, does not properly belong there, and some of the best things he wrote are clearly outside of that division. Secondly, even when he was writing stories based on a crime and its solution, he not only wrote in an individualistic manner, but he included in many of the stories profound and prophetic ideas pertaining to legal and social justice, and keen observations of the changes leading to our present day attitudes and outlook on life.

Through the training and experience he gained as a practicing attorney and as a result of his unusual analytical abilities, Post consistently carried his thinking beyond the immediate concerns and problems of his period. This is particularly true in regard to his opinions on justice. Although from our vantage point much about his life and writing seems tied to the aristocratic and conservative society he served in, in reality he was a rebel and a liberal with an advanced humanistic philosophy that set him apart from many of his contemporaries.

Little, if any, consideration has ever been given this idealistic nature of Melville Post. The principal consideration given him has noted his superb talents and practical techniques in creating short, entertaining mystery fiction. However, a thorough examination of Post's entire work reveals much that is worthy of sincere critical attention and much that should be made more readily available to readers. His faults, which are also many, need to be understood and clarified so that we can better appreciate his successes. It is hoped that this book-length study can be of aid in this respect.

Writing in the *New York Times Book Review* recently regarding "Professionals in Crime," Katherine Davis Fishman said:

> Although they work in a genre which has embraced Joseph Conrad, Robert Louis Stevenson and Somerset Maugham ("Dostoevsky was one of our best," notes one of the pros defensively), mystery writers live mostly in Siberia: writers in other forms refuse to take them seriously, readers apologize for enjoying them, publishers give them a minimum of promotion and critics allow them scanty reviewing space. . . . They have learned to accept a lesser position in society. . . .[4]

Happily, in spite of Mrs. Fishman's observation, the prophecy of Sinclair Lewis is certain to prevail eventually. If this book on the life and writing of Melville Davisson Post plays some minor part in such a renaissance, it will have served fully its purpose.

●●●●●●●●●

I. BIOGRAPHY

    Melville Davisson Post was fond of enigmatic expressions and any study of his life must consider this factor. He was certainly a much more complex personality than his literary accomplishments demonstrate in any obvious manner. A man of cosmopolitan stature and outlook, he traveled almost constantly throughout his adult life, becoming keenly acquainted with some of the most interesting and attractive locales in sundry parts of America and Europe. He often set the scenes of his unique tales in these varied places he regularly visited. His first stories indicate an attraction to the cross-sectioned activities of New York City. Later, he wrote stories with the authentic atmosphere and background of England, Scotland, France, Belgium, Switzerland, and other exotic places, including the wilderness of the Oregon Coast. But while such scenes have a definite place in his writing, he never forgot his birthplace. Post never removed his roots from West Virginia and returned there constantly, not only because it was home, but because he knew it to be most beautiful of all— and it was there, where he spent nearly all of his last years, that he died. It was to the fascinating hills of West Virginia that he turned when he wrote his most rewarding and readable stories.

West Virginia counted among its founders many hardy pioneers who shared in carving out of the wilderness a productive land. In 1773 Daniel Davisson, one of these, settled on a large tract of choice ground at what is now the heart of Clarksburg, in Harrison County.[1] This land, described by a character in an *Uncle Abner* story as "the very best land that a beef steer ever cropped grass on," was, again according to the words written by Post for Uncle Abner to speak, "lands that Daniel Davisson got in a grant from George the Third."[2] Uncle Abner continues, "I don't know what service he rendered the crown, but the pay was princely—a man would do a king's work for an estate like this." Whether or not this is all completely true, Daniel Davisson has been distinguished in various records as a frontier fighter, a major in the militia taking part in the American Revolution, a sheriff of early Harrison County, and as the proprietor of Clarksburg. Over the years he added other holdings of good cattle land, some apparently by means of a fortune in silver he reportedly had brought with him across the mountains. Born in 1749, Davisson lived to be seventy. During the course of his years he married Prudence Izard.[3] Their offspring numbered nine—Lemuel, George, Nathaniel, Henry, Edith, Catherine, Elizabeth, Patsy, and Prudence—four sons and five daughters.[4] Prudence, born in 1788, was the great-grandmother of Melville Davisson Post. She lived until 1876.[5]

Prudence Davisson became Prudence Coplin by marriage. Her daughter, Martha Juliet, married Melville Davisson (of no direct relation) who became the maternal grandfather of Post and the source of his given name. Melville and Martha Juliet Davisson had two daughters, Alice Maud, who died in 1864, and Florence May, who upon her sister's death became sole heiress to the extensive Davisson land holdings and, equally important, to the Davisson family traditions derived from numerous notable ancestors.

Florence May Davisson was born on October 4, 1843, and reared in a family that displayed great respect for its illustrious past, a trait she consistently instilled in her children. With much pride she helped to organize a local chapter of the Daughters of the American Revolution and saw that it took recognition in its name of her great-grandfather, Daniel Davisson. Throughout life she was a thoroughly religious woman, active in Methodist Episcopal church affairs. According to all reports she was a commanding woman who insisted that her family remain true to and fulfill the many worthy social obligations they had inherited. Typical of her times and her station, she exhibited all the regal dignity and grace of a Queen Victoria, whom she somewhat resembled in appearance in her later years. At her death on February 10, 1914, the newspaper obituary published in the Clarksburg, West Virginia *Daily Telegram* noted that she had been an influential woman in her community for many years, one who had managed even through her final days to be unperturbed by the social changes appearing during her lifetime.

On her twenty-third birthday, October 4, 1866, Florence May Davisson was married to Ira Carper Post. Ira, a native of adjoining Upshur County, was born on February 2, 1842. and he too had inherited a family background of note dating back to Colonial times from both his parents, Isaac and Emily (Carper) Post. Ira has been described as being not only a man upright in his relationships with others but one of shrewdness and good intelligence, capable of holding his own in each and every conversation. Honest and hospitable, he formed many lasting friendships and business relationships. Deeply religious, he read and studied the Bible so thoroughly that he gained considerable respect for his extensive Biblical knowledge. He instilled in his family by his example a sense of faith, justice, and honesty—traits which obviously affected the work of his author son. Photographs reveal him a neatly-bearded man of intense spirit. When Ira died on September 27, 1923, at age eighty-one, he had lived a full and successful life, morally and materially.

West Virginia had been legally a separate state only three years when Ira and Florence Post began the first year of their marriage in a frame house located on Raccoon Run, south of Romines Mills, in the central part of Harrison County's Elk District. This house built of hewn timber with vertical siding and a chimney of creek-bed stone was to be their home for approximately the next ten years and the birthplace of Melville Davisson Post, their second child and first son.[6] They brought into the world of newborn West Virginia five children—three daughters and two sons.

Born before Melville was his sister Maud in 1867. Following Melville there were Emma, born in 1872, Sidney in 1878 and finally Florence. The children grew to adulthood in a closely-knit family, and all married. Maud became Mrs. Melville L. Hutchinson and had seven children. Emma became Mrs. William C. Ogden, wife of a popular Fairmont, West Virginia physician. Sidney, educated to be a doctor, followed the profession only incidently, giving his greater attention to agriculture. He married Celia Ward, daughter of a neighboring family. Florence became the young bride of Frank M. Atterholt in 1904 and had two children, one who died as an infant.

Melville Davisson Post, according to the records kept in the family's Bible, was born at one o'clock on the afternoon of April 19, 1869.[7] All published information available from 1903 through 1967 consistently reported him born two years later, but there seems no reason to doubt this record in the family Bible, particularly as it fits other available facts. Whether the incorrect date of 1871 was established as the result of an error or was a purposeful miscue has not been determined. Post certainly would have had ample opportunity to set the public records straight, but no apparent effort was ever made. The true reason for this incorrect date may never be known, along with many other facts of his life, inasmuch as he seemed to avoid regularly any desire, need, or request for revealing biographical details regarding himself in the public records. What little he gave out willingly, particularly that noted in his entry in *Who's Who in America,* remained for years the only factual details of his life available to the general public.[8]

How ambiguous he was when giving out biographical details is illustrated by his elusive answer given to one such request late in his career, long after his name was familiar to at least a million readers of the popular magazines of the time:

> I was born like the sons of Atreus in the pasture land of horses. I was reared by a black woman who remembered her grandmother boiling a warrior's head in a pot. I was given a degree by a college of unbeautiful nonsense. I have eaten dinner with a god. And I have kissed a princess in a land where men grind their wheat in the sky.[9]

Grant Overton reporting on this reply in *Cargoes for Crusoes* calls it a "suitable whimsical reply." The reply was neither suitable nor whimsical. It sums up simply with complete lack of detail the entire life of Post in a brief, elusive statement, as serious as it is poetic.

A member of a distinguished aristocratic family of West Virginia, Melville Davisson Post was indeed born "in the pasture land of horses." The horse was invaluable to nearly every man and boy, and most women in the country in which he spent his childhood. In their cattle-raising occupation it was an absolutely necessary resource to every man involved. To every boy the horse was a means of play and joy as well as an education for the years ahead. And for the women it was the main possibility to travel over the steep, wooded hills. Young Melville knew horses intimately and loved them, holding these creatures in highest regard from his infancy to the last days of his life. His acceptance into the higher courts of the social world, his extensive travels, his wealth and success as an accomplished lawyer and author, nothing supplanted his deep and constant devotion to the horse.

Ira Post was actively engaged in the business of raising cattle and maintained a place with numerous herds and extensive pasture land. Cattle raising was the principal means of earning an income from the hills at this time, and it helped to keep the Post family financially well-established and secure in their inherited status of leadership. A cattle-raising project operated in this manner needed many extra helpers in addition to the regular family members. Among those with the Post family was an attractive negress named Eliza Perkins, no doubt the black woman who reared Melville and told him, believable or not, that she could remember her grandmother in Africa "boiling a warrior's head in a pot." The Perkins family had belonged to the Davissons during the years of legal slavery and had remained on in their service as an essential part of the whole cattle-raising endeavour following the emancipation. Similarly black people were a part of nearly every such establishment there and then, the women taking on the routine household tasks and aiding in the raising of the owner's children; the men working in the gardens, caring for the horses and riding as drovers; and the black children playing with and growing up in the company of the household children. Eliza had a son, said to have been born on Melville Davisson Post's second birthday (the date incidently that Post proclaimed as his also) who became a close, beloved companion of young Melville.[10] Named Orange Jud Perkins, he was immortalized when Post used him as the model for "Jud," the companion of Quiller, narrator in *Dwellers in the Hills*.[11] It is interesting that in the book Post gave no indication of the man's negro heritage except to describe him as "the bronze giant," noting a general description of strength and the fact that he was chosen to wrestle with Black Malan, the negro drover employed by the antagonist, Rufe Woodford.[12] The real Orange Jud Perkins fits this description closely. He was a person of unquestionable physical strength, able, it was said, to straighten a horseshoe with his bare hands, and he could lift a bale of hay straight up at the end of a pitch fork. Jud remained with the Post family throughout his life and served in many capacities as servant and friend. Early pictures reveal him as handsome and proud as he was dependable. Jud and his mother are now buried side by side in a small churchyard burial grounds at the edge of Gnatty Creek amid the beautiful hills they seldom if ever left.

Melville Post seems to have been an active and robust child, healthy and happy in the genial home his parents provided and in the open air and inspiring nature of the surrounding country. His principal companions during his first eight years in addition to Jud were his sisters Maud and Emma. Experiences during these early years sparked his imagination and provided the foundation upon which he built his successful career. From where his parents lived it was only a short distance to the log house where his grandparents Melville and Martha Juliet Davisson lived, a two-story house that brought to mind the pioneer times during which it was constructed. His grandparents, most likely, were the original source of much of the pioneer history and atmosphere and the folktales and legends that appear in several of Post's books. Also his great-grandmother, who lived until 1876, may have told young Melville with her own lips many stories of the earlier days of West Virginia and in particular perhaps related a number of stories about her father Daniel Davisson when he served as the county's sheriff.

Sometime before 1878 Melville's family moved into a finer, brick home they had built nearby, which to some of their neighbors became known as the "big home," but which was named by Melville's mother "Templemoor," a name which it still carries after nearly a century. It was in this newer and larger home that Melville spent the remainder of his childhood and lived intermittently as a young man. It consisted of thirteen rooms connected to spacious halls on the first and second floors and over all an immense attic in addition to a tower room. Constructed of locally-made brick, with walnut woodwork, some walnut paneling, and extra-sized doors and windows, it was an impressive mansion-like house surrounded by a tree-filled lot. In the comfortable, spacious surroundings of Templemoor Melville grew up with great opportunities for dignity, yet with the lessons of nature close at hand, reminding man of his mortality, demonstrating the seasons of life and death, filled with the mystery of eternity. Animal life, especially the rabbits and opossums appeared in abundance in the forest and meadow around him. Wooded hillsides and grassy pastures were his constant playgrounds and he passed through them on his way to the Raccoon School, named for Raccoon Run that flows into Gnatty Creek. Here he had his early lessons in the art he was to practice in his adult years.

As he grew older and was allowed to ride off into the surrounding countryside alone or frequently with Orange Jud Perkins or with groups of neighborhood boys, he grew to feel himself one with the people, the traditions and the hills of his native state, learning at close range the intimate knowledge he later demonstrated of the good and the bad in mankind and in nature. He early developed the skills of horsemanship and grew to love the creatures he rode. He learned carefully all the facts of their nature, their care and equipment, and he learned how to read the prints their hoofs left in a dusty road. Post, in the very first Uncle Abner story he published, has the narrator, Abner's nephew Martin, say what was no doubt the truth regarding the author: "I could ride a horse all day . . . I was tough as whit-leather . . . you must not picture a little boy rolling a hoop in the park."[13]

These jaunts into the hills helped to expand some of the youthful dreams and ideas that had begun to flow through his head as he discovered through books the romance of the written word. This, combined with the oral traditions and tales he received from his elders led Melville early in his life to develop a sense of destiny about himself. This attitude is shown in certain examples of his juvenile writing (early efforts to express his individualistic feelings), some of which are preserved among the Post Family Papers at West Virginia University.[14]

One of these pieces might be titled "My Childhood—An Autobiography," written when Melville was sixteen, probably in January 1886 as a class room assignment at Buckhannon Academy. Later handed to his mother or father and preserved by them, it has survived, unlike the majority of his early work. Written on several sheets of blue-ruled composition paper, it bears on the back of the final sheet a list of errors and criticism by the instructor. There are eighteen errors listed, two-thirds of them calling attention to words misspelled. These are followed by the thoughtful and prophetic comment: "Study the rules for punctuation and orthography carefully.—The thought of your autobiography is placed in concise language." Since this composition contains some of the few available revelations of any events of Post's early years, it can perhaps be most profitably considered here chronologically.

Of great importance is the opening paragraph which obviously confirms the actual date of his birth:

> On the 19th day of April 1869 in the State of West Va. and in the county of Harrison the blessings of peace spread their consoling wings over the surrounding country traversed by the placid little stream of Gnatty Creek. And this national blessing consisted in the birth of a son to a family by the name of Post.[15]

Young Melville then explains some matters in regard to his given Latin name. In the same self-conscious language with which the piece opened, he next states unabashedly, "He was a sweet innocent little child . . ."

Noting next that his grandfather was making a good living, as existing records readily confirm, he reveals that "at a very early age he exhibited a desire for accumulating of wealth and spent most of his time in pursuit of the rabbit and opossum of Raccoon Run." This statement not only suggests the irony and the concise style that he would command in his later career, but it also reflects his lifelong pastime of hunting small game and his outlook on wealth as something that has only to be pursued strongly to be realized.

Somewhat unashamed, if we can believe his next remarks and his tone, Melville states that he was given a horse by his father which he proceeded to sell for 25 cents. With this he invested in a stone pitcher which broke. Here, already, we begin to witness the fanciful mixture of truth and quasi-poetic expression Post frequently chose as a means to mystify his audience.

Next he states that his formal educational experience up until the writing of this autobiography had been received wholly in the small elementary school on Raccoon Run, which he glorifies boastfully as "Raccoon College." There he was in attendance, he says, from his sixth through his thirteenth year. Around this time (at the age of 13 or 14), he mentions, he had a desire to travel, and his father allowed him to go along on a trip to Baltimore. There he nearly reached an early conclusion to his life, as he was almost overcome by gas from a faulty pipe which poured fumes into a hotel room while he slept unaware of the danger. Fortunately he was saved by the intervention of some men who smelled the gas and woke him.

Having spent approximately eight years at Raccoon School, at the age of fourteen Melville apparently was undecided as to the need for further education. Books had already assumed an important place in his scheme of values, and he must have thought that this would hold true for the rest of the world, for at fourteen he decided to become a book agent. This career, perhaps more fancied than realized, ended shortly when he discovered that he was not able to lie. Thereafter, he concluded that his future would perhaps best be served if he applied himself to common labor, and he notes that he toiled for hours hoeing corn.

Finally, again traveling with his father, who during these years was developing something of an affinity for politics in addition to cattle raising, Melville paid a significant visit to the nation's capital. He described it in these words:

> This he followed until his 16th summer when he went to Washington and among other things shake the paw of Grover Cleveland and see what he intended doing with the government. He did shake hands with the President, but also the government he did not have time to investigate. He however took the precaution to leave his address and

> tell Grover that if he needed help to manage things he would know where to send after him. Coming home he prepared to attend the Academy at least one term's work. Here he is again ready to attempt another.[16]

The final statement of this piece of school work is a somewhat satiric stab at humor and pathos, ending with these words: "Sample copies of this Autobiography can be had by application at the den-of-idleness. 25 cents a volume or $1.00 a year. Forever and forever—Amen."

"Mel," as his family and friends now called him, had finished with Raccoon School by mid-1883, shortly after his fourteenth birthday. Until his sixteenth summer he must have been undecided as to his future ambitions. There is no evidence of his attending school for these two years, or until the fall of 1885.

We can believe it was during these years that Post did much of his early reading and consciously or not began to think of writing his own books. A family tradition reports that his mother often observed him sitting out under one of the many trees surrounding Templemoor writing. Fortunately, or unfortunately, the bulk of this practice material he destroyed.

Melville's father appears to have been a man of reason and although he most likely had a great desire to see his son advancing towards a good profession he realized that the boy's choice had to be his own and had to be made in the boy's own time. It may have been that his father, always able to use an extra hand to hoe the corn or an extra rider to mind the cattle range, planned to give the youngster a taste of the day-to-day hardship and drudgery faced in such work. There is a story told of how young Melville, who during these years was riding out to help care for his father's herds, one unusually cold winter day while struggling through deep snow in a far pasture seeking some cattle had his feet nearly frostbitten. The sting of the cold wind-driven snow, the harshness of the biting cold and the pain of numbed flesh on this and other occasions may have helped the young man to decide against the hazards of a cattle-raising occupation. Certainly there was a certain glamour attached to the work and in later years he would describe some of the activities with great affection. But the young man already had a view of the wider world through books and the travel adventures with his father. He could doubtlessly see better and more promising things might be gained through education. Perhaps the significance of his trip to Washington was that it was then the seed was planted that led him to seek an education for an eventual career in law, and thereafter, writing.

In the fall of 1885 Post was enrolled at the Academy in Buckhannon, West Virginia. One principal objective must have been to secure some secondary school credits to prepare the young man for entrance into a university. Whatever else was accomplished, the experience at Buckhannon provided the potential author his first outlet for sharing his literary ambitions and receiving helpful criticism.

No details on Melville's first months at the Buckhannon school have been located, and knowledge of the final months are scant. A few surviving papers, however, do give some insight into his ambitions, attitudes, and personality in his adolescent years. Most items that we can place in this period are class assignments. Perhaps the most useful and interesting is the autobiographical assignment which we have already considered with its insight on Melville's childhood. As noted, it was probably written in January 1886 following the holidays between terms.

Another piece, somewhat autobiographical, but much shorter (two pages), more rambling in content, and of less factual interest is dated February 2, 1886. It is titled "Home of M. D. Post" and bears a note of comment by a Justina L. Steorus, possibly the teacher to whom he was assigned for instruction in English grammar. Its most interesting revelation is a line describing the cellar as "the scene of many a youthful struggle with a cider barrel and straw." It seems certain that young Melville at Templemoor had a typical childhood in accordance with the times.

Less typical is the next piece, a verse written on a sheet bearing the letterhead "Normal and Classical Academy [Buckhannon] Both Sexes Admitted—Academical, Normal, Music, Business, Drawing and Painting Departments." Imitative of the classical verse being studied in his classes, it proclaims its origin as "Composed by R. A. Hall and M. D. Post, March 26, 1886." What portion either composed is not apparent, but a further statement says "Read Friday night by M. D. Post." How much interest young Melville had in poetic expressions is difficult to assess, but no doubt, considering his age and educational experience, it was moderately above average. One other piece of verse, undated but likely to be from this period, is titled "Poem. *Academy Dudes.*" A few other attempts at versification and poetic form are found among the Post papers, some dating more likely from his university days, but none revealing anything more than a talent for mediocre imitations of classical and humourous works. In regard to the latter, he was especially fond of doggerel rhymes, learning them by heart, and in later years reciting them to children, including a nephew who still recollects a few he learned.

A humorous, mischievous and fanciful attitude is revealed in these early examples. Such an example is one piece of prose dated May 1886. It is titled "Parasites." This piece of abstract prose is written beneath the imprint: "*Business*Office*of*Lynch and Post.//Broadway, No. 1//Members of the Philomathean Literary Society//Buchannon, W. Va." Beneath this are the printed names, T. D. Lynch [and] M. D. Post. It is not known how many individuals participated in this group, but the group must have been small and based on close friendships. Always victim of a somewhat stubborn streak of vanity, especially in his youth, Melville must nevertheless have felt as the school term was ending that his literary outpourings were not very world shaking. Thus, he closes his four-page essay, which is in the form of a letter addressed to "Parasite," with these words of warning indicating that he would not easily succumb to the inattention of the masses:

> Thus you perceive that all *all* are parasites there is none that is not *no* not one. Would that I was an exception!! or had the wings of the morning, that I might fly away where essays would cease from troubling and public entertainments would never come, but alas! for the expectations of this world—Vanity of vanities all is vanity.
> Yours truly, M. D. Post[17]

An undated essay titled "The Values of Gymnastics" appears to be related to this period. There also are among the Post papers, notes and manuscripts for debates that possibly are of this period and may be evidence that Melville took part in debates and was developing as an excellent debater even before the more established fame of his university days.

Next evidence of his continuing education are letters to his father and mother written from Morgantown, West Virginia, during the school year of 1886-1887. These would indicate he was being subjected to further preparatory courses for entrance into a formal university program the next year; the name of M. D. Post does not appear on the official roles until 1887-1888. These letters show that he was the typical son away at school, for they often include requests for additional money for expenses such as clothing. One written a few days after his 18th birthday, dated April 22, 1887, indicates an obvious dissatisfaction with his instructors and a desire to enroll in another school. The letter, addressed to his mother, also complains of the harshness of the Morgantown climate, the cold, damp, foggy days which he believed led to the many periods of illness he endured during the winter months. From this letter and other information it seems that although he appeared to be robust and healthy and was active in many things, Post was occasionally plagued by illness, either originating from or heightened by emotional pressures.

Perhaps the subject of changing schools did not arise again during the summer days at Templemoor, or if it did, Melville's desires did not prevail. The records of enrollment at the University of West Virginia for the year 1887-88, [as well as his letters and other evidence,] indicate that M. D. Post was a student there in several subjects. The school's records also show that he continued there during the next three school years taking a normal, well-rounded selection of subjects typical of his aristocratic and agricultural background. In the school of Agriculture he took courses in physics, chemistry, geology, and biology. His studies in the school of Modern Languages show he studied both French and German extensively. He had also had an earlier course in Greek. Although he did not show a special ability with this language, barely managing passing grades at times, later years show he was greatly influenced by the literature of early Greek writers. He also had at least a couple of years study in the school of Mathematics. Other subjects he was graded on include English, rhetoric, anatomy, and metaphysics. His grades ranged up and down, but were consistently above that required for passing, averaging over this four-year period (on a scale of 10) 8.10; thus he can be assessed academically as a good but not exceptional student.

Grades during Post's final year of studies for his Bachelor of Arts degree show he had developed into a strong student.

In reflection, many years later Post stated that he "was given a degree by a college of unbeautiful nonsense." Although this may refer partly to his needs in later years as a writer of popular fiction, he nevertheless seems to have taken his college work seriously. If he had any aversion to education at the time, it was not apparent and not strong enough to keep him from successfully completing his college work.

In addition to his regular studies, Post entered into the spirit of the university's entire program by participating in various activities, such as the Columbia Literary Society and the Cadet Corps, becoming captain of Company C. He directed a presentation of "Richard III" to aid in financing the school's first football eleven, and in his senior year he became co-editor on the student publication, *The Athenaeum*.[18] His experiences at Morgantown removed him from the limitations of the world of cattle raising and put him into the world of ideas. He had had his first debating experience as a student at Buckhannon, and at college he progressed rapidly in debate and also in public speaking. It may have been due partly to his somewhat vain and confident personality that he established something of a reputation for himself in the fields of public speaking and debating which opened a number of important doors for him early in his life.

During these college years, together with his father, who served for some time in the West Virginia State Legislature, Melville was concerned with the popular question of "free silver." Father and son sought information on the subject and there is evidence that Melville probably did some debating on the topic. His father was doubtlessly pro-silver, as a good Democrat could be expected to be. This interest shared with Melville helped to tighten the bonds between them as time progressed. Melville sought the affection of his father and was more strongly attached to him than to his mother and her attitudes. Ira C. Post, conscious of the value of legal knowledge through his experiences in local politics and business, was perhaps the chief influence that lead Melville to study law.

How effectively he had finally adapted himself to the pursuit of knowledge is realized from the fact that after he received his

A.B. in 1891, Post returned to the school for a year of legal studies and earned a LL.B. in 1892. The chief reason for his decision to enter law was no doubt his father's influence; but his family's strong ties with the Democratic party of West Virginia and those associated with it (for it played a forceful and leading part in the state's early life) had early made the course he took inevitable. Certainly his speech-making abilities also had much to do with his decision inasmuch as he had won in his junior and senior years both the intersociety oration and debate contests at the University. With his speaking abilities duly recognized, he was granted the opportunity to make a recommendation speech at the 1892 Democratic State Convention in Parkersburg on behalf of a leading gubernatorial candidate.[19] This won Post his first hour of fame.

Melville Davisson Post was twenty-three when he left the university to start his legal career. He was well-fitted for the work he undertook, for the training he had received during his college education had taught him to examine problems objectively, a talent which was to some extent natural, but which through discipline he was able to develop further and to use effectively. When he made his stand on any matter, it was only after a careful and conscientious weighing of the pros and cons. Post in his law career, in his political adventures, in his study of crytography and criminology, and certainly in the creation of his fictional heroes practiced the intellectual method, selecting a point of departure, building a foundation, and constructing on its solid support. This was also the method he assigned to his fictional characters, particularly to his two most famous, Randolph Mason and Uncle Abner.

Having once become a lawyer, he set about the business in a thorough and efficient manner. Joining into a partnership with John A. Howard, a prosecuting attorney of Ohio County in West Virginia, and working in their office in Wheeling, he spent the next eight years on a variety of cases in the general and criminal legal fields.[20] At the same time he became enmeshed in a number of political responsibilities. In 1892 the Democratic Party of the State of West Virginia selected him as a presidential elector-at-large. Later he was selected secretary of the Electoral College; he was reported to be the youngest person ever to have served in such a position with that group up until that time. There is strong evidence that in 1893 Post had ambitions to run for a public office, but the Secretary of State, William C. Chilton, tactfully turned down his request. Whether hurt by this or later convinced that a public office was undesirable, he gave no further indications of ever wishing to become a political candidate for any office.

Living at the Fort Henry Club during most of his days in Wheeling, he managed to secure a firm reputation as attorney. He became known as an effective collector of bad debts. A number of letters addressed originally to the Wheeling postmaster and requesting forwarding to a "good collector" and "some good lawyer" were regularly put into his hands. His business correspondence, precise and focused clearly on its objectives, shows him usually successful in accomplishing his various clients' goals.

Although actively practicing law and skirmishing in political affairs, as a young man, energetic and anxious to rise above the commonplace, he continued work on his literary ambitions. The hope of achievements in this field were already strong. While delayed by the need to complete his education and to begin his legal career, his hope of achievements in this field had never diminished. It was probably sometime during the years 1894 and 1895 that Post began to look forward seriously to writing for publication. A friend, Dan B. Lucas, reported to Melville on an attempt to find a publisher for a monograph Post had written. Lucas, after talking with some firms in New York City, told Melville that they were not interested in publishing such material unless the author would bear the cost. Melville's friend, in his letter, terms these publishers as "New Yorkers being all gold bugs" and then recommends that the author try some Chicago firms. Nothing apparently ever developed of this venture in 1895. But by the spring of 1896 Post had finished seven stories about an unscrupulous lawyer whose uncanny legal abilities and know-how allowed despairing clients to escape untainted from a variety of ethical and financial problems through loopholes in the law. Post's own professional experiences as a practicing lawyer had obviously furnished him with most of the plots used in these first successful short stories. These tales, centered around the enigmatic

Randolph Mason, were eagerly published by the highly-rated firm of G. P. Putnam's Sons in a volume titled *The Strange Schemes of Randolph Mason.*

In the introduction he furnished for this book, Post states eloquently the unique idea introduced in these stories:

> The high ground of the field of crime has not been explored; it has not even been entered. The book stalls have been filled to weariness with tales based upon plans whereby the *detective,* or *ferreting* power of the State might be baffled. But prodigious marvel! no writer has attempted to construct tales based upon plans whereby the *punishing* power of the State might be baffled.[21]

This inverted approach to the mystery (or problem) story, unusual for its time and uncommon even today, created a mild sensation and, according to the author in the preface of his next book, "provoked large discussion." Sensational murder cases in New York City and in Chicago occurred not long after publication of Post's first book, both of which bore strong resemblances in some respects to the book's first and most controversial story, "Corpus Delecti."[22] In publications and letters Post received favorable and unfavorable comments on his methods. To this extent he had achieved a considerable measure of success.

That the book was also a partial commercial success is evident in that Post and his publisher followed with a second book one year later in 1897. This second book, entitled *The Man of Last Resort, or the Clients of Randolph Mason,* contained five new stories, all in the same vein as the previous stories. The publisher expressed some dissatisfaction with the quality of a couple of the tales and thought there were too few of them,[23] but they seem to have been accepted and printed just as they were presented by their author. Years later, concerning these early stories Post laughingly told his journalist acquaintance, Sam Mallison, "They were pretty terrible in one sense."[24] Yet, despite their outright weaknesses, they do reveal in their inventiveness and in their characterizations a mind with unique powers of inquiry and a keen interest in human behavior. Both books had a successive number of printings over the first three decades of their existence, some of the stories being anthologized several times during those years—and providing we are not too critical of their literary quality, they still have something worthwhile to say to us about men and laws and justice.

At the age of twenty-eight, Post was becoming widely-read and talked-about as an author as well as being established as a capable attorney. His books actually did little for him financially at this time, but his legal profession allowed him a comfortable if not an exceptional income. Although a few years later he would refer to himself in a letter to a cousin, written partly in jest as "a skilled liar," it seems likely that for many years he held his first profession in the highest esteem. In the preface to his second book he said:

> The reader must bear in mind that the law herein dealt with is the law as it is administered in the legal forms of his country, in no degree colored by the imagination of the author. Every legal statement represents an established principle thoroughly analyzed by the courts of last resort. There can be no question as to the probable truth of these legal conclusions. They are as certainly established as it is possible for the decisions of the courts to establish any principle of law.[25]

Post also believed at this stage of his career that all fiction should have its basis in some fact, a belief he held for most of his career as an author.

Every author finds his work criticized, and Post was no exception. From the very beginning he had to defend the course he took and this he did consistently with his skills as a debater and attorney. This produced another attitude that he was noted for throughout life, whether dealing with critics, editors, publishers, friends, or readers. He would listen quietly, usually if not always patiently, then make his own decision and stick to it unwaveringly.

By this time as a result of his varied experiences and travels Melville had assumed a cosmopolitan stature, and no doubt he felt as much at ease in the elite environment of Manhattan as he did at home in his West Virginia mountain country. It is likely that his travels were limited to points in the United States, principally to the Atlantic coast sector. His life was changing during this time because of his minor success as an author, and he obviously felt that certain factors in his world, both professional and personal, were lining up for him and also against him. He was uncertain about what he had gained for himself with his new and promising reputation in literature. There is some evidence that on several occasions he suffered physical ailments and an exhausted mental condition. One rather distraught and melancholy manuscript, called "The Story of a Suicide,"[26] although undated and unsigned, could very well have originated during a part of this period since some of his more fanciful letters of this same period show a similar prose style. This unusual piece, which was probably never intended for publication but no doubt served some usefulness as therapy, rambles along for thirteen pencil-written sheets, beginning and ending with "I am called a dreamer, a visionary, and a fool." Whether this mood resulted from the rejection or criticism of friends, family, or business associates or from some romantic interest, we can not be sure, but it is evidence that beneath the surface all was not progressing smoothly for the young author and lawyer.

Though we do not have an exact date or know all the circumstances of its composition, during this period, in 1901, Post published his third book, a short novel entitled *Dwellers in the Hills*. Most of the manuscript reportedly had been written during a summer's stay at his childhood home, Templemoor. What appears to be the original manuscript is preserved among the Post papers at West Virginia University and indicates steady workmanship with a limited number of changes and corrections. This book, a delightful and sometimes emotionally-directed prose poem, is a sharp departure from the Randolph Mason stories. Written in the first person, it describes a nostalgic return to the environment of Melville's boyhood. It is based on an actual incident a neighbor youth had experienced and makes use of several actual persons and family names. Perhaps because it was so different from the work which first brought him acclaim, it never seemed to catch on with the critics or with the general reading public in America. The novel was given a respectable amount of attention in Great Britain, however, and provided the author a minor literary reputation there for a time. It is an exceptionally beautiful book, and it remains today, although all but forgotten, one of the finest fictional works Post produced in a literary career of nearly thirty-five years. In the honest opinion of those who have read it with thoroughness and reflection, *Dwellers in the Hills* should definitely be rated as a minor classic of American literature.

Perhaps now sensing that bigger things were still to come, Melville decided to shift his major legal activities from the criminal courts to corporation law. In doing this he made good use of his political connections—he had been chosen chairman of the Democratic Congressional Committee of West Virginia in 1898. Thus, around mid-1901, following some correspondence and conversation, he formed a new legal partnership with John T. McGraw of Grafton, West Virginia. McGraw, nearly twenty years older than Post, was one of the more prominent Democrats on the state political scene and a lawyer of exceptional abilities. The new firm of McGraw and Post remained intact for the next five years and reportedly was one of the most powerful in that area, handling among other things, the knotty legal problems of coal mines and railroads. John A. Howard, Post's first legal partner, expressed the following opinion: "This firm was one of the strongest in the State, and for five years was on one side or the other of almost every important suit instituted in the Northern District of West Virginia."[27] Located in offices above and in back of the Grafton Bank, the firm employed several persons for clerical and secretarial work. Also, the firm employed or was associated with a couple of other attorneys who worked in the same office complex. Post seems to have been a considerate employer. One of the young secretaries who worked in the office recalled years later her pleasant visits to the Post home in Grafton and a summer excursion with a group to Templemoor.

The activities of these years left Post a limited amount of time for sincere interest in the opposite sex, but that interest was not neglected. It appears evident that he managed to engage in a normal amount of social activities. A picture published in the October 1901 issue of *The Critic* shows him to have been a good-looking, pleasant, but serious young man. The portrait shows him wearing pince-nez eyeglasses, which he no doubt wore to emphasize his intellectual side, since reports confirm that he had no need of them. He was of a medium height, probably about five foot, eight inches, and weighed about 145 pounds. Dressed in neat, conservative clothes typical of the young professional type, he made a pleasing appearance. Letters indicate that he was witty and adept at jesting, and other evidence shows that he was popular socially, never lacking in friends.

The fact that he had not married and was now past his thirtieth birthday gives cause to wonder about his success in romance. Some evidence may be gathered from his writings particularly from the words of Quiller, the narrator of the 1901 novel,[28] that suggests that perhaps the young author had suffered one or more unhappy experiences with young women to whom he had been attracted. Speculation might suggest that being outspoken and liberal in his opinions of law and religion, with a reputation as being a "ladies' man," a reputation which persisted throughout his life, the conservative families of the most eligible young ladies in his youthful social world would have been hesitant to approve him for their daughters. The events and circumstances of his romantic life before he was thirty and what effect they had upon him and his subsequent literary career, may be only speculated upon and possibly never confirmed.

Nevertheless, Melville Post was not destined to retain his bachelor status much longer, for he soon was considering marriage to an exceptionally attractive and sophisticated young widow, Ann Bloomfield Gamble Schoolfield, a member of a prominent Roanoke, Virginia family. Melville met "Bloom," as she was called by her family and friends, during a ship passage to Europe probably about 1901. He no doubt managed other meetings during the stay in Europe and thereafter.

Although they were in many respects opposites in personality, attractions which they had in common were strong and soon led to a declaration of love. Yet their decision of a wedding date must have been made at a late moment, for four months before the marriage took place Post had written his mother stating his uncertainty about the possibility of the event occurring. Since his tone in that letter was one of pacification, we might assume that his mother, aristocratic but unsophisticated, was reluctant about accepting the match.

On June 29, 1903, in Philadelphia, at the Arch Street Methodist Episcopal Church, Melville and Bloom were married by the Rev. Herbert Fish. Only members of the immediate families were present at the simple ceremony, due to the recent death of Bloom's brother and the fact that it was a second marriage for the bride. George Baird from Wheeling was present as best man. On July 2nd Melville and Bloom set sail on the *Barbossa* for Europe, spending the main part of their honeymoon trip in Glencoe, Scotland.[29]

Bloom has been described as gay and vivacious, and existing photographs leave little doubt as to her outstanding attractiveness. Post was thoroughly devoted to her from their first meeting— maintaining for the rest of his life a deep devotion that never lessened nor ceased.

The couple shared a common desire for extensive traveling and this occupied a great portion of their time during the early days of their marriage. Post and Bloom enjoyed thoroughly a constant mixing in the perpetual social activities centered about the Atlantic Coast. They were in and out of the groups that gathered there with much regularity, going to Bar Harbor in Maine; visiting at Newport, Rhode Island; stopping over at one of the better clubs on Long Island, as the mood fell upon them and the season demanded. At the various resorts they experienced the glittering society life of the wealthy, in groups frequently complete with a multimillionaire or two. There is every indication that for Melville and Bloom that this was a happy time filled with love and romance. They secured a house in Grafton on West Main Street not far from the Grafton Bank where McGraw and Post had their law offices.

In the summer of 1904, Bloom disclosed that she was pregnant, and we can assume that she and Melville anticipated with joy the birth of their first child. A son was born to them on a wintery February 5th in 1905 at their home in Grafton. The child, named Ira C. Post II for his grandfather, brought a promise of happy family life to the couple. In one existent photograph little Ira appears as a happy, healthy child in the arms of his grandfather. Unfortunately, the parents' joy was as short as was their son's lifetime. On August 19, 1906 he died from typhoid fever at the age of only eighteen months. It was an exceptionally difficult and traumatic experience for the writer and certainly for the young bride.

There were other dark shadows cast over these years. They were for Post perhaps the most critical of his life. We do not know all the details, but we do know that Post decided to dissolve his law partnership with McGraw and thus free himself of the entangling responsibilities it carried. Writing of this in 1908, John A. Howard states, "As a result of the labor incident to this partnership, Mr. Post's health was broken down, and he was sent by his physicians to Brides le Bains in the south of France for the cure; but the recuperation has been slow and he has not been able to return to the practice of the law."[30] The salt spring baths at Brides, Savoie, in France contained mineral waters then recommended to patients suffering from liver and digestive canal disorders. It may also be noted that Post was suffering from liver disorders at the close of his life. Exactly how serious his illness was and if it was associated with any emotional disorders is not reliably recorded. We know there are instances in several Randolph Mason stories which suggest that Post was not unaware of a distraught mental state. Some renewed experiences with nervous disorders may have had a part in his disturbed condition at this time.

Because of the emotional shock of their child's death and the ill health of the author, the couple decided, perhaps very wisely, to give their days to traveling, to remove themselves from the scene of their misfortune with respectable haste. They closed their house in Grafton, and some months later decided to sell it, never returning to it. Perhaps partly on the advice of a physician, they sailed in September 1906 across the Atlantic for an extended tour of the European continent. Both Melville and Bloom found many reasons to feel very much at home among the English and in all parts of the British Isles where life conducted in an aristocratic manner was still commonplace. Melville was decidedly impressed with the historical significance everywhere about, and especially he was impressed with the tradition that was maintained in the large homes and old castles. He loved to ride whenever the opportunity presented itself, and at Melton Mowbray he joined into the activities of the hunt clubs. Post's style of dress at this time, and often in the years that followed, was patterned after the English and his clothing was quite likely purchased from English tailors of best reputation.

Dwellers in the Hills had gained for Melville a measure of respect in England as an author and he found himself warmed by the admiration of the British readers. The Baron Anatole von

Hugel proceeded to invite him to Cambridge, Prince Mahadel welcomed him at Harrow, and other invitations followed. He was a guest at the United Service Club in Pall Mall, invited by the Earl of Glasglow, and he was asked to visit at a number of county seats, among such prominent ones as that of the eminent M. W. Calchester Wemyss, who was at this time guardian in Great Britain for the King of Siam.[31]

The sense of nobility and the regal atmosphere won Melville and Bloom over completely. During this period they leased for several months a baronial-style house where they could entertain their many English friends and acquaintances in a very British manner. A picture taken at this time and later published in several newspapers at home shows Bloom dressed like a princess in sweeping folds of rich cloth, glittering with expensive jewels, and holding a large bouquet of roses.[32] It was made on the occasion of June 6, 1907, when Bloom was presented to King Edward VII and Queen Ann in court at St. James in Buckingham Palace through the influence of Mrs. Whitelaw Reid, wife of the American ambassador. On reading the short explanatory caption which accompanied the newspaper photograph, John T. McGraw, reportedly remarked, "As sure as hell, that was written by Mel!" The presentation was surely for Melville and Bloom the thrill of a lifetime. The considerable expense of Bloom's outfit and of their stay in London, Post pointed out in a letter to his father, (as if it had been questioned or was expected to be) was handled entirely by Bloom's brother-in-law, John E. DuBois.

During their stay abroad the Posts set about on various tours throughout Europe. Traveling through the Low Countries Melville was especially impressed by the huge windmills grinding grain for the millers in Belgium. Other days were spent in France, where Bloom had attended school, enjoying the quaint villages and delighting in Paris. There were pleasant days spent in Italy too, where Bloom had many friends and had earlier been presented to Pope Pius X. They also found time to visit the rarified heights of Switzerland. Next to England, Melville preferred the mountains of the Alpine country. He was fascinated by the snow-covered peaks jutting upward into the clouds, and he felt a kinship with the Swiss people, rugged, hardy mountaineers, not unlike his own people back at home in West Virginia. Compared to the bustle and the complexity of the British social scene, Switzerland was a place where he and Bloom could relax and reflect upon things. The country had its long range effect on his life—for years later Post built his own "Chalet" in West Virginia's mountains.

This series of adventures abroad was not only therapy for the author, but it provided him with experiences he would draw upon for many years in the writing of his short stories. The trip served as needed inspiration, coming at just the right time—and the author made the most of it. His own biographical statement, made many years later, revealed the importance of these days spent in the company of royalty when Melville Post would say he "had eaten dinner with a god" and after viewing the giant windmills he could add that he "kissed a princess in a land where men grind their wheat in the sky."

Post, upon returning from Europe in November 1907 well-rested and improved in health, began to pursue his career as an author with new energy, working at several projects. We may note that between 1901 and 1907 there appears almost no published evidence of his doing any significant writing. He had not published a book since *Dwellers in the Hills* in 1901 and had published no fiction in any periodicals—though his Randolph Mason books were still selling and causing comment. *The Strange Schemes of Randolph Mason* had by this time gone through at least twelve printings. Post had maintained an interest in Democratic Party politics, but now participated more from the sidelines. One of the few things he did publish during this period was an interesting article on the Democratic vice-presidential candidate, ex-senator Henry G. Davis, an eighty-one year old man of great wealth and influence in West Virginia; the item appeared in a 1904 issue of *Harper's Weekly*. Otherwise there is no indication of any creative work during these years.

Then beginning with the January 1907 issue of *Pearson's Magazine,* Post appeared in that publication's pages with a story, or part of a story, each month for eighteen months. Three of these stories were published in two parts, and of the fifteen tales published successively at this time, all but two, the first and the last items, made up the contents of his next book, *The Corrector of Destinies; Being Tales of Randolph Mason as Related by His Private Secretary, Courtlandt Parks.*

From available evidence it seems likely, for several reasons, that the stories which make up this group were for the most part written at an earlier date, probably before 1903 and after 1897 when the second Randolph Mason book was published. First, they were not only announced as a "series" at the initiation of their serial appearance, but the rapidity of their appearance would indicate they were done well in advance of publication. Secondly, in *Pearson's* they appeared in exactly the same order in which they appear in book form, clearly indicating that they were published from an existing book manuscript. Thirdly, they match, for the most part, the style and theme of the material in the first two books of Randolph Mason stories, rather than the new style and theme that Post used for his writing from this point onward. And, finally, the editor of *Pearson's Magazine*, Arthur W. Little, states in announcing the stories in the January 1907 issue, "A few months ago we announced that after an effort of about four years we had succeeded in securing from the author of *The Strange Schemes of Randolph Mason* a new series of stories . . . "

It is actually not until the latter half of 1908 that we find Melville Post again performing as a prolific author, his material appearing with increasing regularity in various popular periodicals. For him and Bloom a place of residence continued to remain essentially unsettled, for they continued to travel and to keep up with the social activities they found available. From 1908 through the next six years they divided their time between trips to Europe and regular visits to the Eastern resorts. There were also occasional visits to Templemoor. Because this was the scene of her son's death and because Templemoor was still a busy cattle farm, Bloom's visits there were perhaps more of a duty than a pleasure.

These vagabond days were interspersed with lengthy stays at the home of Bloom's sister Willie, Mrs. John E. DuBois, in DuBois, Pennsylvania—a home referred to by Melville and the DuBois family as "The Mansion."[33] The house was one of grand proportions, having great staircases, large fireplaces and a huge living room. Located about a mile from the center of the town, its grounds were beautifully landscaped and surrounded by numerous trees. From late 1907 through 1914, so frequently and for such extended periods did Melville and Bloom stay at the Mansion with Willie, her husband, and several children that Post used it as his public address during some of these years. It was here also that he completed a considerable amount of the writing he produced during these years. The couple had a three room apartment set aside for their use on the third floor, and Melville when he was not riding or taking long walks would spend his morning hours in the southernmost room working on his stories and articles.

Of the several projects he was engaged in, following 1907, one was a novel. Quite fitting to the mood of his life at this time it developed as a story of romance and adventure. He also was beginning a series of articles which he would publish in the *Saturday Evening Post* under the general title "Mysteries of the Law." And of most importance, he was writing and succeeding in publishing a number of pieces of short fiction in a newly-developed style, stories that for the most part were to become the essential contents of a book which would be published in 1912. This new style of writing was leading him closer toward the superb style that would be used in constructing the Uncle Abner tales.

Publication of the third and last volume of the Randolph Mason stories, featuring the fascinating criminal lawyer, was managed in 1908 through the facilities of the publisher Edward J. Clode. The earlier Randolph Mason stories had created a certain amount of adverse criticism, not necessarily of a literary nature, but most frequent in reference to the conduct of Randolph Mason aiding various of his clients to escape the criminal penalties due them morally, if not legally. Some readers felt that Randolph Mason, who was portrayed as being of unquestionable aid to the hard-pressed clients who managed to secure his attention, was in reality doing society a great injustice by showing criminals that crimes without punishment were possible. As a result of this these last stories present Randolph Mason as an agent correcting specific injustices pressing his clients without the accompanying defeat of the law. There are noticeable changes in Mason's conduct and attitudes, but how successful Post was in reaching towards his newly-defined goal is open to debate.

Meanwhile *The Gilded Chair,* his novel of romance and adventure, was beginning to take shape. It was apparently begun as an attempt to realize a deep-seated ambition to write a popular romance. There is little doubt that the plot of this work comes closer to being that of a novel than any in the other books of

Melville Post. The plot is not an extensively involved one. The story is principally centered around a romance between a young American girl, heiress to a newly-created commercial fortune, and the Duke of Dorset, a British nobleman—a romance that promised to upset some long established traditions. Melodramatic as it would appear, much of it seems to have been drawn from Post's own romance with Bloom. The setting of the opening chapters in England and Scotland surely was a direct result of their extended visit there and the strong influence of the British atmosphere upon Post.

The latter portion of the story is set in the Pacific Northwest, the result of some extensive revisions Post made in the book. This part, adding adventure to the romance, is concerned with an aspect of the Japanese immigrant problem which was the subject of much active debate during the years 1908 and 1909. While the book was not a literary success in any sense of the word, and certainly was not a financial one, yet the book remains interesting and readable if for nothing other than its insight into the author's life and thought.

Correspondence written in regard to *The Gilded Chair* reveals Post's methods of preparing his work for publication during the first half of his career.[34] Writing to Louis E. Schrader of Wheeling, a court reporter and operator of a legal secretarial service and a typewriter sales agency, the author reported on the extensive "structual change" he had decided upon for his novel then in work. Schrader replied within a few days that "Miss (Bertha E.) Baird who copied the original manuscript of the Gilded Chair is at your service . . . "

Post's method appears to have been to first write out his material in a rather small, closely-spaced script, making corrections according to need and the ease with which the work was progressing. The sheets of the handwritten manuscript were then forwarded to Schrader for preparation of the typescript. Frequently Schrader was informed by Post in his instructions to "fiddle around with this," most likely meaning for Miss Baird and Mr. McGinley, a clerk in Schrader's office, to catch any errors in grammar, spelling, and punctuation which had been overlooked. Often when deadlines were involved, Schrader was instructed to send the typed copy of the manuscript directly to the editor of the publication for which it was destined.

Post seems to have felt that his part in the creating of the material was essentially to produce a plot and then to fit it into a meaningful narrative. He was more than anxious to leave the minor details to others. The price of this service to Post is revealed in letters exchanged with Schrader in 1910. The author wrote that some manuscripts were typed for him by secretarial services located in Baltimore and Philadelphia which charged only 10 cents per page. Schrader shrewdly replied that the service he had furnished Post was perhaps somewhat better than that done by these others, noting that his typed manuscripts contained more words per page at his 12-15 cent rates than those of the cheaper services. Not wishing to see Post's business lost, nor wishing to offend a friend, Schrader offered to see what he could do. Providing his employees were not rushed (as was often the case with much of Post's work) he promised to endeavor to reduce his price. The results, while not known, were likely in Post's favor as he continued to use the service for some years following the event.

Post, certainly never lacking in financial means, was a frugal person in many ways. This is well illustrated by observing how frequently [for his handwritten manuscripts] he made use of letterhead paper secured from those with whom he was currently associated. Early examples show he used stationery of the Democratic Congressional Executive Committee of the First West Virginia District. Later he often made use of the stationery of the John E. DuBois Lumber Company. No doubt early training had instilled in him prudence in matters of money. There are an extensive number of stories in which the possession of money is central to the theme of the work.

Beginning around 1908 and through the remaining years of his life, Post appeared regularly in many of the leading American magazines having popular appeal. His first appearance in the *Saturday Evening Post* was on December 19, 1908, with a short story called "The Trivial Incident." This was a minor but interesting tale emphasizing convicting powers of circumstance and rumor. Within the next four years he had made thirty-four appearances in the *Post,* which then claimed "more than a million and a half circulation weekly." Over two-thirds of these appearances were non-fiction items, some belonging to the series "Mysteries of the Law," some to a series titled "Extraordinary Cases," and still others running under individual titles, but all aimed at giving the layman some insight into the legal machinery of the day. Post's interest in writing about the intricacies of the law in his early work outweighs by far his interest in the mystery. Of the tales being written during this period, the majority emphasize legal problems, with only an exceptional tale, such as "A Critique of Monsieur Poe" published in 1910, allowing classification as a pure mystery story.

"A Critique of Monsieur Poe" incidently is one of Post's better-written stories, though it has had little recognition because when published in book format it was buried in Post's unusual but neglected collection entitled *The Nameless Thing*. This story and stories published in the *Saturday Evening Post, The Atlantic Monthly, Harper's Monthly Magazine*, and other publications were woven together into a continuous narrative in the book put out by D. Appleton and Company in 1912. To bring these stories together, Post devised an encompassing plot regarding the meeting of an attorney, a doctor of medicine, and a priest. These three are brought together to investigate the death of a certain Wilfred Druce. The device used here by Post is built around the efforts of these three men to understand the enigmatic death. This they attempt by illustrating their varied viewpoints through the telling of various tales. The book recalls the structures used for the grouping of tales in such works as the *Decameron* and *The Canterbury Tales*. There is a noticeable spread in the quality of these stories, which Post put together with minimal if any revision, and what results is a somewhat uneven book. Yet, while some of the stories reflect Post's work at its least effectiveness, others emerge as some of the more readable and entertaining of his many stories. Unfortunately the book was not successful, and today it is one of the more difficult of Post's books for the reader to come upon.

On June 3, 1911, the *Saturday Evening Post* published the first of Melville Post's most successful series of stories, a series not destined to be published in book form until 1918. This story, bearing the title "The Broken Stirrup-Leather" (which in collected form is retitled "An Angel of the Lord"), was the first to incorporate that unique rural detective who would prove to be the stand-out creation of Post's entire career, Uncle Abner. Several Uncle Abner stories were written and published by the author before the end of 1912. Post by this time was an established short story author of high standing and thus had begun to receive top prices for his manuscripts.

There were a number of authors contributing to the *Saturday Evening Post* about this time, of varying stature but all high in popular esteem, such as Jack London, Rupert Hughes, Emerson Hough, Edna Ferber, T. S. Cobb, Fannie Hurst, and others. These writers gained much of their claim to fame through the pages of this magazine. As a general family magazine under the direction of its long-time editor, George Horace Lorimer, its circulation figures inched upward towards the two million figure. Post continued his contributions to the *Saturday Evening Post* until the end of World War I, selling a total of 87 items of fact and fiction to this one magazine.

Meanwhile, Melville and Bloom continued their habitual travels from year to year, season to season. During the course of his regular visits to the fashionable centers and clubs in the East where he associated with businessmen and politicians, Post took increasing note of the souring world situation. Also he observed the growing intrigue and the tension developing between governments when he took restful visits to the French Riviera. As always, these travels continued amid stopovers at the Mansion with his in-laws and visits at Templemoor with his now-aging parents. He also somehow saved time for his favorite sport, polo on Long Island, and always in England and elsewhere, riding was fit into his plans. Although West Virginia continued to retain first importance in his life and his writings, he had come a long way from the rugged hills in which he grew into manhood. Obviously, as a brilliant, gracious person, it was a change to which he was equal. And Bloom with her European education, her friends on both sides of the Atlantic, and with the charming southern background of her early years, fit perfectly into the social circles she and Melville frequented.

With his outlook broadened, Post increasingly turned his attention to Europe in his fictional offerings, noting the publication in periodicals of several of the M. Joncquel stories. These are woven around the presence of a cosmopolitan French detective. And while still writing an occasional article based on his legal experience and interest, many of his articles were now showing his increased interest in national and international politics. But though these forays into the larger world took much of his time, his attention managed to focus regularly on West Virginia for additional stories of Uncle Abner.

Post returned to West Virginia in sorrow when on February 10, 1914, his mother passed away at the age of seventy-one years. She received a funeral fully in keeping with her many accomplishments in family and civic concerns, including noteworthy tribute from the community, proper services in the First Methodist Episcopal Church and at the burial site in Elkview Masonic Cemetery of Clarksburg, all duly reported in the local press.[35]

The year 1914 brought World War I and to Post the year brought two other significant events. Midway in the year an Uncle Abner story, "The Doomdorf Mystery," was published serially. Grant Overton, writing of this event ten years later, exclaimed, "Who that read in the *Saturday Evening Post* of July 18, 1914 a short story called, 'The Doomdorf Mystery' forgets it now." Post had reached the high point of his career where he would remain for the next decade and more. All other success that followed this was anticlimactic. He had a certain degree of pride (or vanity), as indicated by the wording of his entry in *Who's Who in America* for 1916-1917, which unnecessarily verified his inclusion by stating, "The Corpus Delicti included in the masterpieces of mystery fiction by Review of Reviews, and all short stories pub. in 1915, cited among the distinguished contributions to Amer. lit. during that period by the lit. critic of Boston Transcript." This statement, whatever else it might be, is undeniably objective and true.

The year of 1914 also had a special significance for Post as it was the year he built a large home in the West Virginia hills of his boyhood. It was a house designed essentially for Bloom and himself. He selected a location not far from the place of his birth on a hill overlooking the valley through which Gnatty Creek flows, a site where the Indians had been known to encamp at one time. Bits of pottery and other remnants of the Indians life were uncovered there during the excavation work. Post called the spot

"The Hill of the Painted Men." Having picked the site, he had the architects design a magnificent house of stone and wood construction closely based upon the designs of houses he had often seen in the Swiss Alpine country. The drawings for the house were completed just five days after the armies of the German Empire invaded France at the start of World War I.[36]

Work began at once that summer, with stone from the local quarries being shaped and laid to form the foundation and the walls of the first story. The wood for the second story exterior was Oregon redwood, especially cut and made ready for use by lumber mills in that state. Post used, in his article, "The Mystery Story," an analogy of the construction of a house to the construction of a short story: "One may build any kind of house he likes, but he must build it from material that is real. He must get his stone from the field and his wood from the forest."

The ornamentations were numerous: exact carvings, odd cuttings, and authentic trimmings reproducing that found on similar houses scattered about the heights of Switzerland. The work was an indication of both the love and the money Post invested. A picture reproduced in Grant Overton's *Cargoes for Crusoes* has the author posed in a huge doorway of this house, perhaps the front entrance, set in a wall laid with great chunks of limestone. The heavy wood door is carefully made with triangular panels seemingly constructed of stained glass. Another picture, found in Warren Wood's *Representative Authors of West Virginia,* is a corner view of the entire structure, displaying the magnificent and intricate workmanship in the carvings. Post had waited long for his house and he did not wish to go halfway now.

The foundation was approximately thirty-five by fifty feet, the entire structure being topped by a roof having enormous eaves, in keeping with the general design. The principal rooms of interest were a huge drawing room covering one entire end of the first floor, a library room, and between these a dining room. All were available from a long reception hall.

These rooms had floors of light oak in narrow strips. Some, including the reception hall had wainscoted walls. Other walls and all the ceilings were of plaster. The woodwork in the house was a work of art, the labor of a crew of wood-working specialists sent down by John E. DuBois from his DuBois, Pennsylvania lumber establishment. They erected built-in cabinets for storage, window seats, bookshelves and paneled the walls in dark oak. The workmen erected temporary shelters on the site in which they lived during the months of construction.

The furnishings selected were the finest available, in keeping with the general atmosphere, and among them were many various pieces Melville and Bloom had collected during their trips abroad. In the drawing room there were two desks. One, the favorite of Post when he worked on his manuscripts, was an exceptionally finely finished piece that he was particularly attached to, by either habit or nostalgia. It is probable that he had used it for many years at Templemoor, from his school days on. The principal furnishings were French, perhaps a reflection of Bloom's taste. Heavy blue draperies softened the glare of the winter sunlight. These, closed on the colder days, helped to make the house warm and comfortable. Several fireplaces provided heat in the milder seasons, but Post had provided the house with a central heating system for comfortable steam heat on the colder days. The fireplaces were used as frequently as possible and in front of the drawing room mantel Post placed a set of tall, bronze fire irons together with an array of strangely made fire tools. These were supposed to have come from somewhere in Italy and it was said they had belonged to a king; as to their actual history the author preferred to remain silent, their true origin remaining another personal mystery.

Doors from the dining room opened onto a large, tiled terrace running the length of the building. It was here that Post loved to work when the weather permitted. The area was surrounded with carved railings, and a curving stairway with a stone banister led to a grassy terrace that bordered the wooded hillside. The grounds were thoroughly landscaped, circled with flat-stone walkways, stone benches and cool lily ponds. The drive from the road, its entrance flanked by large stone columns, was paved for its several hundred feet of length with huge, flat slabs of stone. The house was in many ways as fascinating as the secluded Chateau of Cyrus Childers which Post had described in the pages of *The Gilded Chair*, although not built on such an extravagant scale as the imaginary one.

By the spring of 1915 Post and his wife were settled in their home, the last permanent residence they were to share. Basically

Alpine in design, faithfully constructed with his feelings for Switzerland upmost in mind, Post designated his house as "The Chalet." Some nineteen years following Post's death in 1930, a fire struck the house and completely destroyed it.

In December 1914 and in February 1915, Post published two articles revealing the essentials of his literary beliefs. Titled "The Blight" and "The Mystery Story," they set the ground rules which he followed in formulating his short stories. Although they would seem to be of small aid to a novice or to a would-be-writer needing guidance, their tenets guided Post, and although he varied from them as he saw fit, he swore by their implications. Whatever their value to others, they served Post through some of his most prolific writing years.

The war, in full force in Europe and on the sea, had for the present curtailed the visits to the usual resorts. In keeping with the current events Post published a number of articles on the use of secret codes and espionage, an aspect of the war that was then largely unknown to the average person. He had, possibly from the days when he first read the tales of Edgar Allen Poe, an interest in cryptography. Putting this interest to use, he reported on the current arts of spying to the readers of the popular periodicals, giving them some insight into the sinister work. Also, from time to time, he applied this same interest in cryptography to the composition of some of his fiction.

Post also became involved in another campaign, one for proper justice in the courts. This was a field in which he had long maintained a special interest. During the years 1914 and 1915 he served as a member of the Advisory Committee of the National Economic League's study into the "efficiency in the administration of justice." Among those involved in this program were such well-known names in the legal world as Charles W. Eliot, Louis Brandeis, and Roscoe Pound. A preliminary report was issued in 1914,[37] but the fate of the committee or the final outcome of the project, if it was completed, is not known.

Post had set up his own definition of justice some years earlier. In an Uncle Abner short story entitled "The Tenth Commandment," published in 1912, the author wrote:

> "The law is not always justice . . . "
> "Abner," replied Dillworth, "how shall we know what

justice is unless the law defines it?"

"I think every man knows what it is," said Abner.

"And shall every man set up a standard of his own," said Dillworth, "and disregard the standard that the law sets up? That would be the end of justice."

"It would be the beginning of justice," said Abner, "if every man followed the standard that God gives him."[38]

Although Post championed justice, he did not sympathize with the true criminal who was fleeing the law and its agencies. During the months of 1916 and 1917 he published a series of articles focusing on the methods of police detective work as it was conducted in the United States, at Scotland Yard in England, at the Detective Department of Paris police, and elsewhere. Some of these articles were given sub-titles and were grouped under the general title "The Man Hunters," and some were presented independently. They were based on extensive reading as well as on Post's own observations made during his frequent travels and his constant search for short story materials. Since the author's purpose seems to have been journalistic, rather than investigative the pieces allowed little originality. They were published in book form ten years later, and they are the only part of his non-fiction work given this permanence. Post's study of criminology shows up in much of the fictional work, influencing the selection of characters and themes.

In 1917 the United States declared war on Germany and readied its people to enter the conflict. Post, about to reach his 48th birthday, patriotic and civic-minded as he was put most of his talent to use in behalf of the war effort, composing slogans and other copy to be used in recruiting men and money. Subjects related to the war also became the theme of a number of his articles. During the time he worked in support of the country's war goals, there was a sharp decline in the number of short stories published.

The year 1918 is important because of one event that took place that year, the publication of the collection of stories featuring Post's rural detective "Uncle Abner." This book, *Uncle Abner, Master of Mysteries*, would prove to be the crowning achievement of his career. D. Appleton and Company were the fortunate publishers of this work, the only one of his titles to have remained in print, at least until recently. Many of the 18 stories that comprise this volume had already added considerable strength to Post's reputation when published in periodicals over the preceding seven years. They had helped to establish him as one of the highest-paid authors of magazine material of this period. The book, which received good reviews, assured Melville Davisson Post of a lasting and secure place in the annals of American literature. Yet, like so many popular works, *Uncle Abner* has always tended to overshadow much of Post's other work, work often worthy of equal attention.

Always financially secure, Post was now assured of a firm financial position. The public was ready and willing to purchase his stories and the following year, 1919, D. Appleton and Company brought out another collection of Post's short stories. These were selected from the many he had sold to leading periodicals over the recent years, particularly those with plots woven against the continental background. Entitled *The Mystery at the Blue Villa*, which is also the title of the lead story, the book presents readers with several of Post's more unusual and entertaining stories: "The Great Legend," "The Laughter of Allah," "The Miller of Ostend," and others. The writing is a rich display of Post's technical skills. His sharp, economic style led to the development of the "tough-guy" type of fiction that carved a literary field of its own in this century. Post's excellent objective observations and reporting, however, were not always helped by his choice of plots. One reviewer thought the plots, most with remote settings and strange characters, a bit over-dramatic; but reviewers in general were pleased though seldom enthusiastic about the collection. Many people, including former President Theodore Roosevelt, were reading his stories,[39] and thus Post had much to be happy about.

Yet, near the end of 1919, almost coincidental with the publication of Post's latest book, Bloom was placed in a Philadelphia hospital for treatment of skin cancer. Melville and Bloom had been looking forward toward the end of the war and a return to normalcy in Europe so that they might resume their travels on a regular basis. However, during her hospital stay Bloom contracted the dread disease pneumonia. Mrs. Post died on December 17, 1919. Above all other things Melville had been devoted to Bloom and her tragic passing at the prime of her life, when he was at the pinnacle of success as an author, was a blow from which he never successfully recovered.

It is difficult to calculate the full effect Bloom's death had on Post's career. We note that his creative output slowed considerably during the months following Bloom's passing. It was almost two years before he managed to become comparatively productive again, although not nearly on the same scale as he had been before these days of readjustment. Little if any of Post's later work managed to equal in quality what he had published before 1920.

One of the few short stories Post had published during 1919, the "Five Thousand Dollars Reward," was selected as one of the O'Henry Memorial Award prize stories for that year, the only story of Post's ever honored in this manner. Although both Edward O'Brien and F. L. Pattee considered the stories of Post negligible as literature, as they did most all stories they could group under the heading of "mystery stories," they did regularly award him special praise for his high degree of technical excellence. But, Blanche Colton Williams, who led in the selection of the O'Henry prize story, said:

> . . . the committee confess to catholicity of taste, the chosen stories reveal predilection for no one type. They like detective stories, and particularly those of Melville Davisson Post. A follower of the founder of this school of fiction, he has none the less advanced beyond his master and has discovered other ways than those of Rue Morgue. "Five Thousand Dollars Reward" in its brisk action, strong suspense, and humorous denouement carries on the technique so neatly achieved in "The Doomdorf Mystery" and other tales about Uncle Abner.[40]

Blanche Colton Williams also included a chapter on Post in her volume *Our Short Story Writers*, published in 1920, in which she continues her elated praise of his work. Post was now on the verge of receiving the serious consideration his work deserved, but the unfortunate death of his wife surely cast a shadow over these brighter things.

D. Appleton and Company brought out the next of Post's published works in 1920, another collection of mystery and detective fiction. These stories, put together under the title *The Sleuth of St. James's Square*, do not as a whole reach the same level of quality as the Uncle Abner stories, but the stories are readable and good entertainment, especially for the reader favoring the mystery fiction plot. They continue to exhibit the benefits of their author's economic style. Post's prize story, "Five Thousand Dollars Reward," is included here slightly changed and with the title reduced to merely "The Reward." The locale of these stories does not keep to St. James's Square as the title of the book might imply, but the settings include many of the places to which Melville Davisson Post himself had traveled.

The Sleuth of St. James's Square was probably contracted for and mostly put together sometime previous to the death of Mrs. Post. The works collected here, which can be correctly dated, were nearly all published earlier and those couple published later had likely been written earlier and already sold to the publications wherein they first appeared. Most of the stories involve a Scotland Yard-type detective created by Post, Sir Henry Marcus. In many of these stories Sir Henry's part was spliced in, with some logic and a bit of technical fortitude, to permit their inclusion under the title. Reviewers treated the book with a measure of respect and gave it good reports, but in reality it added little to Post's stature as an author.

Post's next book, *The Mountain School-Teacher,* was in many ways a sudden and strict departure in theme from most of the work he had published up to this time. Whatever the origin of this particular book, which was first published serially two years after Bloom's death, it appears that the loss of his wife greatly influenced the direction this story took. We might observe that Post had come at this point through the full circle of religious speculation and experience. From the Christian teachings gathered in his youth, Post, as a young man, turned to consider agnosticism and paganism, then myth and mysticism in the early years of his writing career. In his central years he reflected on the fire and brimstone religion of the Old Testament, and finally returned to a detached but serious consideration of Christianity. Thus, it seems appropriate that we ask the question: What part did Bloom's death have in bringing about this final attitude and this unusual book? Since *The Mountain School-Teacher* was such an absolute and abrupt departure from the themes and treatment of his earlier work and signals a new concern with religion also found in other items of the next eight years, we can speculate that the shock of Bloom's death effected a change in the author's religious outlook.

While our speculations may not give a positive answer to the question, the book in question, with its frank attitudes toward the figure of Jesus, will never let the question rest.

This work, *The Mountain School-Teacher,* published in 1922 by D. Appleton and Company, can be classified as either a long story (196 pp.) or a short novel. The term "allegory" has been constantly applied to the story ever since its publication, but only in a broad sense is the term accurately used. Post has taken as an outline the general story of the life of Jesus Christ as related in the Gospels and has resurrected Jesus in the contemporary world as a "school-teacher." (Although Jesus is never named, the identification is obvious.) There are abundant pitfalls awaiting the writer venturing upon this subject, but Post did exceptionally well, treating it with the upmost reverence and skill. His minor elaborations do nothing to change any essential part of the biblical story. One who had an opportunity to visit the Chalet a few years after Post's death, reported on the author's library:

> One section is made up of works on Christ—lives, interpretations of the teachings of Jesus, and kindred studies. These, no doubt, were obtained by Mr. Post when he was working on *The Mountain School Teacher,* his story of Christ in a modern setting—a motif that two or three other writers have worked up in the time of our generation, but which, it may be mentioned, no one has done quite so well as Mr. Post.[41]

In a work such as *The Mountain School-Teacher,* what the author leaves out, what he includes, and what he emphasizes demonstrate much regarding his personal beliefs and attitudes.

There were some who considered this work worthy of nomination for the Nobel Prize Award, and the critics in 1922 were thoroughly impressed. One critic writing in the *New York Times* suggested that the book contains "such perceptible degree of authentic literary values . . . that most readers must revise their opinion of Mr. Post."[42] Preceding this in the same review, the writer speaks of "a kindling literary ambition in Mr. Post that is not alone concerned with the intricacies of detective fiction, which, after all, is not literature." However, Post's fame was not to rest on such books as this, but, literature or not, on his mystery and detective tales. If nothing else, *The Mountain School-*

Teacher demonstrates the wide range of Post's abilities once and for all. Incidental to this story's merit as literature is the fact that the magazine *Pictorial Review* paid Post $10,000 to publish the serial version of the story in two installments.[43] It was reportedly the highest amount paid up to that time for magazine fiction. Even today's author must look with envy at such a feat.

In the years following Bloom's death, Melville did not resume his former habits of travel. Without Bloom as a traveling companion, he maintained much less interest in the seasonal and migrating social life at the upper levels of society. He instead began to spend more of his various seasons at The Chalet. There he attempted to fill the gaps left in his life by his departed son, mother, and wife. He was now a man who was without the day-to-day companionship of an immediate family. At first he still had his father nearby, who doubtlessly endured the normal symptoms of the aged, but on September 27, 1923, Ira Carper Post passed on at the age of eighty-one years. In many ways Melville had been closer to his father than he was to his mother, and he may have felt this a greater loss, for in his father, Melville had first found many of his strong ideals.

Melville now found himself at The Chalet with many hours of solitude, and he sought ways to make the best of it. The Elk District of Harrison County, among the more beautiful spots in West Virginia, was—with its green, rolling hills populated mostly by cattle—the perfect spot for detached reflection. Apparently Post relished the opportunities he had to be alone, for he seems to have been at times very strict about those who might interrupt his solitude, and he especially disliked trespassers and poachers. A popular story is related of his shooting a lantern out of the hands of a local man who one night crossed the grounds of the Post estate without permission. Fortunately for all, particularly the surprised neighbor, the author, always interested in and skillful with weapons, was an exceptionally accurate shot.

Perhaps because he valued his solitude, a solitude he demanded principally during the periods when he was engaged in putting together one of his story ideas, rumors grew about Post and his magnificent house. There was the idle speculation that it contained secret rooms and hidden passages as well as a fortune in old coins. The house was foreign and strange to those West

Virginians who had not traveled far, like something from another world. To children it may have seemed like something out of a fairy tale, and being awed they sometimes spoke of it in hushed tones. These things did not seem to trouble Post, if in fact they ever reached his ears, as he always seemed to relish an air of mystery about his person and his work.

His writing efforts apparently did not follow a regular schedule, since he usually wrote only when sufficiently inspired by an intriguing plot. At such times the generally understood rule was that he was not to be disturbed in any way. Those close to him knew the signal which indicated they could approach the house without interrupting his work. They would watch his flag pole, for if the flag was not all the way to the top he was at work writing, but if all the way to the top, they were welcome if they wished to visit. It has been stated that Post welcomed occasional visits from various acquaintances and neighbors when made at the appropriate times. According to all reports, he was on these occasions a gracious and pleasant host, whether his guests were distinguished persons or just a group of neighborhood school children.

Post's numerous diversions during these years were perhaps an unconscious effort to fill the gap left by the loss of his loved ones with as busy a life as possible. During these days and for the remainder of his life, he was often seen riding a favorite horse about his property and on the nearby roads, sometimes calling on old friends and neighbors. Other hours were spent with his many expensive sporting guns, searching out the small local game such as the squirrel, rabbit, and particularly the groundhog, long-time enemy of the cattleman. Occasionally when business took him to Clarksburg, about twelve miles away, he could be seen traveling the road from Buckhannon in one of his several cars, a very old Franklin, a handsome Stutz, or his rugged Ford. Orientated as a youth to a world that depended upon the horse, he never became a competent driver and his dependence on the automobile was negligible.

It was the horse which held the highest place in his regular leisure activities. It was the creature he trusted the most and it played a significant part in his life, if only a relative part in his writings. He was fond of posing for occasional photographs astride a horse or dressed for his sport in helmet and riding outfit. One writer recalled Post during these years as "a small man with military bearing, a quiet, intelligent eye, and an apparently unbroken calm."[44] Perhaps it was more of a stoic calm. She also reports that as a neighbor to the Post estate, she frequently heard "the fierce tattoo of the beats of the feet of his polo ponies ... in the distance." Polo had for many years been his favorite sport, and in the meadow down the hill from The Chalet he had built a private polo field. Here he could practice regularly and play games with a group of close friends and relatives.

He kept several polo ponies, among them a favorite named Margo. An unusual and well-trained mount, Margo was frequently assigned to those who were inexperienced at the game. Astride her, a rider had little to do but follow her lead. Stories are told of her ability to follow the ball: for she carefully brought the players into line with the ball but if they missed it during the swing of their mallet, she would stop suddenly, throw back her head, and raise her ears at the ineptness of her rider. Usually on hand for the games was Orange Jud Perkins, faithful as ever to his friend and employer, who attended to all the needs of the players and the horses.

There were many happy gatherings and games at The Chalet, especially during the summer months. Among those usually present were a number of Melville's friends and business acquaintances. Perhaps to compensate for the loss of his own child or partially to lessen the impacts of thoughts of aging, he exhibited a genuine liking for active young people and regularly included a number of them in the various activities. They were neighborhood youngsters, sometimes children of his friends, and whenever vacations from school permitted, several of the DuBois nieces and nephews, children of his wife's sister.

Now an author herself, Agnes Smith Parrish often visited at the Post home during the latter half of the 20's as a young neighbor. She has described in a letter to this writer typical activities of those years at The Chalet as she recalled them:

> During those years I was one of a number of persons of all ages who were guests in his home. We went up for the day, to play polo on his small field and have a picnic lunch after the game was over. With a friend or relative of an age

> to chaperone, at irregular intervals I spent two or three days at The Chalet. We took long cross-country rides during the day and had very good conversation after dinner.
>
> . . . .
>
> There was no formality in our discussion of books, which was often long and heated.
>
> . . . .
>
> As a person, Melville was, to put it bluntly, a darling. Quirky, not like other people; thin, but moving slowly and deliberately; given to long observant silences, often broken by memorable comments or amusing anecdotes. After dinner, while the talk was progressing, he moved from chair to chair, and once explained that it was a sign of approaching old age always to sit in the same chair. I didn't realize it then, but whatever his age he must have been, while I knew him, a very lonely man.

A relative recalls one of the dinners whereat Melville, in his sometimes mysterious fashion, served his guests with a meat that he declined at first to identify. The guests in general were pleased with the delicate, sweet taste of the dish and speculated as to what it might be. Finally their host told them that it was the meat of a possum which he had recently shot.

While to most Melville Davisson Post, during this period, outwardly gave the impression of being a happy and satisfied man, those who knew him best were from time to time made aware of the effects of the stress the changes in his life situation had brought about. There is evidence of his uncertain moods, sometimes apparent in his writing in subtle ways. We might well reason that it was now mostly from force of habit and desire to earn high prices for his work that he continued with some effort in his writing career. The pure desire to create stories was no longer his principal motivation. The record shows that his output diminished, not only in quantity but often in quality, compared to the productivity of the previous ten years.

There are some indications that Post may have changed his working methods drastically. His earlier writing was usually first worked out in a small, handwritten script in close to its final form before being sent along for preparation of the typescript. Reportedly in his later years he would think out his stories in detail first; then, supposedly by memory, he would dictate them to a secretary who would type up the finished manuscript. There is infrequent evidence of handwritten manuscripts for his later stories. Also he seems to have employed for an unknown length of time a secretary named Violet Knight. Thus we might readily assume that these reports are at least partially accurate.

Some of Post's later stories give a definite impression of having been worked out orally, for while still bearing signs of his distinctive technical craftsmanship, they emphasize the tone of conversation over and above that of concentrated thought and sharply turned phrases. Yet, always known to be elusive and ambiguous about his personal life and habits, it may have been that Post, asked by some of his acquaintances about his method of writing, jestingly answered that he merely dictated them to the secretary he employed (more for business purposes than creative), and thus the reports may have more substance as fiction than fact.

An interesting insight on his methods may be gleaned from the same letter quoted above, wherein Agnes Smith Parrish also noted:

> It must have been Melville who told me, I could never have imagined it, that this was the way he dealt with editors. They wrote to him requesting a story; he sent a synopsis; they sent him a check; he wrote the story; they published it.

Certainly one thing that did not change for Post throughout his career was the source of inspiration for his strong plots. From his lawyer-days on he read the newspapers, journals, and law reports noting things he could use in his work. A newspaper account of a trial or crime was often the seed (or "germ" as he termed it) from which his stories grew. It was the method he had used from the first, the use of a factual happening, noticed in print or personally experienced, causing a plot to germinate and a story to spring into being. His stories, while not a point by point recreation, almost without exception had a true incident to which they were related. Once in an unusual "article-story" entitled "Nick Carter, Realist," Post took strong issue with certain critics from a New York daily newspaper who had objected to his unique plots, thinking them overly melodramatic. He cited for these critics, and the reader, a true case that had been reported in published court records of the United States District Court of Nebraska in regular "Nick Carter" fashion. The case, complete with its seemingly melodramatic events and coincidences, concluded with a sensational capture that appeared more imagined than real, but all of it was the actual truth revealed as evidence in a court of law.

Additional evidence of Post's methods is supplied by Samuel Mallison, a journalist, who recalled years later an incident that occurred around 1922. Mallison, on close terms with the author at that time, recalls Melville reading an interesting report of a trial in a newspaper and remarking that he would use it as the basis for a story. The two men then conversed at some length about the story, the journalist noted, and Post went so far as to present a potential plot he would employ, giving it immediately in some detail. Mallison tells that he waited expectantly for a period hoping to soon see the story published by some magazine, but to no avail. Somewhat later, on meeting Post again, he inquired about the progress of the story, and according to Mallison's later recollection, the author replied,

> "I went down to Clarksburg yesterday and I saw this month's *Cosmopolitan* in the window of the newsstand, and on the cover I read, 'In this issue *The Mystery at the Thor Bridge* by A. Conan Doyle,' and I knew then that Doyle had beaten me to it. The funny part about it is that the plot he built around the incident is virtually the same as the one I had planned to use."[45]

We may not wish to rely too heavily upon Post's statement or Mallison's recollection, but the story does serve to illustrate the author's usual source of plots and may help explain the reports that Post would work plots into stories entirely in his head before dictating them. More reliable is the illustration of his continued ambition to do his work as well as humanly possible, found in a letter Post wrote to an editor: "I am taking this care with these stories because I want this to be a distinguished series." This is not the statement of a man who would dictate stories to a secretary with the same indifference that one might dictate a letter. Although the evidence is inconclusive, it appears certain that Post, dictating or not, still gave his work a fair degree of personal attention, as he had always done.

In 1924, the author published a further collection of his

mystery and detective tales in a volume entitled *Monsieur Jonquelle; Prefect of Police of Paris*. For some of these stories he reached as far back as 1913 when the first of the Monsieur Jonquelle stories appeared in print in a weekly periodical, while others of the collection had made their first serial publication more recently. One of these latter, "The Great Cipher," can be rated as an above-average tale. It reveals Post's life-long interest in cryptography, an interest evident in his occasional use of it throughout his literary work. This interest is also manifest to a degree in the stories wherein a character is given the exceptional ability to discover hidden meanings which are overlooked by the majority of people in their observance of commonplace things. This theme, the necessity for one to discover the evidence of truth which is forever lurking behind the seemingly obvious, was a favorite of the author.

Still another lifetime interest led Post in the year 1924 to temporary active participation in politics on the national level. That year the Democratic party selected a life-long acquaintance and fellow lawyer as its candidate for the Presidency of the United States, John William Davis. Davis was born in Clarksburg, West Virginia, just a few years after Post and the two men were in regular contact during the early years of their law careers. Davis served two terms in Congress as a Representative of West Virginia, under President Woodrow Wilson was a solicitor-general until 1918, and then for three years was the American ambassador to Great Britain. Davis was also an advisor to President Wilson during the Peace Conference in Paris in 1919.

Post apparently attended the opening sessions of the convention held in New York City in July of that year, but as the voting dragged on he returned to West Virginia. When Davis was finally chosen on the 103rd ballot, Post wired the *New York Times* on July 10 terming John William Davis as "our greatest citizen." A true Jeffersonian Democrat, a man with liberal tendencies tempered by strong ideals, Davis was indeed presidential material, but he was unfortunate in his timing. He had supported President Wilson's efforts in behalf of The League of Nations, but even his own party was split over this issue. He had recently been employed as an attorney by a number of giant corporations, thus labor did not trust him in spite of his liberal record. On top of all he faced a strong third party candidate, Robert La Follette, and an incumbent president.

Post responded at once to help Davis overcome the pressure against his winning the high office. His first effort was an article, "John W. Davis," published in the August 1924 issue of *The American Review of Reviews,* whose editor termed the author "an enthusiastic fellow-Democratic." Post emphasized Davis' religious influences, his Jeffersonian career, his individualism, his beliefs in law-enforcement, his legal background, and his liberal record. He pointed out that Davis had served labor as well as capital in his legal pursuits. He mentioned, but did not emphasize, Davis' record of opposition to isolationism. Since the article proclaims the candidate a moderate liberal, we can assume it a status in which Melville Davisson Post himself usually felt most comfortable.

Post helped too by leading in the formation of a committee of prominent writers who would supply both oral and printed publicity. Among persons prominent in literature and the arts who Post claimed as members of the committee he headed, we find some of his outstanding contemporaries: Meredith Nicholson, Henry Van Dyke, Charles Dana Gibson, Irvin S. Cobb, Augustus Thomas, Robert Underwood Johnson, and Brand Whitlock. These names are listed with that of Melville Davisson Post on the committee's position paper supporting the Davis candidacy.[46]

The difficulties facing Davis were too strong and the people were of a different mood. The voters selected Calvin Coolidge, the Republican opponent, by an almost 2 to 1 ratio in popular votes. Davis won only the traditional Democratic South, even losing in his native state of West Virginia. John William Davis, nevertheless, appreciated the efforts made by Post, and years later, in 1954, when asked to select a story for the volume *Fiction Goes to Court,* chose Post's "Corpus Delicti." In his introduction to the selection, Davis wrote: "Melville Davisson Post was an old friend of my West Virginia days—a friend who sometimes borrowed my law books to do research for his magnificent lawyer stories."

Immediately following this venture into active politics, Post's writing output was at a low ebb again for a time, as during 1925 he published only one story from December to December. Incidentally these two stories, spaced a full twelve months apart, were stories appropriate to the Christmas season, and they support the assumption of Post having come the full cycle in his religious outlook.

In 1924 he published another collection of mystery and detective type stories. Of the thirteen "chapters" in this book, six formed a continuous narrative, while the seven more loosely connected consisted of items published serially over the preceding three years. Named after the central character in most of the pieces, *Walker of the Secret Service,* the book received mixed criticism from the reviewers, but it also caught the attention of one Joseph E. Walker of New York, a United States Treasury Department operative who brought suit against the publishers, D. Appleton and Company, on August 18, 1925.

In his suit, Joseph E. Walker asked $50,000 damages, asserting that he was the only man in the hire of the Secret Service bearing the name Walker, and inasmuch as the Walker in Post's book was portrayed as a former train robber, his reputation had suffered. Post was reported to have replied (as a witness in court) that to the best of his knowledge, he did not ever discover a "Captain Walker, Chief of the United States Secret Service" as any actual person. The suit dragged on for about eleven months in the courts before New York Supreme Court Justice James C. Cropsey ruled the case dismissed as no cause for action had been established.[47]

During much of this same period Post engaged in an odd dispute over the matter of payments for serial rights in the reprinting of stories from the *Randolph Mason: Corrector of Destinies* volume.[48] The dispute was conducted by correspondence with a W. G. Chapman who represented the International Press Bureau in Chicago, Illinois. Several of the pieces from the book were in the process of being reprinted in issues of *Golden Book.* The book had been reissued by Putnam just a few years earlier along with new printings of the other Randolph Mason works, possibly on the basis of the general interest created in Post during the first half of the 20's by his newer books. Post contended that for any of these stories to be reprinted in *Golden Book* would require that Chapman purchase "3rd serial rights." Chapman replied, in a rather heated letter to Post, that he had some years before transacted business with Edward J. Clode of New York, the publisher of the original 1908 edition, wherein he had purchased the 2nd serial rights for $250 and declared that Post, as a capable attorney, should know that the purchasing of 2nd serial rights allowed the purchaser all future rights—that there was no such thing as any 3rd serial rights.

Whether Chapman was right or wrong in his definition of the serial rights was really not the point. Clode had written in his dealing with Chapman on May 1, 1911: "I will release to you the exclusive serial rights of *The Corrector of Destinies* for $250 . . . latest edition is nearly exhausted and I shall not reprint." Perhaps Post's legal training dictated the inadvisability of disputing the term "exclusive," or the total amount of money involved was too small, or perhaps the matter was unworthy of the time and trouble required to salvage his pride. Nor was Chapman exactly certain of his rights, for he finally offered to share equally with Post the sum of his proceeds in reprinting the stories. Thus, on April 15, 1926, Post wrote the editor of *Golden Book,* Henry W. Lanier, that he had ended his dispute with Chapman. Thirty years in the profession of writing had no doubt taught him he had to move on or be forgotten.

In 1926 he managed to keep his name before the public partly by having a number of earlier stories reprinted. Also, he had collected in book form a series of articles on police work which had seen periodical publication some ten years earlier. Called *The Man Hunters,* it was published by the firm headed by a former Appleton editor, J. H. Sears. This was Post's only non-fiction book. In addition, during 1926, there appeared three new short stories and one longer story in two parts.

Yet, it was a period in which all certainly was not well for Post, though the true nature of the trouble is not obvious. Post was now 57 years of age, and it is possible that he was suffering from certain ailments which he had seemingly overcome for a number of years. Perhaps it was merely the prudence gained from his legal experiences that led Post on December 27, 1926, to write a lengthy will to provide for the disposition of his estate. The eccentricities of this will, along with other reports, indicate that all was not peaceful between Melville and his brother and sisters. The bulk of his estate, The Chalet, and the major portion of the income from his investments was given for life to his nieces, Caroline and Sarah DuBois. His admiration of them was of long standing, particularly following Bloom's death. Sarah DuBois, as a girl in her teens, is said to have spent entire summers at the Post estate as a guest of her uncle. To some extent Melville was on agreeable terms with his brother Sidney as he named him executor of the will and allotted him $2,000 per year for this purpose. Also not forgotten was Orange Jud Perkins who was to be the recipient of $250 per year for life, $50 of this to be used to purchase suitable clothing. Jud survived Melville by only 13 years. It was an unusual will in terms of length and strong legal language, and it demonstrated plainly the complexities of the author.

In general things prospered in the United States in 1927, and they seemed also to prosper again for Post. During the months of January and February *Collier's* published in three parts another long story titled "The Garden in Asia." More important perhaps, Post arranged to have three new Uncle Abner stories published in *Country Gentlemen* and sold a long, two-part Abner story to be published the next year. These four Uncle Abner tales do not bear the marks of being dictated material, lightly handled, or dashed off for a waiting check. They give every indication of being worked on carefully and thoroughly—ranking equal in quality to the best of the earlier Uncle Abner stories and others of Post which reflect the use of skillful composition and technical superiority.

He also sold two short stories to the *American Magazine* and another appeared in the *Ladies' Home Journal*. It has been stated that Post, after gaining his popular reputation, demanded the top price for his material and if not offered what he considered the work's worth in terms of money, he requested the manuscript returned. Much of Post's work shows evidence of being written many months and years before appearing in the magazines. That there was a more than sufficient interest in his work is indicated in the sale of six short stories the next year to one publisher for the then astonishing sum of $30,000—a sum maintaining him among the highest paid magazine writers of fiction during that era.[49]

In addition Post found D. Appleton and Company willing to publish another of the difficult to classify books he was inclined to turn out from time to time. This book was without the complications of even a short novel, being essentially a long story or fantasy set on an unidentified island in the China Sea. It was appropriately called *The Revolt of the Birds.* The economy of Post's prose in this book is nearly extreme. A mood of mystery prevails along with a touch of mysticism—coupled with a faint feeling of pessimism. The specific intentions of Post in writing this book are obscure beyond the fact that he had an unusual fascination for birds. Birds were a subject which consumed many of his free hours. His deep interest in them had resulted in many birdhouses and other conveniences being erected for them on the grounds about The Chalet. Post also collected and read a vast amount of the available literature on birds. It was perhaps through his reading that he picked up the theme which the book argues, one quite advanced for its time and about as unpopular as it was rare in a prosperous America of 1927—the chemical poisoning of birds as a factor in the upsetting of nature's balance. The book thus had little chance for success and the reviewers, in general, were not in the least as enthusiastic or knowledgeable about the feathered creatures as Post. They wrote only lukewarm opinions, and the book passed almost unnoticed by the general public.

The next year, 1928, was equally unproductive for Post, but he still managed to place a few stories in the better popular periodicals. As he was getting top prices for his offerings he could feel justified in his moderate output. Doubtlessly he was fully aware that he was up against more and stiffer competition than he had faced in the beginning years of his career. A new generation of authors had moved onto the literary scene, many of these with exceptional abilities to produce not only popular material, but stories of high literary quality as well. They had rapidly replaced writers who had dropped from the competition because of age or death. Such names as F. Scott Fitzgerald, Ernest Hemingway, Sinclair Lewis, and Sherwood Anderson were being widely recognized, but they represent only a portion of the excellent talent that was now turning out superior short stories in a growing number of publications. Indications are that Post, although aware of the changes taking place, read little of the writings of his fellow fiction writers, with perhaps the exception of certain of the writers of mystery tales, particularly A. Conan Doyle who was still publishing a few new stories. Having had for many years strong feelings about what he considered the necessary ingredients and construction of a short story, he seldom commented publicly about other writers or their methods, preferring quietly his own style and theories so long as his stories were sold and read.

Early in 1929 Melville Post witnessed the publication of his fifteenth book. It consisted of five short stories and two longer tales. These were a gathering of pieces that had appeared in serial publication during the period from 1922 to 1927. Titled *The Bradmoor Murder: Including the Remarkable Deductions of Sir Henry Marquis of Scotland Yard,* it was a potpourri of the talents of its author. Also it was to be the last book from his own hand that he would see in print, the final volume of his work to be a posthumously published collection. This makes it somewhat ironic then that this fifteenth book ends with the words, "In the land where men grind their wheat in the sky!" These words are significantly the concluding words of that fanciful and ambiguous minute autobiography Post had concocted when asked to relate the principal events of his life early in his last decade. This phrase, used prominently throughout the story "The Garden in Asia," the concluding story of the book, refers to Belgium's land of giant windmills. These had had an unusual fascination for Post for many years, appearing first in his 1914 short story, "The Miller of Ostend." *The Bradmoor Murder* received hardly a ripple of attention, although its pages reveal interesting touches of a popular Post theme—how common imagination colors and changes natural events and causes them to appear supernatural.

There are some reports which say that by 1929 Post had virtually withdrawn from the profession of writing after over thirty-four years of producing stories in his unique manner. The half dozen stories which he saw in print during this year, plus one appearing after his death, form part of the contents of *The Silent Witness*. It was the last book which bore his name as author. Arrangements for its publication by Farrar & Rinehart in 1930 were undoubtedly completed by Post somewhat earlier. Due to the fact that no other unpublished work of his appeared following his death, we may assume that those reports of his withdrawal from the profession were substantially correct.

We were told, again by Sam Mallison, that Post had plans for certain stories which were never completed. Post spoke to his acquaintance regarding a novel he had planned, sometime after 1922, which was to be another allegorical story similar in design to

The Mountain School-Teacher. This new novel was to use as the central figure Satan instead of Christ. Plans were for Satan to appear as a contemporary person living in the world of the 1920's, complete with the jazz-crazy, money-minded atmosphere that was then prevalent in New York City and was becoming prevalent in nearly every metropolitan area and in smaller towns across the country. This atmosphere was, in fact, already seeping into the smallest West Virginia hamlet. We do not know much about this proposed story as it must not have passed beyond the first stages of plotting. No evidence of it being put on paper has been uncovered, but it would most certainly have provided a good introduction to the events of October of 1929.

The stock market crash in the world's financial centers probably had little immediate influence on the writer in West Virginia. Post is reported to have had most of his invested wealth in government bonds and similar securities where the financial losses would have been minimal. But Post was also exceptionally sensitive to the general implications of such a disaster, for as a comparatively wealthy man he was naturally closely connected to the world of finance that was then crumbling to pieces and could foresee all the ramifications of that disaster. Included in that crumbling world were the formerly prospering magazines that had paid generous sums for Post's work and also the railroads, coal mining operations, and other commercial enterprises he had been associated with as a corporation attorney. Post, whose outlook was largely cosmopolitan, may have felt the sting of the events more severely in ways other than financial. He had always been a keen observer of his society, and he could see that not only in West Virginia, but in America and in the whole world, the type of life he was accustomed to accepting as the way of things would never again be the same.

It was readily observed by those near Post at this time that his health was becoming troublesome. Nevertheless, he was a determined man, and even though he perhaps had to curtail some activities, there is one he would not. Riding horses was as necessary to his life as it was habitual.

On June 10, 1930, while out riding Margo on the grounds of his estate Post suddenly fell from his mount. Apparently he had suffered a severe spell of illness due to his failing condition. Some reports said he was thrown from his horse, but these have little basis in truth. Gentle, well-trained Margo would not under ordinary circumstances have thrown her master or would have otherwise willfully contributed to his misfortune. Still, there are, or have been, few with better knowledge of these creatures than Melville Davisson Post. Perhaps with some degree of intuition, he had written in "The Devil's Track," a short story published less than three years before this day:

> "Is there any tame horse?" continued Abner as in reflection. "Do not the Scriptures tell us that a horse is a vain thing for safety? And is it not the common experience of man that a horse may be quiet under him for years and then, with no warning, at some inconsequential thing rear and throw him?"[50]

However, we do not know what really caused the fall since there was no immediate witness. As a result of the accident, Post began to hemorrhage and was rushed to the Saint Mary's Hospital in nearby Clarksburg. Examination disclosed his condition to be the compounded results of the fall, varicose veins of the esophagus, and cirrhosis of the liver. After receiving blood transfusions, it appeared to his attending physicians, one of whom was his brother Dr. Sidney H. Post, that the sixty-one year old author was showing signs of improvement. But these hopeful signs were misleading, for nine days later Post suffered a serious relapse, and his chances for recovery lessened. His brother, no doubt knowing the author's hours were limited, was quoted as terming Melville's condition "very grave."

The concern of his physicians was justified, for early on the morning of Monday, June 23, 1930, just a little more than twelve days after his fall from the horse, Melville Davisson Post died in his hospital bed. In his sixty-one active years he had traveled far, made many friends and accomplished much that was worthy of remembrance. Messages of condolence that came to the family from many people in many places, some quite distant, confirmed these accomplishments. The Protestant Episcopal funeral service held on June 25 at The Chalet was short and simple. Omitted were the usual lengthy and belated statements of praise kept for a man of his standing. From The Chalet Post was taken to the Clarksburg Elkview Masonic Cemetery to be permanently laid between his beloved wife, Bloom, and his infant son, Ira.

It was typical of Melville Post to have provided his own epitaph. The words form a profound statement of religious philosophy—a positive statement of faith. Decidedly not an orthodox Christian statement, it bridges boundaries between science and theology, between knowledge and mysticism. In three places it speaks of the "energies of God," an impersonal God not far from the "Nameless Thing," the God of Providence that ruled so many of his plots. In slightly over one-hundred and fifty words it sums up the beliefs by which Post lived and wrote. These words are cut into a large marble slab laid across the grave site:

> The universe toils in some tremendous purpose. Be not disheartened because the understanding of that purpose is denied you. Is not your beloved before you in a world of beauty. How could you have known that the creative energies of God had predetermined on such a world and her when they were lifting the slime life landward out of the old Cambrian seas. If you could not have forseen, then, these excellencies appearing on the way, how much less can you foresee now, the end of that immense endeavor. Reflect, that over aeons, over light years, over ages inconceivably extended, the energies of God, patient and unwearied, have been shaping the design of every earth creature out of the germ of life, and what could you have seen—at any point of that interminable way—in your brief flash of human consciousness, but the rise and fall of tides, the progressions of the seasons, and no change. Go forward with a high face. The mysterious energies of God labor to some divine perfection.

Thus we are made aware at this final stage of a successful writer's life of not only the economy and crispness of his creative art, but that in addition to entertaining through the means of mystery and detective tales, which was his first purpose, he had a more serious purpose in transmitting to us a profound philosophy of things in life as he saw them.

It is interesting to note here that the creator of perhaps the most widely-known fictional detective of all time, Sir Arthur Conan Doyle, the originator of Sherlock Holmes, died on July 7, 1930— just fourteen days after Post's death. Post had admired and read the work of Doyle from their first appearance. But while the fame of Sherlock Holmes' creator has continued undiminished over three quarters of a century, his American counterpart and often his equal, Melville Davisson Post, was soon almost forgotten and his work nearly completely neglected except by a handful of persons. This neglect certainly is not totally deserved. Whatever the final judgment regarding the literary qualities of his work, the short stories of Melville Davisson Post are unique and thus deserve a respectable reading.

II. THE RANDOLPH MASON STORIES

When Post published his first book in 1896, he was all but unknown as an author. He had previously published little if anything of importance. His principal occupation was the legal profession, having in 1892 entered into a partnership in Wheeling, West Virginia with John A. Howard, the assistant prosecutor of Ohio County. As an attorney Post seems to have had considerable success. Also, through his professional and family influence he had become active and prominent in the Democratic Party of West Virginia.

Neither financial security nor the need for success were significant in starting Post on his literary career. He had already achieved a fair measure of both. There was a better reason. From boyhood on he had nurtured a desire to be a writer. Everything in his personal history indicates that he drove himself in this direction unwaveringly in spite of the constant demands of education and profession. It was not an accident of any sort that he became an author of some note in his 27th year. It is likely that he began writing actively shortly after his initiation as a full-fledged lawyer, using the few spare hours that were available. While his first profession left him little time for indulging in his ambition for a second, his thorough acquaintance with the legal world furnished him many characters and plots, not only for the first stories, but for nearly all his work throughout his career as a writer.

The sudden success he managed with the publication of *The Strange Schemes of Randolph Mason* must surely have been welcome, though probably not fully anticipated. The "Introduction" written for this book indicates that Post had done much thinking about the type of literature he wished to create—the planning being as important to him as the actual writing. This piece, although it reflects the vanity, fancifulness, and aristocratic bearing that was a part of his total personality, is an interesting bit of criticism, both of law and literature. The introduction attracted nearly as much attention as his unusual fiction, and still does today among those fascinated by his books and their unique characters. The points he makes may be debatable, but they are vital to a proper understanding of the direction his early literary ambitions followed.

"The teller of strange tales is not the least among benefactors of men."[1] With these words Post opened his first book and his literary career. He believed this statement and in the years that followed never refuted it. Then he spoke of the protest of the "bitter" critic: " 'At best,' he cries, 'the great one among you can produce but combinations of the old, some quaint, some monstrous, and all weary.' " Post answered, "Perhaps the critic forgets that if things are old, men are new...."[2] To him a writer had a mystical power—he was a man with an important responsibility. As a writer he undertook this responsibility with supreme optimism.

"The reader is a clever tyrant," he wrote. So the writer is instructed: "Create mind children, O Magician, with red blood in their faces, who, by power inherited from you, are enabled to secure the fruits of drudgery, without the drudgery.... We know all the old methods so well, and we are weary of them. Give us new ones."[3] Post then refers to the masterpieces of Poe, followed by "the flood of 'Detective Stories.' " He notes how Conan Doyle, upon the creation of Sherlock Holmes, renewed the art; the plots were old, but the trappings were new. "The intent has always been to baffle the trailer, and when the identity of the criminal was finally revealed, the story ended."[4]

Post felt the need for a bold change: "The book-stalls have

been filled to weariness with tales based upon plans whereby the *detective,* or *ferreting* power of the State might be baffled. But, prodigious marvel! no writer has attempted to construct tales based upon plans whereby the *punishing* power of the State might be baffled."[5] Post asked, "Is it possible to plan and execute wrongs in such a manner that they will have all the effect and resulting profit of desperate crimes and yet not be crimes before the law?"[6] Post set out to show indeed that it was very possible.

Speaking of our legal systems, he wrote: "The common sense of the common man is at best a poor guide to the criminal law. It is no guide at all to the civil law."[7] Also, "We are prone to forget that the law is no perfect structure, that it is simply the result of human labor. . . ."[8] Then Post makes his main point, saying, "All wrongs are not crimes [because] a wrong, to become criminal, must fit exactly into the measure laid down by the law. . . . There is no middle ground."[9] This is the way a legal system operates, coldly and objectively.

In the next paragraph he states a fact that is the basis for his early stories. We read: ". . . if one knows well the technicalities of the law, one may commit horrible wrongs that will yield all the gain and all the resulting effect of the highest crimes, and yet the wrongs perpetuated will constitute no one of the crimes described by the law. Thus the highest crimes, even murder, may be committed in such a manner that although the criminal is known and the law holds him in custody, yet it cannot punish him."[10] This prophetic insight led Post to create Randolph Mason.

Suppose that an individual wanted desperately to accomplish some urgent but difficult goal and he could lay his appeal before a lawyer with uncanny genius and knowledge of the law, a knave who would not be concerned with morals but with the letter of the law. That individual could with the guidance offered by this lawyer accomplish his purpose, and although often using unsavory and unethical means, he could find himself protected in the courts under the umbrella of the law. As a practicing lawyer, Post had undoubtedly seen this done, and he certainly read of many cases in the law reports that followed closely such a pattern. All that Post required to emphasize the possibilities of this distortion of the intent of the law was an amoral lawyer to fill his specifications. Just how much invention and how much fact went into the creating of Randolph Mason (a name Post possibly concocted by joining the names of two widely separated West Virginia counties) would be interesting to know, but we have few clues to direct us; thus we must accept him as one of the most unique inventions of popular fiction.[11]

Explaining the possibility of such a personality, Post says:

> An intellect, keen, powerful, and yet devoid of any sense of moral obligation would be no passing wonder to the skilled physician; for no one knows better than he that often in the house of the soul there are great chambers locked and barred and whole passages sealed up in the dark. Nor do men marvel that great minds concentrated on some mighty labor grow utterly oblivious to human relations and see and care for naught save the result which they are seeking. . . .[12]

In the concluding paragraphs of the "Introduction" Post predicts objections to his book which would claim the tales serve to encourage and instruct the enemies of the law; but, his firm position is that "if he instructs the enemies, he also warns the friends of law and order."[13] The prediction was not long in proving itself, for within a short time after publication there appeared objections, many pointing to specific cases in the courts as having been influenced by *The Strange Schemes of Randolph Mason*. Post took pains to point out that his stories were based on actual legal principles, and preceding each piece he documented those points of law which were operative in that piece. This is the law, he says summing up his position, and until we change it we must abide by it in making our legal decisions.

The first story in *The Strange Schemes of Randolph Mason* is titled "The Corpus Delicti." It is one of the stories for which Post is best known, and it has been included in several anthologies. It illustrates best the point Post was trying to emphasize and does so in a sensational manner, since the crime involved is a cold-blooded murder carried out systematically and precisely. This story, more than any of the stories which followed, drew the attention of those who believed Post was instructing the prospective criminal.

In this story Post describes Randolph Mason in full detail much as the character Richard Warren (alias Samuel Walcott) might have seen him:

> He was a man apparently in the middle forties; tall and reasonably broad across the shoulders; muscular without being either stout or lean. His hair was thin and of a brown color, with erratic streaks of gray. His forehead was broad and high and of a faint reddish color. His eyes were restless inky black, and not over-large. The nose was big and muscular and bowed. The eyebrows were black and heavy, almost bushy. There were heavy furrows, running from the nose downward and outward to the corners of the mouth. The mouth was straight and the jaw was heavy and square.
>
> Looking at the face of Randolph Mason from above, the expression in repose was crafty and cynical; viewed from below upward, it was savage and vindictive, almost brutal; while from the front, if looked squarely in the face, the stranger was fascinated by the animation of the man and at once concluded that his expression was fearless and sneering.[14]

Randolph Mason was considered by the author as a "knave" and a "misanthropist." He is all of this and more, a creature for whom sympathy is almost impossible unless one be of a similar makeup, demonic and cantankerous. Under the guise of his gentleman-like conduct we find a mind devoid of humanistic attitudes, devoted to the principles of the law no matter how inequitable they might prove in operation. He appears cunning, dazzling, and daring at times, but beneath he is cold, empty, and unfit for service to his fellowmen. At first Post seemed fascinated by this creature who was more a computer than a human being, but as he wrote more of Randolph Mason he reacted even as the reader reacts who reads of him, the fascination turning to disgust.

When in "The Corpus Delicti" Samuel Walcott goes to Randolph Mason and explains his problem, the evil lawyer not only advises murder as the quickest solution, but proceeds to outline for Walcott a plan whereby he can escape the punishing power of the state if he follows exactly the detailed steps recommended. Walcott is a desperate man who already has a double murder hanging over his head, and even if Randolph Mason had not advised it, he would likely have considered a third murder the only way to resolve his precarious position. With Mason's advice he proceeds with confidence to do what he would otherwise have done in desperation.

Samuel Walcott is actually Richard Warren, having assumed the name after killing the real Samuel Walcott in an altercation over Walcott's wife, the daughter of a Mexican gambler. As the story begins these characters are all living a wild and meaningless existence in the Sierra Nevada mountains in a place appropriately named Hell's Elbow. Walcott depicts the violent incident in telling his tale to Randolph Mason:

> One night, in a drunken brawl, we quarrelled and I killed him. It was late at night, and, beside the woman, there were four of us in the poker room,—the Mexican gambler, a half-breed devil called Cherubim Pete, Walcott, and myself. When Walcott fell, the half-breed whipped out his weapon, and fired at me across the table; but the woman, Nina San Croix, struck his arm and, instead of killing me, as he intended, the bullet mortally wounded her father, the Mexican gambler. I shot the half-breed through the forehead, and turned round, expecting the woman to attack me. On the contrary, she pointed to the window, and bade me wait for her on the crosstrail below.[15]

Had Richard Warren not waited for the woman who joined him three hours later his story would have been different, but fate dictated otherwise. She urges him to assume Walcott's name after revealing a will found among his papers. Going to New York, Walcott claims the dead man's properties which during the intervening years have grown considerably in value, and he thus becomes a wealthy, influential man, a social figure and an eligible bachelor. Tiring of his mistress, Nina San Croix, whom he has furnished living quarters in a suburb north of New York City, Walcott makes plans to marry a sweet, innocent princess of the local society set, Virginia St. Clair. His mistress, realizing she is to be abandoned, threatens to reveal his true identity and the evidence of the murders which she possesses. Richard Warren, alias Samuel Walcott, is trapped—but, at this moment he meets with Randolph Mason.

In this first story Post makes use of the first two of three ways in which, throughout all his tales, he contends a man's destiny is determined—by Fate, circumstantial events, or the Providence of God. Few are the stories he wrote in which one of these does not operate. In "The Corpus Delicti" he depicts Randolph Mason as an opponent of Fate. Post put the scene in these words:

"You are under the dead-fall, aye," said Mason. "The cunning of my enemy is sublime."

"Your enemy?" gasped Walcott. "When did you come into it? How in God's name did you know it? How your enemy?"

Mason looked down at the wide bulging eyes of the man.

"Who should know better than I?" he said. "Haven't I broken through all the traps and plots that she could set?"

"She? She trap you?" The man's voice was full of horror.

"The old schemer," muttered Mason. "The cowardly old schemer, to strike in the back; but we can beat her. She did not count on my helping you—I, who know her so well."

Mason's face was red, and his eyes burned. . . . Walcott could not know that Mason meant only Fate, that he believed her to be his great enemy. . . .[16]

Accepting Randolph Mason's advice, Warren, alias Samuel Walcott, assumes still other disguises. First as a drayman he manages to convey several wine cases of sulphuric acid into the wine cellar of his mistress. Later, he returns in the garb of a Mexican sailor, a disguise he apparently used regularly in visiting Nina San Croix. With little hesitation he plunges a razor sharp knife into the area of her heart. "The hot blood gushed out over his arm and down his leg."[17] Thus the plan for the disposal of the body is carried out. Post describes it in vivid language, creating the scene in detail such as is seldom used in the fiction of this period. In nearly five pages he depicts step by step the actions taken by Richard Warren (now alias Victor Ancona). The description Post creates here is equal to any found in today's bold fiction; today's descriptions may be more sophisticated, but they are never more vivid. The unprepared reader must have found himself shocked. Some members of Post's public protested that such a scene should only be suggested if the work required it, not spelled out in such factual detail.

It is possible to pick out some flaws in Post's description of the disposal of the body of Nina San Croix, but essentially it is presented in a manner both believable and possible. With the body gone, the story moves quickly on. The murderer is apprehended almost at once together with his bloodied murder weapon. Other evidence includes a blood-soaked dress with a slit made by the knife and much blood on the chairs, floor, and on the clothing of the murderer. He is identified as Victor Ancona, since the use of finger print records and other modern methods of identification are not yet a commonplace procedure. Ancona is quickly brought to trial. The Attorneys for the People present to the court all their available evidence—lacking only an eye witness to the crime and, most important, the victim's body.

Here the author introduces the concept of circumstantial evidence into the tale. Circumstantial evidence was of great interest to Post, and he made use of it as the theme of some of his finest stories, but usually to illustrate how circumstantial evidence causes suspicion to fall upon an innocent party. In "The Corpus Delicti" the finger of suspicion points at the guilty party, but Randolph Mason demonstrates that circumstantial evidence, when incomplete, cannot be used to convict the defendant no matter how guilty he may be.

> Randolph Mason . . . faced the judge.
> "If your Honor please . . . the defendant has no evidence to offer . . . but, if your Honor please . . . I move that the jury be directed to find the prisoner not guilty."
> The judge looked sharply at the speaker . . . "On what ground?" he said curtly.
> "On the ground," replied Mason, "that the *corpus delicti* has not been proven."
> The senior counsel for the prosecution was on his feet in a moment.
> "What?" he said . . . "Does he jest? The term 'corpus delicti' is technical, and means the body of the crime, or the substantial fact that a crime has been committed. Does anyone doubt it in this case? . . .
> "Men may lie, but circumstances cannot. . . . It is beyond the human mind to conceive that a clear chain of concatenated circumstances can be in error. . . . Rule out the irresistable inference, and the end of justice is come in this land; and you may as well leave the spider to weave his web through the abandoned courtroom."
> "If your Honor please," said Mason, rising, "this is a matter of law, plain, clear, and so well settled in the State of New York that even counsel for the people should know it. . . . If the *corpus delicti*, the body of the crime, has been proven . . . then the case should go to the jury. If not, then it is the duty of the court to direct the jury to find

the prisoner not guilty. . . .

"The fact that the victim is indeed dead must first be made certain before any one can be convicted for her killing, because so long as there remains the remotest doubt as to the death, there can be no certainty as to the criminal agent, although the circumstantial evidence indicating the guilt of the accused may be positive, complete, and utterly irresistible. . . ."

The judge turned and looked down at the jury. . . .

". . . I am, therefore, gentlemen of the jury, compelled to direct you to find the prisoner not guilty."[18]

The above omits much of the detailed argument Randolph Mason uses to relieve the defendant of the murder charge; the passage deserves a complete reading. Cleared and freed, Victor Ancona drops from sight and Samuel Walcott reappears to wed "the only daughter of the blue-blooded St. Clairs."[19]

The other Randolph Mason stories need to be examined, but in less detail, for it was "The Corpus Delicti" that drew all the attention heaped upon the young author. As Melville had predicted, people were disturbed over the possibilities presented in this story. Early critics note two sensational trials, one in Chicago and one in New York, which followed somewhat the pattern depicted in the story.[20] Law makers were reported, in several instances, to have acted to close the loopholes in statutes of their states as a result of the controversy aroused by Randolph Mason's performance. The amoral lawyer had become established not only as a unique character of American literature but as one to be respected and feared.

There are five more stories presented in this first book, *The Strange Schemes of Randolph Mason,* and although they are profitable reading (particularly if a reader enjoys the intricacies of the legal world) none are of equal importance to the first tale. Yet, in order to obtain a true evaluation of Post's work, particularly his early work, brief consideration of the others is necessary. These other stories are similar to the first in that they are concerned with wrongs which can be committed without penalties under the law. They cannot without distortion be accurately described as either mystery or detective tales; they are problem stories, or crime stories, or legal stories.[21]

"Two Plungers of Manhattan" is illustrative of the above

point.²² Two brothers, gambling in grain futures, need $5,000 beyond their present resources. Going to Randolph Mason, they are advised of a scheme by which they can raise that sum in a real estate maneuver. The trickery is legal, but not at all ethical—nor should it be justified because the elderly rich man from whom they embezzle the money would apparently have used the same means if given the chance. In truth he had at one time taken advantage of their father in a business deal. Of interest to students of Melville Post's work is the reference in the first sentence to Providence, which plays a prominent part in many later stories, particularly in the Uncle Abner tales.

"Woodford's Partner" demonstrates that the greed of men often leads to their downfall. Randolph Mason uses this factor in coaching William Harris to conduct a legal theft under the laws of partnership rights. There is no complicated plot in this story, but the message is strong, a fair warning to the reader to proceed in business matters with great caution, not blinded by the emotions of greed.

For the student of Post's work there are several factors of interest in "Woodford's Partner" beyond any literary value, which is insignificant. First, we meet with the name "Carper" used for the brother of William Harris. Carper was the family name of Post's grandmother on his father's side. Several times in various of his works Post applies the name to a character. Also, we note that the greedy individual in the tale is Thomas Woodford, a cattleman of Bridgeport, West Virginia. The name "Woodford" will appear again in Post's first book-length story concerned with West Virginia's cattle-raising region; there it is applied to another greedy cattleman, Rufe Woodford. Secondly, we should note with interest the excellent description of this region which the author has made a part of "Woodford's Partner," nearly six pages in length at the beginning of section IV. Although too lengthy to quote here, it is essential to those who would wish to understand the region and the people from which Melville Davisson Post originated—a region he used for his most effective fiction. And finally, in this story we are for the first time made aware of the possibility that much of Post's fiction has some basis in fact, but it is almost always difficult to determine where the one begins or the other ends.

The next story, "The Error of William Van Broom,"

introduces [Courtlandt] Parks, Randolph Mason's secretary, in a minor role of no significance.[23] More significant, though, is one of the comments of Mason: "In these problems one pits himself against the mysterious intelligence of Chance,—against the dread cunning and the fatal patience of Destiny. Ah! these are worthy foemen."[24] Post must have felt that he himself was pitted against these forces, as indeed he seemed to be—and thoughts about these led to the telling of some unusual tales. Unfortunately "The Error of William Van Broom" is not one of these. It has a rather weak plot, and its only justification for being read is the warning it offers unwary persons who enter contracts. The principal action in the story takes place in Wheeling, West Virginia, where Post practiced law at this time.

In writing the next tale, "The Men of the Jimmy," Post seemed to be striving for a degree of comedy, something which he did not do well nor often. The title itself seems to suggest this comic factor. A band of thugs needing money to pay for the "escape" of other members of their gang from prison "capture" Randolph Mason and force him to aid them. Mason's plan requires one of the gang to sell information to the father of a kidnapped youngster regarding the boy's whereabouts. Paid in advance and handcuffed to a police office, the thug tosses the reward money to a confederate. Because his information was faked he is brought to trial, but since he has followed the details of Mason's scheme and has broken no law, he is freed. The thugs and the police are both depicted by Post as rather inept characters, and perhaps because the story requires it for comedy effects, or perhaps for deeper, personal reasons, the Attorney for the People shows an utter lack of efficiency. Post himself displays no literary skill in this story, his prose showing all the marks of a rank beginner, but the reader will find this a curious tale with enough suspense to persuade him to read it through.

"The Sheriff of Gullmore" is another story in which the humorous element is noticeable; but, as a circuit judge comments on the act central to the story, "this is no frivolous matter."[25] Post has presented here sharp caricatures to sustain his tale of a mythical West Virginia county, though the name bears a strong resemblance to an actual county.[26] The story, however, is nearly lost in the legal details supporting the conclusion. Mason's secretary, Parks, is used in his first significant role, as an instigator of the plot. The legal embezzlement of funds, in this story and others in the Randolph Mason series, unfortunately has little of the strong impact contained in the human interest issues of murder and other violent crimes.

The concluding title of this first collection is "The Animus Furandi," which is a legal term meaning the intention to steal. Courtlandt Parks in this tale appropriates a Randolph Mason scheme for his own profit, working in partnership with an unsavory detective friend, Braxton Hogarth. (We might note here that "Braxton," also the name of a West Virginia county, later becomes the name of a shrewd attorney who is the central character in a series of stories written and published near the end of the author's career.) Parks and Braxton Hogarth first abscond with a coal mining company's payroll in a conspiracy that resembles a cheap western film plot. Returning to the New York area they use their newly-acquired funds to enter a faro game. The dealer is apparently cheating, so drawing a gun they take their money, plus that of the gambling house, thus completing the second half of the scheme. Post planned this story to illustrate two related points of law, showing first how the intent to steal, necessary for legal charges, could be evaded, and second, how the intent to steal could be absent in a chain of events. The story seems too pat, the author's hand approximating that of a puppeteer; but, there are occasional touches of the color, imagination, and economical style here such as Post masters in his later work.

The Strange Schemes of Randolph Mason succeeded, though not as art, in other special ways. It created attention and debate, as an artless book having something to say occasionally does. It also made Post believe in himself as an author and encouraged him to intensify his writing efforts. As a commercial item the book went through many editions. As a review in *The Critic* said, shortly after publication: "Though far from profitable reading, and utterly improbable, this work opens up a new line of thought, and offers a startling commentary on the apparent vulnerability of some of our laws."[27] This perhaps is the best explanation of the popularity of this most unusual book.

The instant popularity of this first book no doubt caused the publisher to request that Post prepare another as soon as possible.

Thus a year later in November 1897 the second of Post's works appeared, *The Man of Last Resort, or The Clients of Randolph Mason*. These tales, for technically most of these do not fit the general definition of a short story at all, seem to have been done rapidly in a state of excessive confidence. Perhaps some had been completed before "fame" struck Melville Post, but the book's overall appearance is that of a quick, unexpected encore, inadequately planned. The volume contains five pieces, two of which are unreasonably long. While Post makes a heroic attempt to give the book meaningful content, the end result is an overall unevenness and dramatic disaster. Yet, there are occasional flashes of talent suggested, along with portions of significant interest to the student. The book is profitable reading if only for the occasional insights gained into the author.

A letter to Post from G. P. Putnam in 1897 just prior to publication notes the book's obvious defects. The first story is criticized for its unnecessary length and for the introduction of an unnecessary and unrealistic romantic theme. The last story is criticized as ending too abruptly (at least for the taste of that time). The letter suggested that at least one other story be furnished to give the book a more suitable length. Also, the letter led to a compromise about the title. Melville wanted the title *The Man of Last Resort*, the publisher suggested *The Clients of Randolph Mason*; thus the latter became the subtitle. In reprinting the book years later, however, the publishers had their way and switched to *Randolph Mason: The Clients*. Otherwise, in regard to the publisher's comments, Post's opinion prevailed and the stories were published exactly as he had presented them. Perhaps this came about because the first book was then showing good sales and the publisher wished to take advantage of that current situation. However, while the publisher felt the challenge of publishing the stories, he also expressed to Post his doubts about doing so in the face of comments claiming the Mason stories were aiding certain criminal elements.

This second book was dedicated to a cousin with whom Post constantly corresponded and who was an occasional traveling companion, Professor W. M. L. Coplin of the Thomas Jefferson Medical College in Philadelphia, Pennsylvania. Their relationship flourished during these years. In a number of letters to Coplin Melville displayed an unsteady wittiness and indicated some uncertainties regarding his abilities as an attorney. These and other conflicts which Melville hinted at in his letters no doubt had some effect upon his lack of progress as an author as evidenced by the quality of this second book.

As he did in his first book, Post opens the second with an essay, this time termed the "Preface." He again notes how "the skillful rouge" can "render the law powerless." He writes that this point, emphasized in the first book, "has provoked large discussion," and adds that, "no change in the law can properly or safely be brought about except through the pressure of public sentiment." He states, "The duty of the individual to the state is imperative." Despite this ". . . the law, being of human device, is imperfect . . . the evil genius thrusts through and despoils the citizen, and the robbery is all the more easy because the victim sleeps in a consciousness of perfect security."

The first story in *The Man of Last Resort* is almost a novelette in length and structure, being 93 pages long and divided into chapter-like sections. Called "The Governor's Machine," it deals with a trio of profiteers who establish a Western political machine. The tale thus reflects Post's own interest and involvement in politics at this time. Perhaps we might speculate that he also had a romantic interest during this period for he likewise includes a romantic theme. Both of these are treated far too melodramatically. The point of law considered here, the illegality of wagering contracts, lacks shock value. Post describes most of the main characters in picturesque terms, thus contributing to their appearance as mere actors in a melodrama. The significant thing here is that the author is not thinking in terms of the short story but of the novel, and this piece demonstrates that he was striving, none too successfully, in that direction.

The reader who approaches Post's work with a knowledge of the author's life soon realizes that there is a correlation between the two, sometimes strong, sometimes weak, but nearly always present. In "Mrs. Van Bartan," the next tale, Post uses a theme he oftens favors—a charming Southern woman who breaks the heart of a man who since childhood has popularly been assumed to be her intended fiance. In this tale Columbia Summers weds Gerald Van Bartan not for love but for money. Van Bartan's mother, angered, attempts to will her considerable wealth to a church but is foiled by a young lawyer who deliberately writes a faulty will, seemingly because Columbia, before rejecting him, had been his chief romantic interest. The disgraced young lawyer, resigns, heads for Japan, and leaves Columbia Van Bartan with a wealthy husband and a loveless marriage. Post here is the outright satirical commentator. Through Randolph Mason, whose part in this tale is of relative import but is the most realistic and readable part, Post makes such waspish remarks as, "Madam . . . you talk like a diplomat: you say nothing at all."[28] In denying the wealth to the church, we may note certain overtones of contempt. It might also be suspected in the choice of a name for Columbia's wealthy suitor, "Bartan."[29] This whole tale, rather melodramatic and ineptly written, may say nothing at all, but then again diplomatically it may say much.

"Once in Jeopardy" illustrates a widely-known point of law, that a man tried and acquitted for a crime cannot be tried a second time for that same crime. In this overly long story of 82 pages Post's purposes seem to be rather mixed. He has an interesting story filled with sharp observations of people, politics, business, law, doctors, history, and more; but, he unwisely elaborates in documenting the legal factors. Therefore, he uses many pages to completely detail in typical legal fashion much that is obvious. A Post observation which persists in all his writing dealing with attempts at the "perfect" crime is stated here for the first time by the pursued character: ". . . I am entirely convinced that it is almost impossible to cover a crime so that human ingenuity cannot trail down the man who committed it."[30]

In the next story, Post for the second time in his fiction uses a cattle-raising situation, based on his personal knowledge of the West Virginia cattle country of his youth. "The Grazier" exhibits a clear step towards his later use of this situation in his best work. His style is developing, and we catch glimpses of the color he will display in *Dwellers in the Hills*. Also in "The Grazier" are names and qualities of character that will be found in the Uncle Abner stories. Post presents here several pages of background on the development and operation of the cattle industry as it applied to his family. Randolph Mason enters the tale through an accidental incident and offers a plan to save the financially troubled

Rufus Alshire, but the scheme is gallantly rejected.

> "Well," responded the grazier, "whether the plan you are about to propose is a crime or not, it is certainly a moral wrong, and I have no desire to rob a bank by committing even a moral wrong."[31]

The contemptuous reply of Randolph sums up his position.

> ". . . The word moral is a pure metaphysical symbol, possessing no more intrinsic virtue than a radical sign."[32]

Mason, realizing the patient will refuse his miracle medicine, then offers a watered-down, more lengthy and painful solution to Rufus Alshire's financial ills. His concluding ironic summation is offered with an ugly sneer: " 'To the law . . . all things are possible—even justice.' "[33] We note in this story an enigmatic deterioration in the health of the crafty lawyer.

The Man of Last Resort ends with a story entitled "The Rule Against Carper." Post arouses our suspicions of personal revelation, first by giving his chief character a name so closely associated with his own family, and secondly because this story is a soliloquy approximating a therapeutic confession of intellectual and personal disorders. The second of the three sections contains writing comparable to the torments Thomas Wolfe would later, in a more extended fashion, bestow upon his alter-ego heroes.

Post, in some critical articles published eighteen years later, rejects the plotless character story, but here he reveals substantial ability and insight into it. The story which ends the book and portends the self-destructive end of Carper leaves Randolph Mason in a serious state of "acute mania . . . raving like a drunken sailor." Post comments: "The man of last resorts was probably gone."[34]

What private agonies and struggles Melville Post may have allowed to surface in his creative work we are not certain, but *The Man of Last Resort, or the Clients of Randolph Mason* suggests some. We know that the years between 1897 and 1907 were not very productive for the author in terms of literary output, although in 1901 he did publish *Dwellers in the Hills,* his little-read minor classic which we will examine separately. These ten years reveal Post in a state of unrest and transition, engaging in a new and burdensome law partnership, enduring ailments that absented him from the legal profession, meeting and marrying a vivacious young widow, and suffering the loss of his only child. Conclusions about Post's mental state during these years are not easy to substantiate, but his work seems to show the stress of his personal life, unlike the more stable characteristics his later work displays.

The year 1908 saw the appearance of another book of Randolph Mason stories. The contents of the book had appeared serially in *Pearson's Magazine* beginning in the February 1907 issue and monthly thereafter through the May 1908 issue; therefore, it seems probable that the book manuscript existed in total and the serial rights as a whole were sold to the magazine. The book's arrangement follows exactly the order of serial publication. The editorial comments preceding the serial publication shed some light on the origin of the book; they include an explanation by Post of the somewhat different approach to Randolph Mason, presented as a statement signed by the book's narrator, Courtlandt Parks. This explanation needs to be considered nearly complete, together with the opening remarks of *Pearson's Magazine*'s editor:

> A few months ago we announced that after an effort of about four years we had succeeded in securing from the author of *The Strange Schemes of Randolph Mason* a new series of stories built around that remarkable character of fiction.
>
> These stories are to commence in the February *Pearson's*, and we believe that they will prove to be the most interesting stories of the mystery class that have been produced since the original cases of *Sherlock Holmes*.
>
> . . . .
>
> The book (*Strange Schemes*) was fascinating in interest, but it seemed to us that for magazine purposes, a new series of stories would be much stronger, and more universally satisfactory to our readers if Randolph Mason could be made the champion of right instead of the tutor of criminals.
>
> Mr. Post accepted our view of the matter and worked out his cases accordingly. In the stories which commence next month the narrator is *Courtlandt Parks*, the secretary of *Randolph Mason*, and his introduction to the new series explains the change which has come over the Randolph Mason of old; as follows:
>
> > It would take a separate volume to trace the successive stages by which the eminent lawyer, Randolph Mason, became finally dominated by the single idea that all the

difficulties presented by the affairs of men were problems which he could solve; how that one idea absorbed him, rid him of human considerations and led him to demonstrate that every crime, even murder, could be committed in such a manner that, before the law, it was not a crime.

I ought, however, to point out that after Randolph Mason's recovery from his attack of acute mania, this dominant idea took on a further distinguishing phase. He now undertook to find within the law a means by which to even up and correct every manner of injustice. He would consider no case which did not contain this element, a wrong for which the law in its regular course offers no redress. This attitude was, in no sense, a so-called awakening of conscience, nor of any moral origin. I think it arose primarily from the idea that such problems were more difficult than any others. Take a situation so hopeless as to be called fated or inevitable, add, in the correction of it, a necessity to return the injury directly and in an exact measure to the author of it, and one has a difficulty not easily possible of solution to human intelligence.

I have prepared here a record of some of the more remarkable cases attempted by Randolph Mason under this mania of adjustment.

(—Courtlandt Parks)[35]

The stories in the book *The Corrector of Destinies, being Tales of Randolph Mason As Related by His Private Secretary, Courtlandt Parks* are numbered I through XIII, in addition to having a title. It would seem that they were meant to resemble chapters of a novel, indicating that Melville had hoped to develop his talents in the direction of the longer story, as he did in *Dwellers in the Hills* and would next try in *The Gilded Chair*. But there is no time progression, no plot relationships, only the essential characters appearing as needed; thus it must be treated as a collection of stories. Most of these stories, while they are not equal to Post's better work, do show clear signs of the author having begun to master the techniques of creative writing in a definitely professional manner. Much of the technique for which he is justly to be credited, such as economy, suspense, short characterizations, and surprise endings, are found here in increasing prominence.

"My Friend at Bridge" demonstrates Post's growing concern with suspense. The plot is not impressive and there is no thorough revelation of character in this tale, only some skillfully done asides, but the story is better balanced than much of his previous work. The same might be said for "Madame Versay," the second story. "Madame Versay," it can be noted, appears to contain Post's first authentic attempt to use the surprise ending technique. The use of Confederate currency is found later in a couple of other works by the author, but it has long since become outdated and the point of law illustrated in this particular tale would not likely arise today. Thus this story, technically well done, loses whatever punch it might once have exerted.

Post's writings, from the first, indicate a personal and critical relationship with New York City society at the turn of the century. "The Burgoyne-Hayes Dinner" contains a few of his reflections and sharp caricatures. It also provides some good descriptions of Randolph Mason. The story itself, based on a simple point of law, is not forceful, but the banter and conversation of Parks, the narrator, makes up for other deficiencies. The next story of the collection, "The Copper Bonds," again shows Post's consistently more professional abilities, but again he has not developed enough of a universal or useful theme in his plot to give the story a meaningful existence. The theme, as it is in most of these stories, is retribution, but the justice meted out to the villain in this tale seems insufficient for his villainy.

Melville Post possibly never did recognize the full value of dialogue in handling dramatic situations, although he did well with it at times in his Uncle Abner tales. In these earlier stories he overlooked its use consistently. "The District Attorney" has a plot that would have greatly benefited from the use of more dialogue. The technique would have increased tremendously the dramatic effects of the story. Post instead, speaking through the narrator, Parks, explains much too much in lifeless prose. Although he manages a few high points in the piece and makes his points of law clear enough for the layman to grasp, the total effect is one of overwriting. A good, unexpected ending helps lighten the load of the prose preceding it and helps the reader overlook the unnatural smoothness with which Randolph Mason's trickery succeeds.

"The Interrupted Exile" shows Post sharpening his use of atmosphere, which together with a good deal of wit and excellent characterization, plus the introduction of a bit of human interest into plot, puts this story technically a step above most of those presented previous to this point. Unfortunately the plot falters somewhat because of the weak coincidence on which the point of law rests; in fact Post goes to the trouble of inserting a lengthy footnote in an effort to make the incident plausible. Once again the legal situation is one concerned with land transfer rights in West Virginia, a subject in which Post as a corporation lawyer had vast experience. The color provided by the author's familiarity with the Eastern aristocratic set makes this story worth reading.

The next story is called simply "The Last Check," which sums up the plot in three words. Again Post developed his plot around a point of law, here regarding the liabilities of illegal checks, tempering this somewhat with a human interest touch. The sharp views on the morals of politicians presented here carry the weight of the author's close connections with State politics. Also, there appears a touch of the satiric in the closing sentence: "I saw now why the dying man looked upon Randolph Mason as a providence of God."[36]

Tuberculosis is no longer the almost common disease it was once, but nevertheless the picture of the consumptive in Post's "The Life Tenant" moves the reader. The author's portrait of the infected man, of whom Randolph Mason comments that he speaks "the jargon of a cab driver," is done with restraint; yet this story, done basically in dialogue, is a good off-beat, low-keyed drama which entertains more than it instructs. Randolph Mason seems in this tale, despite a few sneers and snarls, much more humanistic than ever before, and even somewhat heroic. Again, in the story which follows, "The Pennsylvania Pirate," Mason assumes the makings of a hero when an unsuspecting villain presents himself at the erratic lawyer's office and is tricked into returning to a group of disappointed investors interest money which the "pirate" had hoped to use for his own benefit. Crowning his defeat of the villain, Mason reveals knowledge of the true value of one tract of land the man had hoped to take title to from the unwary owner. But at the conclusion the shrewd lawyer rejects all appreciation for his altruistic act, saying, "Gratitude . . . like regret, annoys me."[37] This story opens with several paragraphs commenting interestingly on the presence of "pirates" in the modern world of business, and the opening lines are rich in earthy wisdom: "Reforms, it would seem, only cause the devil to change his clothes. The advance of civilization is a progress of disguises...."[38]

"The Virgin of the Mountains" gets its title from a painting credited with miraculous deeds. Unable to purchase the picture, a wealthy American perpetrates the theft of the painting from its place in an Italian villa. The disgraced owner tracks down the American and kills him in cold blood. The dying man, by threatening his killer with revenge, provides Randolph Mason with the necessary situation to save his client from the charge of murder. Post here devised an excellent plot with a justifiable ending but has marred the full effect by including at the beginning a long explanation without dialogue. The plot would appear to be more suited to treatment as a novelette than as a short story. Several isolated sections of the narrative excel, however, and help to redeem its obvious faults.

Post in "An Adventure of St. Valentine's Night" mixed romance into a complicated legal situation, and consequently both suffered. As a corporation attorney, dealing often with the legal problems of railroads, Post may have been acquainted with a case similar to the plot of this tale, but the amount of explanatory material injected causes the story to falter dramatically. This is particularly regrettable since it starts off well with fast-paced dialogue indicating a tight, neatly controlled narrative. Randolph Mason requires only a paragraph at the end to make his point, replacing his usual shrewd methods with cold intelligence.

In "The Danseuse" we find both distressed and distressing adults, plus a pampered child clutching a grotesque, Sir George Fairfeld Porter and "How-de-do." The boy's father has abandoned his first wife and married a scheming danseuse. Divorce, illness, huge sums of money, legal manipulations and schemes backed with bitterness surround the unperturbed child's existence. With a little trickery in two directions Randolph Mason easily resolves the child's fate, likewise that of the mother and the danseuse. The reader of this caricature of a child notices in it some pity for the child plus some satirical touches—but it is difficult to determine which the author actually intended to stress.

The final story in *The Corrector of Destinies,* "The Intriguer," when compared to the early Randolph Mason stories demonstrates how far Post had advanced in confidence and ability as a writer. In spite of a number of dramatic failings, the writing in this story is forceful and entertaining. Dealing with political ambitions, railroad financial affairs, and legal matters, Post assembled here materials most familiar to him and then created realistic characters and a believable atmosphere. The plot is suitably complex and moves through several twists that are well directed. Randolph Mason confounds one man, defeats another, and finds his uncanny wisdom and work wasted due to the unpredictable sympathies and desires of a woman, a near match for the shrewd lawyer. It is a fitting tale with which to end a didactic, but unusual book.

Although the book ends at this point, the career of Randolph Mason was continued in one more story. While never collected in book form, it was published serially immediately following the thirteen tales that make up the final book devoted to Mason. The uncollected efforts of Melville Davisson Post will be considered in a separate section, but it seems more fitting to include this particular item here. Titled "The Marriage Contract," this maverick story involves a romance cramped by custom and warped by money. The man is an American on the verge of losing his inheritance, and the woman an English woman on the verge of losing her man. Randolph Mason's answer that marriage alone can solve their problem seems ambiguous until he proves his point.

While in many ways this story resembles and equals those of the last collection of Randolph Mason stories, various minor deviations make it appear to have been written later. It is the only Randolph Mason story which places Courtlandt Parks in a foreign scene, this being Scotland. Post, about the time this story was composed, was himself traveling in Scotland and England, places that thereafter would be the setting of many of his fictional creations. The story is divided into three numbered sections unlike any stories in the third Mason book (though those in the second book were treated in this manner), and it is told in the first person narrative as are only those of the last book. Some references to Bible verses, made by none other than the seemingly atheistic master lawyer, would seem to set its composition later than the others, placing it closer to the spirit of the Uncle Abner period. The nature of the plot also indicates a later origin.

There is, in the story, one paragraph referring to Randolph Mason's health which, as certain evidence seems to indicate, it possibly reflects the author's own condition:

> I was beginning to wonder how long flesh and blood would stand this tremendous strain. Twice already he had broken down. Once I had taken him to the Riviera, and the sun and the sea of Southern France had got him on his feet; the second time, the credit of his recovery is part of the deserved fame of two New York physicians, unequaled, I think in this world.[39]

Whatever the reason this tale was not included in the last collection of Randolph Mason stories, it was certainly not because of inferior execution. Had allusions that were too personal caused Post, on second thought, to put it aside? More likely, the manuscript containing the thirteen last tales had been completed some time in advance of the writing of "The Marriage Contract." Thus, Post may also have been considering still another Randolph Mason book before abandoning the amoral attorney, when suddenly he realized that Mason's disreputable ethics and manners no longer were applicable to his own moods and the direction in which his creative work was turning.

Post may have symbolically buried Randolph Mason, but a strong character cannot be contained by such a grave. The Randolph Mason books continued to be popular and were reprinted many times, with some editions appearing in the 1920's when Post's fame was still at its highest point. Several of the stories have been anthologized and still others reprinted in serial publications. At one point in 1928 there was a bitter dispute between the author and an agent who had purchased from the publisher many years before certain "exclusive" serial rights to the last Randolph Mason book. Post, in his later years, was himself quite critical of the amateurish style of the Randolph Mason stories. Nevertheless, they have remained long-time favorites of many lawyers seeking out the literature of their profession and have been recognized by various students and bibliographers of crime and mystery stories for their outstanding originality.

●●●●●●●●●

III. TWO NOVELS AND THE NAMELESS THING

1. Dwellers in the Hills.

Taking his correspondence as an indicator, the year 1899 found Melville Post in an unsettled state of mind. He had reached the age of thirty. He was unmarried. For reasons unknown he was approaching a decision to end the law partnership he had entered into at the start of his legal career in 1892.[1] The controversies were still evident surrounding his collections of Randolph Mason stories published in 1896 and 1897. It perhaps appeared to him that he was at a point in life where he would have to decide between literature and law. Taking a summer off from his duties as an attorney he returned to Templemoor.[2] Here at his parent's home where he had grown up in the West Virginia cattle country, he began work on his third book. At the start he had decided it would be a longer work with a vastly different theme. An existent copy of the manuscript shows that the work went well with few changes required. The book was published in the early months of 1901. It was dedicated to his mother.

For *Dwellers in the Hills*[3] the author drew upon material he knew intimately as a boy and a young man. He based the story on some of the problems faced by the West Virginia cattle raisers. Around this he included his intense love for horses, the impressive moods of nature, people he had known in his own youth, and tales he had heard many times about the symbolic "dwellers in the hills" —the mythical little people of the West Virginia mountains.

An article published prior to publication of the book noted that the theme was suggested by someone to Post.[4] This can be only partially true, for a work of this type comes into being only through a deep desire of its creator to put such keen emotions into print. The simple plot is based in part on the true experience of a young neighbor of the Post family, Aquilla Ward.[5] Ten year old Ward was sent to Bridgeport, West Virginia, a distance of perhaps fifteen miles, with a valuable herd of his father's cattle—an outstanding responsibility for a youngster. This event impressed Post and became somehow the catalyst that brought him to a vivid recollection of some of his own experiences as a young rider among the bellowing herds of cattle.

The book received consistently fair to good notices in the reviews, but failed to create any sort of the excitement similar to that of the Randolph Mason books. Reportedly, however, it did create a minor reputation for the author in England. Still, the book has over the years been accorded a measure of praise by the few individuals who have had cause to comment upon it, but the general reading public has long been unfamiliar with it. Perhaps this is because it was never reprinted and except for rare copies has been generally unavailable.

Whether or not this book should be classed as a novel, a novelette, a long story, or a prose poem is difficult to determine. It bears some resemblances to all these categories. Like any creative work that is wrung from the depths of the creator's own experiences, it was not limited by any set literary form, but took its own form. Published by G. P. Putnam's Sons, it runs to 278 pages and is divided into 21 chapters. In cataloging the book the Library of Congress terms it a novel, and most readers would concur. A book of such length and with such an accumulation of varied sensual detail allows consideration as a novel for critical purposes, discounting the simplicity of its plot.

The writing, and this is the most compelling aspect of the work, is that of a prose poem. It fairly sings in certain passages.

Post had a deep affection for the horse and where he touches this subject the sentences ring with authenticity. Also he had a deep regard for nature, which was a forceful influence on the days of his early years, and he describes the details of nature surrounding the three autumn days of this adventure with the strong emotions of poetry, keenly aware of the sights, sounds, smells and moods of the land and the weather. A few uninspired critics wishing that Post had written a pure adventure story, voice disapproval of the occasional "digressions" which they find. In reality, however, few of these are out of place or distracting to the whole work; rather they add a bit of mature seasoning to this story of a boy's adventure related by a reflecting adult. This is a story which cannot be read lightly once and then put aside thereafter to be forgotten— it is a book which demands rereading.

The plot's action can be outlined in a few sentences. Three young West Virginia riders go south on a two day journey to pick up a herd of cattle. They drive the herd north for delivery to a neighboring cattleman. If the cattle are delivered within the contract time limit, the buyer will lose a considerable sum of money because of a price drop in the market. The buyer thus sets his men about to prevent the delivery. The young trio overcome the efforts of their adversary, and he accepts the cattle as agreed. The triumphant riders return home.

Interwoven is the secondary plot which concerns the love affair between the older brother who has sold the cattle but cannot make the delivery because he has been injured and a girl who the narrator suspects to be a traitor—but proves to have been most faithful. Around all this is the theme of the narrator's love for his wonderful horse, El Mahdi—a love real, faithful, and undying.

The story is told by the first person narrator looking back on what must have been three of the most important days of his youth, when he rode out a boy and came back a man. The man who is narrating the tale has achieved an education and a mature mind and reflects on the adventure more calmly and with more digressions than had the tale been dramatized by a boy still in the whirl of the excitement. Its importance has left a clear picture of the events and they are presented in sharp detail. Post, in this book, skillfully handles several layers of thought.

We soon learn that the narrator is called "Quiller" and that his family name is Ward, a clear indication of how closely Post adopted fact for his fiction.[6] The two companions of Quiller are "Ump" and "Orange Jud." Orange Jud is patterned with exactness on the real person of that same name who grew up side by side with Post and who for his whole life worked as a servant for the Post family, along with his mother Liza, who is herself mentioned in the closing paragraphs of the book. Various names scattered throughout the book are familiar names which the author used in either his first two books, or would use again in telling the stories of Uncle Abner. The reader meets briefly with pretty Cynthia Carper, who is the diverting feminine interest of Quiller's brother. We are introduced to the inscrutable Rufe (for Rufus) Woodford, or "Hawk" Rufe, the shrewd competitor of the Wards in the cattle-trading business. Lesser, but typical personalities are Simon Betts, an old wagon-maker; Roy, who operates the distinctly primitive Roy's Tavern; and Nicholas Marsh, another practical cattleman.[7] All these are characters we easily accept as real persons.

As we accept the reality of the characters involved in the adventure, we can also readily believe what happens to them without stretching our imagination too far. The basic plot is simple and progresses in one direction with only the enthusiasm of the author aiding to lift it above the commonplace of a dime novel. It would make an excellent scenario for a motion picture done in widescreen technicolor—but it would take superior direction to capture the intensity of feeling that the author so effectively reports through his economical and elementary prose. Time may prove this book to be a minor classic of American literature. The selection of quotations which follow should help to illustrate the depth of feeling found in its poetic language.

In his opening chapter, Post has the narrator introduce his horse, El Mahdi, the False Prophet; his companion Jud, who rides a great sorrel called the Cardinal; and the hunchback, Ump, who cares for his Bay Eagle with the expertise of a skilled physician. Quiller's description of Ump is the first vivid picture in the book:

> Opposite me in the shadow of the tall hickory timber the man Ump, doubled like a finger, was feeling tenderly over the coffin joints and the steel blue hoofs of the Bay Eagle, blowing away the dust from the clinch of each shoe

nail and pressing the flat calks with his thumb. No mother ever explored with more loving care the mouth of her child for evidence of a coming tooth. Ump was on his never ending quest for the loose shoe-nail. It was the serious business of his life.

I think he loved this trim, nervous mare better than any other thing in the world. When he rode, perched like a monkey, with thin legs held close to her sides, and his short, humped back doubled over, and his head with its long hair bobbing about as though his neck were loose-coupled somehow, he was eternally caressing her mighty withers, or feeling for the play of each iron tendon under her satin skin. And when we stopped, he glided down to finger her shoe-nails.[8]

At the beginning of Chapter II, "The Passing of an Illusion," we are presented the theme of Quiller's introduction to the realities of life. He has just galloped away in tears from his encounter with the antagonist "Hawk" Woodford and the seemingly unfaithful Cynthia Carper:

El Mahdi wanted to run, and I let him go. The swing of the horse and the rush of fresh, cool air was good. Nothing in all the world could have helped me so well. The tears were mastered, but I had a sense of tremendous loss. I had joisted with the first windmill, riding up out of youth's golden country, and I had lost one of the splendid illusions of that enchanted land. I was cruelly hurt. How cruelly, any man will know when he recalls his first jamming against the granite door-posts of the world.[9]

A most notable vignette is the encounter with Aunt Peggy, a typical character of Appalachia, presented vividly by the author with excellent humor, affection, and careful detail:

Aunt Peggy was one of the ancients, a carpet weaver, pious as Martin Luther, but a trifule liberal with her idioms. The tongue in her head wagged like a bell-clapper. Whatever was whispered in the hills got somehow into Aunt Peggy's ears, and once there it went to the world like the secret of Midas.

. . . Aunt Peggy could never be brought to say who it was that told her. One could inquire as one pleased. The old woman ran no farther than "Them as knows." And there it ended and you might be damned.

> . . . .
> She pulled her square-rimmed spectacles down on her nose and squinted up at us. When she saw me, she started back and dropped her hands. "Great fathers!" she ejaculated, "I hope I may go to the blessed God if it ain't Quiller gaddin' over the country, an' Mister Ward a-dyin'."[10]

(Explaining that she had been lied to regarding Ward's condition, Quiller reports her reply.)

> "Bless my life," cried the old woman, "an' they lied, did they? I think a liar is the meanest thing the Saviour died for. They said Mister Ward was took sudden with blood poison last night an' a-dyin', the scalawags! I'll dress 'em down when I get my eyes on 'em."
> . . . .
> "Can you keep a secret?" said Ump, leaning down from his saddle.
> The old woman's face lighted . . . "Yes," she said, "I can that."
> "So can I," said Ump.
> The old carpet-weaver snorted. "Humph," she said, "when you get dry behind the ears you won't be so peart." Then she waved her hand to me. "Light off," she said, "an' rest your critters, an' git a tin of drinkin' water."[11]

As they resume their mission, Aunt Peggy explains to Quiller the legend of the Dwarfs building the bridge. The import of this story is reflected in the stage of the trio's adventure when Black Malan loses his axe into the river. The old woman's parting words to Quiller confirm her belief in the legendary "dwellers in the hills."

> " 'Tain't so certain," said Aunt Peggy, wagging her head, " 't ain't so certain. There's many a thing a-holdin' in the world that you can't see." And she turned around in the door and went back to her loom.[12]

There are other tales of the hills related and folk-talk recorded throughout the book which illustrate the power of these legends in the lives of the people. There are other descriptions of people and places on the route taken by the trio all realistically rendered with exceptional skill. Other interesting characters in addition to Aunt Peggy are Patsy, "a madcap protegee of Cynthia Carper;" Christian, a blacksmith and the very antithesis of his name; the flat ferry boat operators, Mart and Daniel Horton, and Woodford's three riders, Lem Marks, shrewd and cunning, Black Malan and Parson Peppers, the latter who sings hymns as he drinks his cider and goes about his "dirty work." All these illustrate Post's artistry when writing of his own people and land. These little gems enrich the experience of any reader who encounters them.

In a limited examination one cannot exhibit all the facets of the writing that give this book its outstanding value. *Dwellers in the Hills* is equal, many might feel, or even superior to Post's tales of Uncle Abner, his most often critically confirmed classic. But other examples should be presented, particularly some which resemble very closely the language and feelings so often found in the writing of Thomas Wolfe some thirty years after Post's book appeared. Perhaps it is only because both are autobiographical fiction done with the regular use of poetic prose, but the reader must judge for himself. In the following paragraph the similarity is startling:

> When the Golden Land is lost to us, when turning suddenly we find the enchanted kingdom vanished, do we give up the hope of finding it again? We know that it is somewhere across the world, and we ought to find it, and we know, too, that its out-country is like these October afternoons, and our hearts beat wildly for a moment, then the truth strikes and we see that this is not The Land.[13]

Quiller and his companions complete their task, defeating Woodford's attempts to halt the delivery of the cattle. The return trip with the cattle, swimming them across the river when the ferry is found destroyed, and the skirmish with Woodford at the bridge take up over a third of the book, but it is a superbly reported adventure.

Only Quiller's inability to understand Cynthia clouds his success over Woodford in the closing paragraphs. It is a bitter defeat on the heels of a magnificent victory. One early critic alone noted the antipathetic attitude toward women assigned to the narrator throughout the story and reinforced at the end.[14] Could this have been a heart-broken author's own experience surfacing in his fiction? We can hardly avoid the question in light of the autobiographical nature of this work and evidence that we find in other stories.

No reader of *Dwellers in the Hills* goes away from it without having the experience of having ridden along with the narrator. The author's great love for the horse is exhibited time after time. He knew exactly how it felt to be astride this servant of man and expressed it in unforgettable words:

> The moon was rising, a red wheel behind the shifting fog. And under its soft light the world was a ghost land. We rode like phantoms, the horses' feet striking noiselessly in the deep sand, except where we threw the dead sycamore leaves. My body swung with the motions of the horse, and Ump and Jud might have been a part of the thing that galloped under their saddles.[15]
>
> . . . .
>
> . . . The huge Cardinal galloped in the moonlight like some splendid machine of bronze, never a misstep, never a false estimate, never the difference of a finger's length in the long, even jumps. It might have been the one-eyed Agib riding his mighty horse of brass, except that no son of a decadent Sultan ever carried the bulk of Orange Jud. And the eccentric El Mahdi! There was no cause for fault-finding on this night. He galloped low and easily, gathering his grey legs as gracefully as his splendid, nervous mother. I watched his mane fluttering in the stiff breeze, his slim ears thrust forward, the moon shining on his steel-blue hide. For once he seemed in sympathy with what I was about. Seemed, I write it, for it must have been a mistaken fancy. This splendid, indifferent rascal shared the sensations of no living man. Long and long ago he had sounded life and found it hollow. Still, as if he were a woman, I loved him for this accursed indifference. Was it because his emotions were so hopelessly inaccessible, or because he saw through the illusion we were chasing; or because—because—who knows what it was? We have no litmus-paper test for the charm of genius.
>
> Under us the dry leaves crackled like twigs snapping in a fire, and the flying sand cut the bushes along the roadway like a storm of whizzing hailstones. . . .[16]

2. The Gilded Chair.

Melville Post's second novel was no triumph; yet *The Gilded*

Chair deserves at least a limited recommendation, a judgment no less than "interesting and readable." This is not to indicate that it resembles a successful novel, artistically or otherwise, for it is a problem for the critic even as it was for the author. Published in 1910 and dedicated to "Caroline" (his niece, Caroline DuBois), it was Post's fifth book.

That he put a great deal of effort into the completing of the book is seen in the fact that Post made some extensive changes in the work during the year before it was published.[1] Mainly this concerned shifting the locale of the American scene involved from the East Coast to the Pacific Coast, for reasons which can only be speculated on. Moving this part of the action to the West Coast allowed Post to introduce several aspects of the current Japanese problem. One of these was Japan's growing international aspirations. Another was the immigration of Japanese to America, which was thought by some to be a serious threat affecting political, economic and racial matters. Post, as a life-long Democrat, may have used the book as a means of expressing his personal concern for the Republican administration's position on these questions.[2] It is possible that Post could have had his opinion inflamed, coincidentally, by a fictitious account of future history which predicted a war between Japan and the United States.[3] This was published concurrent with Post's last series of Randolph Mason stories in the same magazine at the time he was writing *The Gilded Chair*. Doubtlessly he read it and perhaps any number of the many other opinions being circulated during these years, all concerned with Japan's secret military plans which it was believed would include an invasion of the far western states.[4] While Post might not have seen the major book on this subject, what he did read must have strongly influenced him.[5]

In addition, there are strong possibilities that Post may have made a visit to the West Coast at this time, likely in conjunction with the interests of his brother-in-law, John DuBois, a lumberman who had business connections in the section of Oregon where the story is placed. Such a trip would probably have caused Post to be freshly inspired by the vast wilderness of the area, thus enabling him to write his graphic descriptions. Nor can we overlook that the Pacific Coast provided a suitable location for a remote chateau of uncommon proportions and one which would give it an ambiguous identity, one that would not point too directly at any particular individual or place in the Eastern States where Post had many strong social and political ties and wealthy acquaintances. Whatever the reasons for the changes in his novel, Post did not allow this strong political theme to wholly dominate the book, for he believed entertainment to be the primary reason for the creation of fiction.

The Japanese-threat theme was only one of several apparent themes woven into the story. That they are connected incidentally or loosely rather than organically is the most likely reason for the opinion, arrived at by those few who have given this novel critical attention, that the book is confusing and inconclusive. The central issue, the love theme, is centered on a fanciful romance between a British nobleman and an American beauty. She is heiress to a relatively recent industrial fortune. This romance, treated by the author half melodramatically and half realistically, gives the story its only encompassing interest. Set into this are other minor themes, the childish romance between the wealthy old tycoon of eighty years and the middle-aged American-born widow of an Italian Marquis, and the general and sometimes uncertain comments on religious beliefs. All of these themes are colored by a gentle tint of mysticism, magic, and legend which is most apparent in the choice of chapter titles.[6] These themes, seldom coupled together with invisible joints, tend to jar the reader who expects a simpler, more singular development, such as would be expected in a book using such clear, basic prose as this exhibits.

It should also be noted that violence is displayed here to a greater extent than in any other work of Post to this point, perhaps with the minor exception of "Corpus Delicti," and certainly to a greater extent than in the general entertainment-type literature of its period. The descriptions of violence are not too unlike those common in much of today's light fiction. The hero at one point uses an automatic rifle, capable of firing twenty shots in twenty seconds,[7] in a calculated bloody massacre. Post reports the results of its usage in ambiguous terms, giving no argument for or against its existence or use. He describes its overwhelming effectiveness, however, quite realistically, in a manner rather strong for a love story.

Most worth noting is the author's crisp, simple style, with its directness and its careful and limited use of adjectives. The style is unique and illustrative of what Post was trying to do in the development of his fiction technique. The book is rich with sentences that could easily have served as examples for some of the later writers who adopted the objective or journalistic style of the newsreporter for fictional purposes. Post's prose is nearly always one of understatement, leaving the reader to fill in the definite outline. It allows a quick rendering of successive actions, a rapid pacing of events as the need arises. Post does not deserve any singular credit for development of this style, but he does deserve to be recognized for his early, effective, and extensive use of it. If he had any direct influence on its future use, it was probably in the detective fiction field.

We can render the story Post tells in a brief descriptive sentence, such as: The story is a romance between an English nobleman and an American heiress; or, The story is an adventure of one man protecting himself and two women against a revolting mob; or, The story is about the downfall of a foolish egotist. However, each of these, and all together, leave much to be desired in defining the story for essay purposes. Perhaps only the first would suffice for condensation purposes. An honest approach to this novel requires that we be more specific.

The story opens with the widowed Marchesa Soderrelli making an unexpected call upon the new, young Duke of Dorset. Her purposes are equally to borrow money and to arrange for the introduction of the Duke to some friends at the games in Oban, Scotland. Her friends are two in particular, Cyrus Childers and his niece Caroline, who arrive at Oban aboard an expensive yacht. The Marchesa manages the introduction with ease, and the Duke and Caroline are immediately attracted to each other. The Marchesa later learns that this introduction which she had assumed as her own doings had in reality been done under the strong influence of Cyrus Childers, the eighty year old tycoon, who as a middle-aged suitor had years before been rejected by the family of the Marchesa, who had then been a charming, young Southern belle. The elderly tycoon's desire to marry her remains alive, he invites her to postpone her answer to his proposal until she visits him at his fabulous Chateau in Oregon.

Caroline Childers, as a result of a discussion of marital views with the Duke, momentarily seems to accept the nobleman's statement that one should follow the guidance of one's family in marriage matters.[8] This he emphasizes by telling her the legend of why all the Dukes of Dorset have for centuries never married. As they part, she invites the Duke to stop for a visit at her uncle's Chateau during his projected trip to Western Canada. The Duke, deeply impressed by the beautiful American girl, makes arrangements to be put ashore near the great estate in Oregon. Meeting a mountaineer guide by chance, he arrives at the Chateau some few days before Caroline and the Marchesa are expected. Cyrus Childers invites him to bide the time hunting about the primitive wilderness of the estate. The fabulous home, set deep in the wooded mountains, with beautiful gardens and terraces, the Duke soon learns to be entirely maintained with immigrant Japanese labor exploited by the aged tycoon.

The very day Caroline and the Marchesa arrive the Japanese laborers stage a revolt, shooting a horse from under the Duke—then, as they attack the Chateau, killing Cyrus Childers. The Duke secures an automatic rifle hidden in his luggage and, after shooting a fairly large number of the mob, manages to escape, together with Caroline and the Marchesa, through the wilderness to an old abandoned cabin in the mountains. There the next morning they are discovered by the old, mountaineer guide, who is more or less a circuit rider preacher with no visible congregation other than his mule Jezebel. With his aid and the use of the mule the Duke and the two women manage an escape to the coast. While escaping, the Duke professes his love for Caroline. As the story ends they are married and residing in Scotland. The Duke has been making speeches, according to the final paragraphs, to bring about the breaking of the alliance between Britain and Japan, the uprising at the Chateau having been attributed in part to the secret plans of Japan to engage in a war with the United States.

The Gilded Chair resembles a mosaic built up of many finely shaped pieces assembled into a puzzling, uncertain pattern. The reader no sooner feels that the work is developing in a realistic direction when the emphasis shifts and presents a mood of fantasy. What is rather a stiff romance, a step back into an earlier age, suddenly becomes very modern, coming to life enmeshed in an adventure plot that is nearly thirty years ahead of its time.

Equally disturbing is the shift in point of view. The book begins with a strong emphasis upon the Marchesa and her problems. The Duke is introduced and within a short space the viewpoint shifts back and forth between the Duke and the Marchesa. About halfway through the point of view definitely becomes that of the Duke and remains essentially his for the concluding parts of the book. The problems of the Marchesa are rather hazily resolved at the close of the novel.

The Duke and the Marchesa are allowed some dimension, but the other major characters are only sketched in. Beyond the five principal characters the book is populated only with non-speaking extras. This lack of fully-described characters, a virtue in Post's shorter stories, is obviously one of the book's defects. The reader or critic who demands that all problems be answered, all characters clearly judged, and all scenes presented in sharp focus will without hesitation find the book unsatisfactory.

Whether the structure of the novel shaped up as Post fully intended it to is a legitimate question. As we follow Post's development from the Randolph Mason stories through to his better work, we note a strong emphasis on story-telling technique. Post's masterful accomplishments in the perfection of the modern short story technique is allowed even by some of his most harsh critics. That Post was seeking to try for more modern, quicker paced means of telling a story seems obvious. Such technique proved its value in the short story, and in the hands of other writers would prove itself capable in the short novel. But, in this instance, Post seemed unable to maintain tight control over all the varied elements involved. We are not given a complete understanding of the themes, which leaves us to feeling that he unwisely forced them into what seems to have been first intended as a standard romance. Judgments that the book is "uneven" are thus accurately applied. Had he improved the talented use of point of view displayed in *Dwellers in the Hills* and used it here, together with some wiser editing of subject matter, the results might have proved quite different.

On the other hand, there are certain interesting points that make this book difficult to reject or ignore. First, there is a great deal of Post himself in the character of the Duke, the English nobleman and the sportsman. Post during these years seemed to fancy himself as fitting into this strata of society, traveling freely and visiting the social gatherings of the season, much like an early version of the jet set. His dressing in English riding tweeds, his love for playing polo and hunting are evident and easily permit this conclusion. In the character of the Duke of Dorset we likely see Post much as he saw himself.

Also of critical importance, we see Post making another step towards the characterization of Uncle Abner. In the portrayal of the old mountaineer guide we meet one who like Abner is on a word-for-word basis of familiarity with the Old Testament. At one point in the story we find the mountaineer attempting in detective fashion to assess simple clues left scattered about by the Duke and the women who had escaped into the nearly trackless wilderness. The humble honesty and integrity so much a part of Uncle Abner is definitely a part of the old guide's character. At the time Post was preparing the final copy of the manuscript for this novel, he was only two years away from publication of the first Uncle Abner tale, thus possibly less than a year from the creation of that significant character.

Equally interesting is the continuing revelation of Post's trend in religious thought towards the attitudes of *The Mountain School Teacher.* From the godless Randolph Mason, Post advanced to the pantheism of *Dwellers in the Hills*, and a slightly new Randolph Mason, who emerged in a 1908 book with an increasing amount of moral concern for his client's welfare. This allows speculations that Post felt a growing need to investigate more deeply the mysteries of life as revealed in the teachings of formal religion. In *The Gilded Chair* we find even the skeptical-minded Marchesa greatly upset by the atheism of Cyrus Childers as he proclaims his right to rule from his gilded seat of power.[9] Childer's downfall is later accurately predicted by the Bible-reading old mountaineer with appropriate quotations from the Old Testament. In the attitude of this prophet-like character who believes in having respect for the wrath of a God whose patience is not endless, we read the concerns of the author, conscious or unconscious, regarding the truths of the childhood lessons emphasized by his religious mother and father.

We remember too the traumatic loss to Post and his wife of their infant son, which had occurred only a few years before he was to write the following passage for this novel:

> There is a certain provision of Nature wholly blessed. When one is called to follow that which is dearest to him, nailed up in a coffin, to the grave; when the bitterness of death has wracked the soul to the extreme of physical endurance; then, when under the turn of the screw blood no longer comes, there exudes, instead of it, a divine liquor that numbs the sensibilities like an anaesthetic, and one is able to walk behind the coffin in the road, to approach the grave, to watch the shovelful of earth thrown in, and to come away like other men, speaking of the sun, the harvest, the prospects of the to-morrow; it is not this day that is the deadliest; it is the day to follow—the months, the years to follow, when the broken soul has no longer an opiate.[10]

Although we have judged this book as merely "interesting and readable," we would hope this is a mild miscalculation. There must be better words with which to recommend it.

3. The Nameless Thing.

Most fitting to Melville Post's sixth book is its title, *The Nameless Thing*. Published by D. Appleton and Company in May 1912, it defies a choice of words to describe the essential nature, content, and central theme that combine to give it its form as a book. Although disguised as a novel, basically it is a collection of short stories, twelve in number including the frame tale, used to enclose the others into a book-length mystery. These stories, previously published in periodicals from 1908 through 1912, have been grouped together by a method of literary composition which is really neither original, unorthodox, nor easy. Story tellers long have used similar means for allowing a number of related stories to be incorporated into a continuous narrative.[1] Post, although a late-comer to this method, in this instance has done it boldly and done it comparatively well.[2]

Both because of its length (338 pages) and the manner in which it is broken up into chapters, with most of the individual tales being split once or twice at odd places, *The Nameless Thing* does appear upon casual observation to be a novel. Surely there was considerable deliberation by the publisher and author about the form it was to take, for then, as now, in the history of American book merchandising novels are more consistently salable than short story collections. This deception has had a proven record of selling effectiveness that far outweighs any literary justification. Perhaps Post could better justify his use of the frame method; certainly it does not detract from the entertainment value of the individual stories. Varied as to setting, treatment, and character types, all of the stories have, more or less, a common element. This we discover is *the nameless thing*.

To tie these tales together and allow for a probing of their common element, Post has devised a frame wherein three men, a priest, a jurist, and a doctor, are brought together, each striving to understand the death of a strange individual, Wilfred Druce. Father Jerome and Doctor Lennard had broken into the locked room and discovered the physical evidence, and Judge Flint had read of the incident. Since the judge holds the will in which the doctor is named executor and the priest the beneficiary, they have all met together for a conference. Wilfred Druce had expected to die and in preparation wrote a letter using the vague expression, "I know the design that will accomplish my death." This, together with a collection of material taken from a sealed box found next to the body constitutes the principal data for determining the agency of death.

The priest believes that the death is another example of the Providence of God. The jurist theorizes that the death is the result of an "inevitable necessity" that crimes naturally result in punishment. The doctor presents a theory, a pure mechanical one, that because no man can ever foresee the order of the future, a criminal is helpless to avoid detection and eventual punishment. These three philosophical positions are defended by each man in turn, with different stories being offered as examples of the varied views. The priest tells two stories, the doctor four, and the jurist five. Each somehow manages to interpret his tale to fit his own philosophy, and so they arrive at no single conclusion, other than that they face a semantic problem. The jurist most suitably terms this "the nameless thing."

The stories in this book are not of equal quality, but the majority are sound and at least one could be rated excellent on the basis of its suspense, among other reasons. In composition the stories readily reflect the entire career of Post as an author, although they are principally the result of work done during the four years preceding the book's publication date. Among these tales we still see a touch of the Randolph Mason plot in a couple, the rural locale and the plot development of the Uncle Abner series in a major proportion, and in several the continental, pure mystery atmosphere that predominates in Post's later work. Post's interest in the legal world and its problems are an ingredient found in at least four of the stories.

The book is divided into nineteen chapters. Chapter I is titled "The Mystery." It sets the scene, brings together the principals and establishes the observable facts. Chapter II, "The Strange Data," begins with a revelation of the contents of the metal box.[3] About three quarters of the way through this chapter the priest begins relating the first story. This story, published in the *Atlantic Monthly* in 1911 under the title "After He was Dead" reveals how a dead man through a letter created a device which results in the capture of his murderer. This story continues into Chapter III, which is given the same title as this first story. About four pages from the end of this chapter the first story is completed and almost immediately it is followed by the second told this time by the judge. Titled "The Fairy Godmother," same as the title given to Chapter IV, it is the first of six stories included which were published first in issues of the *Saturday Evening Post*. It follows a young girl's efforts to secure legal help for her father charged with a crime due to circumstantial evidence. The story is interesting for its critical views of various inept legal practitioners, but is overly-long and rambling. Yet, it has a good surprise ending wherein the girl and her father are aided by a strange "woman of the world" who reveals the real killer. The story fills all of Chapter V (entitled "The Ghost") and is concluded several pages into the next chapter of the book. Chapter VI is called "The Trivial Incident," also the title of the next story as it was first published. This story, related here by the doctor, begins in Chapter VI, continues through Chapter VIII ("The Peril"), and comes to its conclusion in Chapter VIII ("The Sign").

"The Trivial Incident" deserves recognition apart from its place in the book. It is a well-executed story with sustained effects and an interesting conclusion. The story begins with a trivial incident as the title indicates.[4] Trapped in a web of increasing complexity, Adolphus Wyatt finds himself on the day of his trial unable to save himself from under the weight of circumstance. The plaintiff's attorney, Asbury Sheits, is a typical pettifogger, but skilled in the verbal trickery of the courtroom. Sheits gets the defendant to admit he is a liar; Wyatt is then left with nothing he can say to defend himself. The jury returns a verdict in favor of the plaintiff, awarding only one dollar in damages; yet, this is such a moral victory over the once-respected town banker that at the tale's end he is left condemned to liquor and dope. The most interesting fact regarding this story, first published in 1908, is that the plaintiff is a young negro boy. The sharp social criticism regarding equal justice that Post has allowed at the conclusion of the story is a unique social comment issued far in advance of its time.

One-third of the way through VIII the previous tale is concluded, and another, narrated by the judge, is begun. This tale was published serially under the title it lends to the book, but not to any chapter, "The Nameless Thing." The relation of the title of the story to the title of the book is only incidental inasmuch as the title is not repeated within the short story itself. This tale, however, contains a pure example of the theme Post concentrates on in the book, and taken alone it is a well-written and an entertaining story. Its principal character is a "doctor" who uses a fake degree to practice in a mining town while he schemes to complete a $600,000 bank robbery. But at the time the theft is to take place, he stops to care for an injured man and thereby unknowingly saves his own life and reputation, this through an error arising from an unpredictable circumstance. The story, concluded four pages into the next chapter, exhibits an outstanding surprise ending for which Post gained a well-deserved measure of recognition.

Early in Chapter IX, entitled "The Sport of Fortune," the doctor begins his second illustrative story, which was published serially in the *Harper's Monthly Magazine* in 1911 under the same title as given this chapter. This tale is about a frugal man who trades horses with a gypsy, demanding twenty dollars in addition, though he knows he can easily cure the gypsy's younger but ailing horse. Suspecting that the gypsy's money is counterfeit, yet being unwilling to part with it without receiving something of value, the frugal man wrecks his honest reputation, only to learn at the end that the money was good and that the gypsy had bargained in good faith since he had at the moment of the trade required a healthy, if older horse. This story is concluded in Chapter X, a chapter titled "No Defense." Another story, which had been previously published serially under this same title, the third tale narrated by the jurist, begins midway in the chapter and is concluded therein. This story is concerned with the misfortunes of a pickpocket who in trying to dispose of the evidence, consisting of a stolen watch, finds that it falls through his trouser leg into his shoe instead of into the snow as he intended. The story has little merit, floundering between humor and realism and missing both marks. At the close of this chapter the priest, the jurist, and the doctor part for the night having decided to meet again the following day.

The three investigators resume their discussion in Chapter XI, "The Pressure," the next day as they dine. The priest reveals he had talked during the night with the dying butler of Wilfred Druce. The doctor says he has a chemist checking experiments which may reveal the cause of Druce's death. Judge Flint reports that he is awaiting information in response to a telegram he dispatched. Then the priest narrates another story concerning a man who is revealed a murderer because after allowing a clairvoyant's message to disturb his composure, he attempts to destroy evidence he thought perfectly hidden. This story ends at the outset of Chapter XII ("The Thief") where the doctor begins another story which is concluded within the same chapter. It describes a motor car ride taken by the doctor at night from Paris to the French Coast. Interrupted midway by motor trouble, the doctor pauses long enough to dine, be approached by a thief, and, by outwitting the thief, come out financially ahead.

Immediately the judge presents a story which lends its name to the next chapter, "The Locked Bag." In this interesting story an insurance company lawyer is upstaged by a local lawyer whose shrewd deductions reveal an attempted fraudulant suit as well as the solution to a crime. Elements of the Randolph Mason stories here give way to elements hinting the approach of the Uncle Abner stories. Completion of this story in Chapter XIII allows the doctor to tell his final tale of a man who was not a criminal, has committed no crime, but receives punishment for his indiscretions. This man, a playboy type of his period, after enchanting a young country girl discards her for a supposed Russian princess. In Chapter XV, "The Goth," the country girl's uncle manages a wedding at pistol point between playboy and country girl. The story has good characterization, but the plot, lacking impact, fails to engage the reader's sympathy. In style, content, and technique, it is in direct contrast to the final tale of the book, this related by the judge.

"A Critique of Monsieur Poe," which is completed in Chapter XVI and which when published serially used the same title as given this chapter, is one of the near perfect stories which Melville Post devised. In addition it is probably the first straight classic mystery story he had published. It originally appeared in the *Saturday Evening Post* issue of December 31, 1910, but has never received the proper attention it surely deserves. All the principal aspects of the good short story are given a well-balanced presentation in this tale which includes a secondary tale as well as a smoothly-handled ending.

The principal plot of "A Critique of Monsieur Poe" is set in Paris. In involves a jeweler who reads mystery stories, a hatter, and the hatter's fiance, who is a shrewd thief. It is this brazen thief who narrates the inner tale, a fast-moving international story of spies and intrigue set in Washington, D.C. M. Duclose, the jeweler, who has followed the thief's suggestion to read Poe, listens with interest to his acquaintance's tale, which is being told to distract him. Having learned from Poe's stories the importance of seemingly insignificant details, the jeweler is not deceived by a clever plan to steal his valuable matched set of pearls. The police arrive at the proper moment, and the thieves are apprehended while engaged in the crime.

The book is completed with Chapters XVII, XVIII, and XIX, titled respectively "The Low Door," "The Coward," and "The Assassin." The judge having received a reply to his telegram reveals "the crime" of Wilfred Druce: he had saved himself from certain death aboard an experimental submarine while the men he commanded were left to perish. This action led to his court martial and discharge from the Royal Navy. The doctor then reveals how the death in the locked room occurred. Druce had been driven by his guilt to hysterical imaginings which caused him to believe that the drowned crew was coming to murder him. In fear he fired away madly with his pistol, backing into a bookcase from which his metal box fell and struck him the death blow on his head.

Post repeated a number of times that his basic intent was to produce fiction for its entertainment value. But whether he intended it or not, there are messages to be discerned in a large portion of his fiction. The Randolph Mason stories point clearly to the need for an improved legal system and a closer examination of the meaning of justice. In *Dwellers in the Hills* a variety of pantheism solidly woven into the background, is exalted, causing it to appear a hymn to nature. *The Gilded Chair* is charged with warnings against materialism and the desire for power and the exploitation of a group of people; and it hints of an Old Testament God able to carry out his stern warnings. That there existed in Post's mind a conflict in regards to certain basic religious principles is almost certain from an examination of his work, a good portion of which reflects a concern for a clearer understanding of the values of religion in life.

An education for law such as he had would of necessity introduce a student of humanity such as Post to philosophy, science, psychology and other specialized fields. Yet, there is some evidence that Post, profound as his thinking was at times, never put any great trust in the growing number of intellectuals of the time. There are some indications of his reading Goethe and Renan, among a few others, and certainly there is his interests in the classics of Greece and Rome. However, there is no indication that he paid any close attention to Darwin, Nietzsche, Bergson, Freud, James, or other profound modern thinkers.

Nevertheless, the problems of modern man make a regular appearance in much of his writing, and although Post seldom does more than touch the surface of these problems, he often proves himself much more modern than his tone would indicate, or than he might admit. And at times he stands out as being quite modern compared with the general popular-fiction writer of the first three decades of the twentieth century. Speaking almost consistently a layman's language in his writing, Post performs as a reporter for the general reader. A casual reader might be almost totally unaware of the thought content, of the basic conflicts that Post fought out in his creative work, and perhaps as objective observers, we note what he himself may not always have been able to see quite clearly. Yet in *The Nameless Thing* we find much that brings to mind the existentialists, the absurdist philosophers, psychoanalytic theories and psychological aberrations, and the questing of modern theologians. How honest then was Melville Post about his true intentions for his fiction? Did he sincerely design his fiction only to entertain? *The Nameless Thing* surely does more than entertain.

●●●●●●●●●

IV. UNCLE ABNER
1.

> Few writers have so conscientious a technique as Mr. Post, such a fine sense of plot. This collection of mystery stories is woven around the personality of Uncle Abner, whose Greek sense of justice is inflexible. All of these stories are masterly examples of the justifiable surprise ending, yet have the logic and dramatic power which we have come to associate with Athenian tragedy. Their effectiveness is largely due to the value of understatement.

This statement was made in a thumbnail review of *Uncle Abner* found in *The Best Short Stories of 1918 and the Yearbook of the American Short Story*, edited by Edward J. O'Brien. Found under a section subtitled "Best Books of Short Stories," it is perhaps the most concise and fair estimate of Melville Davisson Post's seventh book that can be made.

Other detective-story writers have always been among the foremost fans of this collection of Post's short stories, and one of the most enthusiastic of all statements was made in the name of Ellery Queen, the pen-name of America's most proficient mystery-writing team. The bibliographer of the team is reputed to be

Frederic Dannay and perhaps he should be given credit for the praise that is given in this paragraph. Writing in *Queen's Quorum*, the exceptionally valuable bibliographical history of the detective-crime short story, Ellery Queen declares:

> In the same way that Chesterton's *The Innocence of Father Brown*, among all the books of detective stories written by English authors, ranks second only to Doyle's *The Adventures of Sherlock Holmes*, so Melville Davisson Post's *Uncle Abner* . . . is second only to Poe's *Tales* among all the books of detective short stories written by American authors. This statement is made dogmatically and without reservation: a cold-blooded and calculated critical opinion which we believe will be as true in the year 2000 as we wholeheartedly believe it is true today. These four books, two American and two British, are the finest in their field—the *creme du crime*. They are an out-of-this-world target for future detective-story writers to take shots at—but it will be like throwing pebbles at the Pyramids.

Willard Huntington Wright, who in addition to more scholarly work wrote detective fiction under the pen-name of S. S. Van Dine, was another ardent supporter of Post's *Uncle Abner* stories. In his introduction to an anthology he edited, *Great Mystery Tales*, he stated:

> One of the truly outstanding figures in detective fiction is Uncle Abner . . . indeed . . . one of the few detectives deserving to be ranked with that immortal triumvirate, *Dupin, Lecoq*, and *Holmes*. . . . In conception, execution, device and general literary quality these stories of early Virginia, written by a man who thoroughly knows his *metier* and is also an expert in law and criminology, are among the very best we possess. The grim and lovable Uncle Abner is a vivid and convincing character, and the plots of his experiences with crime are as unusual as they are convincing.

Criticism of the *Uncle Abner* tales has not always been quite so favorable, as Howard Haycraft, a reliable commentator on all types of American literature, points out in his volume *Murder for Pleasure*, at the same time defending and praising Post's work in these words:

> Superlatively fine as they are, the *Uncle Abner* stories have not altogether escaped criticism. Their most serious fault, in the opinion of certain critics, is the author's failure in a few of the tales to make all the evidence explicit. In at least one instance this criticism is justified beyond any doubt. But in other cases, one wonders if a basic misunderstanding on the part of the critics themselves may not be at fault? Certainly, we must insist on fair play. But the detective story, whether long or short, does not exist in which there is not *some* "off-stage" work—if only in the detective's mind. To have matters otherwise would be to deprive us of our puzzle in mid-career. In nearly every case, Post's offense is merely the logical extension of this principle; and one feels, somehow, that the writer of the *short* detective story (handicapped and restricted in ways that the author of a novel never knows) should be allowed the widest possible discretion and latitude in this respect. Had Post met the demands of the quibblers to catalogue and label every clue, there would in many instances have been no mystery and no story. . . . It is not without relation that, for all Post's genius in physical device, Abner's detection in the final analysis nearly always hinges on *character*. It is his judgment of men's souls that leads him to expect and therefore to find and interpret the evidence, where lesser minds (including, perhaps, the literal ones of his decriers) see naught.
>
> No reader can call himself connoisseur who does not know *Uncle Abner* forward and backward. His four-square pioneer ruggedness looms as a veritable monument in the literature. Posterity may well name him, after Dupin, the greatest American contribution to the form.

Also, in the article on Melville Davisson Post presented in *Twentieth Century Authors*, edited by Stanley Kunitz and Howard Haycraft, we read this justifiable comment:

> . . . Post himself, in his preoccupation with formula, underestimated some of his greatest literary gifts. The Abner stories are still read and re-read not so much for their intensive plots—highly original in their time but hackneyed by imitation today—as for the author's cogent realization of character, place, and mood. Had Post developed this phase of his talent more, and had he been less concerned with merely commercial success, his stature as a serious artist might have been greater than now seems likely. Even so, his Uncle Abner remains the most distin-

guished American contribution to detective literature between Auguste Dupin and Philo Vance.

These several statements, praising as they do the *Uncle Abner* tales in general, need to be tested through a thorough re-examination of the work. First let us consider Post's own views and theories of short story design, then review the creative transition taken from Randolph Mason to Uncle Abner, and finally proceed to taking a close look at the individual stories.

2.

Although Post was reluctant to reveal details of his personal life, he was not so reticent about his theories of short story construction. The first two Randolph Mason collections both exhibit introductions in which he presents some of his first thoughts regarding the creating of detective and crime stories. He may have included these partly as a defense, because from the very beginning he was subjected to a barrage of criticism from those who could not agree with those unique ideas and methods he brought to his second profession.

The construction of the *Uncle Abner* tales is definitely more complicated than that of the Randolph Mason stories, but some of the rules he practiced in those earlier stories were continued in most of his later and better writings. In his first book Post noted that the critics were ready to declare all efforts at creative writing "combinations of the old . . . and all weary."[1] But Post believed that as each new child brings something new into the world, so each writer can bring something new to the craft. The reader, he wrote, demands believable characters facing a "problem with passion and peril in it."[2] Post pointed out that the public endured a "Flood of 'Detective Stories' until the stomach of the reader failed."[3] Seeking a new approach, in these early stories he created Randolph Mason as an amoral lawyer who gained notoriety because he used legal methods "whereby the punishing power of the State might be baffled."[4] Post was faced quickly with both fame and criticism because of his public revelations of numerous loopholes in the law, which some claimed were inviting crimes to be committed similar to those of the stories. But Post defended his approach in this way: "If the law offers imperfect security and is capable of revision, the people must be taught in order that they may revise it."⁵

Perhaps Post held this as one of his main reasons for writing the Randolph Mason stories, for they apparently did succeed to a certain degree in causing some changes in the laws. But by the time Post was writing the *Uncle Abner* stories, if he had any such high ideology to promote, he approached the matter more subtly. We can also note a complete reversal in his later critical compositions regarding the matter of promoting straightforward ideals through fiction.

About the time that he had written and published at least half of the *Uncle Abner* stories which would appear in the collection, Post produced for the readers of the *Saturday Evening Post* two interesting pieces revealing and defending his theories of the type of short story for which he was so well-known. The first of these, appearing on December 26, 1914, was titled "The Blight."⁶ The second, on February 27, 1915, was presented under the title "The Mystery Story."⁷

Post opens "The Blight" with a question: "Why is it one writer or one magazine becomes greatly popular while others never obtain any considerable hearing?" His answer is that "these authors and these popular magazines give the public what it wants." Then he explains, "The reader is not looking for any form of instruction. If he wishes information . . . he goes to a textbook. The primary object of all fiction is to entertain the reader. If, while it entertains, it also ennobles him this fiction becomes a work of art; but its primary business must be to entertain and not to educate or instruct him." He settles this point, noting, "Did not Thoreau say that if he should hear that one was coming to his house to do him good he would flee as for his life?" Thus we see that Post, by the time of his writing of the *Uncle Abner* tales had set his sights on a new principle. He wanted to be read—and for this reason he wrote principally to entertain, not to propound any special causes. We recognize that he successfully fulfilled this objective.

Post however had not changed one cherished opinion. If anything, he felt even more strongly that "the writer who presents a problem to be solved or a mystery to be untangled will be offering those qualities in his fiction which are of the most universal appeal." Thus, he claims, "a few men . . . have in a measure created the impression that the absence of the problem or mystery in a work of fiction is in some sense a distinguishing mark of the elevated literary class." Having said this, he turns to the Greeks, particularly to Aristotle and his *Poetics*, where Post declares Aristotle "undertook to lay down the principles by which tragedy ought to be constructed" and thereby "gave the common and essential principles for the construction of all fiction—especially for . . . the short story." He then writes: "The plot, as Aristotle says, was considered to be the soul of the thing." While, "Mere delineation of character would never make a work of art; nor would . . . beauty of diction."

After some further explanations, Post says, "The highest form of the short story will be found to run parallel with the highest form of the play, in that both require a carefully constructed plot including the element of surprise and an orderly evolution of tragic incident." Then, he reasoned, "Under the scheme of universe it is the tragic things that seem the most real. Things pleasing and comfortable do not strike us with the same emotions of fear and pity as do things terrible and tragic." Also, Post noted, "A work of art cannot be a mere segment. . . . It must be a complete thing. . . . It must have a beginning, a middle and an end. . . . It must be . . . a whole picture." Finally he points out that "one may shut oneself up and pretend that the opinion of the world does not concern one; but one deceives oneself." Post does not approve of an obscure style, involved and difficult for the reader. "They will insist that the language shall become clear, direct and virile, and that those who write must have a story in their heads to tell."

In his next article of criticism, "The Mystery Story," Post repeats his general premises, spelling them out from various angles, adding a few interesting observations and aiming them more precisely at the mystery tale. Mostly he concentrates on an understanding of the use of plot, saying that before all other things "the short story must have a plot." Yet he realizes that "in spite of the ideas one gets from inumerable stories, the possible plots are limited." Proceeding, he states, "The Greek . . . laid down the formula for all possible plots. The length of the plot should be sufficient for the sequence of events to admit of a change from bad fortune to good, or from good fortune to bad; and it ought not be of greater length than can be easily carried in the memory and comprehended in one sitting." Turning specifically towards the mystery, he noted, "The problem, or mystery story should have a plot that is mathematically accurate."

Post affirms then the source of many of his plots, declaring: "the play or story would be better if its germinal incidents are taken from some actual event . . . as, for instance, the records of some criminal case . . . to give it an appearance of reality." He points out, "In constructing his plot one had better take the basic incidents from life, as the Greeks in their tragedies took them from the experiences of certain great families." And Post then adds, "A well-constructed plot should be single in its issue. It should present one moving event in its complete unity. It should be constructed so that it unfolds itself or builds itself up by a natural and orderly moving of events. Every event should follow the preceding one in inevitable sequence, and the explanation should appear suddenly." But, "After the reader discovers who the criminal agent was he does not wish to read the long explanation."

In this same article Post speaks of the removal of surplusage from the well-written story, a rule that he practiced exactly in the *Uncle Abner* tales and in many of his later stories, with only an occasional serious lapse. Post explained, saying, "This is what Poe meant when he said that a writer who in the beginning of his story, put in a word or sentence which did not have a direct and essential bearing on the ultimate end of the story, had already failed. There must be no word of description, explanation or dialogue that is not as essential to the whole structure of the story as every link is essential to the whole structure of a chain. It is by this elimination that one produces a work of art."

Toward his conclusion, Post states, "This is the great age of the short story. It is to the American people to-day what the drama was to the Greeks." Post's 1915 statement has proved to be exceedingly accurate, perhaps even to a degree which he himself did not foresee. Because he sincerely believed this, he devoted most of the remaining years of his career almost exclusively to the creation of short stories. He found it the medium best-suited to the presentation of his ideas. Except for several instances, in the *Uncle Abner* stories he worked precisely and successfully with these principles that he had termed vital to the making of readable short stories. Post was perhaps one of the most accomplished technicians in the construction of the short story. But many critics who admitted his ability as a technician felt that Post did not have anything significant to say. We might suggest they reached this conclusion only because they did not examine Post's work thoroughly enough. Or, it may be that they were too close to it and were thus unable to judge it against the increasing quantities of short stories created during the first three decades of the twentieth century. Above all, it would seem they reached this conclusion because they were looking for something that Post did not believe should be incorporated in the short story. He knew what he wanted to do, and there are no finer examples of his work than the *Uncle Abner* stories where his success resulted from his doing exactly what he believed.

3.

American literature is essentially a literature of romantic characters, characters which reflect the myriad of American types. Uncle Abner deserves a prominent place in such a tradition. He is the unique creation of Melville Davisson Post, the product of the author's talented imagination; yet, he is so real that we find it difficult to believe that he is only a composite of the author's accumulated experience and vision. Or is he? We can answer with certainty neither "yes" nor "no."

Uncle Abner is as real as any of the outstanding characters who have stepped out of the pages of American literature. Post most nearly accomplished here the definite standard he had set in the "introduction" to *The Strange Schemes of Randolph Mason:* "The reader is a clever tyrant. He demands something more than people of mist. There must be tendons in the ghost hand, and hard bones in the phantom else he feels that he has been cheated."[8] No reader who comes to know Uncle Abner ever feels cheated. A nonprofessional detective, a cattleman riding the hills and pastures of Virginia's western lands in the middle years of the nineteenth century, Abner was a Bible-reading and Bible-quoting champion of justice, favoring the law—but only when it favored justice. Also, without exception, he was a hard-working realist, honest and tough, with an intellect to match his muscle and a computer-like ability to calculate the evildoer of a crime. He was a hill-dwelling Dick Tracy on horseback.

Uncle Abner is very different than Randolph Mason, that first unique character of fiction created by Post. Randolph Mason is a cosmopolitan inhabitant of New York City, a vain and cantankerous individual, an atheist, a crafty lawyer, and an eccentric. Post looked upon him as a misanthrope and a cynic. Uncle Abner is the extreme opposite. His origin is undoubtedly rural. He is kind and considerate to his most flagrant enemies, and he relies heavily on the "Old Testament." His manners are decidedly close to those of the true Christian. The only thing these two men share in common at all is a keen, analytical mind, able to see things that other men easily miss. Clearly the transition from the one to the other was not a sudden passage, and the evidence shows the evolution coming about gradually in the author's work.

Looking at the Randolph Mason stories, we find that although most are set in New York City, Post regularly reached back to his native state of West Virginia for a name, a character, or a situation. Thus a pattern was set here that is evident in all Post's fiction: a swinging back and forth from the cosmopolitan world to the grassy hills of the author's birthplace. We discover that in nearly a third of the Randolph Mason stories there is a direct reference to the West Virginia scene. Several of these references are to cattle trading—the livelihood of Post's father and of Uncle Abner.

In writing the exceptional *Dwellers in the Hills* Post took his next steps. First he changed to the first person narrative. Next, he moved back in time to an earlier period and to a strictly rural setting, placing emphasis upon the concerns of cattlemen. As Post in the novel pits man against man and man against nature in this adventure of cattle raising, he provides at several points for the insertion of detective-like abilities, such as in the resolving of tracking problems. And in Quiller, the narrator of *Dwellers in the Hills*, we recognize the counterpart of the narrator of the *Uncle Abner* tales, Martin. Like Quiller, Martin in the earlier *Uncle Abner* tales is an active participant as well as the narrator. Although Martin seems to be slightly younger than Quiller, referred to as being nine and ten years old, both Martin and Quiller speak as adults looking back upon adventures of their boyhood. The rural countryside in the *Uncle Abner* tales, essentially the same as found in *Dwellers in the Hills*, as suggested by the use of several similar names, predates that of *Dwellers in the Hills* by as many as twenty years or more. We can judge with some accuracy the *Uncle Abner* stories as being placed around 1850,[9] while *Dwellers in the Hills* is indefinite, but best placed as following the Civil War, perhaps close to the time of Post's own childhood.

Dwellers in the Hills incorporates finely-wrought descriptions of the countryside. These descriptions, frequently superior to those found in the *Uncle Abner* tales, overshadow the thin plot of the novel. In the *Uncle Abner* short stories, Post is most economical and uses such descriptions only to set the mood of his story and then with great restraint. Both the novel and the short stories include many of the specialized problems of cattle-handling and trading. The *Uncle Abner* tales place their principal emphasis on plot, which by the time of their writing was the essential ingredient in any short story Post wrote.

The incidental skills of detection which are incorporated in *Dwellers in the Hills* involve tracking horses and determining from the hoof prints the identity of the riders. This skill is most particularly assigned to Ump, the hunchback, of whom Post has Quiller recall:

> But the hunchback knew what he was about. Ward said of Ump that, in his field, the land of the horse's foot, he was as much an expert as any professor behind his spectacles. His knowledge came from the observation of a lifetime, gathered by tireless study of every detail. Even now, when I see a great chemist who knows all about some drug; a great surgeon who knows all about the body of a man; or a great oculist who knows all about the human eye, I must class the hunchback with them.[10]

Such use of simple observation is an indication of the cunning abilities later attributed to Abner. Elementary as it seems, this does show the development of the "detective" element in Post's work.

There is one prominent difference between *Dwellers in the Hills* and the *Uncle Abner* tales that signifies their different creative periods. In *Dwellers in the Hills* the only character who has "religion" is one of the antagonist's hired men, "Parson Peppers," a hymn-singing, hard-drinking cattle driver whose behavior is no fit example of the Christian ideal. The "good guys" are portrayed as being good without the need of any formal religion. Throughout the novel the only "religion" one feels emphasized is the worshipping of nature, a pantheistic mysticism which frequently is felt in much of Post's work, although never quite as strongly as here. This is in great contrast to *Uncle Abner*, for Abner sees his religion as the key to moral living, decisions for the actions he takes constantly being based on his interpretations of the Scriptures.

A minor relationship is the use of Roy's Tavern in the novel and in the first published *Uncle Abner* story, "The Broken Stirrup Leather" (reprinted in the collection as "The Angel of the Lord"), as a setting for important action. Outside of the coincidental use of the name there seems to be no intended connection. However the theme of a youth being given adult responsibilities, used in both, might have been derived from the same actual incident. And we can find no logical connection between the use of the name of "Rufus" for Martin's father and for the chief antagonist in *Dwellers in the Hills*.

During the years between the writing of *Dwellers of the Hills* and the first of the *Uncle Abner* stories, Melville Davisson Post lived some of the most important moments of his entire life. He married, lost an infant son, and suffered ill health that caused him to forsake law for literature. Also he was faced with a barrage of criticism over his Randolph Mason episodes and found little praise coming forth from the critics for his novel-length works. We cannot know if any of these things influenced him to create the character of Uncle Abner, since we have little but creative material to base our judgment upon. Nevertheless, there are indications that Post did begin to move though ever so gradually in that direction. In *The Gilded Chair*, published in 1910 and written over the preceding two or three years, the beginnings of the prose style of the *Uncle Abner* tales are evident, particularly the development of the economical sentence structure.

The themes of *The Gilded Chair* do not readily suggest those found in the *Uncle Abner* tales, nor are the settings similar. But what is most indicative in *The Gilded Chair* of the coming of Uncle Abner is the character of the old mountaineer. This unnamed character, a Civil War veteran, is not similar to Uncle Abner in physical description, nor in his dialect speech, nor in his mode of transportation (he either walks or rides a mule). The mountaineer obviously has an affection for his mule "Jezebel" equal to Abner's affection for his horse, "the great chestnut." But it is in religious outlook, almost wholly, that a strong resemblance to Abner is found in the mountaineer. Post says of Abner in one description, "His god was the god of Tishbite." This reference to Elijah establishes a direct connection between the two characters, for their religious foundation is basically similar, both being like Elijah. Both are fond of the Old Testament Scriptures, both carry a Bible with them on their constant wanderings, and both are ready to quote frankly from its pages at any moment. Both are men guided often by intuition and both are bachelors. Finally the sharp-shooting old mountaineer bears a resemblance to Abner when he attempts to follow the escape route by detective-like methods—though he possesses nothing of the uncanny ferreting powers of Abner.

The remaining transition from the old mountaineer of *The Gilded Chair* through several unrelated short stories to the creation of Uncle Abner is one without further visible steps. Sometime between 1910 and 1911 Post conceived of the character of Uncle Abner and sensed that he would be a useful and exceptional character. Thus he wrote more and better tales around Abner than any of his several unusual but less important leading characters.

4.

Since nowhere in the stories is there a complete description of Uncle Abner, it is interesting to make a composite description using excerpts selected from the various tales:[11]

> His great chestnut stood in the grassplot between the roads, and Abner sat upon him like a man of stone. (p. 21)
> . . . Abner was the right hand of the law. (p. 3)
> He was a bachelor, stern and silent. But he could talk. . . . And when he did, he began at the beginning and you heard him through; and what he said—well, he stood behind it. (p. 41)
> He was one of those austere, deeply religious men who were a product of the Reformation. He always carried a Bible in his pocket and he read it where he pleased. Once the crowd at Roy's Tavern tried to make a sport of him when he got his book out by the fire; but they never tried

> it again. When the fight was over Abner paid Roy eighteen silver dollars for the broken chairs and the table—and he was the only man in the tavern who could ride a horse. Abner belonged to the church militant, and his God was a war lord. (p. 41-42)
> Abner was no respector of men. He stood for justice—clean and ruthless justice, tempered by no distinctions. (p. 186) . . . he was big and dominant as painters are accustomed to draw Michael in Satan's wars. (p. 146)
> Abner sat in his saddle like a man of bronze, his face stern, as it always was when he was silent. . . . He was one of those austere, deeply religious men who might have followed Cromwell, with a big iron frame, a grizzled beard and features forged out by a smith. His god was the god of Tishbite. . . . (p. 212)
> [He was often seen] . . . stroking his bronze face with his great sinewy hand. . . . (p. 222)
> [Abner] . . . was a big, broad-shouldered, deep chested Saxon, with all those marked characteristics of a race living out of doors and hardened by wind and sun. His powerful frame carried no ounce of surplus weight. It was the frame of the empire builder on the frontier of the empire . . . the craggy features in repose seemed molded over iron, but the fine gray eyes had a calm serenity, like remote spaces in the summer sky. The man's clothes were plain and somber. And he gave one impression of things big and vast. (p. 227)
> His great jaw moved out under the massive chin. (p. 256) [When he spoke] His voice was slow and deep. (p. 201) [But, on those occasions when angered, it was] . . . big, echoing like a trumpet. . . . (p. 264) And you noted when He raised his great arm . . . the clenched bronze fingers big like the coupling pins of a cart. (p. 284)
> [To Abner] The horse was a friend and brother. . . . He would go without his dinner, but this horse was fed. He would go without a cup of water, but this horse drank, and wherever he might be this horse was bedded before he slept. ("The Devil's Track." *Country Gentleman*, July 1927, p. 40)

Abner was characteristically seen walking or riding his horse with "his hands behind him." Usually at these moments his keen mind was determining the facts of a crime and preparing to close in on the criminal. At least twice when he is offered a drink of hard liquor, Abner refuses with such emphasis we can assume that he abstains at all times. Also, he apparently does not smoke. This we note in "The Straw Man" when he selects a cigarette that he does not light; he asked for the cigarette box to determine the owner's left-handedness and thus provide the conclusive clue that solves the mystery.

As we observe Abner seeking to unravel some apparent crime, we are provided with only a glimpse of his total personality. But we do learn to know him as a man of strength, a man of broad understanding and sympathy, and as a man accustomed to clean, simple living. He is a man who could have lived in any age; the setting of the tales does not dictate his character.

The source of Uncle Abner is complex and invites speculation. Yet from what we can learn and from what has been pointed out by several writers with first-hand information, we must believe that the essential model for this character was Post's own father, Ira Carper Post. A clue may be the fact that when the *Uncle Abner* stories were collected and published, the book was dedicated to the author's father.

While we can accept as a reliable assumption Ira Carper Post being the chief model for Abner, we must also observe that Post's father around 1850 would have been only a boy about the age of the narrator of the tales, Martin. Martin, in addition to being the narrator, has an active part in all the early *Uncle Abner* tales. Only later does Post move him to the position of an off-stage observer, leaving Abner to become the focal point in the adventures. It is entirely possible to believe that in the beginning Post conceived of Martin very much in terms of his father recalling some events of his youth. Another possibility to consider is that Ira Carper Post might have been the model Post used, perhaps unconsciously, both for Martin and for Abner.

Abner, referred to as "the right-hand of the law," is frequently depicted working with "the law" represented by Squire Randolph, a local justice of the peace. Randolph takes an active part in most of the stories, more often than Martin, Martin's father, Rufus, or any other character. Randolph is in many ways a contrast to Abner, for although both have essentially the same objectives, they have different ways of reaching their goals. While Abner is a character not limited in time, Randolph is more closely a product of his particular day and place. A description of him is also best gathered from Post's writings:

> Randolph was vain and pompous and given over to extravagance of words, but he was a gentleman beneath it, and fear was an alien and a stranger to him. (p. 2-3)
>
> Randolph was constrained with vanity and the weakness of ostentation, but he shouldered his duties for himself. He was a justice of the peace in a day when that office was filled only by the landed gentry, after the English fashion; and the obligations of the law were strong on him. (p. 14)
>
> Randolph came in his big blustering manner and sat down as though he were the judge of all the world. (p. 67) . . . he thundered from behind his table . . . spoke upon the law of accidents sententiously for some thirty minutes. (p. 68) . . . took a pinch of snuff, and trumpeted in his big many-colored handkerchief. (p. 69)
>
> One, short of stature and beginning to take on the rotundity of age, was dressed with elaborate care, his great black stock propping up his chin, his linen and the cloth of his coat immaculate. He wore a huge carved ring and a bunch of seals attached to his watch-fob. (p. 227)
>
> . . . Randolph was a friend and neighbor to Abner. Their lands adjoined; and Abner held him, for his qualities of a man, in high regard.
>
> But his mannerisms were the annoyance of Abner's life. ("The Mystery at Hillhouse." *Country Gentleman*, May, 1928, p. 127)

While it is possible that Post also had a living model for Randolph, the character does not appear to be as authentic as Abner, Martin, or even Doc Storm, the mysterious old doctor of several of the tales. We know some of the characters, such as Nathaniel Davisson, to be actual persons. Yet Randolph gives us the definite impression of being a stock character, a foil for Uncle Abner. No doubt Post met in the course of his legal and political career a fair number of individuals who with a bit of costuming and staging could have served as models for Randolph. It is also conceivable that in some respects Randolph is an alter ego of Post, consciously or unconsciously taking his place.[12]

Few women characters have a part in these tales, and with perhaps one exception Post's women in the Uncle Abner book are typical of those found in most of his work. The young girls are sweet and very pretty. Older women are hardly ever present and when present are stock characters who fulfil the necessities of the plot and little more. The one notable exception, found in the story "The Devil's Tools," is the character of Liza, the black servant of the Randolph family and nanny of Betty Randolph. Although not presented as a full character, and scarcely any of Post's characters could be said to be, Liza comes through realistically and is an individual in spite of the melodramatic treatment she receives. She is viable and forceful regardless of the obvious limitations which Post imposed upon the character. Perhaps the reason Post succeeded in giving Liza an added degree of authenticity is that she is a recollection of his own childhood nanny, Eliza Perkins, whose family served the Davisson family for several decades. Liza in this story is surely a memorial to Eliza. While this type of character has become a stereotype today, in Post's story she was certainly an extraordinary person. Proof of this is in the verbal contest Liza has with the justice of the peace, "Mars Ran." Liza leaves little doubt as to the victor in this battle of wits despite her verbal handicaps and her full-blown admiration for Randolph's abilities.

In addition to Liza and Randolph, Post has peopled these stories with an interesting array of other secondary and supporting characters. Some are drawn sharply, some just a flitting shadow, but always they are useful in the creation of the suspense and vital to the plot. None, however, is near the commanding figure that Uncle Abner is, calm, collected, and knowing. When he speaks everyone listens and Post tells us that he spoke "in his deep even voice." (p. 60) "And when he spoke his voice was like a thing that has dimensions and weight." (p. 62)

5.

Turning our attention now to individual stories in *Uncle Abner, Master of Mysteries*, we see at once several courses we might follow in planning our examination.

First we have the choice of following the order of the book exactly as published in 1918. The stories collected therein are numbered as chapters, I through XVIII, beginning with "The Doomdorf Mystery" and concluding with "Naboth's Vineyard." This arrangement seems quite illogical, lacking as it does any form of continuity. Perhaps Post or his editors had a scheme they followed, but it is difficult to discover the rationale for the arrangement as it is thus presented. Some theories might be attempted, but these need to be forced to apply at all. One explanation that comes to mind seems rather too simple, that is considering "The Doomdorf Mystery" placed first because of its seemingly greater popularity and closing with "Naboth's Vineyard" because the tragic courtroom-ending provides a suitable closing scene. Such speculation however, gives us no useful plan of criticism.

We must recognize the obvious fact that numerous publishers of that time (and now) put their faith in statistics which suggest that novels sell better than short story collections. Thus they reason that disguising a collection as a novel may sell additional copies. This certainly had some direct influence on the decision to give the tales Roman numerals in their collected form. Neither can we overlook the possibility that Post himself could have wished to give his collection the appearance of a novel-length work. He had already done this with considerable skill in *The Nameless Thing* and would do it again with subsequent collections. We know that he earned only limited success with his novels; therefore he may have tried partially to fulfil his ambition to write novels through the secondary means of producing pseudo-novels. It remains, though, that for Uncle Abner not much serious thought seems to have been given the book's arrangement. As it stands, the book has little more continuity than if the tales had been shuffled in the manner of playing cards.

A second way of approaching the stories of this collection would be in a strict chronological order, particularly the order in which they were composed. But there are difficulties in determining such an arrangement. First we have only fragmentary factual information upon which to base an arrangement done chronologically in the order of composition. Secondly, the date of publication is of use only in some instances inasmuch as the pieces were not always published serially in the order in which they seem to have been written. Indeed three offer no indication of any publication previous to their appearance in the book. We have some evidence in regard to six of the stories. These we find originally handwritten in an inexpensive, bound composition book, indicating the apparent order in which they were created.[13] A check reveals that the publication dates of these same stories vary over a period of about five years, during which time Post wrote and published other Abner stories used in the collection, plus stories unrelated to this particular series. Not only can we not look at the Abner stories as having been written one after the other in the fashion of a novel, our evidence eliminates all possibilities for arriving at any strict chronological order that might provide a useful critical frame.

Having these limitations, we have either to accept the printed order of the book or to devise a third means. We can devise a meaningful order based principally on the obvious and logical developments of the stories themselves combined with the available chronological information. This rearrangement of the stories was finally determined the soundest method to adopt. Such a rearrangement reveals several important patterns not easily discernible in the book's arrangement. Once the rearrangement had been accomplished in this manner we noted that there is little probability of its being inaccurate. We can believe it approaches very closely what was the actual order of composition.[14]

A general examination of the stories in their serial form did not reveal any significant difference from their collected form, except for one complete change in a title. This is typical of nearly the entire body of Post's work published in both serial and book form. Perhaps Post seldom released a story until he was certain every sentence and every word was exactly as he wanted it to be. Thus there would never be any need for revising a finished piece of work. But more likely, once he had done a story he lost interest in it, giving his prime interest only and always to work yet to be done.

Also included for critical examination here are four Abner stories which were published some ten years after the collection was made. These were published in serial form only, but they are logically considered here. These last four stories rate among the best of the entire group of stories Post wrote about Uncle Abner, the most endurable of all the characters he created.

The first *Uncle Abner* story published exhibits definite signs of having been the first written. It is numbered III in the collection and titled "The Angel of the Lord." It was published first as "The Broken Stirrup Leather" in the June 3, 1911, issue of the *Saturday Evening Post.* The narrator, who is simply called "Martin," tells the story as a firsthand experience that occurred when at the age of nine years he was selected by his father to deliver a large sum of money on an overnight journey. We note that the part Martin plays in this story is hardly secondary to the part of his Uncle Abner. Looking at the construction of the story, it seems that Post may have first conceived of it as a story about Martin and realized only afterwards the importance of Uncle Abner. Thus the story begins as Martin's and ends as Abner's. Also obvious evidence of the early origin of this story is the use of Roy's Tavern as a stopping place on the overnight journey, a carry-over from Post's *Dwellers in the Hills* that reappears in this story only. We might profitably note that the theme used here is also similar to that of the short novel—the placing of adult responsibilities upon a mere youth.

There are also, few as there are, more details brought out here about Martin than in any other Abner stories. We should also note that because this was apparently the first use Post made of Abner, the details revealed here regarding him are all the essential ones adhered to, for the most part, throughout the later stories.

Martin sets the story in action by describing the beginning of his adventurous journey and his meeting up along the way with the evil-appearing Dix. Dix is a neighbor of Abner, who has apparently come upon hard times and would conceivably resort to any crime to attempt to change his fortune. Martin is suspicious of Dix, especially when Dix at the last moment decides to stop at Roy's Tavern, where Martin plans to spend the night. There Martin feels Dix eying the saddle bags which contain the money. Martin's fears mount after he has gone to the loft to sleep. After a short sleep Martin awakes and observes, through a crack in the floor, Dix in the final stages of convincing himself to commit robbery and perhaps murder.

We have been prepared earlier for Uncle Abner's entrance, and at this crucial moment he enters Roy's, arriving just as Dix has started up the ladder to the loft. As Abner enters, Dix stops and decides to leave, but Abner detains him. There follows a dialogue between Abner and Dix that is typical of many others in later stories. Abner, while seemingly talking in riddles, tells Dix all he knows about the man and the crime which is already on his hands, though known to no one except Abner. He tells in his deliberately indirect fashion how he discovered Dix had murdered a partner and buried the body beneath the man's dead horse in an old abandoned well covered with a huge stone slab. Unlike some later tales, Abner does not deliver the criminal over to the local law authority, for justice of the peace Randolph has not yet appeared on the scene. Instead, feeling that the man will be justly dealt with by an avenging Lord, Abner sends the man on his way with a gift of his coat and a hundred dollars—his sympathy for Dix hidden beneath a stern threat to the man's life if he should ever appear in the hills again.

The central theme to this story is one that is constantly found in Post's work, particularly work done about this time. It is the theme of "the providence of God." Post seemingly was bent on confirming its existence, not only to his own satisfaction, but also to the reader's. This theme, in combination with other minor themes, is used time and time again in many of the Abner stories. Although a theme that lends itself to triteness, Post in most instances uses it skillfully and with moderation, as he did in "The Angel of the Lord."

Post published two more Uncle Abner stories in 1911, "The Wrong Hand" and "The House of the Dead Man," numbered II and VII in the collection. In these we again find Uncle Abner cornering the criminal and charging him with murder, and in both we note a continuing pattern as Abner leaves the criminal to other judgments than the law. In "The Wrong Hand" the criminal left to his own devices hangs himself, and in "The House of the Dead Man" Abner, satisfied with the recovery of the stolen money, says, "Let him go . . . for his father's sake. We owe the dead man that much."

Also we note that the narrator, Martin, is on the scene to report both of these stories firsthand. This too is a pattern found in the first ten stories woven around Abner's crime-solving activities. We also find Post giving the central place in these stories to Abner with Martin's usefulness being relegated almost totally to reporting. In "The Wrong Hand" Post has Martin explain his presence thus: "Abner never would have taken me into that house if he could have helped it. He was on a desperate mission and a child was the last company he wished. . . ." Post provides a similar explanation in "The House of the Dead Man," but it is obvious that Martin is along with Abner as an observer and nothing more.

In both these stories Post has set his scenes, various as they are, with the utmost skill. There is an echo in both of these stories of the language found in *Dwellers in the Hills*. Also quite apparent is Post's development of great economy in the telling of these tales, following closely his rule of paring a story down to not a word more than that required to convey the plot, while still making it believable and entertaining.

Numbered IX in the collection, "The Tenth Commandment" retains Martin as a firsthand observer. The tale, incidently, contains a reference to Squire Randolph in regard to the writing of a deed; it is the first use of the name "Randolph" for any purpose in the Abner stories. Here he is referred to "off-stage" only and otherwise does not have a part in the story. Also there is an interesting mention of the origin of the Davisson family lands, the first significant indication that Post in the Uncle Abner tales is dealing, if only remotely, with certain historical facts. The story "The Tenth Commandment" is one of the author's best, not only because it outlines clearly Uncle Abner's philosophy of justice, but also because it uses very effectively a number of unexpected twists in the plot and a good surprise ending.

Uncle Abner's idea of justice, put forth in this tale, is one with which many persons might agree. Abner is discussing with a man named Dillworth the latter's acquisition of a tract of land. Abner states his premise, saying, "The law is not always justice." This causes Dillworth to ask, "How shall we know what justice is unless the law define it?" Abner replies, "I think that every man knows what it is." Dillworth counters with, "And shall every man set up a standard of his own? That would be the end of justice." Perhaps only too aware that a man like Dillworth will not understand, Abner states the keystone of his philosophy, saying, "It would be the beginning of justice if every man followed the standard that God gives him." Dillworth is baffled and says, "But, Abner, is there a court that could administer justice if there were no arbitrary standard and every man followed his own?" Abner's reply is, "I think there is such a court." It is difficult to think of Post, with his legal background, taking such an unorthodox position. And seeing that this is but a variation on the recurring providence-of-God theme, it alerts us to the difficulties of separating Post's feelings from those of his well-wrought character, Abner. Indeed at times it seems almost impossible. Also very apparent in this scene is an echo of Plato's Socrates.

A page later than the above conversation Post has Abner submit, "But under the law the weak and the ignorant suffer for their weakness and for their ignorance, and the shrewd and the cunning profit by their shrewdness and their cunning." Written to be entertaining, there is certainly more to these so-called mystery and detective tales of Post than most critics have admitted in their reviews. Perhaps they failed to notice the substance in these stories and it is only now, at this time in history, that Post can be appreciated.

How much of this philosophy of justice is Post's own, how much his father's or his ancestors', and how much just created for the purposes of fiction poses a question which, although we may not have the answer to, we should not overlook in any attempt to understand these stories and their author. No doubt, from some of the facts we know, if Abner's philosophy was not Post's publicly-stated opinion, it was nevertheless a part of his private thinking. Post had inherited an artistocratic social status, but he was a keen student and observer of the modern world. His writings indicate he clearly saw the changes that were taking place about him. They reveal a mind which could look beyond the common philosophies of his contemporaries to fresh approaches to persistent problems.

The next six stories written were put down in an inexpensive notebook referred to earlier. They are in Post's tight script, three on the forward pages and three on the reverse sides. In the first of these six, titled "The Devil's Tools" and numbered X, Post continues to use Martin as an on-the-scene reporter, as he still does in the remaining five, but Martin's duties are kept to a minimum. In this story Martin "ages," being given an age of ten years; yet he is obviously treated more as a child than when introduced in the earliest story. In this tale he lurks in the background only, spying and observing like a shadowy espionage agent who is never discovered taking down his notes.

This story is also the first in which Squire Randolph is given an active part, but he has not yet set out accompanying Abner in search of criminals. In fact in this particular episode the "criminal" strikes right at the heart of the Randolph household. Prominently involved besides Randolph are his daughter Betty and Liza, the girl's nurse and substitute mother, who is guardian apparent of all that takes place on the Randolph estate concerning the servant help. How Uncle Abner solves the mystery of the missing emeralds reveals his full powers of uncanny deductive reasoning, his shrewd knowledge of human psychology, his persuasiveness, and his crafty maneuvering in a delicate situation. Post in the writing of this story comes as close to the technical perfection dictated for successful popular magazine fiction as in anything he ever produced. Probably written in late 1911 or early 1912, it demonstrates that he had nearly mastered the short story form he formulated.

The next story, "A Twilight Adventure," numbered VII in the book, has a theme which Post used several times. Here he uses it most effectively. It is the theme of circumstantial evidence and how it can entangle an innocent man.

In "A Twilight Adventure" Martin continues his on-the-scene observations with only a limited part in the action, while Uncle Abner demonstrates again his exceptional cunning and wit by staving off a lynching and bringing about a legal trial.

Perhaps of some interest here to the critic and student is Post's use of a number of family names familiar to the readers of Post's other Abner stories and also his *Dwellers in the Hills*. Their use indicates almost certainly the early origin of this tale published first in 1914, but written at least two years earlier. Most of the characters presented are to a degree authentic. Post again in this story sets his scene with excellent descriptive details and employs use of atmosphere with full narrative power. He then ends this successfully told tale with a light but effective twist.

In what appears to be the seventh Abner story Post wrote, Squire Randolph makes his first appearance as an accompanist of Abner. Martin is also in the company of the two men as the story "The Hidden Law," eleventh in the collection, begins. Post makes it plain to the reader what Martin's purpose is to be when Martin says, "I was overlooked as a creature without ears; but I had the ears of the finest and I lost not a word." Thus excused, Martin reports the adventure with only slight intrusions to remind the reader of his presence.

Post's creative powers were at full strength when he wrote this story. In it, along with its references to gold and bees, are allusions to Shakespeare, the Holy Bible, witches, eminent law makers from the past, and miscellaneous bits of vital truths. Betts, an old miser, does not wish to share his hoarded gold coins with his son, who has left home for college, nor with the daughter, who remains at home. A fearful and superstitious man, Betts has come to believe that some unnatural creatures have stolen his treasure, carefully guarded and hidden as it was by the miser. Uncle Abner sniffs out the secret, but concurs symbolically with the old man's explanation regarding the crime. Abner assures Betts a portion of the gold will be returned in time. As Abner leaves with Martin and Randolph he reveals how the girl, the brother, and the bees are all involved. There is no need of legal action. An abbreviated telling of the story cannot suffice—it must be read as Post wrote it. It is a delightful story as well as one of Post's best.

In "The Riddle," the story numbered XII, the riddle reads, "Why don't you look in the cow?" But Abner is not the only one to discover the answer. On the way home from the grand jury investigation into the death of the riddle's maker, Uncle Abner, who is accompanied by Martin, decides during the snowy ride to stop over at the supposedly abandoned house, but he discovers Doc Storm, a strange old country doctor, already there. The plot unfolds, but with many sharp turns. The atmosphere is superbly created in this story which doubles back and confuses the reader who is not alert. Because of a breach of Post's rules regarding singleness of plot, while it repays a close reading, the plot does not resolve itself with the sharpened clarity of Post's more typical and effective tales. "The Riddle" does show, however, that Post, whether he wished to do so here or not, did on some occasions permit certain questionable obscurities in his stories. While as in the case of "The Riddle" they may make a story more difficult to read, to the serious reader they offer a challenge and invite additional readings.

The theme of the next story we consider is another variation of the providence-of-God theme. Abner sees justification for a murder, which Randolph in his blundering manner has recorded as an accident, and retaining his secret (except for Martin's eavesdropping) allows the murderer to take his justice at the hands of God. Numbered IV of the collection, it is titled "An Act of God."

In this story Post uses an obvious example of the "covered trap door technique" to bring off his surprise ending. Those who have taken time to be critical of Post's short story techniques have often focused their attention on this example. Howard Haycraft has written regarding this story:

> In the Abner story, "An Act of God," Post proves by a phonetic misspelling the forgery of a document purportedly written by a deaf-mute. The brilliant solution is spoiled by the fact that he does not allow the reader to scan the document. Had he done so, the tale might well be ranked as one of the most perfect in all the literature.[15]

Although Post may have overlooked this imperfection in the story, the idea behind the story is an ingenious one and as difficult as any to bring off perfectly. Other than this one defect, the story is told with excellent style and color. Martin is merely an eye-witness—uninvolved again, but lingering as a shadow in back of his uncle—while Squire Randolph appears on the scene in his legal role and fulfills his principal literary purpose of being a foil to Abner, whose keen mind is awarded the total triumph.

Although last in the book, the next story was not the last written by any means. "Naboth's Vineyard," although first published serially in 1916, can be seen to easily fit the earlier patterns. We can judge with some certainty that it was written between early 1912 and early 1914. It is the last of the six stories found in the bound composition book which apparently contains, in the order of creation, the fifth through the tenth story of the Abner series. These other stories all date between 1912 and 1914. "Naboth's Vineyard" is also the last story in which Post uses Martin as an on-the-scene reporter, for with "The Doomdorf Mystery" published in September 1914 this pattern changes, and although hereafter we assume Martin to continue as narrator, he is no longer named or present at the action.

We find a somewhat more involved plot and more supporting details in this short story than in most of Post's more direct tales, which have given him his greatest measure of fame. "Naboth's Vineyard" is numbered XVIII in the collection. It is a fitting final story because of its intense courtroom scene and because like the grand finale of a theatrical production, the entire principal cast of the Uncle Abner stories appears.

The plot begins when one Elihu Marsh is found murdered. Circumstantial evidence points to the hired man Taylor as the man who fired the shot and ran off. The details are revealed in the court of Judge Simon Kilrail.

But, just as the case against Taylor tightens, the girl who was Marsh's cook attempts to confess the crime. With her confession the legal proceedings are shifted in a new direction and the court adjourns until the next day.

Abner, Doc Storm, and Martin ride along with Kilrail on the way home, stopping for a short time at the judge's house. There Abner manages to discover Kilrail's watch key missing and Doc Storm finds a certain page in a book of poisons is the only one cut. The following day, Abner, backed by the citizens of the county, confronts Kilrail in court charging the judge with the crime. Abner then presents his evidence, explaining the murder of Marsh, together with a deed book conveying Marsh's land to the judge in an unindexed entry. With the crime solved, Post has the judge provide, by means of a self-inflicted, fatal bullet, a fitting and sudden end to the case.

Of all Melville Davisson Post's stories, "Naboth's Vineyard" is the only one which, to public knowledge, has ever been adapted for use in the theater. Adopted for the stage in 1945 by Elizabeth McFadden under the title "Signature," it lasted for only two performances at the Forrest Theatre in New York City. This was long enough for it to receive a mild panning by the critics; for example, *Newsweek* summed it up as "that kind of melodrama." But the blame here does not rest on Post, for although it is far from his most effective work, it is an entertaining story and profitable to read for its characterization and its unusual legal maneuver.

"The Doomdorf Mystery," given first place in the book, has probably drawn more attention to Post than anything that he ever wrote. It is a well-written story, and though certainly not the best Post wrote, it has drawn comment from its various critics far out of proportion to its real importance. It has been reprinted several times in anthologies, particularly as an outstanding example of the "locked-door-mystery." In it Post relied heavily upon the possibilities of circumstance—not impossible circumstances, but remote circumstances—and this, perhaps, is where most of the arguments lie. Stranger things happen in truth, but some literary theorists argue that they should not in fiction. Post may well have had a real incident upon which he built "The Doomdorf Mystery," but whether he did or not, in this instance he most certainly refused to cater to the idea that fiction needs to be more plausible than truth.

"The Doomdorf Mystery" is apparently the eleventh story featuring Uncle Abner that Post wrote. We note that here Randolph becomes the prime companion to Abner. Martin, who no longer reports from firsthand knowledge, continues to be recognized as the narrator because of the use of such terms as "my uncle" and an occasional unidentified "I."

Squire Randolph, whose function and character are clearly brought out in several lucid sentences, hereafter remains Abner's principal companion in the investigations of crimes in all of the other tales with the exception of four. Two of these omit Randolph and leave Abner working entirely alone, and two feature Abner working alone through almost the entire story, with Randolph appearing on the scene at the conclusion. It should be noted that of these four stories, one of each type is collected in the book, and one of each is among the Abner tales that saw magazine publication some ten years later.

Post apparently felt that Randolph made an excellent contrast to Abner, a perfect foil for Abner's sharp intellect, a role which a child like Martin could not reasonably satisfy. He also recognized the possibilities for a wider choice of plots that Randolph's companionship provided. This change in the pattern of the Abner stories resulted in the loss of the "immediate presence" of the narrator, who must hereafter appear to have received his information by a secondary means.

As the story opens, Doomdorf has already met his death. At the scene of the death are two strange and suspicious characters: Bronson, a fire and brimstone preaching circuit rider, and a woman of foreign blood and broken English. To Randolph, both are reasonable suspects with sufficient motives to have taken the victim's life. Both in fact believe they have been instrumental in bringing the death about—the preacher through appeals to his wrathful God to send fire from heaven, and the woman by the black magic act of piercing a wax model through the heart. Abner suggests to Randolph that neither is guilty of the murder, but that there is a third suspect involved whom they should wait for. The ending is a baffling surprise and Post, with his powerful narrative skill, makes a somewhat implausible occurrence plausible by having Abner give proof of what happened through a reinactment of the event. Setting the story on a tract of land adjoining the Daniel Davisson lands, at a point on a mountain neglected by the early surveys, Post challenges us to accept it as history.

Next we note Post's outstanding technical skills in another expertly told story, "The Treasure Hunter," number V of the *Uncle Abner* book. This story is charged with an atmosphere of violence and with strong suspense. The chief characters are strange and forbidding persons drawn in vivid lines of angry-black and blood-red. It is one of Post's trick stories with a double surprise, the last and most effective coming in the very last sentence. Justice of the peace Randolph accompanies Abner in this adventure, promptly pouncing upon the obvious solutions to the mystery and baffled as always by Abner's seeming unwillingness to accept his simple explanations. But Abner, with his careful judgment, his knowledge of his fellow man, and his ability to realign the jumbled facts into a meaningful solution, skillfully explodes Randolph's rational conclusions.

"The Age of Miracles" when published originally in *Pictorial Review*, was not an Uncle Abner story.[16] But, in the *Uncle Abner* book version we may continue to assume that Martin continues as the anonymous narrator, although he is obviously not present during any part of the action. This story, eighth in the collection, finds sober-minded Abner on his way to observe the remains of a man readied for burial. The departed is believed to have died from the accidental discharging of his fowling piece. Accompanied by Randolph, Abner meets an attractive young woman at the entrance to the estate. As finally revealed at the end, Abner sees what Randolph blindly misses—the victim was not killed accidentally, but murdered by his brother. Frightened, he had tried to protect his face with his hands. The brother then covered the hands of the corpse with gloves to hide the truth, that both hands were peppered with shot marks.

Using his secret knowledge as a wedge, Abner causes the

remaining brother to return to the rightful owner, the young woman, property which the murderer and his brother had obtained through a faulty deed. The story is well told in economical fashion. It has also another of Post's surprise endings, although not the most successful. Above all, it is worth reading for its sharply-drawn characters, realistically described. Post, describing the murder victim as a man constantly shooting both game and song birds, wrote: "One would believe all the birds had done him some harm and thus he had declared war on them." The theme of this story given in one word is "justice."

An entertaining story which leads up to a striking solution of a murder is Post's "The Adopted Daughter," XVII of the collection. Here we find evidence that Post frequently enjoyed playing word games with the reader. This fact is illustrated by the irony of the title—which at first glance suggests a melodramatic piece, but actually describes a facade for a bitter depravity. Abner, who goes to view the body of the brother of one Vespatian Flomoy, is accompanied by Squire Randolph and Doc Storm, both acting in their professional capacities. Vespatian explains to the trio that his brother dropped dead suddenly the preceding night. Inasmuch as there is no mark on the body or other evidence of foul play, Randolph and Doc Storm are willing to accept the words of the drunken Vespatian. Vespatian boasts to his listeners that he shall possess the beautiful girl his brother had called an "adopted daughter," but whom he had discovered to be in bondage as revealed by a bill-of-sale found in his brother's possessions. Abner, who had not been so quickly deceived, step by step, aided with some coded hints from the girl, ferrets out the hidden elements of violence. He proves that Vespatian, a crack shot, had fired a light-charged dueling pistol with the bullet striking his brother directly in one eye. Then, as the brother was prepared for burial, Vespatian inserted the top sawn from an ivory chess pawn into the death wound and closed the eyelid over it.

This story is a first rate example of Post's principle of economy—no line is used that does not play a part in the total artistry of the composition. It appears to have been written soon after Post had put the formula for his story-telling into essay form, and it actually echoes directly at one point the very words he used in his essay almost as if they were being quoted.

We note that Melville Post, in most of these stories, does not inject more than a fragment of his philosophical tenets. Only occasionally he emphasizes a favorite concept. When he does he usually speaks through Uncle Abner, as in the following excerpt from "The Straw Man," which is XIII in the book. Here Post reveals one of the fundamentals of his individualistic beliefs:

> "Sire," replied Abner, "I cannot think of God depending on a thing so crude as reason. If one reflects upon it, I think one will immediately see that reason is a quality exclusively peculiar to the human man. It is a thing that God could never, by any chance, require. Reason is the method by which those who do not know the truth, step by step, finally discover it." (p. 234)
>
> "Then, sir," said Mr. Esdale Moore, "you do not believe that the criminal can create a series of false evidences that will be at all points consistent with the truth."
>
> "No man can do it," replied Abner. "For to do that, one must know everything that goes before and everything that follows the event which one is attempting to falsify. And this omniscience only the intelligence of God can compass. . . ." (p. 235)

Thus, the lawyer nephew of the murdered man, attempting to throw suspicion on his blind cousin, is identified as the killer because of his left-handed habits, another proof that the truth cannot be successfully distorted. This is a lively story, vividly told and full of suspense. The reader who follows the writings of Post from his earliest tales to his last will note that the point made here that there can be no perfect crime is one that is often expressed in his fiction. It is the basic premise upon which the majority of his plots turn. As it is stated in this story, in the words of Uncle Abner, it is stated more clearly than in anything else the author wrote.

In choosing a title for his stories, Post often exhibits his exceptional adroitness by selecting a title with depth of meaning, as we noted in regard to an earlier story. "The Edge of the Shadow" is another prominent example of such a case. This title prefaces a story which is simple on the surface, but touches on many vital factors that are pertinent to our age. Numbered XVI in the collection, this story provides us such up-to-date elements as: the theologian versus the humanist; special rights versus civil rights; fact versus fiction; law versus lawlessness; and aberrations versus normality.

Particularly in one short passage, we find words which might easily be applied to life today:

> "Shall a fanatic who stirs up our slaves to murder," said Mansfield, "be tried like a gentleman before a jury?"
>
> "Aye, Mansfield," replied my uncle, "like a gentleman, and before a jury! If the fanatic murders the citizen, I would hang him too, without one finger's weight of difference in the method of procedure. I would show New England that the justice of Virginia is even-eyed. And she would emulate that fairness, and all over the land the law would hold against the unrestraint that is gathering."
> (p. 295-6)

Here Abner's justice joins hands with Randolph's law and order. It is one of the few places we find Abner and his creator standing explicitly for capital punishment. But the story ends with an explanation of the killing which emphasizes one of the strongest of reasons for opposition to capital punishment—and for greater faith in Abner's Providence. Since Abner constantly holds out for the workings of the providence of God, we must believe that essentially this would be Post's final position regarding capital punishment.

In this story we again see evidence that Post probably drew often on his personal life experiences for models from which to create realistic characters. In this instance we see a remarkable resemblance between the Cyrus Mansfield of this story and Cyrus Childers of *The Gilded Chair*. When Mansfield says, " 'I will not be held back from laying hold of the lever of the great engine merely because the rumble of the machinery fills other men with terror,' " (p. 291) the relationship is unmistakable. These two characters were undoubtedly inspired by the same model—someone from the author's past who had made a deep impression. Had Post been less reticent about his personal affairs it is likely that the model he used in this instance could be discovered, but unfortunately, lacking all the necessary knowledge, at best we might only approximate a close guess. So we must settle for not knowing and enjoy the story as complete fiction.

This story, "The Edge of the Shadow," for all of its innocence, should give even the more sophisticated reader something to consider and argue. It will more than repay the effort expended in reading it. Such stories make it difficult for one to be reconciled with the opinions of those critics who thought that behind his brilliant displays of technique Post had nothing to say. It causes one to question which stories such critics may have neglected to consider.

Martin, as we have assumed, is the narrator of all the Uncle Abner tales, even if only visible in some through the phrase "my uncle." Also, we have noted that when Martin was not usually on the scene as a firsthand witness, Squire Randolph was about—but we must note an exception in four stories, two of the book and two of the uncollected tales. In each of these four instances Abner is essentially on his own, except for the final moments when Randolph and his men arrive on the scene. The two stories from the book in which Abner solos are number XIV, "The Mystery of Chance" and number XV, "The Concealed Path." The principal virtue of both of these stories is their entertainment value, and they rate high in dramatic atmosphere. Also, scattered throughout both we note some pointed remarks by Abner concerning such subjects as gambling, God, liquor, and vengeance.

"The Mystery of Chance" takes place in a river town on the Ohio, somewhat out of Abner's usual territory. Abner's presence and purpose among the river boats is well explained as a part of his cattle-raising livelihood. In bringing this special adventure to a fitting conclusion, Abner in a somewhat unusual fashion makes use of brawn as well as brain. Well-written, the story is thoroughly suspenseful and colorful due to Uncle Abner's individualistic character.

Throughout the various tales we are introduced to a number of races and nationalities that have come to the western land of early Virginia—Negro, Italian, German, French, and others. In "The Concealed Path" we meet the Scots. It is to the credit of Post's art that his characters appear in general authentic representatives of their types. This is especially true of the Scots in this particular tale—set in an atmosphere as bleak and cold as their northern homelands. We actually feel chilled as the plot slowly unfolds in this stark wintery atmosphere. Abner, in his usual cautious fashion, solves the case just in time for the arrival of Randolph and his aides. Post's talents are at near peak in this interesting and moving tale.

We have listed these last three tales as the sixteenth, seventeenth, and eighteenth of the Abner tales essentially because the way they fit the pattern of development we have followed. Further, they are the only stories among those collected in the book which seemingly were never published serially previous to their book publication. They are well-polished tales, their workmanship a credit to Post's reputation for technical craftsmanship. It is difficult to understand why they missed magazine publication originally unless they were written close to the time the book's manuscript was turned over to the publisher and the author gave no other thoughts to the stories.

So much for the eighteen tales of the book. We can now conclude our examination of the individual Uncle Abner stories with some consideration of the four later stories which had serial publication only. They show few distinguishing characteristics to place them apart from the collected tales, other than a heightened religious imagery in the first three and the extra length of the fourth.

These four additional tales were all published in the magazine *Country Gentleman*. The first appeared in the July 1927 issue and it was titled "The Devil's Track." The unofficial rural detective takes off on these remaining adventures with this sentence: "It was a trivial matter that took my Uncle Abner onto the Dillworth lands." It is almost as if he had not been in retirement for ten long years. There is, however, good reason to believe that these stories were written at least several years before they saw print, so perhaps what we have are only delayed reports on the activities of Abner.

In "The Devil's Track" Uncle Abner, proceeding as a solitary agent, discovers an unreported crime. The Devil leaves his footprint and Abner follows the trail and discovers the criminal—whereupon he shrewdly sends a message to Randolph and his men while completing his case against the greedy neighbor, Dillsworth. A minor connection to the 1901 *Dwellers in the Hills* appears in this 1927 tale; a hired hand by the name of Twiggs serves as a messenger in both instances. Only the name and the function seem to connect the two; yet we wonder why the name was used again.

Post surely had an unlimited supply of names equally unusual from which to draw if he pleased. Was it a mere coincidence?

"The God of the Hills" was placed in the September 1927 issue of *Country Gentleman*. All the important ingredients of the preceding Uncle Abner stories are included here, and they fuse into a good mystery-problem story with an added element of tragedy. There is a thorough display of religious concern and symbolism; there is Abner's magnificent intuition, skills of detection, shrewdness, and legal wisdom; there is the near blundering of Randolph, an innocent girl in need of protection, and a strong supporting cast. The action is quick and decisive with the suspense sustained throughout. Its theme, cunningly contrived and executed, is the major one of Post, the providence of God. It is evident from the opening line ("Abner used to say that one riding on a journey was in God's hands") to the ending ("It was the fulfilling of the prophecy").

Third of the later stories appearing in the same magazine is "The Dark Night" in the November 1927 issue. Religious imagery is again strong in this story in which Abner, again alone, pits his intelligence and shrewdness against a calculating, vicious criminal who has no faith in Abner's God. In truth he tries to use the symbols of Abner's religion for his advantage and therein meets his downfall. Post has skillfully woven these symbols into an effective story, as we note in these lines:

> "I mean," replied my uncle, "that these things, the candle and the Book and the manger, are symbols used in the service of God, and you have used them, Brant, in the service of the devil."
>
> He went on, his words, slow and even, like a pronouncement of doom.
>
> "They are symbols of life, Brant, and you have made them symbols of death! . . ."

It is Brant's "locked Bible" which in the closing lines reveals the final and convicting evidence—in one of Post's best-constructed and most convincing stories.

The final published tale and the twenty-second in which Uncle Abner appears is particularly unusual because of its length, being more nearly a novelette in length and partly in construction. It was published in two parts, the first installment appearing in

Country Gentleman in May 1928, and the second installment the following month. Post titled this long tale "The Mystery at Hillhouse," and it is probably the most complex case of any Abner ever faced, complete with four prime suspects. He introduces Abner and the scene of his adventures with a thoroughness not found in most of the stories, revealing smoothly his character and his occupation. We meet again with Randolph, designated in this story alone by both the terms "Squire" and "justice of the peace" and characterized as always as "vain, pompous and enamored with the extravagance of words." Some of the situations and actions remind the reader of those found in other stories, but here they are tightly knit into the total plot. We meet again with an unsavory character named Dix, who appeared in the first of the Uncle Abner tales, where Abner gives him a chance to leave and live, so long as he does not return to the scene of his crime. Is this the same Dix and has Abner forgotten his pledge? Or, does this story, seemingly written last, precede the first in terms of time? Probably there is no relationship, or the relationship is meaningless. Nevertheless, giving this some added thoughts, we can imagine this last story as a very fitting tale with which to open a collection of Uncle Abner stories.

"The Mystery at Hillhouse" ends not with a solution to a crime, but with an explanation for the death of the victim. The circumstantial evidence we have followed in seeking the murderer is brushed aside, and the death is pronounced officially by Randolph as an "accident." Or, as Uncle Abner termed it, " 'Now that . . . will depend on how you are willing to regard it.' " Surprisingly or not, Post all but abandons his providence-of-God theme here and returns to the myth and mysticism of the mountains. We are reminded again of Post's great and abiding interest in these commonplace mysteries—demonstrated most clearly in the ambiguity prominently found in both text and title of his first novel, *Dwellers in the Hills.* In this regard we note that the victim of this final Uncle Abner short story was actually brought to his fate by the *dead*, the "ancient people on the mountain." This fate was predicted at the end of the first installment by the eccentric old woman who runs the tavern, a character also reminiscent of one found in the earlier work. These "dwellers in the hills" lurk in the background of many of Post's tales. Neither related to a God nor to human beings, these shadowy figures are suggested as real and effective forces.

In Uncle Abner we have one of the noteworthy folk characters of American literature, a fascinating man involved in a fascinating series of adventures. These stories have been unjustly overlooked, largely because they have been relegated to the mystery-tale classification, where few serious critics have dared to tread. There is much more in these so-called "mystery" stories than has readily been recognized. Certainly, as the author himself stated, Post's first principle was the production of entertaining plots, but he did not neglect art totally in preference to entertainment. He stated and proved that a properly-written story creates its own "art." The Uncle Abner stories are the crowning achievement of Post's distinctive methods and talents. These tales need to be preserved and read and discussed, and the sad fact is that up until now they have not been given their just due in any of these respects.

The birthplace of Melville Davisson Post, located in a wooden rise above the Clarksburg-Buckhannon Pike near Romines Mills, W. Va.

"The Mansion" in DuBois, Pa., formerly the home of John E. DuBois, a brother-in-law of Mrs. Post. Melville and Bloom stayed here frequently in a three room apartment on the third floor during the years 1903-1914. Much of Post's best writing during this period was worked on here.

The gravemarker of Melville Davisson Post in the Elkview Mason Cemetery in Clarksburg, W. Va. It shows the true year of Post's birth and the unique epitaph he provided for his grave which lies between that of his infant son and his wife.

The grave of Orange Jud Perkins, playmate, servant and lifelong companion of Post. It is in a tiny church graveyard beside Gnatty Creek in Romines Mills, W. Va.

The front entrance to Templemoor, the boyhood home of Post on the Clarksburg-Buckhannon Pike.

Taking afternoon tea on the grounds of Templemoor, about 1907, are Post's mother Florence May Davisson Post, his sister Florence Post Atterholt, his nephew Frank Atterholt, and serving are Eliza Perkins and her son, Jud.

Post in one of his favorite modes of dress, standing near the back terrace of The Chalet, his noted West Virginia home. This picture dates about 1920. The home was destroyed by fire about 1946.

Orange Jud Perkins observing Post, the rider on the extreme right, with a group of polo players at The Chalet's polo field. One of the ponies is probably Margo, though which was not determined.

Post, who spent his lifetime riding horses, is seen here in a typical view before the main entrance steps to The Mansion in DuBois, Pa.

The Davisson family coat of arms.

V. FOUR SHORT STORY COLLECTIONS
1. The Mystery at the Blue Villa

By the end of World War I Melville Davisson Post was known to millions of readers, and he had among his many admirers a number of the nation's outstanding citizens. Certainly one of the most notable of these and also one of the most enthusiastic was the 26th President of the United States, Theodore Roosevelt. The two men are reported to have been on friendly terms, and Post had met several times with the colorful Colonel Roosevelt. Roosevelt was very much interested in the methods Post used in the composition of his stories. Always a great lover of books and an avid reader, Roosevelt carried with him a plentiful supply of reading material wherever he journeyed. Having been informed of the publication of Post's next book, likely by the author himself, Roosevelt wrote in a letter dated September 6, 1918, from his New York office:

> My dear Mr. Post:
> When that book comes I shall without doubt find that I could pass an examination in each separate story; because I never see anything of yours I don't read! But equally

without doubt I shall read them all over again with the utmost pleasure.

With hearty thanks,
Faithfully yours,
Theodore Roosevelt[1]

Roosevelt must have been writing in reference to Post's collection of stories about Uncle Abner which were being issued late in 1918. Indeed we may accept the fact that Roosevelt had already read in serial form many stories in that collection as well as other stories of Post appearing in a variety of popular magazines. Because the former president died just four months after sending the above note to Post, it is not certain that he ever had an opportunity to read the book itself.

While this letter does not refer directly to *The Mystery at the Blue Villa* collection, nevertheless it does show the sort of praise which Post received frequently for the work he was then publishing. With his career at its peak, Post seems to have issued his next book principally to make money. *Uncle Abner* was already being accepted as a minor masterpiece, and without doubt it was good business to get another book before the public. Between the publishing of *The Nameless Thing* and *Uncle Abner* six years had elapsed and Post had accumulated a sufficient stock of stories from which to assemble a book without much labor.[2]

Regarding this next book, published late in 1919 by D. Appleton and Company, critics in general were somewhat reserved in their opinions. The reviews of *The Mystery at the Blue Villa*, while certainly not enthusiastic, were for the most part more than fair, noting the excellent parts and ignoring the bad. Most of the reviewers had probably read and recognized the superior quality of the *Uncle Abner* tales and finding these new stories not equal to the previous book's material, decided to adopt a wait-and-see attitude.

The *New York Times* critic reported on the new book's stories in stock terms: "They have variety and freshness and if occasionally overemphasized, they are never trite."[3] Another reviewer, writing in the *ALA Booklist* regarding these seventeen stories, was more to the point, giving an accurate and enlightening opinion which noted: "In several there is an atmosphere of psychic horror and dread and a common theme in some unexpected contact between the social 'upper' and 'underworld.' Though somewhat overdramatic and artificial, the plots are clever and interesting."[4]

If there is a common theme to the book, it is as the latter critic suggested, the "contact between the social 'upper' and 'underworld.' " Post was familiar with both, belonging to the "upper" and well-acquainted through his first profession as a criminal courts lawyer with the "underworld." As a writer of fiction and a sometime student of criminology he continued his interests in both.

All of the stories in *The Mystery at the Blue Villa* had appeared between 1914 and 1918 in such periodicals as *Pictorial Review, Saturday Evening Post*, and *Hearst's Magazine*. The locale of these stories varies widely and includes for the most part territory with which Post was familiar. The titles are all rather flat, descriptive titles with hardly a touch of irony or obscurity. The stories are numbered I through XVII without any significance attached to their order. Twelve of the stories were rated in various degrees of excellence in the annual listings of *The Best Short Stories*, edited by Edward J. O'Brien, but the judgments of Mr. O'Brien are not indisputable.

The book takes its title from the lead story, a tale set in Port Said, "the devil's half-way house." "The Mystery of the Blue Villa" received a high rating in *The Best Short Stories* and must have received other acclaim to be awarded first place in the collection, but relative to today's measurements it appears a minor accomplishment. The tale is told in the words of an acquaintance of the unknown narrator, while aboard an ocean liner crossing a wintry Atlantic. The plot evolves in an exotic atmoshpere ranging from the strange to the macabre. It is well-constructed technically, but for the reader of today it contains no outstanding shock value. Post's ability to paint colorful word pictures of the characters and the events keeps the story alive and moving. But the surprise ending to the story is what sets it apart and makes it worth reading. Post at the story's end dispels the mystery with a very human explanation.

"The New Administration" also got a good rating from O'Brien, but the surprise technique used in this story falters, perhaps because it is a reversal of the first. The story evolves as a normal situation with the twist being a shocking, ghostly ending. Although Post makes good use of low-keyed language and short sentences, there is not much in the way of action or effective atmosphere to heighten the reader's interest. Today's more sophisticated reader will, in general, find the story dull going. Still, the author's revelations of the double dealings occurring in the legal, business, and financial worlds may have stirred a few minds at the time it was written.

"The Great Legend" is well-told. It makes effective use of its atmosphere and its split scenes. The action alternates between an eerie Algerian desert where the tale is being told to the fantastic events in Paris under attack. The plot unwinds with an air of mystery that grips the attention and maintains the suspense until the very end. Using as a background World War I, it reveals a story, believable or not, that is not likely to be found in the history books. Either as colorful folklore or merely as entertainment the story deserves a definite place in literature. Stories using a surprise ending seldom hold up well in a second reading, but this does better than most.

"The Laughter of Allah" is another story presented as an ordinary experience, but halfway through, it shifts to a psychic experience. Since there is a logical explanation given, the reader's doubts are clearly satisfied. Told with good use of descriptive passages, plenty of action, and an atmosphere of foreign excitement, the story manages to trick the reader pleasantly. The standard Post romance which is inserted is weakened somewhat through use of coincidence but is partly saved by a telescoping of time.

Post, having sailed the Atlantic a number of times, makes use of his experiences in several stories to write descriptions which are authentic and interesting. In "The Stolen Life" he uses his knowledge with exactness to create a mood, although the plot of the piece has hardly the value of a melodrama. Only when looking upon "The Stolen Life" as an analogy of the dilemma which the civilized world faced in 1914 do we see any value in it.

Post in several stories makes use of the espionage activities of World War I. "The Girl from Galacia" is one such instance.[5] Since Post more often than not took the idea for his plots from factual sources, we might assume that this tale had a real counterpart. The story is interesting, particularly if it really happened, but it does not deserve more than a "fair" rating.

"The Pacifist" is another story using espionage. This time Post shows his life-long interest in cryptography, making the use of a secret code a central factor in the plot. Again the story is interesting, but it does not have the shock value it may have had in 1917 when the story first appeared in the *Saturday Evening Post* in the midst of World War I.

In its use of legal affairs and detective work, "The Sleuth of the Stars" is a typical Post story, but it is unusual in that the first person narrator is a young girl. It includes an astronomer known as "Sir" Henry,[6] his niece Sarah, a will, an innocent orphaned child, her negro nurse, and a false heir in a truly melodramatic tale. Other than the young girl as narrator of the story, there is little that is new or interesting. When first published serially the story rated three stars on the O'Brien honor roll, but it lacks sincerity of purpose, contains little suspense, and has a well-worn plot. Today's reader must wonder the reasons for its original acclaim.

Set in Nice, France, "The Witch of the Lecca," despite a seemingly contrived plot, maintains a certain measure of interest with its treatment of real and supposed sorcery. The story's action moves quickly, developing a mood and an atmosphere of suspense which leads to an interesting and satisfying conclusion. The surprise ending is a plausible one and could be based on a true occurrence.

World War I also provided the plot for "The Miller of Ostend." The atmosphere in this story is grim and urgent. The touches of realism that Post worked into the narrative make it as interesting and believable as a set of photographs. Even the irony, which could easily be written off as contrived coincidence, fits the situation. The effect of the war on the little people caught in its web is not overly melodramatic. The ending is unusual, a surprise ending with some element of horror, though not a shock to the modern reader more conditioned to violence. The use of the German zeppelins is interesting from a historical viewpoint. Whether or not Post used the giant windmills at the end in a symbolic fashion is open to speculation. Windmills held a special fascination for Post from his first view of them.

Writing from some of his Swiss experiences, Post contrived the plot of "The Girl in the Villa," a puzzling story, but one lacking in real suspense. He used here the elements of love and adventure, which he never used well. The story has an air of fantasy although again the plot could well have had its origin in a factual case. Post's descriptions of the broken-hearted Randolph could easily be an accurate description of his own feelings at one time.[7]

"The Ally" is again a story using as background the battle of France against the World War I armies of Germany. It uses espionage as the basis for the plot and in a better-than-average manner for Post. Into this plot Post brings an aide to the commander of the Russian token troops in France, a Major Lykoff, and a beautiful girl working as a dress maker's assistant. They are placed against a backdrop of wartime Paris. The theme, not an unusual one, is a man's weakness for a pretty woman. Woven into the special circumstances of the plot, this theme not only proves to be different and consistently interesting, but it reveals the seldom observed rakishness in Post. Also, from this angle it seems a somewhat bold story for a so-called "family magazine" of its day, published as it was first in the *Saturday Evening Post* of 1915.

Post was always on the lookout for an incident around which to build a plot, and "Lord Winton's Adventure," as unbelievable as it might seem, is not really so very implausible. The story is done in the author's semi-oral style. It proceeds at a rapid pace allowing just enough suspense, and it includes colorful descriptions done boldly and movingly. The story has within itself a second "story" and Post presents this conspiracy in a way that holds the reader's complete attention, springing his trick ending with enough of a humorous effect to allow this story a rating of "excellent." The incidental use in this story of a guilt-ridden submarine commander who had saved himself while his crew perished is interesting because such a character is found earlier in *The Nameless Thing*.

In most of his stories Post approaches the subject from the viewpoint of the corrective force or the victim, but occasionally, as he does in "The Wage-Earners," he tells his story from the point of view of the criminal. His portrayal of the criminal element may seem quite primitive to today's reader acquainted with the "tough-guy" literature of later years, but relative to the time Post was writing, he was exploring a new and only partially explored territory. Thus his criminal types, crude as they are in this instance, played a part in introducing this new "outlook" to the readers of popular fiction. We must note that those few scholars who have approached the history of this type of literature are unanimous in overlooking Post's contributions. The theme of this story—that the wages of sin are death—earned the story, when first published in 1917, a "good" rating. By present standards we can judge as only "fair" this somewhat shoddy melodrama.

"The Sunburned Lady" is again a standard Post plot involving Sir Rufus Simon, a British solicitor who also takes part earlier in "The Stolen Life." Whatever the factual basis for this story, and it is not apparent, the author did not succeed in unifying the plot and the characters into as good a story as the material warranted. The characters are stiff, and the woman is especially unconvincing, the drawing of effective women characters being one of Post's weaker points. The plot expanded and used as a basis for a popular novel would have been more effective. It is strongly reminiscent of the plot of a grade-B motion picture of the 1930's.

One story which fared well in O'Brien's ratings in *The Best Stories of 1916* and which also impressed Grant Overton is "The Baron Starkheim." In the years before World War II a story like this could be accepted as a good, popular adventure story. Measured against today's standards, however, such a plot seems melodramatic and dull. It is a short story that leans heavily on character, a type of a story which Post himself had declared unsuitable for popular fiction. Baron Starkheim's antics are almost as humorous as they are pitiable. The former U-boat commander is presented as detestable with no sympathy being allowed him by the author. The Baron's guilt is too great for the confines of a short story. In spite of an explanation by Post and the actual plausibility of the Baron's mental state, we cannot wholly believe his failure to adjust to the reality that dooms him.

"Behind the Stars,"[8] the closing story in *The Mystery at the Blue Villa*, is in a somewhat different key than the other stories in the book. Post again uses a split-scene technique, with the narrator reporting on a story told him by an acquaintance while they are seated in a concert hall listening to a piano artist, unnamed, but descriptive of the great Paderewski. There are constant flashes of good description that stand in isolation, and the story, which is essentially a fantasy using real people, is like a piece of program music, moving through a variation of moods to a crescendo conclusion. Because it does not have adequate characterization, the story does not develop as effectively as the sensitive subject matter demands. Still it is a satisfying story having about it a captivating atmosphere that Post handled with his usual admirable skill. This story, which adds a new dimension to his talent, rates at least a "very good."

Of the seventeen stories in this book, six have some possible literary merit. Three of these are stories using World War I incidents as the basis for plots. They are "The Great Legend," which is based on the inspired French army's battle to save Paris; "The Miller of Ostend," which reveals the primitive horror of the vastly changed methods of modern warfare with its unhuman attacks on civilians from the air; and "The Ally," which in its truly ironic title reminds us of another unnerving phase of modern warfare, the double dealings of espionage agents. These three stories deserve several readings, and the first two deserve a place in the literature of World War I.

The other three stories, "The Laughter of Allah," "Lord Winton's Adventure," and "Behind the Stars" are alike in their effective development of mood. "The Laughter of Allah" with its psychic adventure is a nightmare that has the quality of prophetic truth. "Lord Winton's Adventure" is a mixed bag of humor and human frailty, presented tongue-in-cheek fashion. "Behind the Stars" catching the mood of music, tells a modern day fairy tale.

These six stories save *The Mystery at the Blue Villa* from mediocrity. They illustrate that the art of the short story was being advanced by the professional skills of writers like Melville Davisson Post to the point where it now has a secure position in the realm of serious literature.

2. The Sleuth of St. James's Square

In arranging this collection of stories, Post once more tried bringing together into novel form pieces which had not been written with this purpose in mind. Striving for this end, he makes use of Sir Henry Marquis, chief of the Criminal Investigation Department of Scotland Yard. Because he has a residence there, Sir Henry is known as "the sleuth of St. James's Square." In most of the stories gathered in this volume Sir Henry originally had no part as they were written and published serially, the "sleuth" only being incorporated by diverse means at the time they were collected for the book. Even in those stories which did originally incorporate him as a character, he does not come off as an outstanding character, but always rather secondary to the other characters who sustain the action. The mating of Sir Henry with most of these stories has therefore not been wholly successful—and in several instances stories which are good stories in their own right suffer his needless entry without benefit of improvement. And some would have remained better stories had Sir Henry remained secluded in his St. James's residence.

Sir Henry Marquis does not have the clear, fine stirring qualities of an Uncle Abner. Neither is he as interesting a character as Randolph Mason. If anything, Sir Henry seems a snob, though we do not have much evidence by which to judge him since the author did not allow him anywhere in these stories the substance and importance needed to make a major figure. The best stories of this uneven volume stand on their own merits regardless of this character who Post had hoped would draw the various tales together.

Critical comment on the book is rare, but usually favorable. A reviewer in the *New York Times* said of *The Sleuth of St. James's Square* tales:

> . . . they are not only unusual in construction, they are very well written, and with but few exceptions, close with a twist which will surprise even the skilled and habitual reader.[1]

This observation is a fair estimate of their character, but the comments of Edward J. O'Brien, made in his 1921 yearbook, seem too elusive and difficult to fully justify. His statement, in part, said:

> This volume contains the best of Mr. Post's well-known mystery stories. . . . These stories show all the resourceful virtuosity of Poe, and are models of their kind. While they

seem to me to possess no special literary value, they have solved some important new technical problems, and I believe they will repay attentive study.[2]

It is impossible to agree that this volume contains the best of Post's stories, and although they do have a resourceful virtuosity of their own, it does not compare equally with Poe's. Mr. O'Brien's use of "literary value" is perhaps the most elusive of terms.

These stories all have as their common motivation the occurrence of a crime, using the word in some instances in its broadest definition as "an evil act." Post, due to the unnecessary emphasis he gave here to such a character as Sir Henry Marquis, helped to add to his reputation as an author of mystery and detective stories, ignoring the fact that his best talent did not fit comfortably into this category. He seems not to have realized the real value of his plots, which pivoted on matters other than the mystery and detective elements. Omitting Sir Henry Marquis's minor part from the stories in this book, these tales, with their variety of scenes, situations, and characters, obviously only border on the category of mystery and detective tales. They amply illustrate that Post's work is much more than mere entertainment.

Of the sixteen stories in *The Sleuth of St. James's Square* there are at least two which deserve a better reputation than they have heretofore received. The remaining stories are fair, though most all show the unique talents of the author, and perhaps a few of these deserve to be read more than they have been.

"The Thing on the Hearth," which opens the collection, begins as an effect story. A seemingly mysterious killing is described by a strange defendant. A logical explanation is provided by the court, but it gives way to a trick ending with the final truth being divulged by Sir Henry Marquis in the decoding of a cryptographic message. Strange things appear to happen as the author brings together a chemist who has discovered a way of producing synthetic gems, a mysterious oriental figure, a Scotland Yard detective, and an unusual andiron. The andiron, depicting Romulus carrying off the Sabine woman, may have been descriptive of one which Post had in his own drawing room at this time. Although interesting in places, the story does not seem convincing, partly because of a rough, unfinished quality which it fails to overcome with the brief, surprise conclusion.

Placed second in the book is the only story of Post's ever awarded a prize rating by an annual short story collection. This story when first published in the *Saturday Evening Post* was titled "Five Thousand Dollars Reward." Post, in including it in this collection, shortened the title to "The Reward," possibly because the shorter title was more ironic. Blanche Colton explained the editors' selection of the story as an "O'Henry Memorial Award Prize Story" as due to "its brisk action, strong suspense, and humorous denouement."[3] It does display these qualities, but in no greater proportion (and in some cases in lesser proportion) than other stories by the author. Thus this story's selection as the only story awarded such an honor as it received might be considered a spurious action.

As originally published "The Reward" did not include Sir Henry Marquis, and his interjection weakens the structure. He must be transplanted to Washington, D. C., without sufficient reason, and because he is a famous criminologist and expert detective he should have ready answers to several puzzling factors which the original narrator (described as a man of letters) would not have had.

Captain Walker of the U. S. Secret Service, who was made the central character in another of Post's collections, is introduced here, but not to his advantage. The story is a confession of his unfortunate meeting with Mulehaus, a master criminal, and of his failure to apprehend the man. There is some mild suspense, a certain air of mystery, but it is the tongue-in-cheek humor plus the craftiness of the master criminal that sets the story apart.

Despite its apparent weaknesses, "The Reward" contains some of the slickest and most deceptive writing Post ever produced, with hardly a word being wasted. If read uncritically and with no questions asked, it seems almost a superior story worthy of all the special recognition it received. But, on rereading and examination, the incidents presented are too pat or coincidental. It is questionable that a man of Walker's position would have been duped so easily. Post perhaps realized this inasmuch as he has Captain Walker admit his stupidity. The story is captivating and might well seem one of the better ones in this volume; yet the technique used is obvious and the marks of construction are too plain.

Post's ability to come up with ambiguous titles was one of his better talents and one that has been sadly overlooked by most reviewers. The twist in the story he had titled "The Lost Lady" is one of the most effective. The narrator, a would-be hero, is baffled by the "lost lady." Only through Sir Henry's belated appearance does the confused man understand what has happened. In this story the problem plot is secondary to the psychological description of a man's head skillfully being turned by a beautiful and crafty woman. The secret is given away bit by bit as the tale progresses, thus the ending has no real surprise value. Although the twist in plot is sharp, it merely discloses a resolution that the reader has been prepared to expect. While the plot lacks punch, the emphasis on character redeems it from complete failure. In this and several other stories, Post, despite his own rule that the first demand of a story is a strong plot, lets characterization play a fundamental part in the development of the action.

Aware of woman's increasing importance in the twentieth century, in "The Cambered Foot"[4] Post makes a good use of a modern woman as narrator and heroine. She is representative of the new type of woman that appeared with the social upheaval surrounding World War I. Such a woman finds herself pitted against the fading Victorian world. This quiet struggle between the two social climates gives the story an added dimension of suspense. The story is told in a captivating manner, the reader's attention being held by an interest in both the outcome of the girl's position with her intended inlaws and in the outcome of her adventures with Sir Henry Marquis and his suspect. The ending is a surprise, without the use of trickery, and wraps up the plot neatly.

"The Man in the Green Hat" was originally published with Post's critical article "The Mystery Story"[5] in which he discusses some of his guide lines for a successful and entertaining story. Just why Post used this particular story to illustrate his points is difficult, perhaps impossible to determine—for it does not exemplify the standards he advocated in the article as effectively as he may have thought, or as effectively as other tales of his would have. The narration of the story takes place as part of a discussion being held in a European villa, but it concerns an incident that took place in Post's home state of West Virginia. Its basic element is a point of law, one both interesting and unusual, but the division of attention between the discussion of the point of law at the villa and the tragedy of the West Virginia hills that illustrates it in operation hinders all chances for unity in the tale. It would have been better had Post held strictly to one scene. Finally, in readying this story for the book, the author merely played a game of musical chairs with his narrators and then slipped Sir Henry Marquis into the whole with nothing gained or lost.[6]

The next three stories presented are related in that they are purported to be taken from a diary which came into the hands of Sir Henry Marquis through a branch of his mother's family who we learn had settled in Virginia during the 1850's. Otherwise, they have nothing to do with Sir Henry and all are principally concerned with a certain Pendleton, a justice of the peace. The diary's author is reputedly Pendleton's daughter. These stories are all very much in the vein of the Uncle Abner type tale. The girl who narrates is the equivalent of Martin, narrator of the Abner stories. Pendleton is a combination of the character of an Uncle Abner serving the functions of a justice of the peace such as Randolph.

These stories, "The Wrong Sign," "The Fortune Teller," and "The Hole in the Mahogany Panel," are all carefully composed using the successful combinations of special ingredients that Post used so skillfully in his better-written stories. Using nearly the same precise, masterly balance of suspense, action, and atmosphere as he did in putting together the Abner stories, he has produced here three entertaining pieces that are a rewarding reading experience. The Sir Henry Marquis element which was added to these three tales is inserted as a preface; thus it is unobtrusive and serves no purpose other than as a connecting link to place them into the collection.

Occasionally Post has authored an outright failure and "The End of the Road" appears to be one in this category. The plot has possibilities, featuring an unusual woman as a chief character, an element of espionage, a brutal murder and a glimpse of the criminal mind. However, Post fails to bring out the possibilities inherent in this material. The woman is not convincing, he resorts to pure circumstance and he provides a weak ending with the solution of the murder, as Sir Henry Marquis again pops in at the end.

"The Last Adventure" will prove interesting to some, but mediocre and dated to others. It is done in the manner Post favors, using a secondary tale to tell the prime story. This is a method he found very effective for much of his material. The adventures described here have paled somewhat in the decades since they were recounted, but they are meaningful and an accurate description of their particular time. There is a strong thread of suspense woven through the action and the ending is a trick one with an added element of humor.

Sir Henry Marquis has been worked into the collection version of "American Horses" most skillfully by Post, though he was absent in the original magazine version—and in this instance he may have added something to the effectiveness of the story. The criminals in this drama have considerably improved on the old "shell game." Post makes the events sound very believable with his unusual abilities to set his scenes with short, energetic sentences that give movement to this story. The suspense is well-managed and the resolution is a satisfying surprise. The master criminal Mulehaus makes a reappearance in this story in partnership with a feminine fugitive. As with Post's other women of the criminal class, this one too has charm and class, but, again like the others, is tagged by the author with the most unfortunate name of "Hustling Anne."

"The Spread Rails," a story of only mixed quality, was admitted to the collection under the pretense (according to the first three sentences) that it was told at a dinner party in the St. James's residence of Sir Henry Marquis. No literary benefit is gained by this addition. Yet, the story deserves some attention for other reasons.

Under pressure to fit the story in, Post made an oversight that weakens a story already poorly-organized according to his usual standards. The tale is told, according to the third sentence, by Lisa Lewis, an American Ambassadress. The narrative is presented in the first person, but the narrator is addressed by the heroine at one point early in the piece as "Sarah," then only later near the end as "Lisa." Not being presented with any other reason to explain the conflict in names, one must assume it to be an example of faulty editing by the author. This is the most obvious sign of carelessness on the part of Post in putting this particular book together.

"The Spread Rails" as a short story is surely much longer than it need be. A long passage, for example, is devoted to an awkward and somewhat unrealistic discussion of abstract matters between the track boss of a railroad and a woman student of law. At this point a reader looking for entertainment would not likely continue reading, or if he did, would not likely be entertained. But once the reader reaches the conclusion, it appears a well-handled surprise. This story proves fair the criticism that had Post put more time and effort into some of his work, it would have been much more effective and worthy of consideration. In allowing this story to be published as it was, he opened himself unneedfully to such criticism—which frequently put him aside without consideration of his good work.

"The Pumpkin Coach" is another of the tales unreasonably forced upon Sir Henry Marquis. Published first in *Hearst's Magazine* in 1916, it appears to have been written much earlier; in fact it compares closely on many points with another early story which was called "The Fairy Godmother" and which became a part of Post's *The Nameless Thing* in 1912. In both pieces there is a frustrated woman seeking to secure justice for an innocent loved one, and both secure aid from a strange woman. Also, in each case a nephew of the victim proves to be the real thief and killer, being unmasked in the courtroom with the stolen property hidden in his coat. Unfortunately the characters are not well-drawn, the plot not compelling, and the ending not a real surprise. Other than for the acidy comments Post makes here regarding the legal profession and the courts, the story contains little to arouse any unusual attention.

There are several weak instances in "The Yellow Flower," but overall this story is interesting and readable, if not one of Post's more successful tales. The important action is revealed mostly through the dialogue. The tale thus moves slowly, and the twist to the plot, sharp as it is, does not redeem the melodramatic conclusion. The characters are unusual persons, each in a special way, but related through a tangle of unusual circumstances. An air of mystery and suspense is sensed, but not fully exploited as it might have been.

In "A Satire of the Sea" Post has written one of his better stories, and it follows closely his precise guidelines for a successful short story. St. Alban, an Englishman around whom the story centers, finds himself a hero by default. His heroic image is due to a gallant incident in the course of World War I. The ironic St. Alban had replied boldly to a German submarine commander who had threatened a hospital ship crossing the English Channel. His brave and distinguished words were, " 'Don't threaten, fire if you like!' " Sir Alban's self-inflicted death, a quietly-kept secret, therefore presents an unusual mystery.

The explanation for St. Alban's quiet despair is made clear to the narrator in suspenseful steps by Sir Henry Marquis. He reveals the secret details of how the people's hero was in truth an utter failure, a victim of the very thing he had been assigned to keep from occurring. That which he had worked so efficiently to prevent others from doing, he had done unwittingly himself. Post, who looked to the Greek tragedies as ideal plots, found here a fitting tragic incident to match them. A favorite quotation of Post is injected in this story as Sir Henry Marquis comments: " 'Man is altogether the sport of fortune!' I read that in Herodotus, in a form at Rugby. . . ." A short story published first in 1911 had been titled "The Sport of Fortune," and in an article written in 1924 on John W. Davis, the unsuccessful presidential candidate, the quotation is used again. This is a theme running in and out of Post's work from the first to the last, sometimes stated, sometimes suggested. To have been repeated so often, Post must have believed this statement quite sincerely.

"A Satire by the Sea," while not generally recognized as the excellent short story which it is, surely deserves more attention than it has received. This is also true of the next and final story of this collection. "The House by the Loch," while it lacks the tragic element of the tale preceding it, is made excellent by Post's masterly ability to create an atmosphere of suspense and mystery and combine it with a strange plot that is revealed only at the end with a sharp twist. The scene is set in Scotland, bleak and fogbound, complete with a foreboding house and unusual characters. The narrator, a young American visiting Great Britain, looks up an eccentric uncle whose hobby appears to be the impossible one of casting a special form of Buddha. The plot unfolds slowly and smoothly, the ending being an unexpected conclusion that should catch the reader off guard.

As a whole this collection of stories should not be accorded any special acclaim, for the quality of the whole is not equal to Post's best work. Only several of the tales presented here can be said to have any real worth as literature. The air of mystery, the feeling of suspense, and the surprise endings are used consistently throughout these stories, usually with the technical skill that so many have praised in reviewing Post's work, but the principal flaw seems to be that in nearly all these pieces the mechanics are too obviously exposed. In *The Sleuth of St. James's Square* the criticism of Post's work that is most frequently repeated and most justified certainly applies, that had he given a little more attention to art and a little less to technique, his worth as a writer would have been greatly enhanced.

3. Monsieur Jonquelle

The collection of twelve stories issued in 1923 under the title *Monsieur Jonquelle, Prefect of Police of Paris*, is in several ways next in quality to *Uncle Abner* among the books of Melville Davisson Post. These stories, most of which are principally concerned with the activities of a shrewd French detective, are of a moderately uniform quality throughout the book. The plots, with few exceptions, are well contrived with paradoxical features that contribute to the suspense element, and most skillfully conclude with a catchy twist or surprise ending.

While there are some minor similarities, M. Jonquelle cannot be considered as unique a character as Abner. Both are shrewd, both humane, both incorruptible, but in the rural American we feel these qualities more intensely. The Frenchman, being the head of a police department in one of the world's most outstanding cities, must necessarily be an exceptional person, a thorough cosmopolitan with qualities above average and with outstanding powers of investigation at his command. We must accept him immediately as such and Post does not try to make him anything more—thus as a character he lacks the distinctiveness of the backwoods amateur. This lack of individuality reduces his impact upon the reader and suggests one reason to rate the book of secondary importance.

At times M. Jonquelle's riddle-like method of questioning a suspect reminds us of Abner's ambiguous and indirect probing for facts, but too infrequently. Although the two characters share somewhat similar basic philosophies regarding the inability of a criminal to commit a crime which cannot be detected, a theory which is actually a favorite of the author, M. Jonquelle's philosophy ends far short of Abner's unshakeable belief in the Providence of God.

Another obvious reason for considering this collection of secondary quality is the continual shifting of viewpoint. While this is of no harm to the tales considered individually, it gives the book a somewhat uneven pattern. Unlike the *Uncle Abner* work wherein all the stories are first person narrations by the nephew, Martin, these stories use both first person and third person viewpoints. Also the narrators are several and often we are not sure of the narrator's identity. To ignore this disturbing quality in reading the stories as a collection requires some extra effort by the reader.[1]

While the *M. Jonquelle* collection appeared nearly three years later than *The Sleuth of St. James's Square*, several of the stories featuring the Frenchman ("Found in the Fog," "The Alien Corn," "The Ruined Eye," and "The Haunted Door") predate any of the stories written around the British sleuth. Records indicate Post created M. Jonquelle during the early years of the peak of his career, about two years after the first Abner tale appeared. Thereafter for several years Post switched regularly between his two heroes as the mood struck or the circumstances dictated.

There is no one outstanding story in the collection, but all are entertaining and most are intriguing. This is perhaps the best description for the opening story of the collection, "The Great Cipher." Appearing archaic and unsophisticated in many respects to the literature of today, it nevertheless strongly resembles one type of science fiction currently popular, the distortions of the disorientated mind.

The narrative frame into which "The Great Cipher" is set is

worthy of special notice. Its outer frame is that of an unidentified third person reporting a conversation of M. Jonquelle's taking place on "the southern portico of the Executive Mansion" with an unnamed President of the United States. From Post's description of the voice and manner we readily assume the President to be Theodore Roosevelt. The scene is perhaps descriptive of an audience Post himself reportedly had with the famed, adventure-loving President. Although M. Jonquelle is telling the tale in Washington, D. C., the story he tells takes place "in the great wilderness of Central Africa, a little north of the Congo." This inner tale is also narrated in the third person since the French detective's personal involvement is also merely that of narrator. The author, thus twice removed from the central adventure, can stretch his imagination as far as he might dare—and Post does skillfully. The story is well-paced in carefully thought-out steps, moving smoothly to a logical but unobvious conclusion. Well-received by its first critics, it perhaps deserves a bit more attention than it has been given.[2]

Air pollution greets M. Jonquelle on his visit to London in the second tale, "Found in the Fog." " 'Diable!' he commented . . . 'these Britons have lungs of brass.' "[3] Nevertheless, the thick fog does not cloud his mind or handicap him in any manner. In fact he has the case already solved and he merely needs to trap the suspect. Much like a confident spider he weaves a seemingly delicate but inescapable net around the object of his search. His parting remark at the conclusion, couched in a point of law, reveals his crafty success.

"The Alien Corn," next in the book, concerns an artless romance heightened with intense descriptions of a Riviera carnival season. The tale is related as a first person experience by an aide-de-camp of the French detective's staff. The naive young man parts from M. Jonquelle with instructions to enjoy a holiday in Nice. Soon he finds himself involved in an infatuation and later is an unsuspecting foil for those very criminals that M. Jonquelle is pursuing. At the end the criminals, the fascinating young woman, and her conniving father escape, much to the relief of the aide-de-camp and to the perplexity of the Prefect of Police of Paris.

"The Ruined Eye," in spite of its trick ending and its concentration on the shrewd talents of M. Jonquelle, is one of the weaker stories in the collection. The plot, obviously contrived, struggles to a quick, easily-anticipated conclusion.

Although far from being among the best of Post's work, the fifth tale, "The Haunted Door," is a more unusual and suspenseful story. Set in the twilight months before World War I, its plot, concerned with espionage activities, keeps its secret until the final scene. With its interplay of normal activities and violence, hinted at instead of openly displayed, it resembles the subtle, wit-disturbing form of spy tale rather than the flashy, unrealistic and melodramatic type that passes for contemporary espionage fiction.

"Blücher's March," the next in order, also uses espionage as a basis for its plot. It rates well in its use of the elements of suspense, and it includes a burst of action near the conclusion. The story involves a bird which whistles a military tune belonging to the enemy and an American meatpacker who proves to be the spy in addition to being a former Junker Lieutenant. The tale can be recommended as intriguing entertainment only. In both of these spy stories, M. Jonquelle keeps his identity a secret until the closing sentence.

In several of his stories, Post has plotted variously around the suggestion that certain ferocious members of the Parisian underworld were of unusual value to France during the 1914-1918 struggle with Germany. In "The Woman on the Terrace," an average story kept interesting by the twists in the plot, the heroine prevents an economic disaster for her country by destroying the work of a counterfeitor. Her secret is her underworld connections. Once again the villain has an American background with pointedly German sympathies. M. Jonquelle displays his shrewdness well in this tale.

The eighth story of the collection, "The Triangular Hypothesis," presents M. Jonquelle unravelling the mysterious death of an alien. The plot revolves around a foreign envoy's attempt to collect an idemnity for the apparently murdered man. It is well put together with elements of suspense and indirection. The French detective performs effectively and the reader is led to a rewarding surprise ending.

"The Problem of the Five Marks" is among the more entertaining and colorful stories woven around M. Jonquelle. It is narrated as a first person adventure by a young American who has come to aid the Frenchman investigating the death of an aunt. Although a graduate of Harvard, the American is naive and a complete romantic. M. Jonquelle takes him to Ostend, Belgium, and leaves him. Later, the detective is observed secretly working in the background as the youth "discovers" an attractive "exiled Russian" girl and her father. The youth, whose head is clouded with visions of a story-book romance, ends up, as M. Jonquelle had planned, an unsuspecting dupe for his new acquaintances. The story comes to a surprise conclusion in the deceased aunt's house in Paris. With the recovery of a valuable necklace, the French detective steps out of the shadows and reveals the intrigue operated by a French criminal in partnership with an American actress from the *Folies Bergères*.

The technique of "The Problem of the Five Marks" is perhaps overly smooth, although Post effectively bridges the coincidental features with great skill. Post in most of his work avoids any hint of sexual experiences, but in this and several other stories of this collection he touches the subject briefly but timidly. This particular story being almost wholly an amusement might not withstand closer examination, but it does serve to draw our attention to this facet of Post which was buried under an almost Victorian attitude in most of his writings.

The next two stories are written as third person narratives. The first, "The Man with Steel Fingers," has good dramatic action and portrays the French detective as a man with shrewd abilities, but the plot produces some unsolved questions. At the end we learn that M. Jonquelle had been present at the scene shortly before the murder. Why then did he not learn of the victim's death? He had vital information. Why did he not know of the trial and offer his testimony? The trial was newsworthy and would have received ample publicity. Does he delay and wait to trap the murderer only as a convenience for the author? Such defects are death to a mystery story and do nothing to enhance the character of the hero detective.

"The Mottled Butterfly," the next story, is not only a more carefully-written and better-plotted story, it also has touches of life-like color. M. Jonquelle not only appears as a crafty, versatile member of his profession, but he shows a knowledge of human nature and an appreciation of its entanglements. "The Mottled Butterfly" takes its name from the orchids in the bouquet in which the detective discovers the conclusive evidence that proves his theory of the crime. It also might apply secondarily to the character of the playboy figure who supplied the flowers. Post's surprise ending in this story is one of his most effective.

The final story of the collection, "The Girl with the Ruby," is a first person narration by M. Jonquelle, but his only active part in the piece is acting as reporter of a story told him by a Russian exile living in France. It was told to explain why the Russian has chosen to marry a woman of wealth and social standing, but with little beauty. The tale told by the Russian details an experience with synthetic rubies, a beautiful and innocent appearing young girl, and her "secret." At the end we discover the girl, who leaves such a vivid impression on the Russian, is a member of a notorious band of French criminals. This is a commonplace twist which Post uses often and sometimes with skill, as here when he ties it to the unique conclusion which explains a Russian romantic's marriage.

This collection, whatever its faults, and they are several, does much to explain the popularity Post enjoyed in his peak years as a writer of magazine fiction. As entertainment these stories, when they succeed, succeed principally because the author was a master of technique. Each story presents a surprise solution. Post does this while practicing a most economical use of language and while including perfectly chosen touches of color. If these alone were their only qualities, they could fall forgotten along with ten thousand other stories, but Post has put his mark upon these tales, a quality that is difficult to analyze other than to say that he has added to them something of his own personality in giving them their final shape. Whether or not this allows them sufficient literary quality to deserve continued attention, it does furnish them with an individual character, something lacking in the greater number of their kind.

4. Walker of the Secret Service

Melville Davisson Post had created an efficient, shrewd French sleuth in the person of Monsieur Jonquelle and had attempted the same with the shadowy British detective, Sir Henry

Marquis. His patriotism perhaps at a high pitch due to World War I, Post sought to create an American master of criminal investigation in the person of Captain Walker, chief of the United States Secret Service. Hardly equalling the efficiency claimed for him and seldom emerging from the background, Walker never seemed to attain the status the author had likely envisioned for him.

The American Secret Service Chief made his initial appearance in a 1919 *Saturday Evening Post* story titled "The Five Thousand Dollar Reward," the author's only story ever to earn him an O'Henry Memorial Award.[1] Walker's first literary adventure did not flatter him as a professional manhunter, but for Post it was a worthy achievement in that it is one of the few stories he wrote with successful comic overtones, intended or not.

During the next two years Walker appeared in three more stories, "The Girl in the Picture," "The Inspiration," and "The Diamond"—hardly enough material to justify a collection. But Post was at the peak of his career, and the public was buying his books. Thus when the demand for another collection arose, the Chief of the United States Secret Service was awarded a starring role. This was managed by means of a bit of literary legerdemain. Post united an uninspired assortment of weak materials with the several existent Walker stories. Although as a whole the book proves to be unsatisfactory, some of the stories are well-written and interesting when considered individually.

The book consists of thirteen "chapters" or stories. Of these, the first six have a relationship apart from the remainder and form an introductory section. These first six have a continuity resembling a novel-like story, although each depicts a separate incident. Unfortunately, this group is of poor quality compared to the author's better writing. These pieces, while conversational in tone, suffer from a lack of actual dialogue to enliven their dramatic passages. Their one interesting characteristic, a singular virtue, is their clipped, economic, objective prose, related to and perhaps an inspiration for some of the "tough-guy" prose that was soon to win popular attention, first in detective stories and eventually in nearly all popular literary offerings. Admittedly Post's chapters here are primitive examples; nevertheless they clearly point in the direction of the development of that style.

Post, who possibly wrote these first six parts with another

objective in mind, had tentatively titled the project "Incidents in the Career of a Train Robber."[2] None of these parts saw serial publication. Strangely, the first-person narrator is never once identified by name, a problem Post rather laconically sought to solve by adding an explanatory paragraph at the end of number VI, which says:

> And so came Walker into the United States Secret Service. The story of his way upward in that service is not written out here. If you wish to hear it ask his charming wife whose memories go back to the time when the big tent of a circus was the Kingdom of Romance. But you find in the chapters to follow, some adventures in mystery with which he was connected.[3]

While the introduction of Walker, a Captain of the United States Secret Service, as a former train robber, allowed Post to use some otherwise unused and unrelated materials, it also proved to be the factor which brought about a distasteful libel suit against the publisher.[4]

This introductory material admittedly gives Walker an unusual background for an expert secret service detective, one combining toughness and inside knowledge of criminal methods—but Post fails to use this background to any real advantage. In the first piece, "The Outlaw," the narrator (who we only learn later to be Walker) is from the very start presented as a rather naive person, even for an ordinary young man; thus he seems hardly choice raw material for a future super-sleuth. Later at one point he pictures himself thus: "I must have presented a ridiculous appearance, a big overgrown boy as uneasy as though he were being photographed for his mother."[5] In similarly simple, almost etched prose, Post allows the narrator to describe his initiation into the art of train robbery.

Walker having left home visits a circus and there meets up with Mooney, the chief plotter of the robberies, and White, a partner. The planning and execution of Walker's first criminal venture is outlined here step by step. Young Walker, without protesting, accepts $20.00 for his share, after Mooney falsely explains that they failed to get the loot they had hoped to find. Impressed with the powerful youth's unquestioning performance, Mooney invites him to meet the circus again at the next town.

At the beginning of "The Holdup," the second adventure, the youth obtains a job caring for the circus' horses and discovers a pretty girl who rides in the show.[6] The next robbery, executed several days later, is a thoroughly-planned, complex performance for the trio. Dressed as trainmen during their escape, Mooney drives the getaway car containing himself, White, and young Walker into a group forming a posse and coolly directs it off in an opposite direction.

The third robbery finds the trio newly-disguised. It is now obvious that Mooney plans each crime minutely. Described under the title "The Bloodhounds" we learn how Mooney with Walker enters an express car and skillfully blows a safe to obtain the loot. This is then passed to White, disguised as a passenger, through an exchange of pieces of luggage. Mooney and Walker are quickly pursued. Mooney avoids the pursuing bloodhounds by applying turpentine onto his and Walker's shoes and clothing. Their escape route proves successful, although it presents some difficulties and allows some close brushes with the lawmen in pursuit.

The section titled "The Secret Agent" displays fully Mooney's daring and genius as a criminal. Posing as a secret agent of the Federal government, he is allowed to guard the safe in an express car. Undisturbed, he manages to pilfer the contents. His strict demands made to the local authorities that everything be kept absolutely secret is followed to the letter and the trio depart unpursued.

In "The Big Haul," the fifth adventure, the trio pick up a loot of $102,000 in unsigned bank notes.[7] These, with rubber-stamped signatures, bring about the trio's downfall as the series numbers are traced. As they split up, the narrator is given only $500 as his share and is sent back to the circus, accepting Mooney's explanation that the loot was worthless. Mooney and White divide the remainder and go different ways, but White is soon captured. White's capture, escape, and recapture are detailed here and his fate sealed finally with a sentence of twenty-five years.

In the last of the six related parts the chief instigator's fate is revealed under the title "The Passing of Mooney." Mooney, trapped between a fatal struggle with pneumonia and recognition by a former victim, surrenders to the law officials as he dies. His downfall and White's as noted by the narrator, is reminiscent of Post's often used Providence-of-God theme. The narrator says: "A strange fatality seemed to follow White and Mooney . . . something they seemed unable to anticipate. . . ."[8] This factor is later explained to the narrator by a Federal agent, who states: " 'The thing is so certain to happen that it seems to look as though there were a power in the universe determined on the maintenance of justice. . . .' "[9] But the narrator's fate is saved by the intervention of the young circus girl's guardian, the old woman. She comes into possession of Mooney's share of the loot, and offers it to the government in exchange for allowing the narrator a chance to redeem himself. Thus, the narrator, though then an untried and naive youth, is offered an opportunity with the Secret Service, and Walker's future according to Post is set for the remaining adventures of the book.

Of the remaining seven pieces in the book, three, "The Diamond," "The Inspiration," and "The Girl in the Picture," originally appeared with Walker in an active detective role. The other four stories were "attached" to the collection rather haphazardly with no apparent reason other than to increase the volume's size. "The Symbol" gives Walker only an insignificant walk-on role, while "The Expert Detective," "The Mysterious Stranger Defense," and "The Menace" are loosely related to Walker, who takes no active part in them.

"The Diamond" resulted perhaps from the author's interest in the precious gems. The diamond was Post's birthstone, and he became a fond collector of these stones, developing also a skilled interest in the various facets that add to their charm. The story is told by an unnamed person interested in such gems. The narrator, having a synthetic gem he wants examined by an expert jeweler, witnesses a transaction involving a suspicious character who is accompanied by a young girl. Later, when Walker arrives, he hears what has occurred and along with the narrator commands a taxi to Grand Central Station. Quickly and shrewdly devising his attack, Walker borrows the narrator's fake stone and creates an incident which allows him to identify the suspect as a known forger. He signals for the arrest of the forger and the girl. The girl, we learn, had stolen blank bank drafts and letterheads, then accompanied the suspect to the jeweler's store for her award of a $5,000 ring. Post uses this simple plot well to make an interesting story, one of the more successful concerning Walker inasmuch as it displays him as an efficient investigator equal to his high ranking title.

The next stories, "The Expert Detective" and "The Mysterious Stranger Defense," are introduced in a specially-constructed opening paragraph which explains their inclusion in the collection. The stories are selected by Walker to illustrate two detective types, the "professional" detective and the amateur. They actually prove little other than what any specific ficticious instance would prove—even should we choose to believe Post adapted them from true cases as he often did in practice.

"The Expert Detective" is a good but minor courtroom drama in which a crafty defense lawyer praises the detective in the case for his skill, then suddenly, after seemingly throwing his case away in face of that investigator's expert testimony, proves the detective the real criminal and reveals the stolen money hidden in the man's clothing.

There is a twist of sorts also at the end of "The Mysterious Stranger Defense." This tale evolves around a common trial defense technique of weakening the State's case, then turning suspicion for the crime upon an unknown person. The woman defendant is freed as her attorney succeeds in both measures in a smooth, subtle fashion—but we learn at the end that his success was possible principally because he had arrived immediately on the scene of the murder along with the chief of police and had skillfully managed to hide important evidence.

Most likely it was because of Post's fascination with England's drawing room society that he sent his Chief of the U. S. Secret Service across the Atlantic for the next two stories of the collection. "The Inspiration" finds Walker playing the role of a soft-shoe cupid. To the young Englishman who seeks Walker's aid in saving a girl from a dishonest explorer and his scheme, Walker pleads that his only advantage over the "superior intelligence of Scotland Yard" could come from an inspiration. Walker's lukewarm inspiration does arrive in the form of an unfrozen bottle of ink used by the pseudo-explorer to have a guardianship request witnessed by members of his expedition. The still usable ink supposedly had been conveniently available beside the deeply-frozen body of the girl's father at a sub-zero Antarctic death site. Whatever their initial capacity, such plots have lost their power to shock later readers.

"The Girl in the Picture" finds Walker at an English country estate where a fugitive he had sought for the theft of bonds in Washington is found dying of tuberculosis. The shrewd criminal reveals an unusual story of "saving" a young girl from her undesirable marriage for financial reasons. The narration occurs in England, but the principal events leading up to the story occurred at Bar Harbor, Maine. Post himself had spent many a fashionable season there. It was there the criminal hid out, supposedly only to become impressed by some of the members of the elite society that gathered there, particularly the troubled girl. His method of preventing the mercenary marriage is accomplished both through his criminal skills and his strange alliance with "religion." Post has worked some comments on religion into this story by casting their entry in a humorous tone, obscuring the obvious sincerity he expresses. One interesting passage has the hardened professional criminal telling Walker:

> ". . . I limped down to the fashionable church. . . .
> "You see I had to have a little help on this job. It had a big loose end.
> "I went in and sat down in a pew. It was dim and quiet and I went right down to business. I didn't run in any of the prayer-book curtain-raisers. I put the thing right up to the boss.
> " 'Now, look here, Governor,' I said, 'has a helpless little girl got a pull with you, or is it bunk? Because I'm a-goin' to call you, and if the line your barkers are putting out is on the level, you've got to come across with the goods. If there's nothing to it, the Government ought to shut 'em up on a fraud order—I'm a-goin' to carry one end of this thing; get busy at the other end!' "[10]

The petitioner's reliance on Uncle Abner's *Providence* works in spite of his bare, brutish language—while the author, disguised as a sentimental master criminal, reveals his impatience with the pomp of formal religion. Whatever else it might prove, it is a typical Post story told in a uinque manner with a surprise ending.

The last two stories of the collection also exhibit unusual

moral and religious overtones such as are often noticeable in Post's work in the years following the death of his wife. Published first as "The Man Who Threatened the World," the first of these was introduced into the Walker collection with the shorter, more realistic title, "The Menace." It can be numbered among those stories that illustrate the author's keen insight into human nature—its foibles and its triumphs.

It is adapted to the collection in an opening passage that describes it as a magazine story suppressed from distribution by Walker and his department in the interest of the Prohibition Amendment. Its narrator is unidentified. The story is not a detective story but a trick-ending mystery which is both crafty and entertaining. It concerns a wealthy, frustrated former distiller who seeks revenge for the act of the people that put him out of business. He boasts: "This country's goin' to hell, an' I'm goin' to give it a shove along." He soon learns of a fantastic elixir from a chemist who turns out to be an apparition. This concentrate reproduces the taste and reactions of a coveted distilled liquor, but has wrecking side effects in that it suppresses all the finer desires of human beings, including love. Post gave the reader of the 1920's a brief prediction of things to come as he describes the manufacture of the substance, simple to produce in a clay pipe from a common weed seed and purified with the help of a fungus culture as available as bread mold. Little wonder such a "revelation" would need to be repressed by the government. Fortunely revenge is subdued by love and all ends well.

The final story of the collection displays Post's talent at its best. Having a Christmas setting, the story concerns an unusual crucifix, from which is derived the title, "The Symbol." Walker's part in the story is an outside one, his presence and status made known early in preparation for his slender last minute appearance and moment of heroic action. The story is actually a story within a story, a favorite device of the author. It moves from the Christmas Eve setting back to an incident growing out of the Boxer Rebellion of China. Carefully constructing his story with the help of a pair of unsavory but useful characters, Post fills out the piece with interesting facts, sidelights, opinions, descriptions, and an occasional leering remark that set the story far above the material used to open this collection. It is a story which must be read to be appreciated, both for its entertainment value and its technical superiority.

Prophetically, in the opening paragraph of this last Walker story, the chief female character receives a telegram reporting on a decision by a United States Circuit Court of Appeals, revealing what were for her the unhappy words of "reversed and dismissed." However, in regard to the libel suit which this book brought about a short time later, these proved to be happy words for Post and his publisher.

VI. THE NOVELETTES

1. The Mountain School-Teacher

Although seemingly a minor point, it might prove profitable to consider why in writing this story, Melville Davisson Post placed an inconspicuous hyphen between "school" and "teacher." Almost without exception, those who have made reference to this book have neglected to include the hyphen. We are not sure just why Post used this hyphen, whether out of habit[1] or for a shade of difference in meaning—whatever the reason, it is there. In *The Mountain School-Teacher* we have an intended work of art, a model of simplicity and economy, whatever else it's worth. Taken as a whole the book does not seem to contain a word more or less than the author needed—each seemingly selected with care. We do not know precisely how much time Post spent writing this story; perhaps the economy of language and the smoothly flowing, simple prose came as a result of practice alone. We are aware though that he prepared himself well for the task by examining many books related to the subject.[2] Therefore he must have been engaged with the preliminary work over a lengthy period before he wrote the first word of his story. Surely he gave thought to the use of the hyphen in his title.[3]

The Mountain School-Teacher was, in a public sense, an unusual book to come from the pen of a "detective" story author. To classify Post as such was, of course, a convenience. The truer picture shows that even his best detective tales cannot really be labeled "detective" stories without distorting the definition of the term or limiting the evaluation of the work. This book, different though it seems from everything else the author wrote should not have come as a complete surprise to anyone familiar with the exceptional variety found in Post's work up to this point. The book is not so much an exception as it is an outgrowth of what preceded it.

The term "allegory" was immediately applied to this story upon its publication, and in almost every mention of the work since that time it has been conveniently repeated. If we use a very simple and inclusive definition, such as: "An allegory is the description of one thing under the likeness of another," then the terminology fits. More accurately what we have is a selective rendering of the Gospel story transferred in time to an Appalachian community.

There shall always be some question as to why Post wrote a work of this nature. Yet this should not pose a problem for the serious reader of Post, for in nearly everything he wrote there is an indication that he was truly concerned with the problem of man's relationship to the idea of God. As we have noted elsewhere, Post's religious outlook had by 1922 come full circle. Raised and influenced from infancy by Christian parents, from his college years through his early years of professional writing he progressed from near agnosticism to a mystical paganism, then from a concern with the religion of the Old Testament prophets gradually back to a consideration of the ideas of Christianity. That Post would have found a certain consolation in Christianity in his later years is understandable, for although he knew considerable financial and professional success, life had not been easy for him. We may note the indications of a disappointment in romance, the breakdown in health in the midst of his apparent success as lawyer and writer, the early death of his only child, the death of his beloved wife, and the keen insight he had into the accelerating and uncomfortable pace of change in the world all about him. All these were things that directed his thinking.

But we must not be led to think, as many incidental critics do, that this story, which recasts in modern terms incidents from the Gospels regarding Christ, is just a simple retelling of the happenings. Post's religion was not orthodox or formal in any real theological sense—it was individualized much as that of Thomas Jefferson. This story is in a certain sense a partial summation of what Post's beliefs were. Beyond this, it is a social-religious comment upon the men and institutions which have insistently claimed that they have stood for the Christian concepts. And it is, in many ways, a bitter comment.

In this simple tale we find some harsh criticisms of the institutions of law, medicine, and the church. These are obvious targets, open to easy criticism, but we feel as we learn about the author that they also may have been personal targets to some extent. Everyone will not agree with Post's comments, but the reader can accept them or disregard them in the light of his own experience. Certainly there is much truth in them. To the student of Post these reflections on society and religion provide additional evidence of the author's keen ability to sense the diseased areas of our civilization. Aristocratic in his origin, Post nevertheless could not ignore the obvious injustices which confronted his sensitive nature.

Some specific points should be noted in Post's tale of Christ's reappearance in an Appalachian community. Summarizing these points we can arrive at a fairly accurate estimate of the author's conception of the historical figure of Christ and what he means to humanity. We can begin by noting that Post does not refer to the birth story and its mythical overtones. The mountain School-teacher, when he comes into the community where he will teach, is a young adult. He looks fit, youthful, and unblemished. There is no mention or concern for his origin. He comes into the story ready and prepared for his task.

Tracking through a nearly overgrown path on the mountainside, the School-teacher meets and aids a small boy. David had been taking a sack of corn to the mill by ox when the sack had slipped off and he could not lift it back across the animal. The School-teacher helps him out of his difficulty and accompanies him to the mill. We note the *immediate* trust the boy has in the stranger. The mill's operator is a husbandless middle-aged woman with a small daughter. When she discovers the School-teacher has arrived she says that they had looked for him the day before. "Somethin' kept you back, I s'pose." "Yes," is his simple reply. She then tells him the big boys and girls will be busy at work, all he can expect at the school are the small children. "I would rather have the little children," he replies. As she serves him supper she learns that he will stay at Nicholas Parks' house. The woman is amazed, for ". . . ole Nicholas . . . He's the meanest man that ever drawed the breath of life!" The newcomer leaves for the schoolhouse, where later that night Martha, the woman's daughter, notices lights "like they went up an' down through the tree tops." "I suppose he's carryin' water down from the spring on the mountain," the woman replies. Up to this point we have had many hints but no conclusive evidence of the School-teacher's *real* identity.

There are several points that Post has emphasized. The School-teacher is a healthy, unblemished man who is fond of children, a man to whom children are attracted. His origin is a mystery, for we know nothing of it. He had been expected sooner than he had come. The "grown" children are too busy at their work to attend to his lessons. He is going to have something to do with "ole Nicholas Parks" (Old Nick?) who represents his opposite. And we see that the child beholds something mystic in the moving lights up on the mountain, but the mother sees only the practical explanation. Having given us nothing more than this, Post continues with his story.

The next morning at sunrise the miller learns from the local doctor that "ole Nicholas" has died during the night. The woman wonders why the doctor went out to see Nicholas for he would not have expected to be paid. The doctor replies, "If he didn't pay me, I wouldn't go. . . . I've quit bringin' 'em in or seein' 'em out unless I get the cash in my hand." The doctor also explains that the old man has left everything to the new teacher. When the woman next goes up to the house for the funeral, she finds the men waiting for the preacher. The grave has already been dug, apparently by the young stranger. The preacher, a tall man with one eye nearly blind, arrives to learn that the School-teacher is up at the house. The preacher is surprised and says frankly, "I didn't know the new School-teacher had come."

The two children, David and Martha, stay close to the School-teacher as the preacher conducts the burial. Then the preacher approaches the School-teacher, asking, "Do you think that you are old enough to teach the children the fear of God?" The School-teacher's reply is, "I shall not teach them the fear of God." Then looking at the preacher's face, he adds, "Isn't there something growing over your eye?"

Another day arrives and the School-teacher, now living in the house of the recently-deceased Nicholas Parks, sets out for the schoolhouse. At a spring, he meets a woman who has a two year old boy and a dog. The woman, after some conversation with the new School-teacher, entrusts her son to the teacher's care when the boy asks to go with the man who shows such an interest in children. The woman gives them both some lunch and they leave. When they come to a stream, the little boy stops, unsure of how they can cross it. The dog, who has also come along, swims across. The child loses his fear, and the crossing is made in safety. As they cross, the child notes that the dog walks in the water. Post does not say how the School-teacher crosses. Perhaps it is from stone to stone, perhaps by means of a successful jump clearing the stream; or, as the author leaves it open to our opinion, perhaps he walks across the water, while the dog, as the child remarks, walks *in* the water.

Next, as the children of the school are playing games in the schoolyard, they see a young couple they recognize coming along the road. The young man has his arm in a sling as the result of an injury he received when chopping trees to clear a field. The school children are sent into the building and the School-teacher talks with the couple. The woman discloses that they have only five dollars to pay the doctor who will do nothing unless he is paid in advance. The School-teacher tells her not to worry. What happens next is best told in the author's own words:

> He went over to the man. What the School-teacher did precisely, these persons were never afterward able to describe. The event in their minds seems clouded in mystery. A wonder had been accomplished in the road, in the sun, in the light before them, but they could not lay hold upon

the sequence of the detail. The voice of the School-teacher presently reached them as from a distance.

"It's all right now," he said.[4]

We have, to this point, seen the School-teacher do several unusual things. He has replaced old Nicholas Parks in the community. The husbandless women find him consoling and helpful, and they trust him although he is a complete stranger. He answers frankly the man who represents God in the community, telling him he will not teach the children to fear God. Then, looking directly at this preacher, he informs him that he has limited vision. Also, he "demonstrates" faith, the faith the little two year old child has in him. Then he performs what seems to a young couple a miracle as he restores the young man's arm to usefulness almost instantly.

In the next chapter, following his day in the school, the School-teacher meets two men approaching him along the road. They are riding in a buckboard pulled by a gaunt, tired horse. One is a black-bearded man, the other a big hump-shouldered man. The latter queries the School-teacher about his right to the Parks property. The newcomer says it belongs to his father. The man on the buckboard contends the land belongs to the state and says to the School-teacher, " 'So you can make up your mind to get off.' " The School-teacher watches them leave, his face filled with misery.

Another day brings a new event. Along the road the School-teacher hears a woman approaching, singing a sensuous tune. She is young and buxom, and she walks with a swagger. Her hair is yellow and smells of cheap perfume, and earrings hang from her ear lobes. Her lips are deeply-colored from eating wild grapes, her face whitened with powder, her clothing vividly colored. The author has not needed to use the term; we know along with the School-teacher that she is a harlot. Seeing the School-teacher she stops as though stricken and apparently recognizes his "real" identity. He refers to her as "poor child!" She runs off. That night on returning to his place he eats supper and sits awake all of the night before the fireplace. Post tells us, "He sat in the fantastic glow of the fire with its agony on him." Near morning he hears a sound and finds that the young woman has returned after discarding her cheap symbols of harlotry.

In the next episode the children have put their meager resources together and secured the School-teacher a hat. This hat is a difficult symbol which Post weaves effectively into the story. Its meaning is definitely abstract, not explained at any point and never made clearer than in these lines from the book:

> . . . From the day that he received it, he had never ceased to express his appreciation of it. He continued always to regard it, as if in it were merged, as in a symbol, all the little sacrifices of every child, and all the love that had strengthened each one to bear what the thing cost him.[5]

The School-teacher admires the hat with the greatest of pleasure and the children are very proud of it—handling it they have left on it their tiny finger marks. The preacher, learning of this gift, is appalled and at once goes to see the School-teacher. There he charges that it proves the School-teacher unfit to teach the children.

Jerry Black is the recipient of the next "miracle." His eye has been bothering him since the thrashing of the wheat, and he has been waiting for the doctor. When the doctor does come he finds the man's ailment cured by the School-teacher. The doctor asked, " 'Now how do you suppose he done it?' " The answer follows:

> "I don't suppose how he done it," replied the doctor . . . "I know how he done it. Ole Jerry got a wheat husk in that eye when he was thrashing, and it stuck against the lid back of the ball. The fools that looked into his eye by pushing the lid up couldn't see it. But when anybody come along with sense enough to turn the lid back he got the husk out and the eye got well."[6]

This logical explanation is followed by the doctor's statement that the shoulder joint of the young man's arm, which the School-teacher had healed earlier, had only been dislocated. Then the miller asks if the doctor has ever seen the dead returned to life. She goes on to explain how the little two year old boy had fallen into the millrace and from all appearances had drowned. While she had run about in panic, the School-teacher somehow restored the child's vital functions. There is no mention of the use of any of the usual methods of resuscitation nor is there any definite statement that the School-teacher did not use such a technique. The doctor says only that the miller is a fool if she believes in such an event as the raising of the dead.

The School-teacher's performances are explainable in two ways. Whether or not they are "miracles" is dependent upon the viewpoint of the witness. Perhaps they seem miraculous to the person unskilled in the knowledge needed to perform them or too emotional to observe what actually occurs. To others they are not necessarily supernatural events, but natural events performed by one with superior knowledge. Post implies that an understanding of these miracles, especially for those most affected, is not needed to appreciate or to benefit from them. He also seems to say that the motive of one performing such humane acts needs to be love and not profit.

We see this latter point illustrated in the next group of incidents which Post depicts. They conclude with a rather mystical dialogue between the School-teacher and the doctor. The doctor goes to Black's house to collect the fee he feels due merely because he came to perform his work, although the patient was already cured. Black refuses to pay and the doctor leaves in anger, looking for the School-teacher. Arriving at the house where the School-teacher lives the doctor finds the former harlot whom he addresses as "Yaller Mag." She offers him some money the School-teacher had found in the house, left behind by the deceased Nicholas Parks. Then she says that she has been told to feed the doctor's horse. The doctor cannot bring himself to settle the question so easily, so he rides off again seeking the School-teacher at the place of the woman with the two year old boy, whom he terms "the woods-colt." There he finds the School-teacher on his knees husking corn. The School-teacher rises and they converse in a strange manner, each seeming to be concerned with separate matters:

> "I understand you're practicin' medicine," said the doctor.
> "Your horse is tired," replied the School-teacher.
> "There's a law against practicin' medicine without a license," said the doctor.
> "Your horse is hungry," continued the School-teacher.
> The doctor, riding on, replied with an oath.
> "You're going to get into trouble," he said.[7]

In the next chapter the School-teacher is confronted by P.

Hamrick, the school trustee who has placed a notice on the schoolhouse door saying the school is closed. The trustee finds it difficult to explain the closing of the school, but finally after extensive questioning he as much as admits that the action is the result of certain "good men" complaining about the School-teacher. He mentions specifically the minister and the doctor. Then he points out that he disapproves of the harlot living in the same house as the School-teacher; but, when challenged to tell her himself to leave, the trustee turns the other way. Leaving in his cart, his parting question, which is not answered, is that he wants to know why the School-teacher is "always carryin' that bastard brat around."

 The School-teacher begins telling the children, individually, that soon he will have to leave them. "On Thursday evening this secret became the common property of all. The schoolteacher was going away! There would be no more school."[8] Then after returning the little boy to his mother, he goes to tell the harlot he is leaving, and when she sobs he chastises her. Still being followed by Martha and David he walks down the mountain path toward the town. As he bids the last two children goodbye at the schoolhouse, two men approach on horseback, one carrying a rifle. As the children watch they see the men take the School-teacher into custody and leave in the direction of the town.

 In the next chapter we learn that the School-teacher's arrest has come as a result of a meeting at the church between the sheriff, the doctor, and the minister. They had the sheriff arrest the School-teacher on a contempt charge for remaining on the Nicholas Parks' property after he had been ordered to leave. Also, they agreed to have the doctor charge him with the illegal practicing of medicine. Finally, to assist the deputy in making the arrest, they hired Jonas Black. Black demands to be paid what seems to them an excessive fee of five dollars, so they settle for three dollars. As a part of the deal, they agree that Jonas should also guard the two prisoners already being held in the jail, who are "bad characters." Jonas is then paid off in silver coins taken from the church's collection—twenty-six dimes, three nickels, and a quarter—thirty pieces in all.

 The School-teacher is taken to the courthouse of the county seat where he is brought before a circuit judge, then a justice of the peace, and again before the circuit judge. Finally, when he is committed to a term in the county jail, the accusers protest that the commitment order refers to the "School-teacher of Hickory Mountain District" which they declare is incorrect inasmuch as the trustees had not employed him. But the judge refuses to change the wording of the order.

Those several persons who had brought about the School-teacher's jail sentence are disturbed that the sentence will not retain the prisoner for long, and so they meet to devise a plot to get him out of the community. Carrying out their plan, the sheriff goes to the jail house that same night and unlocks the cell where the School-teacher and the two men jailed for larceny are kept. He tells the School-teacher, " 'The door's open . . . you can get out of the county before it's daylight.' " The two men do not hesitate as the School-teacher does, but at the last moment he suddenly follows them, catching up and stepping between them and the door. A rifle cracks out and the School-teacher falls mortally wounded.

The School-teacher's friends, some women and children, come for the body. They bury it on the crest of the hill between two hickories above the Nicholas Parks' place. In the morning, leaving the grave, the burial party turns to look back and they see the sun, a golden disc, rising between the two great trees.

It is now obvious that, while he has in many details followed the passion drama as recorded in the Gospels, Post has taken liberties with the story, some perhaps for the convenience of his art, but some, certainly, for other reasons. These liberties are both omissions and variations, doubtlessly made because Post wished to depict the passion drama in accordance with his own views, placing his personal values on these events. These events are, of course, by their very nature and due to the methods of their historical recording, open to various interpretations. Thus, some interpretations may suggest an orthodox or traditional view, and others a moderate or liberal view. Post's interpretation, we quickly assay, belongs to the latter classification.

Through this story we are made aware of two possible views of Christ by Post: the historical Christ who actually lived and died the passion drama of the Gospels, and the Christ who can return and re-enact the passion drama. And this modern reenactment presented here is Post's view of the effect that the reappearance of Christ would have on the world of today.

Insofar as the historical picture is drawn, we find Post's Christ to be a man of mystery rather than a myth; a performer of miracles, if only for those who lack the knowledge that explains them; a teacher rather than a prophet or a preacher, one with a general divine relationship, rather than a specific relationship; a doer of deeds rather than a speaker of parables; a mystic rather than a saintly creature; and a symbol of God in nature, rather than a spirit of an unseen God.

Post's modern day Christ is represented as highly involved with the children, loving them and being loved in turn. He is sympathetic and helpful to women of misfortune. And Post's teacher helps two men with their physical disorders—and the one proves to be the father of his assassin. He is not afraid to use his hands in productive labor, repairing the schoolhouse and equipment at the mill, digging a grave and shelling corn. He is a pacifist, one who turns the other cheek rather than meet violence with violence. Also, quite striking and noticeable is the relationship of the School-teacher to the church that supposedly has been established in Christ's name and spirit. The preacher, half-blind physically and totally blind spiritually, we must suppose represents the attitude of Post in regard to the organized church, seemingly a perverted institution. Likewise, Post apparently does not find any concern or understanding for his School-teacher in that group represented by the doctor, the intellect and scientist. Nor does Post give more than a slightly higher rating to the men who represent the legal instruments, the legislature, the court and the enforcement agencies.

This picture that Post gives us of a Christ in our century is a shocking one. Not because we are unaware of unchristian behavior in our society, not because we know of Christ's rejection by individuals, but because the very institution which supposedly speaks in his name and for his cause puts him in the position where he is assassinated in cold-blood. Here we have a prophecy of the very violence which rules the days of this century. Each day and in each town, if we properly read this parable, we re-enact the passion drama over and over again.

Post's use of his economical style, his short and easy to

grasp sentences, his employment of a minimum of descriptive terms, his choice of crisp and natural dialogue do not succeed in making this work a first-rate literary accomplishment, although they do strive toward that end. Yet, they do help to produce a book which is very readable and rewarding entertainment. A critic for the *New York Times* noted ". . . there is such a perceptible degree of authentic literary values contained in the book that most readers must revise their opinion of Mr. Post."[9] This was doubtlessly an ill-considered judgment—for the true literary values of Post are best found in his other work, namely the *Uncle Abner* tales. *The Mountain School-Teacher* is imaginative, but it is not seriously dramatic.

The above noted critic also predicted that this book "should win new laurels for its author." This, of course, did not happen, for while the idea of placing the Gospel drama in an Appalachian community is stimulating, it is not significant. The book was read and commented upon in the limited fashion it deserved, and it is read occasionally today by those fortunate enough to find it on a library book shelf. While the novelette is not the crowning achievement of Post's career, neither is it his least. It should be approached in this spirit.

2. The Revolt of the Birds

Melville Davisson Post often appeared an enigma and something of this passed into much of what he wrote. Very early he drew from critics comments on a lack of style or polish. Some critics hastily judged that he had a tendency to incompleteness or inept plotting. No one took an honest reflective look at his stories. Those looking for bright, flashy commercialism decked in arty style passed over his work quickly. Midway through the 1920's his popularity began to diminish.

Post had always sought simply to produce entertainment, a quality his work seldom lacked; but work based on this factor alone is readily lost in the steady flood of such materials. Post's superb technical skill, unique plots, and guarded endings were rapidly matched and surpassed by other able authors. The only thing that remained and gave his work individuality was its enigmatic quality, but this feature has been consistently ignored.

Nothing he wrote was ever more enigmatic than the novelette *The Revolt of the Birds* and hardly anything more completely ignored. It does not deserve to rank with his best work, but it is an interesting item to analyze, though somewhat less interesting to read. It is at once handicapped because it is essentially a fantasy, but stranger tales are true and the margin of truth in this story is part of the enigmatic element.

The extreme economical style used in this story impairs our final judgment of the book. Post had developed over a period of years an economical style in his short story writing that was technically useful and easy to read—but here he has pared his material so thoroughly that at times it seems hardly more than the form of an outline. Many of the paragraphs are no more than simple sentences. What was good in the limitations of the short story does not lend its magic to this longer tale.

There is some indication that at this period Post was dictating his stories to a secretary rather than putting them down in longhand as he had done earlier. This may account for the overall conversational tone of the work and at times its uncomfortable roughness. Editors eagerly awaited his stories and Post accepted their offered checks, oftimes expending only what effort was necessary to put the material into an acceptable form. Usually approaching writing as a profession rather than as an art, only at rare moments did he give thought to the permanence and literary value of his work.

Intentionally or unconsciously Post pursues elusive objectives in this piece, but either because the story was written first for periodical publication or because of its economical style, or both, the indicated goals are not wholly reached. We also sense in the writing a struggle to make this fantasy believable. The story is woven into a first person narrative which automatically gives it the advantage of personal reportage. This is first brought to our attention on the third page through the simple statement: "I had drifted here on my mission." But the "I" is never identified beyond some hint that the narrator might be a secret service agent. Shortly thereafter, Post shifts to his favorite device of having various characters within the narrative spell their stories. This continual change of viewpoint keeps the material in a hazy focus, and the reader needs to be alert.

The story opens with a description of a seaman's clubroom in Hong Kong at the offices of the Wu Fang Company, a dingy shipping company whose personnel and business affairs are questionable. Here the narrator meets several men: Bennett, later identified as an American, a ship's officer of sorts; Captain Chillingsworth, an Englishman; a German called Baron Nordheim; and a shadowy Italian who reads an Italian translation of *The Passing of Arthur* quietly to the side. Of this edition of Tennyson's ambiguous poem Post has the narrator note that it contains "quaint pictures of the three queens who came, in the legend, in a mystic barge to take Arthur to Avalon." The substance of this poem suggests the imaginative, mystic frame into which Post's story is set. The Englishman, the German, and Bennett contribute objective, visual material to reinforce the mood of the tale while adding to the knowledge that the narrator possesses.

It is almost an abstract picture which Post has the narrator sketch of the room in which these men meet:

> I am trying to make you realize this place and the men I found in it. It did not seem to belong in the world. The men and the place seemed to belong in some form of nightmare; some vague conception of a hell where men maintained the forms and manners of the world from which they had descended.
>
> But it was all a sort of abominable pretense.
>
> They spoke with exaggerated courtesy. They were careful to accord each his title and distinction. They listened attentively when one spoke and made some remark at the end of it or some courteous interjection. But one felt, as I have said, that it was all a ghostly pretense.[1]

This room is subtly symbolic of the *actual* world man has made for himself, suggesting the hell it is as opposed to the *ideal* world of the mind.

Early in the book the Englishman relates the experiences of a trader with a persistent dream, or what would now be termed as an extra-sensory experience. In his vivid dream the trader sees a coastline and a grove of coconut trees. This vision appears so real that he has an artist make a detailed water color picture of the place on which he marks the two trees between which he believes a treasure has been buried. As the dream keeps returning "with the regularity of a cyclic monomania of the mind," the trader, already a fugitive criminal, works like a slave to get enough money together to find his coastline, "doing anything about the brothels, with petty thefts thrown in."

Finally, buying a dangerous old hull for a ship, the trader sets out to find the coastline and his treasure. He does find it—but his craft breaks up in a storm and he is washed ashore, drowned at the very spot he sought. There a native resident discovers his body and buries him. Bennett's comment on the story is forthright: "Hell . . . that man was tricked into hunting for his own death. . . ."

Post places this incident in the book to suggest the possibility of truth found in dreams. At the date of the book's composition scientific interest in ESP phenomena was as yet slight, but as myth or superstition the possibility of dreams having content corresponding to reality has long been noted in literature—from the Bible, the Greek plays, to Tennyson's stories of King Arthur. Post thus hints that there is always a margin of truth in a fable.

The elusive nature of time is another matter which has long fascinated men. As a factor to measure reality it figures in a tale told by the Baron Nordheim. This is placed immediately following the narrator's reporting of the initial part of Bennett's strange story. The Baron's contribution is one of misfortune, symbolic of his nation. He had dueled over a girl and lost, but after the duel he had killed his opponent and fled. Later, while working aboard a ship, he caught his foot in a line being played out and was flung into the sea. There he almost drowned, but in that brief moment he recalled every second of his unfortunate duel. The narrator states: "That was the point Nordheim was making. That time was merely a condition of the mind."

Post next has the narrator report a further experience which Nordheim related concerning the nature of time. It concerns a contraband cargo and the effects of drugs. It is interesting to note Post's treatment of drugs in this neglected and puzzling book. Here are the words he furnished for the narrator:

> The resident in his thatch house at the end of the sluggish river explained it to Nordheim. Hashish had a strange effect on the human mind. It lengthened one's conception of *time*!
> The resident said:

"I get drunk; I take the drug, and so it happens that in one afternoon I enjoy myself for a month."

It was a finger's touch on an immense mystery.

A lost German in a forest of Asia was on the way to one of the greatest discoveries of the age. He had outwitted time; he had hit upon a plan to extend the pleasant periods of it.

Nordheim said there was no doubt about the effects of the drug. It did extend the consciousness of time. Grave professors had experimented with it in the universities of Berlin. In half an hour one could traverse the length of Unter de Linden. But if one swallowed a portion of the drug, a very limited portion, one seemed a whole afternoon in the pleasant walk. Strange that this astounding quality in the Asiatic hemp should have received so little attention from the savants of the world! What an immense control one would have over one's life if one could extend for a long period, brief, happy moments in it.[2]

Having made this point the book returns to the relating of Bennett's tale, which the narrator suddenly recognizes as the adventures of an American he himself knew, named Arthur Hudson. The narrator relates what he knows about Hudson's affairs. Briefly, Arthur Hudson had fallen in love with an English girl of social prominence. Because he had inherited from his father some failing coal mines, he returns to America and works to restore his fortune in order to be able to support the girl he desires. After some years he makes the necessary financial gains, but upon returning to England he discovers that the girl he had longed for has been seduced by a notorious Lord X_____. Meanwhile, he realizes that he had never dreamed of his British girl, but only of a strange girl, "a delicate ethereal beauty like a dryad in a sacred grove, or a fairy woman." He notes also that always a flock of birds moves about this strange creature. Having lost his first dream, that of the *real* world, he sets out in search of the less objective dream.

At this point Post allows the narrator to make some comments concerning the liberation of the female. Post had seen the beginnings of the change in the status of women, but his statements are truly a prediction of things which were to come. Here, again, the writer's words are best quoted:

What was the matter with the American?

>   Did he expect to crack a roc's egg and find a woman within it?
>
>   The world had changed! The new generation had made up their minds to live—to have all they could in the time they had. And the more experiences one had—the more reactions—the more one lived.
>
>   Did he expect to find her waiting for him, a little country innocent in a blossomed pasture!
>
>   In what sort of saccophagus had the man been entombed?
>
>   Women had come into their inheritance of freedom at last. And they proposed to make the most of it. Life was too precious to be risked blindly as it was too precious to be wasted. Imagine going to live with a man for one's life when one knew nothing about a man! Did any man of us enter an irrevocable situation, until after he knew, pretty thoroughly, all about it? And experience was life.[3]

In the concluding section of the book the narrator relates Bennett's account of the final adventure of Arthur Hudson. Some of the details are those that Bennett observed and some are from the lips of the delirious and nearly-dead Hudson. This portion revolves around a facet of ecology which was considered only lightly, if it was considered at all, in 1927 when the book was published.

The story Bennett has been telling concerns an incident that occurred on the China Sea. He was at the time master of a decrepit ship of the Wu Fang Company. Bennett's Chinese crew had spotted an object in the distance. At first he cannot see it with his glass, but as they came closer it seemed to be an odd-shaped cloud above a small craft. Suddenly the cloud rose, moving away from the vessel and leaving it adrift. When Bennett reaches the small boat an exhausted man is discovered aboard it.

Bit by bit, Bennett pieces together a strange tale from what the debilitated and delirious Arthur Hudson tells after being brought aboard Bennett's ship. Hudson tells of his very compelling desire to reach a certain island. Post propounds, through the narrator, the instinctive nature of this dream:

>   It doesn't get us anywhere to reject such a theory with a smile.
>
>   When one has a profound feeling there may be some lure of direction in it. What guides the birds in their migrations and the schools of fish that travel in the sea?[4]

For his purpose Hudson had obtained a ship, but when he found the island his Chinese crew, out of fear, refused to take him ashore. Thus, he went ashore alone in a bare-rigged sampan which had been lashed to the deck for emergency purposes. Arriving at the island he immediately discovered the reason for the crew's reluctance. The entire island was swarming with insects. "It was a death island." Seeing smoke coming from a house down the shore he managed to make his way there by walking the distance through the water, avoiding the insect covered beach.

The house he found was built at the water's edge and was thoroughly screened to ward off further invasion by the insect hordes. There Hudson discovered a dying missionary and his daughter. With them was an Oriental servant. The missionary died the night of Hudson's arrival, almost as if he had been anticipating the moment. But Hudson had found the girl he was seeking. Post sketches this meeting in the barest details with "the fragments Hudson gave in his mad talk."

At this point we are introduced to Post's principal thesis, the likely motive for the origin of his tale. He had a great interest in birds and observed them regularly about his home in West Virginia. There he had constructed birdhouses, feeders and other conveniences to attract them. He read as much about them as he could obtain. Thus Post approached, some thirty-five years before Rachel Carson and *Silent Spring*, essentially the same argument in this short novel that has only now caused the general public to become aware of the problems of survival and concerned with ecology, that to seriously disturb the balance of nature can have disastrous consequences.

The idea Post presents had not been widely-discussed or considered in 1927. It was presented, when at all, mostly in neglected government agricultural pamphlets and touched only briefly in the popular journals. Post sums up the subject in these words:

> . . . insect life and man were in a terrific struggle for possession of the earth. The birds alone held the earth for the race. The prodigious procreation of insect life was simply incomprehensible.
>
> Five billions of birds in the United States of America stood between the human population of that country and

the devastation of death.[5]

Few, if any, who read Post's story in 1927 were prepared to accept the importance of such a statement.

The narrator sums up his knowledge about the birds. The island had once been a fertile rice-producing land. Then greed led the rice growers to poison untold numbers of the island's bird population because they ate a portion of the crop. None noted that a considerable part of the bird's diet was also the island's insects. As many of the birds died, the remainder *revolted* and avoided the island, allowing the insects to multiply unchecked until they devastated everything and completely controlled the island.

The missionary's daughter had befriended the remaining birds by feeding them unpoisoned rice, and soon these began to flock around her. Shortly after Hudson's arrival and the death of the girl's father, Hudson was attacked by the Oriental servant. Hudson's superior strength overcame the Oriental's judo techniques, but in the course of the battle the protective screening was smashed, thus destroying the last refuge from the insect hordes. The dead Oriental was left to the insects as the girl and Hudson sought the safety of the sea in a sailless sampan. In vain the two paddled the sampan against the current. Only with the miraculous arrival of the birds the girl had befriended, settling en masse on the boat's rigging and forming somehow a sail, did the craft move out from the beach. This is the explanation for Bennett's sighting the sampan and the "cloud" which accompanied it. Bennett at this point in his tale picks up the Italian translation of *The Passing of Arthur* and sets it away on the shelf.

Ending his tale, Bennett admits that he is unsure about what actually happened. There was no evidence of how long the couple had been at sea or what distance they had traveled. Since the girl was not in the sampan when it was discovered, he believes that she might have slipped into the sea from exhaustion. Bennett notes that Hudson also vanished from the deck of his ship one night, perhaps by rolling into the sea. He conjectures in his concluding statement: ". . . or the two of them may have passed with the birds to some earthly paradise. . . . Anyway, he was gone one morning and the native lookout said he saw the cloud pass."

Post did not succeed in all his aims in creating this fantasy, but he did produce a book that deserves more attention than it has received. As a fable it lacks the impact of having a definite hero—its real hero being the multitude of birds. Whether defined as a long story or as a novelette, *The Revolt of the Birds* attempts to cover too much territory, treating its characters as silhouettes, some being blurred and nameless. Its thematic moments are hardly realized because of the brief treatment they receive. In spite of these handicaps, Post does manage to impose a certain loose form on the material. He thus creates some suspense and a certain degree of narrative interest.

Post was always an observant student of the evolution of social attitudes, as is shown in his earlier works in his prophetic views on justice. In this book are brief hints of some of the principal social concerns that engage us some forty years later, the effects of drugs, interest in the psychological facts of time and in ESP, equal rights for women, and growing concern for ecology. His hints are brief and limited, but visible. The enigmatic quality of the book remains even after analysis and repeated readings, just as the enigmatic qualities of its author have persisted.

In a piece for *The New York Times Book Review* the critic does an excellent job of summing up the plot in a couple of well-written paragraphs, but in his final paragraph he rejects the book, saying that Post "seems almost afraid of his theme; he has not the boldness to drain it of its possibilities; he faces his situations almost apologetically and with numerous side excursions into the doings of the Wu Fang Company, derelict skippers, and other matters of but little relevancy."[6] Thus, caught up in the story, this critic missed the importance of the themes half-hidden in the framework of this story. He was not alone.

VII. NONFICTION AND UNCOLLECTED WORK

1. Nonfiction

Critical comment on Post's work has been concerned almost exclusively with his fictional writings. Whether justified, or not, this situation is not likely to change. Nonfiction articles, however, account for at least one-third of Post's professional writing which appeared in serial publications. Proportionately less of his nonfiction writing has been put into book form; only one of his sixteen published books consist of nonfiction material. That one book, *The Man Hunters*, was given its form, it would seem, for commercial reasons and not for its literary value, as it contains some of the least valuable work of its author.

Very little of Post's nonfiction work has any obvious literary or journalistic value for the reader of today. It is principally useful, if at all, in throwing some light on his personal attitudes, his political beliefs, his legal and literary philosophy, and the sources of many of his plots. Thus, there is justification for the larger portion of his nonfiction work remaining neglected. This being the case, we will comment upon the major part of Post's nonfiction articles in general, emphasizing specifically only those items which demand some attention or deserve a place in the final judgment of his total literary accomplishments.

Speaking in this manner, however, we must not allow the impression that most of Post's articles were poorly done in the technical sense, for they were not. This applies in general to much that we shall all but ignore, being of interest only to the exceptional student who is exercising specialized aims. A good percentage of the nonfiction, particularly the earlier items which treat matters related to the courts, law, and the judicial process and are written principally for the benefit of the layman, are well constructed and researched. Post was adept at weaving together in these articles illustrative vignettes of human interest in wise proportion to his personal opinions and his prosaic themes. This aided in making them interesting to read and doubtlessly boosted their popularity with both editor and reader when they were of current interest.

Post's ability to write in a fashion both readable and convincing derived first from his exceptional skill and practice as a debater in school and then later in the courts and political circles. This experience taught him to sharpen the point of his argument, to express it in clear and concise language, and then to arrange it in a manner that demanded the attention of his audience. The evidence we have, which may be partially incomplete, shows that he made the step from spoken to written argument quite readily— perhaps owing a great deal to his unique personal assets and to his early desire to excel as a man-of-letters.

The first indication that Post was interested in writing factual articles on a professional basis is found in a letter dated February 12, 1897, which he wrote to The Century Company, publishers of *The Century Illustrated Monthly Magazine*.[1] In his letter Post queried the editor with the suggestion that: "The death of Captain P. N. McGiffin suggests that you might be interested in a paper dealing with the career of this remarkable man." Post went on to note his personal acquaintance with the subject and some of his close associates and the availability of the subject's papers. Since G. P. Putnam's Sons were at this time in the early stages of preparing to publish Post's second book of short stories, he closed his inquiry with a note of reference to that firm. Whether the editor pursued the matter further, we do not know. No doubt, a minor hero of his times, McGiffen's career would have lent itself better to fiction than fact.[2]

In the 1898 February and April issues of *The Law Student's Helper*, Post made what appears to be his first appearances in a regular serial publication with two short stories. His third appearance, in the July issue of this publication, was also his first nonfiction material accorded general publication. It dealt with one of his distant relatives, Nathaniel Copeland. Other than a brief piece in *The West Virginia State Bar Association Report* in 1899, there is no record of the serial publication of any other fiction or nonfiction serial of Post's until 1904.

Perhaps because he had secured by now a minor reputation as an author of three books or because he was a respected and active member of his state's Democratic Party, Post made his next nonfiction appearance in a widely-read publication, *Harper's Weekly*, with an article entitled "Ex-Senator Henry G. Davis." The piece, appearing in the August 6, 1904, issue, was politically motivated, inasmuch as the subject was a unique eighty-year-old candidate for Vice President of the United States with the misfortune to be matched with Alton B. Parker against the formidable Theodore Roosevelt and Charles W. Fairbanks. Post's essay, a combination biographical, political, and bravado assemblage, aided Davis' candidacy little, if at all, but it was well-written in all respects—good usage of language, smooth arrangement of arguments, and carefully researched information of general interest. It was a model example of political journalism, one worthy of limited praise.

The next appearances of Post in print with nonfiction material occurred in 1909 in *Pearson's Magazine* following a two-year-long series of stories in that publication. These articles, only two in number, marked Post's first attempt at interpreting the processes and problems of the judicial system for the average citizen. Titled "Shall We Burn the Court House?" and "The Failure of the Jury System," they were the first of his many informative essays on the administration of justice, a subject involved in approximately half of his nonfiction production and woven frequently into his fiction. Both are well-written pieces which demonstrate professional standards, and according to the editor's comments regarding the first, the public response included "almost as many viewpoints expressed in criticizing Mr. Post as there were critiques."

Meanwhile, Post made his first sale of a short story to the *Saturday Evening Post* (1908), but it was not until May 1910 that he continued his decade of association with the *Post* by publication of the first of his series of seven articles under the general title, "Mysteries of the Law." These pieces are rather uniformly constructed using many actual instances which the author had accumulated from his personal experience in the courts and from his extensive reading of legal reports. A good number of these illustrations later found their way into the plots of many of his stories. Here again, it might be worth comment that the larger part of Post's fiction apparently is built on real situations or occurrences from a variety of sources, personal and secondary.

"Mysteries of the Law: Fact and Fiction," the first of the seven associated pieces, opens with a statement of theme that is not only emphasized in the remaining articles, but is central to a large part of Post's writing throughout his career. Here he states that theme very simply and clearly: "No man can perpetrate a crime without leaving some clew behind." Also, in this piece Post notes: "For weird tales of crime Poe has never had an equal." Then he goes on to answer some of the critics of Poe who had declared his stories "exaggerated." Post recounts here an actual case that duplicates the weird, unlikely elements of a tale by Poe.

In the sixth piece, "Mysteries of the Law: The Nicks in the Knifeblade," Post covers thoroughly a case with which he was personally familiar and which probably dated back to his days as a lawyer in Wheeling, West Virginia. Perhaps one of the more interesting items in this article is his description of a criminal named Mooney. Post wrote: "This man, Mooney was a notorious criminal. . . . He was a fearless, daring, vindictive desperado." What relation he bears to the Mooney in *Walker of the Secret Service* is uncertain, but one can infer that there is a strong resemblance to the crafty criminal who gave Walker his early lessons in the criminal arts.

Further evidence of Post's use of actual events in his fiction is found in the final piece of this series of articles, "Mysteries of the Law: The Will in the Teapot." That this practice was merely a following of tradition is one of the points that he subtly suggests. First, he says, "The lost will was a cherished device of the old-fashioned playwright; with it he created, it would seem, every variety of incredible situation." Later, he writes, "The missing will was equally dear to the early novelist." Post quotes from the legal records and experiences of his law career some incredible situations of this type, and as anyone who has read many of his stories knows, he himself has frequently resorted to various types of wills, missing and present, for dramatic motivation.

Also in this piece, in line with the theme that runs through his unique fictional accomplishments, Post observes Hippolyte Adolphe Taine commenting on Mill: " 'Here Mill is right. Chance is at the end of all our knowledge. . . .' " Then Post observes, "But may not this factor in all human events be exactly the thing that Greenleaf and Wharton call Providence?" He then goes on to cite instances which account for the intriguing plots in several of the *Uncle Abner* tales that would appear within the next few years. Among these stories, one of the best and most compelling is "Naboth's Vineyard." There, despite an air of authenticity, reinforced by the use of a number of names of actual persons at one point, the reader wonders at the seemingly contrived event that enables Abner to throw proof of the murder on the least likely suspect. This event is the locating of a book on poisons, the pages uncut except at the very place of the poison used in the crime. Citing the actual case from which he drew the device that he later used in his plot, Post wrote:

> Here one who had committed murder by poison was apprehended by this curious incident: In his library, at his residence, there was found a volume on poisons. . . . Now the finding in this library of a work on poisons would have meant little had it not been that the pages of this volume were all uncut except at a single place, where the effect of this particular poison was described.[3]

Anyone bent on taking Post to task for employment of the *deus ex machina* device in many unusual plots had better first examine these nonfiction articles of the author, most all but forgotten. Ironically, it might be a fact that truth is stranger than fiction.

In "The Border Land of the Law," his next published article,

Post discusses a wrong which is often voiced, that wealthy men often escape criminal prosecution. He says, "If it be true that wealth and influence enable one to evade the law, then our system of justice fails." Later, taking up another current theme, he states, "there could be no safety for anybody unless those things that a citizen ought not to do be clearly and accurately defined." Otherwise, "one might be haled into court and tried for anything that those in authority might conceive to be wrong."[4] Midway in the article he restates some of the ideas in the introductory sections to his first two Randolph Mason books. Near the conclusion of this piece, he begins to sound like an advocate for late twentieth-century situation ethics philosophy as he observes:

> There is no clear marking line between right and wrong, as there is none between blue and green, as there is none between sane and insane, as there is none between sounds that constitute music and those that do not, as there is none between flowers that have odor and flowers that have no odor.[5]

Although Post would not be in perfect agreement with those who today have pushed certain of these philosophies to their extremes, it hardly seems either that he would be completely shocked by their suggestions. Almost unnoticed, Post was a rebel in his own fashion. Perhaps here we might find some clue toward understanding why Post, disturbed by some sort of a conflict with his first profession, chose to remove himself from active practice in the legal world.

Post next began publishing a series of articles with the overall title "Extraordinary Cases." Five of these appeared in order and two were later added under the same heading before it was dropped. "When one touches the mystery of human identity he seizes upon a golden property of romance," he wrote in opening the first, "Extraordinary Cases: The Sealed Packet." Defending again the truth-is-stranger-than-fiction theory, he said:

> . . . the realist, insisting on truth, will thrust his tongue into his cheek and put down the book. Such adventures in their nice, intricate adjustment do not happen, he tells us with a judicial air. But they do happen![6]

In this piece Post cites a lengthy, true case involving proof of identity, one which is a match for any melodrama a writer of fiction might conceive.[7]

The third of this series, "Extraordinary Cases: Fabricated Defenses," amplifies Post's often repeated conclusion, that in instances of criminal behavior the truth will always prevail somehow over the events of a constructed explanation. In other words, a lie cannot overcome the truth. Post makes one of his most complete statements regarding this idea here:

> If one carefully examines any natural event he will presently realize that if an intelligence placed it there then that intelligence must necessarily have known everything that preceded and everything that followed this event with an infinite sweep of comprehension. The human mind is, no matter how intelligent, limited in its knowledge.[8]

This obviously deterministic statement perhaps tells us more about Post than it explains the actual cases the author cites to support his theme—and his fiction. This belief was the keystone to his approach to existence, and it ruled his thoughts in almost every situation of life.

In "Extraordinary Cases: The Hidden Tenant," his next article, Post shows us that he is alert to the difficulties of making uncontestable judgments on matters relating to human beings.

> Whether we believe man is a spirit or a fungus, that manifestation of him which we call his consciousness is a profound mystery.
>
> * * * *
>
> It is important to carry this in the mind when one comes to consider insanity as related to the question of the administration of the criminal law. Ground for an insanity plea, a judge ruled, must show the defendant was unaware of the nature and quality of the act he was committing.
>
> There is hardly a criminal case in which insanity is not present to some degree.[9]

One of the most interesting parts of "Extraordinary Cases: The Gashed Finger," fifth of the series, is Post's revelation of the source for the solution of the *Uncle Abner* mystery tale "An Act of God," wherein a deaf-mute is murdered and a note, purportedly written by him is proved a forgery done by the murderer to right a wrong. This unusual murder's solution motivates one of the finest short stories that Post ever wrote.

Turning his attention again directly to the nation's courts and writing with the ordinary citizen in mind, Post next published three articles concerned with the accuracy of the judicial process. In writing "The Layman and the Law" and "The Citizen in Court," Post includes material that we can relate to a number of his short stories, including a reference to the point of law which he covered so vividly in his earlier and provoking Randolph Mason tale, "Corpus Delicti." Focusing more closely on the difficulties plaguing the courts, in "Reforms in the Legal Procedure" Post presents a well-written review of the subject. How much this particular article helped to arouse the legal minds of the country we cannot know, for Post was not entirely alone in this field. Yet, this article, along with others he wrote, surely was part of the reason for bringing Post to the attention of an elite group of the country's legal minds when they were formed into a committee to investigate the "efficiency in the administration of justice."[10] Whatever resulted from this group's project is difficult to determine as its activity seems to have been stifled by the pressures of World War I. With increasing frequency and broadening application, this subject has in the intervening years continued to draw attention, not only in the legal world, but in general among all men. It is well-worth noting that a number of suggestions which Melville Post brings out in this article are still valid and need to be acted upon.

Returning to his series, Post next published an article, "Extraordinary Cases: The Fragments of Plaster," which incidentally throws some light on one of his more interesting stories, "American Horses." This story is not concerned with *horses* as such, but with counterfeitors. Also here, illustrating his often overlooked enigmatic talent and his ability to move the reader with simple, colorful prose, we read a renewed and broadened approach to the core of his philosophical meanderings.

> The madhouses are crowded with men who have endeavored to solve the mystery of chance. The inquiry presently enters that bloody angle wherein the adherents of design and those of coincidence contend with the bayonet. Nevertheless when one looks closely he seems to observe a certain percentage of chance against the criminal agent. Does this mean that the criminal is usually a person whose intelligence is below average, or does it mean that the Thing behind the machinery of the universe—mind, impulse, call it what you

like—is laboring at some great work, and that all those who are useful to its purpose, who aid it, it endeavors to preserve, and all those who are useless or harmful it endeavors to destroy—as Nature in the plant or animal develops the organ that is useful and eliminates the one that is not?[11]

With the publication of "Science and the Forger" and "Extraordinary Cases: The Red Peril," we meet with the first of Post's nonfiction given a controversial measure of permanence, being slipped into the only collection of his factual prose in book form. That book, *The Man Hunters*, will be discussed here later when we deal with the main body of material incorporated under that title. These two articles show Post principally as a reporting journalist—with one main exception, his sharp personal attack on the use of psychological tests and early models of the lie detector. He declares: "The disposition of a citizen's life, funds or liberty cannot be made to turn upon the results of psychological tricks or mechanical devices that he does not understand."

With the publication of his article, "Are We Governed by the Supreme Court," midway through 1912, Post's nonfiction material turned in a slightly new direction toward the politics of jurisprudence. Here he concerned himself with the effects of the Supreme Court on government and consequently on the democratic processes—of which Post was an ardent defender. Some of the attitudes of the Supreme Court, its operation, and the effects he lists sound very familiar and almost contemporary, even after the passage of over fifty years of our history. Post claims: "The original idea of the jurisdiction of the Supreme Court of the United States did not include the review of legislative acts." Noting that the people can remedy errors of the legislative branch, while they have no remedy for errors perpetuated by the final court, Post insists that the power of full government must be returned to the people.

In his next article, "Recall of Judicial Decisions," Post makes a prediction which is, if anything, more applicable to the mood of today's people than it was to the reader of 1912. This piece was the lead item in a 1912 issue of the *Saturday Evening Post* and was illustrated by a cartoon drawing by Herbert Johnson. Continuing in the steps of the argument of the previous article, Post wrote:

> There is a disadvantage in the accumulation of power by any department of a state—namely, that as the power accumulates, the resistance to it also accumulates. It seems to disturb the political balance—to disturb the natural equilibrium which an even distribution of power in the hands of the whole people maintains in republican forms of government. It is a sort of law, and, not unlike those to be found in Nature, if persons or groups of persons assume the exercise of this sovereignty the result will be a resistance which, in the end, takes the form of violence.[12]

Is there not something ironic here, something strangely inappropriate in our methods of scholarship, that one so prophetic can be assigned no other recognition in our encyclopedic records than that of authorship of mystery and detective entertainments?

Continuing his attack in the article, "Courts and their Critics," Post warned the reader, "Those, therefor, who exercise sovereign power in a state do not permit criticism of their acts." That this is no original line of thought he has been pursuing, Post acknowledges, quoting from the teachings of Socrates. He also notes that Jefferson, Jackson, Lincoln, and Theodore Roosevelt all held that the people alone have the right to say by what laws they are governed. His closing statement in the article sums up effectively his attitude toward the inevitability of change, a subject into which he showed great insight. He wrote:

> Civilization advances and becomes more complex; new situations arise; broader obligations are recognized and broader opportunities are insisted upon. A greater distribution of the perils which fall upon certain classes, a wider enjoyment of the natural resources of the whole country, a larger equilibrium in the benefits and disadvantages of life are coming more and more to be demanded. Laws must be enacted to carry forward and accomplish these things, and the courts must not stand hostile in the way. This is the race at its great work. This is man on his tremendous journey; and if he can find an iron wheel or a canvas wing to carry him faster the courts must not compel him to travel in an ox-cart.[13]

These, it would seem, are hardly words that any but a liberal thinker would allow in public view. Post, without any doubt a believer in law and order, was against revolution and violence, but he could foresee that, given no other recourse, this was the direction in which the people would act.

Post was warmly critical of the judicial system and of the men who administered it, a position hinted at frequently in his fiction, but increasingly so in his nonfiction. Other than the reasons he states in his public writings, there is no other indication how this position came about. More than any other reason, it seems to be the natural course of development of his personal philosophy and experience. We cannot speculate beyond this. In "Justice and the Justice," he directs his thoughts to the justice-of-the-peace systems, saying, "The failure of a justice-of-the-peace system is a striking example of how a wise and sound institution may be changed by the exigencies of civilization into one inadequate and vicious." His descriptions of Squire Randolph in the *Uncle Abner* stories, satirical as they are, were a bit more mellow. Post continued his attack on the entire system in his next article, "The Bench and the People," before dropping the subject for a time.

Certain instances in his fiction show Post's acquaintance with the gambling habits of society and indications are that he must have been a visitor, on a number of occasions, to the great gambling resorts of Europe. His sudden condemnation of gambling in his next article, "The Immorality of Chance," since we have not been prepared for it, comes as a mild surprise. Here he reviews the history of Monaco and praises its Mediterranean beauty; but, of those who gamble at the tables, he perceives, "The faces of the players look like those of persons waiting for the arrival of the greatest event, as the verdict of a jury determining the issues of life." He declares the atmosphere is tense, while systems to beat the house are sought, but none really succeed for the operators take no chance. After quoting an old English judge who said, "It encourages a hope of reward without labour," Post concludes:

> . . . Chance is the great enemy of all human progress.
> * * * * *
> All the struggle and effort of the race, from the time it emerged from the slime of the old Cambrian seas, has been directed toward one object—to escape the dominion and tyranny of chance.[14]

Although one can agree to some degree with the arguments Post establishes in his next essay, "The Immortal Millions," one is disturbed to note that he directs them against the legislation that allowed the founding of the Rockefeller Foundation. Sounding thoroughly conservative, he wrote, "One of the most perplexing things in this world is to decide how far we may sacrifice what we call a principle in order that good may result." While the attitude is a legitimate one, understandably so from Post's perspective, it nevertheless seems a regressive one in light of his usually forward-looking views. Other statements in the article reinforce this assessment of the essay as Post exhibits a strong distrust of the real objective of the foundation and questions the authority of the Congress to grant such charters. He argues that he follows the opinions of Jefferson in his questioning. Perhaps, because we today can see the overruling results of philanthropy that have accrued, we wonder at Post's apparent inability to accept philanthropy as a motivation for the establishment of the fund. His closing statement reveals some likeliness of personal bitterness that guided his comments on the subject.

> We would know what to do with the great buccaneer who offered us the accumulated gains of his buccaneering; but do we know what to do with the great financier who offers us the accumulated gains of his financiering.[15]

Post favored strong individualism—but he is unrealistic when at times he seems to expect that all men function easily with such an attitude of individualism.

"The Lesson of the Roosevelt Trial" again shows us evidence of a sort of change in the author. The Melville Davisson Post of 1904 had been opposed politically to Theodore Roosevelt and, we must assume, to some of his principles. But in 1913, in this piece, we find Post siding very firmly with the former President, at least on the issue involved. Somewhere, sometime during the years the two men had met and talked several times—and no doubt, Post recognized in the personality and acts of the fiery Roosevelt some of the individualism and idealism that had governed his own outlook.

The occasion for this article was Theodore Roosevelt's views on the administration of justice which he had announced in several public addresses. Some enemies of the position he took had apparently made innuendoes regarding the former President's habits, suggesting the origin of his forthright doctrine might not have resulted from a sober mind. Post wrote in defense of Roosevelt's views:

> Stripped of misleading commentary, there was nothing revolutionary in Mr. Roosevelt's doctrine of justice. He was asking for but two things: that the whole body of the electorate should at all times and under all circumstances be the ones to say by what law they should be governed; and that the administration of justice should be humanized.[16]

This is obviously the same doctrine that Post had been exhorting in a large body of his nonfictional writings. Post concludes his arguments by praising Roosevelt for the faith he showed in the law when he took the libelous charges to the courts.[17]

In "Government by Magic," Post ranges, at times seemingly haphazardly, further than he does in most of his articles. His theme here is that the law is not meant to cure our many ills, its purpose rather is to provide the ground rules, while the opposing forces work to put things in order. He makes an easy summation with an eerie ring of truth, when he notes:

> When the moon was threatened with extinction by an eclipse the savage always saved it by beating a tom-tom. And when a form of civilization is threatened in modern times politicians are accustomed to save it by formulating planks in a platform.[18]

In this swirl of thoughts, attacking party platforms, agricultural tariffs, and socialism, Post declares, "All progress rests on just one thing and nothing else, and that is the incentive to individual effort." Going on, he warns of the "vain dreams of the intellectual Nihilists in Turgenieff's novels," debates the economic philosophy of Karl Marx side by side with that of Marcus Hanna and Pierpont Morgan, and notes the scarcity of truth of the "School of Contraryists" of which Bernard Shaw acted as literary apostle.

But at the end Post mellows and is optimistic, noting these schemes must fail, but "right" shall prevail. Easing on his idealism, he wrote, "If human nature were perfect a perfect system could be formulated." Saying that there is some good in all these ideas, he however points out that *magic* will not accomplish the needs of men.

Having previously defended Roosevelt's plea and made known a few of his personal thoughts on the subject, in "Humanizing the Law" Post makes perhaps his best argument for the need for general improvements in matters of the law. "The science of the law awaits a great constructive intelligence," he wrote. Reviewing a limited history of the law, Post emphasized the slowness of change and oftimes abusive usage of common law. "Every change is resisted as an instrumentality of destruction," he exclaimed, while pointing out the fact that there have been many changes in human relationships.

In discussing various human relationships, Post appears to be an early champion of the women's rights movement. How he came to accept more readily than most men this new attitude is better understood when one considers the strong individualism found in the character of his wife. No doubt there were other reasons too for his position, for he was known as an admirer of women in general. Post commented eloquently on the emotional subject when he wrote:

> We seem about to recognize that the accident of sex shall not make a difference in the benefits accruing to the individual from our modern civilization. The early philosophy of the law was conspicuously unfair to women, and it remains so in many jurisdictions today.[19]

Also, here in this 1913 article, he takes an admirable swipe at the divorce laws and the unreasonable treatment accorded those unfortunate enough to have themselves tagged, to any degree, with the term "criminal." "We have come to see that the criminal is often a sort of cripple or a sort of child," he reports, but notes that we must not relax our laws foolishly. Hopefully perceiving a period of enlightenment, he voices a truism that echoes prominently in the opinions of many persons, perhaps being heard even more urgently some sixty years later:

> Civilization has tremendously advanced within the last decade, and we have come to see that there is an intolerable discrepancy in pretending the philosophy of the New Testament in our churches, and enforcing the philosophy of the Old Testament in our courts.[20]

Next, returning to the purpose of explaining facets of the courts and legal devices for the lay reader, Post published "Keeping Out of Court." In his opening statement he exclaims, "The average man looks on a lawsuit as a calamity. He regards going into court as among the evils from which—in the prayer book—we beg to be delivered." Some dozen years later, long separated from and discouraged with his first profession, having been wearied a bit by the twists and turns of life, no longer as adept at dragon-slaying, he experienced days when he likely found himself more in sympathy with the average man.

"What is the Monroe Doctrine?" finds Post making an excursion into international law and politics. His interpretation of the ramifications of this document and its part in our history is both informative and unusual, if limited. He believes that the policies of Jefferson and Monroe described in this significant paper were distorted and inflated by commercialists who had, he declares, taken over the power of government. It is an interesting approach to a controversial subject and deserves not to be totally overlooked.

Renewing arguments he had used before, Post states in his next article, "The Jury and the Judges:" "This is true today. . . . The judge is a presiding officer whose duty it is to see that trials are conducted in an orderly manner and who is to advise the jury what the law of the land is; but the jury is the supreme tribunal." Post disagrees with the typical judge who lords over the court and treats the members of juries as though they were "upper servants of an imperial bench." He concludes:

> Self-government goes forward on two legs—the people are the source of authority and the poeple are the source of justice. To amputate either is to put democracy on crutches.[21]

This simple and well-worded statement might well deserve the attention of every public servant—not only the masters of the courts.

In writing "Our Continental Policy," Post again focuses on international politics—here, with some success, invoking a reason for better understanding the meaning of the Monroe Doctrine and coming to the defense of Theodore Roosevelt's position which sought realistic interpretation of its purpose. Sounding prophetically like an advocate of the United Nations, Post wrote: "There can be no doubt that a concert of Powers to police disorderly places of this world is an advance." Then Post gives some wise advice that the latter-day leadership of this government might well have profited from and which certainly more Americans are beginning to now recognize as irrevocable truth. He suggests: "The joint action of civilized nations carries more weight and incurs less antagonism than that of a single power." Had Post expanded on some of these significant thoughts in book form, he might today be better known as the political prophet who also wrote mystery and detective fiction. A wider and wiser application of some of the far-reaching principles he touched on in a number of his essays would perhaps have helped us avoid participation in four costly wars and uncounted instances of civil strife.

Post contends in his next published essay, "Business at Judicial Discretion," that when the Supreme Court in 1910 inserted the word "undue" before "restraint of trade" in the 1899 Sherman Antitrust Law, that legislative action was amended in a fashion that prevented it from being used in accordance with its original intent. He places the blame on greedy, powerful interests that have the ability to purchase, in one manner or another, men in influential positions. It appears a case of Post playing the wise and brave David to the Philistine Goliath. Aiming the rocks of his slingshot at a shrewd, tenacious target, Post needs to be admired, if not for his wisdom, at least for his bravery.

Most of Post's nonfiction pieces have not enough vital substance, except for a few scattered lines, to make them useful for today's reader, but "Trial by Jury" may be one of the principal exceptions. In this article Post was again concerned with the jury system used in the courts of the United States, and although repeating some of his previous arguments, here he has taken his best aim at this subject. "The basic thing from which the jury system suffers is a lack of dignity," he wrote and then went on to compose a well-balanced debate upon that statement. Here, also, he has couched his points in some of his most readable prose. One might recommend it as enlightening reading material for anyone who is to serve on a jury, and anyone interested in improving our courts and justice will find it a well-reasoned plea for improvements. While there have been some noticeable changes for the better in the jury system since this was written, judges and lawyers involved in the daily administration of justice will find suggestions worthy of their consideration in this essay. Post concluded that the principal reason for the jury system is "that the letter of the law may not be permitted to destroy the spirit of justice." One would suppose that most democratic-minded citizens of this land would agree with that statement.

Turning abruptly from politics and legal concerns to literature, the next two articles Post published stand almost alone among his nonfiction accomplishments. "The Blight"[22] and "The Mystery Story" both reveal many of the principles that guided Post in writing his most successful short stories, particularly those of the *Uncle Abner* book. We have discussed these aspects of the two articles in the section devoted to that work.[23] In the first of these articles Post answer's the question, "What is it the public does want?" It becomes apparent that Post believed quite passionately that the principal objective in writing fiction is to provide the reader with entertainment. He was not formulating here an elaborate series of excuses for not concentrating on literature as an *art*—he had shown by this time that he had talents that could have been focused in that direction. A number of his better stories are classic examples of what a short story should be, either as literature or entertainment. No thorough fan of Post's work can afford to miss reading these two articles detailing his views on the kind of writing he did best.

From the days of his youth, when he was first enchanted by the writing of Edgar Allan Poe, Post had nurtured an interest in cryptography. With the outbreak of World War I when it became necessary for the author who wanted to publish nonfiction material to engage himself with a facet of the war, Post turned to espionage. He produced between 1915 and 1918 at least eight articles in this category, and he used the theme of espionage in a number of his fictional works. One of the eight articles became Chapter XIII of *The Man Hunters*, but the rest were never reprinted. They are all uniformly alike and can be discussed readily as a unit.

The credit for first treating espionage on a scientific basis is given Germany, and Post emphasizes consistently the size and efficiency of Germany's spy network. He says, "We know with what care, patience, and ingenuity the Teutonic mind sets about the solution of any problem. . . ."[24] Post notes that "no less than fifteen thousand [spies] were known to the authorities of Paris."[25] In contrast to this, Post contends that France, Great Britain, and later, the United States had been almost reluctant to develop an espionage apparatus to counter that of Germany. Sometimes assumed, sometimes stated, the intent of these articles is to awaken the readers and officials of the United States to the need for being prepared to cope with this modern menace that has the power to destroy a nation.

In these pieces Post also explains many of the methods used in spying, with considerable emphasis on cryptography. Some of the simpler methods of relaying secret messages are unique and interesting, particularly to anyone not acquainted with the subject, but Post never gets much beyond these fundamental schemes. A weakness of these articles is that Post drew heavily on secondary sources for much of his information and these pieces consequently become mere reportage, a summing up mostly of the superficial aspects of the subject. Since the time of the publication of these essays espionage has become more esoteric, more efficient, and certainly more important; thus, Post's articles on this subject, helpful as they might once have been, can be of only small value to the person who today is interested in the subject.

Following publication of the first four of his spy pieces, Post returned briefly to the subject of law and published an article titled, "The Rule-Ridden Game." Equating the courtroom trial to a game, he discusses a number of areas involved in the conduct of court cases; however, very little of significance stands out.

Next, Post published the first of a series of eight "Man Hunters" articles. The first was called "The Man Hunters: Scotland Yard;" the next, "The Man Hunters: The Detective Department of Paris;" and so on. In these he reported on the contrasting police methods of the European countries and America. The eight articles, plus eight others which were related to the subject but which had not originally been part of the series, were put into book form.[26] Since they were given this permanence, it is proper to judge them in total as a book.

The Man Hunters was a mistake in several ways. First, the articles in it are among the least effective pieces that the author wrote. They have been, in most instances, compiled from secondary sources rather than through original investigation. Whatever value they have as reportage is not balanced with any of the values of new concepts. Secondly, the material is seriously dated. The book was published in 1926, some ten years after most of the articles first saw serial publication, and by that time many of the methods reported on had changed and those still in use were already common knowledge to a great extent. Two of the articles collected went back even further, having been published serially in 1912, and the material from which Post drew his information in some instances went back to the previous century. Almost no effort was made to update any of the material, the one exception being the piece that treated Russian police methods, but, even here, considering the great upheaval in that country, the changes made were very few. Thirdly, there is no outstanding, uniform theme to the book as a whole other than a remote suggestion that American police methods did not in general compare favorably with those of Europe, a theme which had a measure of truth. Possibly to make the book more saleable, an attempt was made to make *The Man Hunters* seem more authoritative and thorough by adding a lengthy index of some ten pages. But the book is so devoid of information of real value that no index seems justified at all. Since Post in many instances had written factual material of more worth than that of this collection, publishing the book was an unfortunate event.

There remain only three other nonfiction pieces to recognize. The first of these was called, "Nick Carter, Realist." This is a unique piece, a reply by Post to several persons who had taken issue with him over the plotting of stories. Their claim was that Post was "not adhering . . . to the actualities of life" in his plots. Post, in rebuttal, recounts an actual case from official legal records to show that it contains all the melodrama of a Nick Carter adventure complete with baffling coincidences. It was unlikely that Post convinced his adversaries of his own methods, but at least Post felt that he had dealt them a blow. Post concludes with these words:

> . . . And now, my critical gentlemen of the "curate and tea-party novel," I suggest a dreadful doubt. Suppose--and I whisper it lest the idea escape into the world--suppose it should ultimately happen that Nicholas Carter is a truer realist than you are?[27]

Second of these three pieces, "Mobilizing the Whole Nation," contains Post's ideas on how the United States could best prepare itself to overcome the problems of a war economy while winning in World War I. He sees no exceptions permitting personal profit, and no reasons of any kind should be allowed to interfere with the nation's one objective, that of putting forth a total war effort for the cause of victory. Post contends here that certain individuals in past wars had profited excessively while others were "impoverished or on the firing line" and that this "was at the bottom of all social unrest in nations in a state of war." Lost in shallow thoughts, Post was burdened here with pronouncements of idealism, and it made all his noble efforts seem quixotic and little more.

Shortly following publication of the above piece, almost as if thwarted by a continual neglect of his ideas, Post stopped writing nonfiction. He returned only once in the last decade of his life to the essay form, for a similar reason that he had written one of his earliest pieces, to aid the political efforts of a personal acquaintance who was a candidate for the highest executive office of the United States. Ironically the man's family name was again Davis (no relation to the earlier candidate) and, running against overwhelming odds, he also proved to be a loser.[28]

Each reader, according to his own experience and need, perhaps would come up with a different opinion as to the lasting values of Post's various nonfiction performances. Whether or not the materials deserve the amount of attention we have given them is an open question—certainly they deserve some attention and until now they have received practically none. At their best the nonfiction pieces are exceptionally well done, at their poorest they are best forgotten.

2. Other Items

Very early in his life Post had ambitions to become a writer. Much of what he wrote in his earlier years has been destroyed except for a few items found in the collection of papers at West Virginia University Library. Some of these items we have mentioned in treating his life in the Biography section. The remainder are of no value other than to illustrate that Post was at first uncertain as to what direction his literary ambitions might turn. Among these items are papers used in debates, a few bits of verse, and some attempts at playwriting. He had great success and a reputation in debating, perhaps because he was both well-prepared and an able speaker. His few lines of verse show neither poetic skills nor originality—surprisingly since some of his prose shows indications of latent poetic ability. This holds true also for the few examples of his dramatic work that remains. Other than these items and some newspaper and magazine pieces of little significance, there remains only the slightly more than a dozen uncollected short stories.

Nearly all of the fiction written by Post was presented first in serial publications and later put into books. Of his total fictional output, only about fourteen short stories do not appear in any of his collections. There are indications also of some missing items, but they are few in number.

As noted earlier, Post's first appearance in any regular serial publication was in *The Law Student's Helper*. "The Ventures of Mr. Clayvarden" in the February 1898 issue of that publication and "The Plan of Malcolm Van Staak" in the April issue for the same year mark the beginning of Post's long career of writing magazine fiction. Neither of these two stories has any importance beyond this fact, and the author chose well not to include them in any collection.

In *Pearson's Magazine* for January 1907, Post made his next appearance with a short story, also one that was never added to any of his books. Called "A Test Case," it is narrated by a character named "Coleman Winter." It illustrates how a bank might easily be defrauded by a clever criminal who has knowledge of the law. Although it seems to have this lesson in mind, the story is well-written, has an element of suspense, uses smooth dialogue, includes some sharp social criticism, and has a good ending. It shows Post as a capable professional writer and it is an obvious improvement over the writing seen in most all of the Randolph Mason tales. We can note a number of indications of the methods and talents that Post would improve upon in his stories of the next two decades.

A series of thirteen Randolph Mason stories, those which became Post's fourth book, appeared monthly next, followed by a fourteenth which for some reason was not added to the collection. Called "The Marriage Contract," it was discussed in the section dealing with the Randolph Mason stories where it properly belongs.[1]

Carolyn Wells in writing "The Technique of the Mystery Story," one of the first full-length books treating that subject in a how-to-do-it fashion, refers to a story by Post with the title "The Missing Link." This story does not appear in any of Post's books and information regarding where and when it was published serially is also missing.

Between 1916 and 1925, there appeared at least five additional stories never put into any collection. Three of these are stories with a Christmas background. The last of these three, "The Other Mary," is partially forced into that category—the basic plot bearing mostly on a type of mysticism. The plotting and the lack of real suspense unfortunately indicate a decline in the skill of the author.

Four uncollected Uncle Abner stories, which appeared quite surprisingly during 1927 and 1929, are among Post's best work. It is indeed unfortunate that they have never been put into any book. They were discussed at the end of the section on the *Uncle Abner* book because of their intrinsic relationship to that work.[2]

One other uncollected item has been noted, a story titled "The Mystery at the Mill." It appeared in 1929, but for some reason was not collected in 1920 in *The Silent Witness* along with the other Colonel Braxton stories. It seemed best to discuss the story with the material to which it is related.[3]

●●●●●●●●●

VII. THE LAST STORIES

1. The Bradmoor Murder

This group of seven stories comprises the last collection Post was to see released in book form before his death in 1930. The work represented here is certainly not Post's best work, but it is also far from his weakest effort. All these tales demonstrate his definite professional abilities and attitude in short story writing. They reflect distinctly his mastery of the form and his use of suspense, mood, economy of description, and surprise endings.

Whether by coincidence or because Post had begun to feel indications of advancing age, or because by chance he had some psychic premonitions (an interest of his during these years), these stories have the shadow of death cast across their pages. Although death had been a part of many of Post's narratives, it is more bitterly motivated in these stories, often more absurdly envisioned here than in most earlier stories. In the book preceding this collection, *The Revolt of the Birds*, Post had framed his tale in Tennyson's "The Passing of Arthur," with its theme of the death-struggle ending in a mystical and comforting passage into another state of life. In this last book, however, death is treated as totally final and unrewarding. This feeling is effectively summarized in "The Garden in Asia," the concluding tale of the collection, in the attitude of one character expressed through the narrator's words:

> But the fear haunted him that the land he beckoned toward was not, in fact, one of living man. And it was as a living man that he wished to possess this alluring, heavenly creature. He wanted her in life; in this life. He didn't care about sight and hearing, so long as the living sense of feeling remained.
> That was the whole thing.[1]

Published in America under the title *The Bradmoor Murder: Including the Remarkable Deductions of Sir Henry Marquis of Scotland Yard*, the title reflects the fact that the British detective has a part in five of the seven stories. The book was also issued in England by another publisher with the first and last stories placed in reversed positions and the book's title thus changed to *The Garden in Asia*. Reader interest in mystery tales was reaching a new high, but Post's book, facing tough competition in every direction, received only slight critical mention. The "hard-boiled" detective story had materialized and was beginning to attract the principal attention of the reading public and the press.

Although published serially over a period of several years and in six various journals, the stories in this book are uniformly alike and make a balanced collection. Of the seven, one was first published serially in 1922, others in 1923 and 1924, while two were first presented to the public in 1927. All are basically "British" in setting and atmosphere, all examples of Post's long standing and intense interest in polo, cryptograms, explorers, and England's aristocratic society. All have definite touches of the unnatural quality and stylisms of the gothic novel. They take place in the same mysterious atmospheres indulged in by two favorites of the author, Poe and Doyle. Still it would be neither fair nor correct to indicate that they are imitative, for all have the distinctive qualities that Post brought to the development of the mystery short story.

"The Bradmoor Murder" is an extended-length, "locked-room" mystery written in three parts. The story opens with a note by the author introducing a narrative purportedly written by the present Duke of Bradmoor. The former Duke is dead, supposedly murdered. The death weapon is missing and certain strange circumstances surround the event. Several experts who have been called in, including Sir Henry Marquis, are unable to explain what has happened. A famed alienist blames a family curse. A fellow explorer deems it the work of an exotic African god. Part II presents the details of the curious discovery of this god by the late Duke of Bradmoor. He, with the explorer, had come upon it secluded on a remote mountain deep in the waste regions of the Lybian (Post's spelling) desert. The plot at this point follows the stereotype of a typical, low-budget movie. In the final part, with its insipid romance, the young Duke and his love learn the vital clues that unravel the bizarre and puzzling method of death—one that had baffled the finest minds of England. The more promising qualities of this story are lost in the unfortunate length of the narrative, and what could have been one of Post's most effective stories results in a padded melodrama.

A typical Post puzzle story is "The Blackmailer" with its misleading and inverted clues woven through a twisting narrative to a surprise ending. It is told in an interesting, yet not a compelling manner. Because of this, the weird collection of characters and unusual events lose some of their potential impact. The ending, a totally unsuspected one, will allow a momentary jolt to the unwary reader. The author leaves the reader to make his own final conclusions with the ambiguous closing words: "You cursed —you blessed—Jezebel, he's here!"[2]

Post, in many of his later stories, for some reason strained to add romance to his mystery plots, but seldom did he do so with any success. His talents were for the unusual, the unexpected, the curious situation, with the plot cut up into pieces like a puzzle. Often he liked to work a simple cipher into his narrative to keep the reader guessing. In "The Cuneiform Inscription" he did this with great skill, making it the pivot point for one of his awkward romances. The surrounding material, the background of decaying British aristocarcy, the appearance of a mysterious but rewarding relative, and the trick cipher keep the story alive and worth reading.

Drawing from his long standing interest in the methods of criminology, Post based his story "The Hole in the Glass" on a simple fact emphasized in training manuals for police work. A bullet passing through a pane of glass leaves a definite clue to its direction of travel. Weaving his story once again around suspenseful African adventures and an unusual woman, the reader is kept guessing to the very end what direction the plot will finally take. While the deductions of Sir Henry Marquis do not prove to be truly "remarkable," his determined and colossal pursuit organized in quest of justice appears quite remarkable. As he frequently does, Post manages to devise a twist amid the closing lines of the story.

The catalytic object in nearly every one of Post's many problem or mystery stories is invariably some sort of wealth, whether an inheritance, cash money, or valuable gems. In "The Phantom Woman," an expensive ruby bracelet is the important object. The narrator, Sarah Whitney, accompanies Sir Henry Marquis to the scene of the "crime." The narrator's deceased mother had pledged the ruby bracelet, a family heirloom, to her daughter—but the stepfather, a repulsive, titled fiddler, who refuses to fulfil the pledge, claims the bracelet stolen by a servant. Sir Henry notes that the evidence points to a phantom as the suspect. Then, after making an unusual deal with the fiddler, he produces the bracelet from in back of a seemingly undisturbed picture frame solidly encased in spiders' webs. Such would make it appear that only a "phantom" could have penetrated the strands without leaving them broken. With the bracelet returned to the narrator, Sir Henry reveals the logic of his reasonings and the absence of an otherworldly suspect. Post, having created a story with excellent and deft touches of mystery, disappoints the reader at the end with an overly-simple solution.

Continuing with the use of material wealth as the pivot point for his plotting, Post titled the next story "The Stolen Treasure." Once again, the tale reports on events connected with the exploring of untracked regions in the Lybian (Post's spelling) desert. There a treasure of gold located by the explorers "vanishes" as they split into two groups on the return trip. Post weaves into the plot an independent American girl. The narrator, a representative of Sir Henry Marquis but otherwise left unidentified, describes this girl as "the loveliest creature in the world." Then he goes on to reveal how her romantic interest succeeds in unraveling the mystery of the missing gold. Using a fashionable Long Island club such as he himself frequented as a setting for the narration, Post allows the mystery of the African expedition to be solved. He leaves the reader puzzled, however, as to why the narration takes place at that random location.

"The Garden in Asia," the final tale, turns out to be much less than *a garden in Asia*. Among other disappointing aspects, this is perhaps the most devastating. Led to expect more by a beginning which sets up a compelling mood of mystery and suspense, the reader must read through an excessively long presentation of the facts documenting the origin of the strange garden. This unusual place is stumbled upon by the narrator in the dusk of a rainy evening while wandering through an unfamiliar Belgium countryside. A series of Canadian scenes and events which follow are done deftly with imagination and mounting suspense, but these are drawn out to such length and filled with so much detail that their importance is distorted. Some matter-of-fact events eventually grow into a puzzling account of apparent witchery. The insight into the mystery is supplied to the unidentified narrator by the same alienist who dabbles in the events of "The Bradmoor Murder" at the start of the collection. "The Garden in Asia," again originally serialized in three installments, has been padded with many minor details, interesting in themselves, but detracting constantly from the essential puzzle with which the story is concerned. The conclusion, which reveals and explains the reason for the mysterious garden and its odd inhabitants, rounds out the long tale with several artful dodges. Among those things deciphered is the curious and enigmatic phrase, "the land where men grind their wheat in the sky." This phrase had a meaning for the author beyond that allowed in the confines of the story.[3] Finally, disregarding the faults of its construction, "The Garden of Asia" can be counted as a unique story, one which bears all the indelible marks of its author's talent and interests. It displays many facets of originality and use of special techniques typical of Post's work.

This can be said for most of the tales found in this collection. Yet, readers of this book must approach it aware that it does not have all the sharply etched lines of the tragic nor the strong characterization of the *Uncle Abner* work, nor any of the subtle philosophy displayed there.

2. The Silent Witness

The Colonel Braxton stories collected in *The Silent Witness*, plus one left uncollected, indicate that Post was concerned after 1925 with regaining some of the prestige which the *Uncle Abner* tales had allowed him a decade earlier. Published serially by *American Magazine* during the final four years of his life, these fourteen pieces form a unit patterned somewhat on Post's most successful work. Certain events and attitudes demonstrate that he felt the remaining years of his life were limited and that his writing years were nearly done. He hoped naturally to finish strong.

In these stories starring Colonel Braxton, Post again turns back to the Uncle Abner period of about 1850. The western lands of old Virginia are the setting, but rather than in the cattle-raising region, these stories are set principally in the area along the Ohio River, the definite scene of only one Abner story. Abner was a cattleman, the livelihood both Post's father and grandfather followed; but Colonel Braxton is a lawyer, as Post first was himself.

Braxton has much of the keen insight that Abner was reputed to have, the same abilities to discover the proper clues and unravel puzzling situations. His method of interrogation and investigation resembles Abner's slow, ambiguous style of keeping the suspect unwary until the trap is baited. Thereafter the similarity decreases, for Abner was strictly a rural character, although well-learned. He was rugged, raw, and best viewed in the out-of-doors. Colonel Braxton, while not so fully described, seems more accustomed to the trappings of civilization, more at home seated in a well-furnished room than out in the saddle. Braxton has a basic religious philosophy, but it is not made so prominent a part of his character as is his skill at devising victories for his clients in the courtroom battle. He seems a more commonplace character than the unique Abner, who almost resembles an Old Testament prophet. As a lawyer, Braxton keeps close to the justice of the courts and the letter of the law. Only on a rare occasion does he deliberately allow the guilty person the uncertain punishment of banishment or a fate through the working of Providence, as Abner often did to settle the score.

Somehow, for these reasons, these stories do not have the commanding appeal of the *Uncle Abner* tales, nor do they have the rare and delicate nuance of tragedy that elevates most of the Abner pieces to the potential of classics. Of the Braxton stories, all but two are strictly third-person narratives—lacking the personal warmth which Abner's nephew maintained. The narrator is left unidentified except for a few brief lines in the opening tale, "The Metal Box."

There is some tendency in several stories to set up a clerk of the circuit court, a Mr. Dabney Mason, as a foil for Braxton, but never in the able manner that Post used Squire Randolph as a contrast to Abner. Whereas Post created Abner as a believable individual with sufficient vitality and warmth, Colonel Braxton lacks color and appears frequently an automated creature. Abner seems fully alive, but Colonel Braxton seldom exhibits more than a single dimension.

Thus, aiming high, the book would appear to be disappointing in terms of total results. The central character is a potentially strong hero. He uses his sharp knowledge of the law, the faults of human beings, and the manners of the courtroom to overcome murderers, thiefs, and assorted evil-doers. Philosophy and religion are woven into the tales in tasteful proportions. But the final product is not smoothly finished, and consequently it sometimes bores more than it entertains.

Post develops some interest, but seldom creates suspense in a degree we would expect. While most of the plots are pregnant with possibilities, the opening parts of these stories drag. Done mostly in straight prose, these parts, sometimes amounting to fifty percent of the entire tale, lack the dramatic impact of dialogue. Greater use of dialogue in these parts would enliven the action and draw the reader more readily into the events. Instead, we are treated too often to the steady drone of the faceless narrator. When, usually about midway in these pieces, Post switches to dialogue, the stories improve immensely—though they are lopsided as a result.

In a number of these stories, as he does in "The Metal Box,"[1] Post goes back to use ideas that appeared first in some of his non-fiction presented many years earlier.[2] The fact introduced into the fiction here is the contents of the metal box. This we learn is a microscope rather than some bizarre secret, and Colonel Braxton uses it, as Post had described in his earlier article, to prove that the signature on a will was written before the paper had been folded, and that the legal conveyance was a later addition. Post wrote this tale skillfully, but at the end it seems little more than a puppet show controlled by the author. Most interesting in this piece, one of the two first-person narratives in the collection, is the section where the narrator identifies himself as a great-grandson of Post's notable great-great grandfather. This is brought out in a paragraph where the boy narrator's grandfather speaks:

> "In my father's house," he said, "there used to be a little circular glass window on which three names had been scratched with the diamond setting of a ring: 'Aaron Burr;' 'Harman Blennerhassett,' and 'Daniel Davisson.' It was a meeting of conspirators; but my father, Daniel Davisson was not one of them. Burr was a relative and a guest, but he told him the truth. 'You're an infernal fool,' he said, 'and Tom Jefferson will hang you!' "[3]

The second tale, "The Dead Man's Shoes," is one of the better ones in the book. The clues and the events are carefully plotted and the mood is somber and effective. Its principal fault is that of most, the opening paragraphs are a monotonous prose, unlightened with dialogue to heighten the dramatic aspects of the plot. Yet, it does end strongly with a neat, simple twist.

"The Invisible Client," the next story, makes prominent use of Post's favorite proposition, which governed his philosophy, his religion and, on occasion, his legal views—the idea of the providence of God. Post, in his later years, leaning again toward his Christian background, has Colonel Braxton comment in the closing sentence, "Dabner . . . you name the power correctly. . . . It was the King of Kings!" Also apparent here is the somewhat extrasensory outlook that Post flirted with in some of his later writings. Again, while well-written, the plot is too simple and the action too obviously contrived to fit the overly-simple clues furnished by the author.

In the fourth piece, "The Survivor," the plot again hinges on the tell-tale marks a bullet leaves in a pane of glass revealing to the knowledgeable investigator the direction of its travel. Here he uses the fact doubly, because two bullets are involved and the clues show which victim died first, which second, and who consequently was, if only momentarily, the true survivor. This allows a good surprise ending to a dramatic courtroom scene which the narrator has termed "the strangest case that ever happened in Virginia." The story, however, is hampered somewhat by the melodramatic romance which is interwoven in a careless fashion.

Perhaps the trickiest of the stories collected here is that one titled "The Guardian."[4] Colonel Braxton is effective here as a shrewd lawyer "hero" and proves himself an able agent of "The Guardian of the Fatherless." Although the plot hangs delicately on the melodramatic, it is an entertaining bit resulting from the author's outstanding abilities with the mystery short-story form.

Published serially under the more fitting title, "The Forgotten Witness," the next story was retitled in the collection "The Cross-Examination." It is based on an actual case mentioned many years earlier in Post's nonfiction work. This factual basis does not, however, influence its value as fiction. It is a good illustration of the author's often emphasized proposition, that the criminal who sets up a fabricated system of events always neglects to complete the chain at some point. In this case the criminal overlooks a door, and the door proves to be the shrewd attorney's sole, but convincing witness. A light tale, almost too obviously contrived, it lacks impact and entertainment value at the end.

Post once stated the benefits to dramatists and novelists that wills provided,[5] and during his long career as an author he used almost with reckless frequency the devices of inheritances and wills as a motivation for the crime and mystery problems of his many plots. In "The Heir at Law," he uses the material again, but this time in one of his more effective manners. The trick to the story is not in the will, but in the cunning and foresight of the attorney. Here Post succeeds somewhat in increasing the suspense and dramatic content, while effectively avoiding the melodramatic. The result is an entertaining, readable tale with an added degree of realism.

The eighth story of the collection, "The Guilty Man," is set in a courthouse where a Grand Jury investigation is taking place. After we are presented with two suspects, in a thoroughly melodramatic fashion Braxton baits his trap and uncovers the real murderer. Caught by the attorney's shrewd maneuvering and the presentation of damaging evidence, the guilty man brings the case to a quick conclusion by taking his own life. The final and complete evidence shows up in the lining of the murderer's coat, a device employed for surprise endings by Post in several stories of earlier collections.

"The Mark on the Window," next in order, has strong dramatic possibilities—the murder of a judge, an angry mob, and a courtroom scene that reveals the solution to the crime in a well-written surprise ending. Post again uses a simple clue, but manages enough suspense to carry the reader's interest toward the concluding events. With a stronger beginning the dramatic conclusion would have been better balanced and the story a more successful example of the author's talents. The closing statement of Colonel Braxton is particularly effective as a concluding paragraph.

> "Yes," he said, "I forced you to write your own indictment . . . for it was an ancient custom of our father's, in a particularly atrocious and cold-blooded murder, to compel the guilty man to dig his own grave before they hanged him!"[6]

Tenth in order, "The Vanished Man" is perhaps the best of the stories in the book. After a baffling presentation of the facts, the "vanished man" is left undisturbed by the lawyer, his whereabouts revealed, and the reasoning behind the "crime" explained. Colonel Braxton puts compassion above principle and sums up the matter in a sentence conceived in terms of another variation of the author's often repeated proposition:

> "For I have learned one thing—one thing in a long experience of life—I have learned to keep silent and to stand aside when the inscrutable Providence of God is moving to the adjustment of some troubled matters in the affairs of men!"[7]

Such an ideal policy is difficult to maintain with the ease allowed Colonel Braxton, and earlier allowed Uncle Abner—but Melville Davisson Post at several points in his life was fully aware of this difficulty.

Going back again to lift a bit of scientific criminology from his earlier nonfiction writings, Post based "The Mute Voices"[8] on the fact that the pattern droplets of blood make on a surface indicate the direction in which a wounded individual has traveled. The delicate situation involved in the murder, together with the suspense in the courtroom as Colonel Braxton awaits the proper time to promote his defense of the accused, make this story potentially exciting. In a fashion typical of his methods, Post arranged the events to allow for a conclusion in which everything is finally solved—the innocent saved and the true murderer revealed. It is an excellent plot, but Post has again put too much of the story into straight descriptive and explanatory prose, thus robbing his work of the full dramatic possibilities available. Post says himself in the third sentence at the beginning of this tale: "There was in it very nearly every dramatic incident." This is true, and disregarding some apparent defects, the story remains an interesting and readable piece of short fiction.

Returning to the first-person narrator in "The Leading Case," Post identifies the narrator only as "I" and as a young spectator. This young spectator has no personal involvement in the trial depicted in this tale other than at the end to be the surprised recipient of a kiss from the comely young lady who was the victorious defendant. This light touch alone justifies the use of the first-person narrative. This girl, described as "of all lovely things she was the perfection of God's work," is near the point of losing title to a tract of valuable land. But Braxton, with a simple observation of a document presented in evidence, proves forgery on the part of the plaintiff. The author, as usual, made a skillful selection of words and language in constructing this mild tale, but he has weighed it down with overly-long sections of flat prose where dialogue would have given added interest.

How dialogue helps to enliven a short piece of fiction is amply illustrated in "The White Patch," the concluding piece of the collection. This is perhaps the best balanced tale of the book. As he usually did, Post kept his scene, time, and characters well within the classic limits and—mixed with good portions of dialogue, plus economy of language—he created here a tale with all the vitality of drama. The plot, a story of libel and ruined lives, has many of the dimensions of tragedy. Colonel Braxton's shrewd investigating and cunning questioning lead to a fitting conclusion. "The White Patch" is a first-rate story, closing an ambitious book and career.

For some undetermined reason, one additional story featuring Colonel Braxton was not included in *The Silent Witness*. It should be considered as an equal to these others. Titled "The Mystery at the Mill" and published serially, as were all the others, in *American Magazine*, its plot is arranged with all the professional finesse of which Post was capable. Called by the editor, a "great story of the inscrutable justice that moves behind the deeds of men," it follows the sharp-witted attorney on an adventure in which he solves a cruel murder and then observes what seems to be the avenging agency of God settling the misdeed in representative Old Testament-style.

The Colonel Braxton stories, as indicated earlier, found Post striving to match the success that he had experienced at the peak of his career. Drawing together many of the assets and ingredients that had worked well for him and brought him a well-earned popularity, he wrote about a past history with which he was thoroughly acquainted. He blended together in his chief character many of the attributes of Uncle Abner together with some of the eccentric lawyer, Randolph Mason, along with a touch of the abilities given his British and French detective heroes. While Post has created in this last collection interesting and entertaining tales, all worth reading, they lack the gleam, the originality, and the force that rightly earned the more successful tales their fame. *The Silent Witness*, while not equalling the ambitions its author had for it, is a firm work and one that any professional author with goals similar to those of Post need not regret.

IX. A FINAL EVALUATION

Judging the lifetime literary accomplishments of Melville Davisson Post is not a simple task. His present fortune is to belong to that group of authors, due to some seemingly unwritten law, who are subjected to near-total neglect. This is partly traceable to the phenomena that mediocre work and sometimes inferior work, which meets a public fancy, will draw all attention away from those items which do have a significant value causing what is worthy of critical attention to be ignored. Thus, only with a thorough application of research and item by item review can we conclude that Post has not received proper recognition for his several contributions to the literature of America. While there are no reasons to judge his contributions either as unmatchable or indispensable (terms which can be used only rarely), what he did accomplish may still be considered of importance, even if only of minor importance because of the depreciated rating of short fiction at this time. Also, we must allow that his contributions are not in any great quantity—much of what he wrote has been fairly judged and assigned to the limbo it deserves.[1]

The most obvious injustice to his neglected accomplishments has resulted, ironically, from the recognition granted Post as an author of mystery and detective stories. Undoubtedly, this restricted praise is the product of an erroneous view, one which once established is mirrored by those who avoid doing original investigations. A prime objective of this book-length study has therefore been to provide evidence to effect a change in this unreasoned classification. The necessity for a reordered recognition of Melville Davisson Post is plain—however, viewed realistically, this does not guarantee the possibility of its success. Too often, history reports, such efforts tend to fall victim to the same obstacle they strive to overcome.

It appears that Post was attracted to enigmas; in fact he created them when they did not exist. Therefore, he undoubtedly brought upon himself, to a large extent, the very enigma that has been the legacy of his career as a writer. Post wrote to make money, and having such a goal, he proceeded on the basis that an author's principal aim should be primarily to write material that would entertain the reader. Post assumed that such work would attract the most readers, be most saleable, and earn the greatest sums of money. These points he developed with great success and remarkable skill. The result was that he became in the years between 1910 and 1930 one of the more frequently read writers of magazine fiction, and he received the top prices for his work. As his fame as a writer of mystery and detective tales grew, he accepted the role and even promoted it. Seeing perhaps the profit in being himself a mystery, he limited published knowledge of his personal life to a few guarded facts and ambiguous statements. Thus, by revealing to the public only his shadow and by ignoring his real talents. Melville Davisson Post aided his own demise.

The history of the mystery and detective story as a type of literature is lengthy and complex if one seeks to trace every one of its features back to their earliest source.[2] The mystery and detective story, as we are most familiar with it, had its principal modern advent in the work of Edgar Allan Poe. Almost all of today's mystery and detective fiction can be said to have evolved from Poe's efforts in this category. There were a number of near-imitators of Poe's work who contributed memorable tales over the next several decades, plus some works less imitative. Following

Poe, the modern mystery and detective story flourished as readers, writers, and books grew steadily in number. When A. Connan Doyle came upon the scene after 1887 with his cleverly-drawn detective, Sherlock Holmes, whose name is almost synonymous with the term "detective," he added impetus to the form. As Post noted in the "Introduction" to his first collection of stories in 1896, the reader was caught in a near "flood" of such stories. It was for this reason, being already enigmatic and unique in his approach, Post sought to invert the commonplace plot. In his attempt he created Randolph Mason, not as a detective, but as an attorney, waging a personal vendetta against Fate and lacking any moral standard but his own. Mason abetted various criminal acts, including murder, by casting his extraordinary powers and intelligence against the laws of the state. This was Post's first contribution, one which, while it never predominated, nevertheless is found in varied modes with great regularity in the modern tale of this field.

Despite success and fame as a result of two books of Randolph Mason stories (unique offerings, but mostly mediocre in construction), Post's next contribution was another complete change of style. *Dwellers in the Hills* is not only a minor masterpiece, but is completely removed from the mystery and detective category. This short novel is an ode to childhood, to nature, to adventure, and to life. The relationship of a remarkable boy and a magnificent horse recorded here has been seldom matched by any other writer. *Dwellers in the Hills* is a worthy contribution to American literature, but it is almost totally unknown to the general reader, even those who have read Post's more popular materials. More persons need an opportunity to read this short, but beautifully written and exciting book.

In Post's next three books there is again much mediocre and some inferior work. Although the third Randolph Mason book, *The Corrector of Destinies*, the novel, *The Gilded Chair*, and the unusual, disguised collection, *The Nameless Thing*, all have instances of brilliance, for the most part they deserve a measure of the neglect they have been accorded. Again in these three books little appears to assign Post to the mystery and detective tale classification exclusively. Only in *The Nameless Thing* do we find some such material. This last is a little understood collection, never properly criticized, put together in an interesting if not original fashion. It also contains one of the best and most neglected of Post's mystery and detective tales, first published serially under the title "A Critique of Monsieur Poe."

Post had been writing and publishing tales about his finest character, Uncle Abner, for seven years before they were collected into the deservedly famous *Uncle Abner, Master of Mysteries*. It is not only the best of Post's work, but one of the truly great collections of mystery and detective stories of all time. The chief contributions made here by Post are through his character, Abner. Here is the first great "non-detective" who solves crimes. Also with Abner, we find a character who does not wait upon the law, but administers justice as he sees it in accordance with the powers of Providence—although he often cooperates with and always sides with the law in a manner justified in the frontier setting of the tales. Perhaps Abner's method of solving crimes is one of the most important contributions, for he operates not only on shrewd intelligence in sorting out significant clues, but he has the added ability to read human nature. In these Abner stories, in nearly every instance, Post has devised plots that have various aspects of the tragic drama. Many good things have been said about these stories and many more remain to be said—they are a supreme accomplishment.

Profiting from his fame, Post was able during the remaining years of his life to publish nine more books, but none a challenge to his *Uncle Abner* stories. Six of these books have many elements in them that give credence to the classification of Post as an author of mystery and detective tales. In them are found some of the more commonplace detective characters he developed, the Britisher, Sir Henry Marquis; the Frenchman, Monsieur Jonquelle; and the bungling American Chief of the Secret Service, Walker. Also in these six books there are other elements which permit the further opinion that although it is partially correct to classify them as mystery and detective works, they are only borderline cases. Many of their stories and features are not closely related to the typical mystery and detective tale, but are significant in having a wider appeal. The last of these books again features a lawyer hero, Colonel Braxton, who operates much in the manner of Abner—but unfortunately these stories were not written with an equal skill. Discounting Post's one nonfiction book as inferior, there remain two other works, both novelettes and neither having any resemblance to a mystery-detective work. Both of these are unique books, but only mediocre in execution. *The Mountain School-Teacher*, a reconstruction of the life of Christ, appeals to a limited audience and perhaps says more than most readers realize. *The Revolt of the Birds*, a hazy tale, almost a fable, enlightens momentarily, then struggles to a dreamy conclusion.

Through all his work, the good and much of the bad, Post also added other worthy contributions that deserve more notice than they have been given. In Randolph Mason, Post helped lay the ground for acceptance of the anti-hero. He introduced often into his stories criminals as leading characters and, in a minor, primitive way, gave a start to the hard-boiled facet of the field. More generally, but also more importantly, he helped develop the sharpened technique that improved the form of the plotted short story. This he coupled with an economical use of language that helped to give short fiction some of the fast-paced action that is a distinctive feature of the modern variety. Although no single author deserves any special credit for this development of style, Post deserves as much credit as any should have earned.

Melville Davisson Post, in addition to being an author of many mysteries, was a man of many mysteries. He was an enigma in life and remains an enigma—a man who received some fame and praise, but not enough—and that he received for the wrong reasons.

NOTES

INTRODUCTION

[1] Joseph Shearing, *The Golden Violet: the Story of a Lady Novelist.* With a forward by Sinclair Lewis. (New York, 1943). The author's name is a pseudonym of Mrs. Gabrielle Margaret Vere Campbell Long.

[2] Ibid., p. 5.

[3] Edmund Wilson, "Why Do People Read Detective Stories?" *Classics and Commercials, a Literary Chronical of the Forties*, (New York, 1950) pp. 231-237.

[4] New York *Times*, CXIX (April 26, 1970) 7:2. Mrs. Fishman also observes later in her article:

> The line between the straight mystery (whodunit) and suspense (we know whodunit; how will he be caught?) is blurring. Now the traditional roman policier is being updated with anti-heroes, ethnic sleuths and social commentary.

Post in creating the character of Randolph Mason in his first stories in 1896, a character who can easily be described as an anti-hero, proved himself an unique innovator many years before the above noted trend took hold.

I. BIOGRAPHY

[1] Writers' Project of the Works Progress Administration in the State of West Virginia, *West Virginia: a Guide to the Mountain State* (Oxford University Press, 1941) p. 210.

[2] *Uncle Abner, Master of Mysteries*, p. 159.

[3] Little is known regarding Prudence Izard Davisson, but she is reported to have been a cousin of Aaron Burr.

[4] According to the will of Daniel Davisson made July 16, 1810. See: "West Virginia Estate Settlements," *West Virginia History*, XXII (Oct. 1960) 38.

[5] Jack Sandy Anderson, "Melville Davisson Post," *West Virginia History*, XXVIII (July, 1967) 271-281. This article, by a distant relative of Post, produced for the first time in public print many of the essential and valuable biographical facts regarding M. D. Post's personal and family history.

[6] Charles Carpenter, "The Harrison County Homes of Melville Davisson Post," *The West Virginia Review*, XIV (March, 1937) 195.

[7] Anderson, p. 273.

[8] *Who's Who in America, 1903-1905* (A. N. Marquis & Co., 1903). This and superseding editions print the 1871 birth date. Similarity of nearly all reference elsewhere indicate this to be the prime source for all information to date. One variation was noted: Oscar Fay Adams, *A Dictionary of American Authors* (5th ed., Boston, 1905, p, 544) gives birth date as 1870.

[9] Grant Overton, *Cargoes for Crusoes (D. Appleton, 1924) p. 59.*
[10] Anderson, p. 274.
[11] Ethel Clark Lewis, "West Virginia's Most Noted Writer," *The West Virginia Review*, VIII (December 1930) 81.
[12] *Dwellers in the Hills*, p. 146 and p. 195.
[13] *Uncle Abner*, p. 42.
[14] Post Family. Papers, 1842-1926. [Includes misc. papers, early school work, and misc. mss. of M. D. Post as well as various family papers.] *West Virginia Collection* (No. 538) West Virginia University Library, Morgantown, W. Va.
[15] Ibid. [16] Ibid. [17] Ibid
[18] Anderson, p. 274. [19] *The Critic*, XXXVIII (April, 1901) 293.
[20] John A. Howard, "Melville Davisson Post," *Library of Southern Literature* (Atlanta, Ga.: Martin & Hoyt, 1929 [c1907, 1909]) p. 4167. This essay on M. D. Post by his first law partner, introducing a selection of Post's writings, although brief in regard to their relationship, presents a variety of otherwise useful and accurate information.
[21] *The Strange Schemes of Randolph Mason*, "Introduction," p. 4.
[22] Howard, p. 4168. [23] Post Family. Papers.
[24] Sam T. Mallison, The Wheeling Daily *Intelligencer* (Dec. 9, 1936) 7.
[25] *The Man of Last Resort, or the Clients of Randolph Mason*, "Preface," p. xii.
[26] Post Family. Papers. [27] Howard, p. 4170.
[28] This point regarding Quiller's attitude toward women was noted in a review of *Dwellers in the Hills* published in *The Critic*, XXIX (Oct. 1901) 375, but has been ignored in all subsequent written opinions of the book.
[29] Wheeling Daily *Intelligencer* (June 30, 1903) 4.
[30] Howard, p. 4170.
[31] *The Illustrated Monthly West Virginian*, II (Oct. 1908) 41.
[32] Baltimore *Sun* (June 20, 1907).
[33] Presently a part of the University of Pennsylvania, Du Bois Campus.
[34] M.D. Post, Correspondence. *West Virginia Collection* (Nos. 1143, 1635) West Virginia University Library, Morgantown, W. Va.
[35] The Clarksburg *Exponent* (Feb. 12, 1914) 1.
[36] Carpenter, p. 194.
[37] National Economic League, *Preliminary Report on Efficiency in the Administration of Justice*, prepared by Charles W. Eliot, et al. (Boston [Castis-Claflin, 1914?]).
[38] *Uncle Abner*, p. 161-162.
[39] Warren Wood, *Representative Authors of West Virginia* (Worth-While Book Co., 1926) p. 185.
[40] Blanch Colton Williams, "Introduction," *O'Henry Memorial Award Stories 1919*, Society of Arts and Sciences (Doubleday, Page, 1921) p. xiii.
[41] Carpenter, p. 195. [42] New York *Times* (Oct. 1, 1922) 18.
[43] Mallison, p. 7.
[44] Isabelle Minear, "Visit a Literary Shrine," *West Virginia Review*, XII

(Oct. 1934) 21.
[45] Mallison, p. 7.   [46] New York *Times* (Oct. 29, 1924) 4:4.
[47] Ibid. (May 11, 1927) 42:7.
[48] Post Family. Papers.   [49] Mallison, p. 7.
[50] M. D. Post, "The Devil's Track," *The Country Gentleman*, XCII (July, 1927) 40.

II. THE RANDOLPH MASON STORIES

[1] *Strange Schemes*, p. 1
[2] Ibid., pp. 1-2   [3] Ibid., pp. 2-3   [4] Ibid., pp. 3-4.
[5] Ibid., p. 4   [6] Ibid., p. 4.   [7] Ibid., pp. 4-5.
[8] Ibid., p. 6.   [9] Ibid., p. 6   [10] Ibid., p. 7.
[11] A typescript copy of "The Men of the Jimmy" located among Post's papers at West Virginia University Library shows the piece as being part of a work tentatively titled *The Strange Schemes of J. Hatley Mason*. "J. Hatley" is scratched out and "Randolph" is written above. Similarly, in a typescript copy of "The Corpus Delicti," we find "Randolph" entered in blank spaces left in front of the name "Mason."
[12] *Strange Schemes*, pp. 8-9.   [13] Ibid., p. 9.   [14] Ibid., p. 21.
[15] Ibid., p. 28-29.   [16] Ibid., p. 24-25.
[17] Ibid., pp. 43-44.   [18] Ibid., pp. 55-63.   [19] Ibid., p. 67.
[20] In Chicago, Adolph L. Luetgert was charged with the bizarre murder of his wife. Owner of a sausage factory, Luetgert was accused of killing his wife there on May 1, 1897, and disposing of her butchered body in a vat of boiling caustic potash. Shortly thereafter, in New York City, Martin Thorn was accused of killing William Guldensuppe, a rival suitor, on June 25, 1897. Police believed he cut up the body and disposed of the pieces in various locations about the city. Some mutilated parts of the body were found, excepting the head, and identification of these was doubtful. Neither of these accused murderers were, however, as fortunate as the accused of Post's "Corpus Delicti." Luetgert was convicted on February 9, 1898, after a sensational series of trials and sentenced to prison for life. Thorn was convicted on November 30, 1897, at the conclusion of a second trial and died in the electric chair at Sing Sing Prison on August 1, 1898.
[21] The publishers, in an advertisement for *Strange Schemes* placed in back of the 1923 reprint edition of *The Corrector of Destinies*, noted in an overly-restrained statement:

> Unlike the leading characters of practically all mystery stories, Randolph Mason is not a detective with uncanny powers of deduction, nor is he a clever young newspaper man. On the contrary, he is a calm, collected, almost sinister lawyer whose specialty is in advising clients how to evade the law.

[22] A typescript copy of "Two Plungers of Manhattan" shows the piece to have been first titled "High Grade Robbery as a Fine Art."
[23] A typescript copy of "The Error of William Van Broom" shows the

first intended title to have been "The Chemical Bank of Duluth."
[24] *Strange Schemes*, p. 149.   [25] Ibid., p. 246.
[26] Gilmore County, W. Va.
[27] *The Critic*, XXVII (March 27, 1897) 218.
[28] *The Man of Last Resort*, p. 101.
[29] It is hard to escape concluding this when we read of "the Episcopal minister, Rev. Mr. Boreland, and . . . an obscure practitioner named Gouch." (Ibid., p. 124.)
[30] Ibid., pp. 177-178.   [31] Ibid., p. 252.   [32] Ibid., p. 253.
[33] Ibid., p. 257.   [34] Ibid., p. 284.
[35] *Pearson's Magazine*, XXIII (January 1907) 120.
[36] *The Corrector of Destinies*, p. 150.
[37] Ibid., p. 188.   [38] Ibid., p. 167.
[39] "The Marriage Contract," *Pearson's Magazine*, XXV (June 1908) 598-607.

III. TWO NOVELS AND THE NAMELESS THING

1. Dwellers in the Hills

[1] Post had joined John A. Howard in Wheeling, W. Va., in 1892, but would soon establish a more prominent partnership with John McGraw in Grafton, W. Va., about 1901.

[2] Charles Carpenter, "The Harrison County Homes of Melville Davisson Post," *West Virginia Review*, XIV (March 1937) 217.

[3] Originally in manuscript form the book was titled "The Four Hundred." This was changed at least twice before Post settled on the well-chosen published title.

[4] *The Critic*, XXXVIII (January 1901) 6.

[5] In the summer of 1969 this writer had the privilege to speak with Mr. Aquilla Ward, then a man of some eighty years, and to hear his version of the incident Post used. Mr. Ward still resided nearby Templemoor where he had lived all his life. The Ward and Post families were very close and Melville's brother, Sidney, married Mr. Ward's sister, Celia. For the principal character's name Post used "Quiller," a shortened form for Aquilla.

[6] Mary Meek Atkeson, "The Development of Literature in West Virginia," *Semi-Centennial History of West Virginia* (Semi-Centennial Commission, 1913) p. 567. Mrs. Atkeson wrote about Post's first novel, saying "and particularly in 'Dwellers in the Hills' (1901) has drawn many pictures of his friends and neighbors of Harrison County."

[7] Among the places these names are used we may note: (Carper) "The Rule Against Carper," *The Man of Last Resort*, p. 261; (Woodford) "Woodford's Partner," *Strange Schemes*, p. 95; (Roy's Tavern) "The Angel of the Lord," *Uncle Abner*, p. 41; (Betts) "The Hidden Law," *Uncle Abner*, p. 191; (Marsh) "Naboth's Vineyard," *Uncle Abner*, p. 323.

[8] *Dwellers in the Hills*, p. 2.   [9] Ibid., p. 21.   [10] Ibid., p. 76.

[11] Ibid., pp. 78-79.   [12] Ibid., p. 85.   [13] Ibid., p. 128.
[14] *The Critic*, XXXIX (October 1901) 375.
[15] *Dwellers in the Hills*, pp. 142-143.
[16] Ibid., pp. 146-147.

2. The Gilded Chair

[1] Mentioned in a letter dated June 14, 1909, to Henry S. Schrader of Wheeling, W. Va., whose secretarial service prepared the typescript of this book and other work of the author. M. D. Post Correspondence, *West Virginia Collection*, West Virginia University Library, Morgantown, W. Va.

[2] The Republican Platform in 1908 ignored the Japanese immigration question, but both the Democrat Party Platform and that of the Independence Party for that year took a strong stand for legislation to limit "Asiatic immigrants."

[3] Atherton Brownell, "Our War with Japan, A Brief History of Events Ending March, 1917." *Pearson's Magazine* XVII (May 1907) 480-496.

[4] According to Jabez T. Sunderland in his book *Rising Japan* (New York, G. P. Putnam's Sons, 1918) on page 67 of the chapter entitled "Menace of A Japanese Invasion," the predictions of a war between Japan and the United States were numerous. He wrote: "Mr. George Kennan has compiled a list of twenty-two of these sinister yarns. Mr. Kanakami in an article in the *Atlantic Monthly* refers to six others. Ever since 1906 the pot has been kept boiling."

[5] Homer Lea, *The Valor of Ignorance* (New York, Harper & Bro., 1942). Published originally in 1909, Lea's book made some accurate predictions of the military strategy used by the Japanese in 1941 and thus gained new recognition. Although *The Gilded Chair* was not reprinted, library records do show it received a surge of reader interest during the years of World War II because of this theme Post has incorporated.

[6] (e.g.) Chapter XVI, "The Lesson in Magic," Chapter XVII, "The Stair of Visions;" Chapter XVIII, "The Sign by the Way;" etc.

[7] "Within twenty seconds the Duke emptied the magazine of the Mannlicher four times into the mob—a shot for every second." *The Gilded Chair*, p. 293.

[8] A reversal of the romantic situation Post used in "The Marriage Contract," the last and only uncollected Randolph Mason story, published in *Pearson's Magazine*, June 1908.

[9] The following selection from the section wherein Cyrus Childers and the Marchesa discuss their ideas of religion is also an excellent example of the simple, objective style of writing Post used throughout much of this book:

> "Ah, Marchesa," he said, in his big voice, "what do you think of this night?"
> The Marchesa looked out at the bay flooded with its soft topaz color.
> "It is wonderful," she said. "It makes me believe that

somehow, somewhere. our dreams shall come true by the will of God."

The old man's jaw tightened on his answer.

"Who makes the will of God?"

"It is the great moving impulse at the heart of things," said the Marchesa.

"Nonsense," said the old man. "One makes the will of God for himself. The moving impulse is here," and he struck his chest with his clenched hand. "What we dream comes true if we make it come true. But it does not if we sit on our doorstep or shut outselves up to await a visitation."

He made a great sweeping gesture. "How can these elements that are dead and an appearance resist the human mind that is alive and real?"

"But providence," said the Marchesa, "chance, luck, fortune, circumstance, do these words mean nothing?"

The old man laughed.

"Marchesa," he said, "if a man had a double equipment of skull space he could sweep these words out of the language."

"Then you do not believe they stand for anything?"

"They stand for ignorance."

"We are taught from the cradle," continued the Marchesa, "that there is in the universe a guiding destiny that moves the lives of each one of us to a certain fortune."

"It is the wildest fancy," replied the old man, "that the human mind ever got hold of. . . ." (*The Gilded Chair*, pp. 112-114.)

For some readers the comment of the Marchesa, ". . . providence . . . chance, luck, fortune, circumstance, do these words mean nothing?" may bring to mind the often quoted line of Hemingway's *Farewell to Arms*: "Abstract words, such as glory, honor, courage, or hallow were obscene beside the concrete names of villages. . . ."

[10] *The Gilded Chair*, pp. 337-338.

3. The Nameless Thing

[1] The best known examples of this method would be Boccaccio's *Decameron* and Chaucer's *Canterbury Tales*.

[2] For reasons such as the order of serial publication, style, and settings, it seems most unlikely that Post conceived of the book as a whole before most of the individual stories were written—their common though many-faceted theme being the catalyst that brought about their union in the unique manner the author adopted.

[3] (A) Post gave only enough information about the contents of the box

to whet the imagination, scarcely enough to allow an "armchair detective" to devise any accurate conclusion before the explanation is unravelled by the author at the book's end. Post's method was not to furnish all pieces of the puzzle as later mystery writers have practiced for the entertainment of the reader who desires to outguess *the detective*. Those who have criticized the author for not doing so, have criticized him unfairly in this respect.

(B) The greater part of the contents of the box consisted of numerous newspaper clippings, all having "some relation to the general idea of retributive justice." It might be that the box is a somewhat accurate description of one the author himself maintained to provide a source of plots for such tales as this book includes. Post, in addition to using names and events from his own experiences, often described in his stories various personal objects to which he assessed extraordinary value.

[4] A similar incident reportedly happened to Post himself one day during a walk in DuBois, Pennsylvania, and perhaps as he mulled it over, he realized how it could be magnified, by unrelated circumstances, out of proportion to its real importance.

IV. UNCLE ABNER

[1] *Strange Schemes*, p. 2.
[2] Ibid., p. 2.   [3] Ibid., p. 2.   [4] Ibid., p. 3.
[5] *Man of Last Resort*, pp. ix-x.
[6] *Saturday Evening Post*, CLXXXVII (Dec. 26, 1914) 21, 25-26.
[7] Ibid., (Feb. 27, 1915) 21-23.
[8] *Strange Schemes*, p. 2.
[9] Post gave no clues to the definite time period for the adventures of Abner, but the use of the term "abolitionist" in one case (p. 293), Doc Storm's father described as a physician in the Napoleonic Wars of 1800-1815 (p. 322), and Nathaniel Davisson (a son of Daniel Davisson) described as being very old (p. 336) puts the time period in the general vicinity of not more than 10 years before the start of the Civil War and the birth of West Virginia as a separate state.
[10] *Dwellers in the Hills*, p. 104.
[11] Pagination for all quotations in Chapter IV not otherwise identified refer to *Uncle Abner, Master of Mysteries*.
[12] Similarities between Randolph and Post are several: both were adept at speech making; both dressed to emphasize their social status; both were short of stature; and both practiced the profession of law devotedly.
[13] Post Family. Papers, 1842-1926. *West Virginia Collection*, West Virginia University Library, Morgantown, W. Va.
[14] The following is the order of printing in the collection, followed by a number in parentheses indicating the theoretical order of the writing of each tale—and thus the order in which we have treated them here.

I. The Doomdorf Mystery. (11)	X. The Devil's Tools. (5)
II. The Wrong Hand. (2)	XI. The Hidden Law. (7)
III. The Angel of the Lord. (1)	XII. The Riddle. (8)
IV. An Act of God. (9)	XIII. The Straw Man. (15)
V. The Treasure Hunter (12)	XIV. The Mystery of Chance. (17)
VI. The House of the Dead Man. (3)	XV. The Concealed Path. (18)
VII. A Twilight Adventure. (6)	XVI. The Edge of the Shadow. (16)
VIII. The Age of Miracles. (13)	XVII. The Adopted Daughter. (14)
IX. The Tenth Commandment. (4)	XVIII. Naboth's Vineyard. (10)

[15] Howard Haycraft, *Murder for Pleasure* (New York: Appleton-Century, 1941) p. 96, footnote.

[16] The serial version of this story, published in the *Pictorial Review* of February 1916, used a Judge Jackson in Abner's role and a Mr. Greenleaf, a clerk, in the Randolph role. Only the names of these characters differ, otherwise it is a typical Uncle Abner tale. Also it has proved one of the more popular having been anthologized at least four times.

V. FOUR SHORT STORY COLLECTIONS

1. The Mystery at the Blue Villa

[1] Quoted from: Warren Wood, *Representative Authors of West Virginia* (Ravenwood, W. Va.) p. 185.

[2] Post published some thirty-eight pieces of fiction during the years 1913-1918.

[3] *New York Times Book Review* (April 18, 1920) 191.

[4] ALA *Booklist* XVI (April 1920) 246.

[5] Published serially under the different title, "Some Girl" in the *Ladies Home Journal* XXXIII (May 1916) 13, 78-80.

[6] Not to be confused with Sir Henry Marquis, but may have played some part in the creation of "the sleuth of St. James's Square."

[7] *Blue Villa*, pp. 223-224. Post's use of the name "Randolph" for his broken-hearted suitor adds strength to the suggestion we have noted here.

[8] Published serially under the longer and more descriptive title, "Against the Sky of the Theater," in *Ladies Home Journal* XXXV (August 1918) 11.

2. The Sleuth of St. James's Square

[1] *New York Times Book Review* (December 12, 1920) 21, 23.

[2] Edward J. O'Brien, *The Best Short Stories of 1921 and the Yearbook of the American Short Story* (Boston: Small Mayard & Co., 1922) p. 432.

[3] Blanche Colton Williams, "Introduction," *O'Henry Memorial Award Prize Stories* 1919 (Garden City, N. Y.: Doubleday, Page, 1921) p. xiii.

[4] First published serially as "The Man from America, Whom a Girl from London Picked Up," *Ladies Home Journal* XXXIII (November, 1916) 9-10.

In this first version Post used the name of Sir James McBain instead of Sir Henry Marquis for his detective.

[5] *Saturday Evening Post* CLXXXVII (February 27, 1915) 21-23.

[6] An Italian *Count* originally occupied the place taken by Sir Henry Marquis in the collected version.

3. Monsieur Jonquelle

[1] The varying viewpoints in these stories were noted very early by Grant Overton in his Melville Davisson Post essay in his *Cargoes for Crusoes* (New York: D. Appleton & Co., 1924) p. 55; however, his "explanation" for the mixture explains nothing. There is no logical explanation other than the stories for the most part were collected as they were first published serially with an apparent lack of desire on the part of both author and publisher for any extensive revision.

[2] Willard Huntington Wright in the "Introduction" to his anthology *The Great Detective Stories* (New York: Scribner's, 1927) stated: "The story called 'The Great Cipher' . . . is, with the possible exception of Poe's 'The Gold Bug,' the best cipher story in English." (p. 24)

[3] *Monsieur Jonquelle*, p. 28.

4. Walker of the Secret Service

[1] This first Walker story was collected in *The Sleuth of St. James's Square* by adding Sir Henry Marquis to the cast of characters and changing the title to "The Reward." See p. 155 (Section V, 2. Sleuth).

[2] This tentative title is noted on a copy of parts of the manuscript material filed with the *Post Papers* at West Virginia University Library.

[3] *Walker*, p. 120.

[4] This incident is detailed in the "Biography" section of this book. See p. 55 (Section I Biography).

[5] *Walker*, p. 115.

[6] In its original typescript form Post gave this story a more picturesque and fitting title, "Spook Faces."

[7] Originally titled in typescript form "The Dime Novel Desperado."

[8] *Walker*, p. 101.

[9] Ibid., p. 117.   [10] Ibid., p. 215.

VI. THE NOVELETTES

1. The Mountain School-teacher

[1] Although almost always combined today, old usage sometimes dictated separation of the words "school" and "teacher" with a hyphen. While the combined form came into common use during the period of Post's writing career, his early schooling perhaps suggested the method he followed.

[2] See p. 46 (Section I Biography).

[3] Post was writing symbolically, and it is apparent that the "teacher" symbol fits his conception of the Christ figure of the Gospels, thus the

hyphenated term emphasizes this aspect. One might also speculate on the capitalization of "School-teacher" which Post uses consistently throughout the story, but the reason for this is no doubt the obvious one.

⁴*Mountain School-teacher*, pp. 90-91. ⁵Ibid., p. 122.
⁶Ibid., pp. 129-130. ⁷Ibid., p. [149]. ⁸Ibid., p. 163.
⁹*New York Times Book Review* (October 1, 1922) 18, 22.

2. The Revolt of the Birds

¹*Revolt of the Birds*, pp. 7-8
²Ibid., pp. 50-51.

There is some degree of truth in the narrator's statement, or more properly the author's statement, that little attention has been given Asiatic hemp by the *learned men* of the world; but, a closer look seems to refute most of the statement's strength—for over the centuries, a modicum of research will reveal, a goodly number of persons (wise and not so wise) have investigated the uses of the various forms of those substances derived from the hemp plant, still considerable controversy as to their real values, or hazards remains. Only recently has any serious scientific research been directed upon the matter in force.

³Ibid., pp. 73-74. ⁴Ibid., p. 91. ⁵Ibid., p. 128.
⁶*New York Times Book Review* (October 2, 1927) 27.

VII. NONFICTION AND UNCOLLECTED WORK

1. Nonfiction

¹The New York Public Library. Manuscript Division.

²Philo Norton McGiffen (1860-1897) was noted as a soldier of fortune who upon receiving an honorable discharge from the United States navy in 1884 accepted a commission in the Chinese navy. Also, he taught in the Chinese Naval College and commanded a Chinese warship in a battle with the Japanese in 1894. His family home was in Washington, Pennsylvania, not far from Wheeling, West Virginia, where Post practiced law at this time.

³"Mysteries of the Law: The Will in the Teapot," *Saturday Evening Post* 183 (October 15, 1910) 24-26.

⁴That we are only now slowly changing this situation is illustrated by the following lines from a recent newspaper article:

> Until recently, arrests for "common prostitution" were also fairly frequent. Under that city ordinance, a woman who had once been arrested for engaging in prostitution could be charged as a "common prostitute" any time she was found loitering on the street.
>
> However, in December 1969, Judge Doan ruled this law unconstitutional.
>
> —"Oldest Profession on Decline," *The Cincinnati Enquirer* (February 7, 1971) 6-A.

[5] "The Border Land of the Law," *Saturday Evening Post* 183 (May 20, 1911) 10-11, 46.

[6] "Extraordinary Cases: The Sealed Packet," *Saturday Evening Post* 184 (September 23, 1911) 10-11.

[7] The Tichborne case. Mark Twain was in England in 1874 and took exceptional interest in the trial. See: Paine, A. B., *The Biography of Mark Twain*, Chapter XCII.

[8] "Extraordinary Cases: Fabricated Defenses," *Saturday Evening Post* 184 (November 11, 1911) 16-17.

[9] "Extraordinary Cases: The Hidden Tenant," *Saturday Evening Post* 184 (December 30, 1911) 12-13.

[10] For details, see: p. 41 (Section I Biography).

[11] "Extraordinary Cases: The Fragments of Plaster," *Saturday Evening Post* 184 (April 20, 1912) 21-22, 72.

[12] "Recall of Judicial Decisions," *Saturday Evening Post* 185 (August 31, 1912) 3-4.

[13] Courts and their Critics," *Saturday Evening Post* 185 (September 21, 1912) 18, 61.

[14] "The Immorality of Chance," *Saturday Evening Post* 185 (November 16, 1912) 11-12, 50.

[15] "The Immortal Millions," *Saturday Evening Post* 185 (June 14, 1913) 14-15, 33.

[16] "The Lesson of the Roosevelt Trial," *Saturday Evening Post* 186 (July 12, 1913) 6, 33-34.

[17] Roosevelt, upon winning his court case, would accept only six cents in damage payments from the defendant.

[18] "Government by Magic," *Saturday Evening Post* 186 (August 2, 1913, 11, 32-33.

[19] "Humanizing the Law," *Saturday Evening Post* 186 (December 15, 1912) 9-10, 32.

[20] Ibid.

[21] "The Jury and the Judges," *Saturday Evening Post* 186 (May 18, 1914) 19, 65-66.

[22] "The Blight" was given a degree of recognition by being included in Herbert S. Mallory's anthology, *Backgrounds of Book Reviewing* (Ann Arbor, Mich., G. Wahr, 1923).

[23] See: pp. 113-116 (Section IV, part 2. Uncle Abner).

[24] "Secret Ciphers," *Saturday Evening Post* 187 (May 8, 1915) 8-9, 69.

[25] "The Invisible Army," *Saturday Evening Post* 187 (April 10, 1915) 3-5.

[26] For titles included, see: Section X. Bibliography.

[27] "Nick Carter, Realist," *Saturday Evening Post* 189 (March 3, 1917) 14-15, 59.

[28] For details, see: pp. 53-54 (Section I Biography).

2. Other Items

[1] See: pp. 85-86 (Section II. The Randolph Mason Stories).
[2] See: pp. 141-144 (Section IV. Uncle Abner).
[3] See: p. 228 (Section VII. The Last Stories).

VIII. THE LAST STORIES
1. The Bradmoor Murder

[1] *Bradmoor Murder*, p. 291.
[2] The Duke of Dorset and his American wife, chief characters of Post's 1910 novel, *The Gilded Chair*, are important characters in this tale, which could in a sense be termed a sequel to the novel.
[3] See p. 31 (Section I Biography).

2. The Silent Witness

[1] Published serially under the title "The Witness in the Metal Box."
[2] "Science and the Forger," *Saturday Evening Post* 184 (May 18, 1912).
[3] *Silent Witness*, p. 17. Daniel Davisson's wife, Prudence Izard, was reported to be a cousin to Aaron Burr.
[4] Published serially under the longer and certainly less effective title, "Colonel Braxton Chooses a Client."
[5] "Mysteries of the Law: The Will in the Teapot," *Saturday Evening Post* 183 (October 15, 1910). See pp. 198-199 (Section VII Nonfiction).
[6] *Silent Witness*, p. 203.   [7] Ibid., p. 233.
[8] Published serially under the title, "Colonel Braxton Hears the Silent Voices."

IX. A FINAL EVALUATION

[1] Much of this work has been rated "entertaining" and "interesting" for the purposes of this book-length study, but in general it does not deserve more than minimal critical attention. Most of it deserved publication as entertainment at the time it was originally published—best judged now, not as inferior, but as dated. Post met most of the standards of his time for the production of entertaining fiction. The individual reader who takes the time to search out this material will find varying amounts are still entertaining today.
[2] Two excellent short histories of mystery and detective fiction are presented as introductions to two of the best anthologies of this type of story, these being namely: *The Great Detective Stories* by Willare Huntington Wright (1927) and *The Omnibus of Crime* by Dorothy Sayers (1929).

X. BIBLIOGRAPHY

1. Books

The Strange Schemes of Randolph Mason. New York: G. P. Putnam's Sons, 1896. Reprinted as: *Randolph Mason: the Strange Schemes.* New York: G. P. Putnam's Sons, 1922.

The Man of Last Resort; or, The Clients of Randolph Mason. New York: G. P. Putnam's Sons, 1897. Reprinted as: *Randolph Mason: the Clients.* New York: G. P. Putnam's Sons, 1923.

Dwellers in the Hills. New York: G. P. Putnam's Sons, 1901.

The Corrector of Destinies: Being Tales of Randolph Mason as Related by His Private Secretary, Courtlandt Parks. New York: E. J. Clode, 1908. Reprinted as: *Randolph Mason, Corrector of Destinies.* New York: G. P. Putnam's Sons, 1923. Reprinted again as: *Randolph Mason, Corrector of Destinies.* Freeport, N. Y., Books for Libraries Press, 1971.

The Gilded Chair. New York: D. Appleton, 1910.

The Nameless Thing. New York: D. Appleton, 1912.

Uncle Abner, Master of Mysteries. New York: D. Appleton, 1918. Reprinted: *Uncle Abner, Master of Mysteries.* New York: Collier Books, 1962. (Paperback edition.)

The Mystery at the Blue Villa. New York: D. Appleton, 1919.

The Sleuth of St. James's Square. New York: D. Appleton, 1920.

The Mountain School-teacher. New York: D. Appleton, 1922.

Monsieur Jonquelle, Prefect of Police of Paris. New York: D. Appleton, 1923.

Walker of the Secret Service. New York: D. Appleton, 1924.

The Man Hunters. New York: J. H. Sears, 1926. Also: *The Man Hunters.* London; Kingsport, Tenn.: Hutchinson, 1927.

The Revolt of the Birds. New York: D. Appleton, 1927.

The Bradmoor Murder: Including the Remarkable Deductions of Sir Henry Marquis of Scotland Yard. New York: J. H. Sears, 1929. Also published, with contents rearranged, as: *The Garden in Asia.* London: Brentano's, 1929.

The Silent Witness. New York: Farrar & Rinehart, 1920.

2. Fiction in Serial Publications

"The Ventures of Mr. Clayvarden," *The Law Student's Helper*, 6 (Feb. 1898) 40-42. (Uncollected)

"The Plan of Malcolm Van Staak," *The Law Student's Helper*, 6 (Apr. 1898) 119-121. (Uncollected)

"A Test Case," *Pearson's Magazine*, 17 (Jan. 1907) 103-113. (Uncollected)

"My Friend at Bridge," *Pearson's Magazine*, 17 (Feb. 1907) 210-221. (*Corrector of Destinies* . . .)

"Madame Versay," *Pearson's Magazine*, 17 (Mar. 1907) 310-317. (*Corrector *of Destinies . . .*)

"The Burgoyne-Hayes Dinner," *Pearson's Magazine*, 17 (Apr. 1907) 391-400. (*Corrector of Destinies . . .*)

"The Copper Bonds," *Pearson's Magazine*, 17 (May 1907) 568-577. (*Corrector of Destinies . . .*)

"The District-Attorney," *Pearson's Magazine*, 17 (June 1907) 634-643. (*Corrector of Destinies . . .*)

"The Interrupted Exile," *Pearson's Magazine*, 18 (Part I, July 1907; Part II, Aug. 1907) 45-53, 168-175. (*Corrector of Destinies . . .*)

"The Last Check," *Pearson's Magazine*, 18 (Sept. 1907) 328-335. (*Corrector of Destinies . . .*)

"The Life Tenant," *Pearson's Magazine*, 18 (Oct. 1907) 417-432. (*Corrector of Destinies . . .*)

"The Pennsylvania Pirate," *Pearson's Magazine*, 18 (Nov. 1907) 481-490. (*Corrector of Destinies . . .*)

"The Virgin of the Mountain," *Pearson's Magazine*, Part I, 18 (Dec. 1907) 664-671; Part II, 19 (Jan. 1908) 28-37. (*Corrector of Destinies . . .*)

"An Adventure of St. Valentine's Night," *Pearson's Magazine*, 19 (Feb. 1908) 144-153. (*Corrector of Destinies . . .*)

"The Danseuse," *Pearson's Magazine*, 19 (Mar. 1908) 318-326. (*Corrector of Destinies . . .*)

"The Intriguer," *Pearson's Magazine*, 19 (Part I, Apr. 1908; Part II, May 1908) 417-424, 539-547. (*Corrector of Destinies . . .*)

"The Marriage Contract," *Pearson's Magazine*, 19 (June 1908) 598-607. (Uncollected)

"The Trivial Incident," *Saturday Evening Post*, 181 (Dec. 19, 1908) 10-11, 24-27. (*Nameless Thing*, pp. 95-128)

"No Defense," *Saturday Evening Post*, 183 (Aug. 13, 1910) 17-18. (*Nameless Thing*, pp. 183-193)

"A Critique of Monsieur Poe," *Saturday Evening Post*, 183 (Dec. 31, 1910) 20-21, 34. (*Nameless Thing*, pp. 296-319)

"The Locked Bag," *Saturday Evening Post*, 183 (Feb. 4, 1911) 8-9, 40-42. (*Nameless Thing*, pp. 239-262)

"After He Was Dead," *Atlantic*, 107 (Apr. 1911) 464-472. (*Nameless Thing*, pp. 27-49)

"The Fairy Godmother," *Saturday Evening Post*, 183 (Apr. 15, 1911) 8-10, 37-40. (*Nameless Thing*, pp. 50-94)

"The Broken Stirrup-Leather," *Saturday Evening Post*, 183 (June 3, 1911) 12-13, 65-66. (*Uncle Abner . . .*; retitled: "The Angel of the Lord.")

"The Nameless Thing," *Saturday Evening Post*, 184 (July 8, 1911) 5-6, 32-33. (*Nameless Thing*, pp. 30-154)

"The Wrong Hand," *Saturday Evening Post*, 184 (July 15, 1911) 5-6, 40. (*Uncle Abner . . .*)

"The House of the Dead Man," *Saturday Evening Post*, 184 (Sept. 30, 1911) 30-32. (*Uncle Abner . . .*)

"The Sport of Fortune," *Harper's Monthly*, 123 (Oct. 1911) 707-716. (*Name-

less Thing, pp. 156-181)
"The Pressure," *Metropolitan*, 35 (Feb. 1912) 9-11. (*Nameless Thing*, pp. 199-217)
"The Thief," *Popular Magazine*, 23 (Feb. 15, 1912: Month End Ed.) 107-113. (*Nameless Thing*, pp. 219-238)
"The Tenth Commandment," *Saturday Evening Post*, 184 (Mar. 2, 1912) 12-13, 62. (*Uncle Abner . . .*)
"The Riddle," *Metropolitan*, 36 (Sept. 1912) 16-18. (*Uncle Abner . . .*) Reprinted in *Illustrated Sunday Magazine* (Jan. 21, 1917).
"The Alien Corn," *Saturday Evening Post*, 185 (May 31, 1913) 7-10, 29-31. (*Monsieur Jonquelle . . .*)
"The Haunted Door," *Saturday Evening Post*, 186 (Aug. 30, 1913) 12-13, 41-42. (*Monsieur Jonquelle . . .*)
"Found in the Fog," *Saturday Evening Post*, 186 (Sept. 13, 1913) 6-7, 38. (*Monsieur Jonquelle . . .*)
"The Ruined Eye," *Saturday Evening Post*, 186 (Oct. 11, 1913) 6-7. (*Monsieur Jonquelle . . .*)
"An Act of God," *Metropolitan*, 39 (Dec. 1913) 28-29, 50-51. (*Uncle Abner . . .*) Reprinted in *Illustrated Sunday Magazine* (March 4, 1917).
"The Stolen Life," *Saturday Evening Post*, 186 (Jan. 17, 1914) 3-4, 39. (. . . *Blue Villa*)
"A Twilight Adventure," *Metropolitan*, 39 (Apr. 1914) 29, 46, 48, 50. (*Uncle Abner . . .*) Reprinted in *Illustrated Sunday Magazine* (Jan. 2, 1916) 9-10, 12-13.
"The Doomdorf Mystery," *Saturday Evening Post*, 187 (July 18, 1914) 9-10, 26. (*Uncle Abner . . .*)
"The Hidden Law," *Metropolitan*, 40 (Aug. 1914) 41-43. (*Uncle Abner. . .*) Reprinted in *Illustrated Sunday Magazine* (Oct. 8, 1916) 3-4, 14-15.
"The Miller of Ostend," *Saturday Evening Post*, 187 (Oct. 31, 1914) 3-4, 34. (. . . Blue Villa)
"The Man in the Green Hat," *Saturday Evening Post*, 187 (Feb. 27, 1915) 23-25. (*Sleuth . . .*)
"The Laughter of Allah," *Pictorial Review*, 16 (July 1915) 18-19, 58. (. . . *Blue Villa*)
"The Ally," *Saturday Evening Post*, 188 (July 10, 1915) 6-7, 45-46. (. . . *Blue Villa*)
"The Treasure Hunter," *Saturday Evening Post*, 188 (Aug. 14, 1915) 12-13, 53-54. (*Uncle Abner . . .*)
"The New Administration," *Saturday Evening Post*, 188 (Nov. 20, 1915) 16-17, 52-54. (. . . *Blue Villa*)
"The Spread Rails," *Hearst's Magazine*, 29 (Jan. 1916) 30-32, 49-50. (*Sleuth . . .*)
"The Age of Miracles," *Pictorial Review*, 17 (Feb. 1916) 16-17, 37. (*Uncle Abner . . .*; revised: see Uncle Abner Notes: No. 15)
"The Sleuth of the Stars," *Saturday Evening Post*, 188 (Mar. 4, 1916) 24-25, 81-82. (. . . *Blue Villa*)

"The Hole in the Mahogany Panel," *Ladies' Home Journal*, 33 (Apr. 1916) 23, 90-92. (*Sleuth . . .*)

"The Witness of the Earth," *Hearst's Magazine*, 29 (Apr. 1916) 258-260, 313-315. (*Sleuth . . .* ; retitled: "The Wrong Sign," and with added material which introduces the three Pendleton stories.)

"Some Girl," *Ladies Home Journal*, 33 (May 1916) 13, 78-80. (. . . *Blue Villa*; retitled: "The Girl from Galacia")

"Naboth's Vineyard," *Illustrated Sunday Magazine* (June 4, 1916) 7-8, 16-17. (*Uncle Abner . . .*)

"The Great Legend," *Saturday Evening Post*, 188 (June 10, 1916) 8-9, 34, 37. (. . . *Blue Villa*)

"The Adopted Daughter," *Red Book*, 27 (June 1916) 243-252. (*Uncle Abner . . .*) Reprinted in *Illustrated Sunday Magazine* (May 13, 1917) 3-4, 13-15.

"The Baron Starkheim," *Collier's Weekly*, 57 (Aug. 12, 1916) 5-7, 32, 34. (. . . *Blue Villa*)

"The Mystery at the Blue Villa," *Pictorial Review*, 18 (Oct. 1916) (. . . *Blue Villa*)

"The Pumpkin Coach," *Hearst's Magazine*, 30 (Oct. 1916) 218-220, 268-269. (*Sleuth . . .*)

"The Man from America," *Ladies' Home Journal*, 33 (Nov. 1916) 9-10. (*Sleuth . . .* ; retitled: "The Cambered Foot")

"American Horses," *Saturday Evening Post*, 189 (Dec. 23, 1916) 12-13, 34. (*Sleuth . . .*)

"The Witch of the Lecca," *Hearst's Magazine*, 31 (Jan. 1917) 13-15, 64. (. . . *Blue Villa*)

"Lord Winton's Adventure," *Hearst's Magazine*, 31 (June 1917) 447-449, 490-491. (. . . *Blue Villa*)

"The Straw Man," *Illustrated Sunday Magazine* (June 10, 1917). Reprinted here, original serial publication source undetermined. (*Uncle Abner . . .*)

"The Wage-earners," *Saturday Evening Post*, 190 (Sept. 1, 1917) 5, 81. (. . . *Blue Villa*)

"The Devil's Tools," *Illustrated Sunday Magazine* (Dec. 9, 1917). Reprinted here, original serial publication source undetermined. (*Uncle Abner . . .*)

"The Pacifist," *Saturday Evening Post*, 190 (Dec. 29, 1917) 3-4, 48. (. . . *Blue Villa*)

"A Satire of the Sea," *Hearst's Magazine*, 33 (Feb. 1918) 114-115, 150-151. (*Sleuth . . .*)

"The Girl with the Ruby," *Ladies' Home Journal*, 35 (Mar. 1918) 17, 86, 88. (*Monsieur Jonquelle . . .*)

"The Girl in the Villa," *Hearst's Magazine*, 33 (Apr. 1918) 270-272, 302-304. (. . . *Blue Villa*)

"Against the Sky of the Theater," *Ladies' Home Journal*, 35 (Aug. 1918) 11, 45, 47, 49. (. . . *Blue Villa*; retitled: "Behind the Stars")

"The Fortune Teller," *Red Book*, 31 (Aug. 1918) 75+ (*Sleuth* . . .)
"The Sunburned Lady," *Hearst's Magazine*, 34 (Dec. 1918) 416+ (. . . *Blue Villa*)
"Five Thousand Dollars Reward," *Saturday Evening Post*, 191 (Feb. 15, 1919) 12-13, 106. (*Sleuth* . . . ; retitled: "The Reward")
"The Thing on the Hearth," *Red Book*, 33 (May 1919) 23-25, 88. (*Sleuth* . . .)
"The Yellow Flower," *Pictorial Review*, 21 (Oct. 1919) 12-13, 48. (*Sleuth* . . .)
"The House by the Loch," *Hearst's Magazine*, 37 (May 1920) 35, 64, 66-68. (*Sleuth* . . .)
"The Lost Lady," *McCall's Magazine*, 47 (June 1920) 10-11, 52. (*Sleuth* . . .)
"The Expert Detective," *Everybody's*, 43 (Oct. 1920) 15-18. (*Walker* . . .)
"The Unknown Disciple," *Pictorial Review*, 22 (Dec. 1920) 14-15, 93-94. (Uncollected)
"The Man Who Threatened the World," *Hearst's Magazine*, 38 (Dec. 1920) 8-10, 62. (*Walker* . . . ; retitled: "The Menace")
"The Girl in the Picture," *Pictorial Review*, 22 (Jan. 1921) 26-27, 91. (*Walker* . . .)
"The 'Mysterious Stranger' Defense," *Everybody's*, 44 (June 1921) 32-36. (*Walker* . . .)
"The Mottled Butterfly," *Red Book*, 37 (Aug. 1921) 60-64, 98-100. (*Monsieur Jonquelle* . . .)
"The Last Adventure," *Hearst's Magazine*, 40 (Sept. 1921) 9-11, 67. (*Sleuth* . . .)
"The Man with Steel Fingers," *Red Book*, 37 (Sept. 1921) 34-36, 94, 96, 98, 100. (*Monsieur Jonquelle* . . .)
"The Triangular Hypothesis," *Red Book*, 37 (Oct. 1921) 82-85, 120, 122. (*Monsieur Jonquelle* . . .)
"The End of the Road," *Hearst's Magazine*, 40 (Nov. 1921) 37-39, 57. (*Sleuth* . . .)
"The Great Cipher," *Red Book*, 38 (Nov. 1921) 76+ (*Monsieur Jonquelle* . . .)
"The Inspiration," *Red Book*, 38 (Dec. 1921) 67+ (*Walker* . . .)
"The Mountain School-teacher," *Pictorial Review*, 23 (Part 1)(Dec. 1921) 10-11, 55-59; (Part 2) (Jan. 1922) 6-7, 52-55, 58. (*Mountain School-teacher*)
"The Woman on the Terrace," *Pictorial Review*, 23 (Mar. 1922) 8-9, 73. (*Monsieur Jonquelle* . . .)
"The Diamond," *Red Book*, 39 (June 1922) 93+ (*Walker* . . .)
"The Problem of the Five Marks," *Woman's Home Companion*, 49 (Nov. 1922) 27-28, 129-130. (*Monsieur Jonquelle* . . .)
"The Cuneiform Inscription," *Pictorial Review*, 24 (Dec. 1922) 26, 28, 76, 100-101. (*Bradmoor* . . .)
"The Laughing Woman," *Red Book*, 40 (Feb. 1923) 56-59, 124, 127. (Uncollected)

"The Hole in the Glass," *Woman's Home Companion*, 50 (July 1923) 23-24, 104. (*Bradmoor . . .*)

"The Phantom Woman," *Woman's Home Companion*, 50 (Aug. 1923) 21-22, 81. (*Bradmoor . . .*)

"The Great Symbol," *McCall's Magazine*, 51 (Dec. 1923) 7-9, 28, 34, 49. (*Walker . . .*; retitled: "The Symbol")

"The Blackmailer," *Harper's Bazaar*, 59 (Mar. 1924) 52+ (*Bradmoor . . .*)

"The Miracle," *Pictorial Review*, 26 (Dec. 1924) 6-8, 36, 72-73. (Uncollected)

"The Other Mary," *Ladies' Home Journal*, 42 (Dec. 1925) 8-9, 101, 103. (Uncollected)

"The Revolt of the Birds," *Ladies' Home Journal*, 43 (May 1926) 10-11, 110, 115-116, 119, 121; (June 1926) 28-29, 164-165, 168, 171. (*The Revolt of the Birds*)

"The Forgotten Witness," *American Magazine*, 102 (Sept. 1926) 20-23, 112-114. (*Silent Witness*; slightly revised and retitled: "The Cross-Examination")

"The Survivor," *American Magazine*, 102 (Oct. 1926) 10-13, 138. (*Silent Witness*)

"The Invisible Client," *American Magazine*, 102 (Dec. 1926) 20-23, 149-152. (*Silent Witness*)

"The Garden in Asia," *Collier's Weekly*, 79 (Jan. 29, 1927) 5-7; (Feb. 5, 1927) 15-16; (Feb. 12, 1927) 20-22. (*Bradmoor . . .*)

"The Heir at Law," *American Magazine*, 103 (Feb. 1927) 12-14, 120, 122, 124-125, 128. (*Silent Witness*)

"The Leading Case," *American Magazine*, 103 (June 1927) 20-23, 98, 100. (*Silent Witness*)

"The Stolen Treasure," *Ladies' Home Journal*, 44 (June 1927) 28-29, 181-182. (*Bradmoor . . .*)

"The Devil's Track," *Country Gentleman*, 92 (July 1927) 3-5, 40-41. (Uncollected)

"The God of the Hills," *Country Gentleman*, 92 (Sept. 1927) 6-7, 38, 40, 43. (Uncollected)

"The Dark Night," *Country Gentleman*, 92 (Nov. 1927) 6-7, 101-104. (Uncollected)

"Colonel Braxton Chooses a Client," *American Magazine*, 105 (Apr. 1928) 20-23, 86, 88, 90, 92, 95-96, 98, 100. (*Silent Witness*; retitled: "The Guardian")

"The Mystery at Hillhouse," *Country Gentleman*, 92 (May 1928) 3-5, 119-124, 127; (June 1928) 18-19, 100-105. (Uncollected)

"Colonel Braxton Hears the Silent Voices," *American Magazine*, 106 (Sept. 1928) 16-19, 145-146, 149-150. (*Silent Witness*; retitled: "The Mute Voices")

"The Vanished Man," *American Magazine*, 107 (Feb. 1929) 10-13, 112, 114, 116-117. (*Silent Witness*)

"The Mark on the Window," *American Magazine*, 107 (Apr. 1929) 50-53, 80, 145-147. (*Silent Witness*)

"The Dead Man's Shoes," *American Magazine*, 107 (June 1929) 30-33, 145-147. (*Silent Witness*)

"The Mystery at the Mill," *American Magazine*, 108 (Aug. 1929) 68, 70-71, 151-153. (Uncollected)

"The Guilty Man," *American Magazine*, 108 (Sept. 1929) 16-19, 152, 155, 156. (*Silent Witness*)

"The Witness in the Metal Box," *American Magazine*, 108 (Nov. 1929) 42-45, 134, 136, 138. (*Silent Witness*; retitled: "The Metal Box)

"The White Patch," *American Magazine*, 110 (Sept. 1930) 40-43, 100, 104. (*Silent Witness*)

3. Nonfiction in Serial Publications

"The Statement of Nathaniel Copeland, One Time a Circuit Judge of the Virginias," *The Law Student's Helper*, 6 (July 1898) 242-244. (Uncollected)

"The Plan of the Other Wise Man," *The West Virginia State Bar Association Report of the Thirteenth Annual Meeting*, (1899) 84-89. (Uncollected)

"Ex-Senator Henry G. Davis," *Harper's Weekly*, 48 (Aug. 6, 1904) 1206-1207. (Uncollected)

"Shall We Burn the Court House?" *Pearson's Magazine*, 21 (Apr. 1909) 345-352. (Uncollected)

"The Failure of the Jury System," *Pearson's Magazine*, 21 (June 1909) 643-650. (Uncollected)

"Mysteries of the Law: Fact and Fiction," *Saturday Evening Post*, 182 (May 14, 1910) 3-4, 66-68. (Uncollected)

"Mysteries of the Law: The Bit of Lint," *Saturday Evening Post*, 182 (May 28, 1910) 6-7, 40-42. (Uncollected)

"Mysteries of the Law: The Bit of Paper," *Saturday Evening Post*, 182 (June 18, 1910) 10-11, 45-46. (Uncollected)

"Mysteries of the Law: The Blue Stain," *Saturday Evening Post*, 183 (July 30, 1910) 10-11, 28-30. (Uncollected)

"Mysteries of the Law: The Inner Voice," *Saturday Evening Post*, 183 (Aug. 27, 1910) 10-11, 57-58. (Uncollected)

"Mysteries of the Law: The Nicks in the Knife Blade," *Saturday Evening Post*, 183 (Sept. 24, 1910) 28-30. Uncollected.

"Mysteries of the Law: The Will in the Teapot," *Saturday Evening Post*, 183 (Oct. 15, 1910) 24-26. (Uncollected)

"The Border Land of the Law," *Saturday Evening Post* 183 (May 20, 1911) 10-11, 46. (Uncollected)

"Extraordinary Cases: The Sealed Packet," *Saturday Evening Post*, 184 (Sept. 23, 1911) 10-11. (Uncollected)

"Extraordinary Cases: The Curious Ring," *Saturday Evening Post*, 184 (Oct. 7, 1911) 10-11. (Uncollected)

"Extraordinary Cases: Fabricated Defenses," *Saturday Evening Post*, 184 (Nov. 11, 1911) 16-17. (Uncollected)

"Extraordinary Cases: The Hidden Tenant," *Saturday Evening Post*, 184 (Dec. 30, 1911) 12-13. (Uncollected)

"Extraordinary Cases: The Gashed Finger," *Saturday Evening Post*, 184 (Jan. 13, 1912) 24-26. (Uncollected)

"The Layman and the Law," *Saturday Evening Post*, 184 (Feb. 3, 1912) 7, 61-62. (Uncollected)

"The Citizen in Court," *Saturday Evening Post*, 184 (Mar. 16, 1912) 14, 73-74. (Uncollected)

"Reforms in Legal Procedure," *Saturday Evening Post*, 184 (Apr. 13, 1912) 20-21, 45. (Uncollected)

"Extraordinary Cases: The Fragments of Plaster," *Saturday Evening Post*, 184 (Apr. 20, 1912) 21-22, 72. (Uncollected)

"Science and the Forger," *Saturday Evening Post*, 184 (May 18, 1912) 9, 61-62. (*Man Hunters*)

"Extraordinary Cases: The Red Peril," *Saturday Evening Post*, 184 (June 1, 1912) 18-19, 57-58. (*Man Hunters*)

"Are We Governed by the Supreme Court," *Saturday Evening Post*, 185 (Aug. 10, 1912) 9-10, 46. (Uncollected)

"Recall of Judicial Decisions," *Saturday Evening Post*, 185 (Aug. 31, 1912) 3-4. (Uncollected)

"Courts and their Critics," *Saturday Evening Post*, 185 (Sept. 21, 1912) 18, 61. (Uncollected)

"Justice and the Justice," *Saturday Evening Post*, 185 (Oct. 12, 1912) 33-34. (Uncollected)

"The Bench and the People," *Saturday Evening Post*, 185 (Oct. 19, 1912) 22, 40-41. (Uncollected)

"The Immorality of Chance," *Saturday Evening Post*, 185 (Nov. 16, 1912) 11-12, 50. (Uncollected)

"The Immortal Millions," *Saturday Evening Post*, 185 (June 14, 1913) 14-15, 33. (Uncollected)

"The Lesson of the Roosevelt Trial," *Saturday Evening Post*, 186 (July 12, 1913) 6, 33-34. (Uncollected)

"Government by Magic," *Saturday Evening Post*, 186 (Aug. 2, 1913) 11, 32-33. (Uncollected)

"Humanizing the Law," *Saturday Evening Post*, 186 (Dec. 15, 1913) 9-10, 32. (Uncollected)

"Keeping Out of Court," *Saturday Evening Post*, 186 (Jan. 31, 1914) 6, 38. (Uncollected)

"What is the Monroe Doctrine?" *Saturday Evening Post*, 186 (Apr. 11, 1914) 8-9, 57. (Uncollected)

"The Jury and the Judges," *Saturday Evening Post*, 186 (Apr. 18, 1914) 19, 65-66. (Uncollected)

"Our Continental Policy," *Saturday Evening Post*, 186 (June 6, 1914) 19-20, 71. (Uncollected)

"Business at Judicial Discretion," *Saturday Evening Post*, 186 (June 20, 1914) 8-9, 50. (Uncollected)

"Trial by Jury," *Saturday Evening Post*, 187 (Aug. 15, 1914) 17-18. (Uncollected)

"The Blight," *Saturday Evening Post*, 187 (Dec. 26, 1914) 21, 25-26. (Reprinted in: *Backgrounds of Book Reviewing*, edited by Herbert S. Mallory. Ann Arbor, Michigan: G. Wahr, 1923)

"The Mystery Story," *Saturday Evening Post*, 187 (Feb. 27, 1915) 21-23. (Uncollected)

"The Invisible Army," *Saturday Evening Post*, 187 (Apr. 10, 1915) 3-5. (Uncollected)

"Secret Ciphers," *Saturday Evening Post*, 187 (May 8, 1915) 8-9, 69. (*Man Hunters*)

"Spy Methods in Europe," *Saturday Evening Post*, 187 (May 15, 1915) 5, 32-34. (Uncollected)

"The Great Terror," *Saturday Evening Post*, 187 (June 12, 1915) 17-18, 30-31. (Uncollected)

"The Rule-Ridden Game," *Saturday Evening Post*, 188 (Dec. 18, 1915) 23, 26-27. (Uncollected)

"The Man Hunters: Scotland Yard," *Saturday Evening Post*, 188 (Jan. 22, 1916) 6-7, 48. (*Man Hunters*)

"The Man Hunters: The Detective Department of Paris," *Saturday Evening Post*, 188 (Jan. 29, 1916) 14-15, 43-44. (*Man Hunters*)

"The Man Hunters: The Dragnet," *Saturday Evening Post*, 188 (Feb. 19, 1916) 7-8, 73-74. (*Man Hunters*)

"The Man Hunters: German Detective Methods," *Saturday Evening Post*, 188 (Mar. 11, 1916) 20-21, 69-70. (*Man Hunters*)

"The Man Hunters: American Instances," *Saturday Evening Post*, 188 (Mar. 18, 1916) 19-20, 44-45. (*Man Hunters*)

"The Man Hunters: Italian Criminal Orders," *Saturday Evening Post*, 188 (Apr. 22, 1916) 12-13, 47. (*Man Hunters*)

"The Man Hunters: The Austrian University System," *Saturday Evening Post*, 188 (May 6, 1916) 26-27, 70. (*Man Hunters*)

"The Man Hunters: The Swiss Method of Preserving Evidence," *Saturday Evening Post*, 188 (June 24, 1916) 25-26, 29-30. (*Man Hunters*)

"Codes and Signs of the Underworld," *Saturday Evening Post*, 189 (Aug. 16, 1916) 7, 61-62. (*Man Hunters*)

"Going Through the Bank," *Saturday Evening Post*, 189 (Sept. 23, 1916) 25-26. (*Man Hunters*)

"The Study of Footprints: The Bare Foot," *Saturday Evening Post*, 189 (Feb. 3, 1917) 14-15, 73. (*Man Hunters*)

"The Study of Footprints: The Shod Foot," *Saturday Evening Post*, 189 (Feb. 17, 1917) 12-13, 65. (*Man Hunters*)

"Nick Carter, Realist," *Saturday Evening Post*, 189 (Mar. 3, 1917) 14-15, 59. (Uncollected)

"Spy Stories," *Saturday Evening Post*, 189 (Mar. 10, 1917) 24-25, 106. (Uncollected)

"Alien Enemies," *Saturday Evening Post*, 189 (Mar. 17, 1917) 24-25, 71.

(Uncollected)
"Protecting America from Espionage," *Saturday Evening Post*. 189 (Mar. 24. 1917) 14-15, 50. (Uncollected)
"Mobilizing the Whole Nation," *Saturday Evening Post*. 189 (Apr. 14. 1917) 8, 106. (Uncollected)
" 'The Old Rounder,' " *Saturday Evening Post*. 190 (Sept. 1. 1917) 11. 78, 81-82. (*Man Hunters*)
"German War Ciphers," *Everybody's*. 38 (June 1918) 28-34. (Uncollected)
"John W. Davis," *Review of Reviews, America*. 70 (Aug. 1924) 149-156. (Uncollected)

INDEX OF TITLES

"Act of God, An," 132-133, 201, 248.
"Adopted Daughter, The," 137, 249.
"Adventure of St. Valentine's Night, An," 84, 247.
"After He Was Dead," 103, 247.
"Against the Sky of the Theater," See: "Behind the Stars."
"Age of Miracles, The," 136-137, 248.
"Alien Corn, The," 162, 163, 248.
"Alien Enemies," 254.
"Ally, The," 150, 152, 248.
"American Horses," 158, 249.
"Angel of the Lord, The," 36, 119, 126-128, 247.
"Animus Furandi, The," 75.
"Are We Governed by the Supreme Court?" 203, 253.
"Baron Starkheim, The," 151, 249.
"Behind the Stars," 151-152, 249.
"Bench and the People, The," 205, 253.
"Blackmailer, The," 219, 251.
"Blight, The," 41, 113-114, 211, 253.
"Blücher's March," 164.
"Border Land of the Law, The," 199-200, 252.
Bradmoor Murder: The: Including the Remarkable Deductions of Sir Henry Marquis of Scotland Yard, 59, 217-222, 246.
"Bradmoor Murder, The," (story title) 218-219, 221.
"Broken Stirrup-Leather, The," See: "Angel of the Lord, The"
"Burgoyne-Hayes Dinner, The," 82, 247.
"Business at Judicial Discretion," 210, 253.
"Cambered Foot, The," 156, 249.
"Citizen in Court, The," 202, 253.
Clients of Randolph Mason, The, See: *Man of Last Resort, The*
"Codes and Signs of the Underworld," 254.
"Colonel Braxton Chooses a Client," See: "Guardian, The"
"Colonel Braxton Hears the Silent Voices," See: "Mute Voices, The"
"Concealed Path, The," 140-141.
"Copper Bonds, The," 82, 247.
"Corpus Delicti, The," 23, 38, 54, 67-72, 96, 202.
Corrector of Destinies The: Being Tales of Randolph Mason as Related by His Private Secretary, Courtlandt Parks, 31-32, 33, 55-56, 80-86, 231, 246.
"Courts and Their Critics," 204, 253.
"Critique of Monsieur Poe, A," 36, 106, 232, 247.
"Cross-Examination, The," 225, 251.
"Cuniform Inscription, The," 219, 250.
"Danseuse, The," 84, 247.

"Dark Night, The," 142, 251.
"Dead Man's Shoes, The," 224, 251.
"Devil's Tools, The," 124, 130-131, 249.
"Devil's Track, The," 61, 141-142, 251.
"Diamond, The," 167, 170, 170-171, 250.
"District-Attorney, The," 82, 247.
"Doomdorf Mystery, The," 38, 44, 133, 134-136, 248.
Dwellers in the Hills, 12, 25-26, 29, 31, 73, 78, 79, 81, 87-94, 100, 107, 117-119, 127, 129, 131, 141, 143, 231, 246.
"Edge of the Shadow, The," 138-140.
"End of the Road, The," 157-158, 250.
"Error of William van Broom, The," 73-74.
"Expert Detective, The," 170, 171, 250.
"Ex-Senator Henry G. Davis," 31, 197, 252.
"Extraordinary Cases: Fabricated Defenses," 201, 252.
"Extraordinary Cases: The Curious King," 252.
"Extraordinary Cases: The Fragments of Plaster," 202-203, 253.
"Extraordinary Cases: The Gashed Finger," 201, 252.
"Extraordinary Cases: The Hidden Tenant," 201, 252.
"Extraordinary Cases: The Red Peril, 203, 253.
"Extraordinary Cases: The Sealed Packet," 200-201, 252.
"Failure of the Jury System, The," 197, 252.
"Fairy Godmother, The," 103, 159, 247.
"Five Thousand Dollars Reward," See: "Reward, The"
"Forgotten Witness, The," See: "Cross-Examination, The"
"Fortune Teller, The," 157, 250.
"Found in the Fog," 162, 163, 248.
Garden in Asia, The, See: *Bradmoor Murder, The*
"Garden in Asia, The," (story title) 57, 218, 221, 251.
"German War Ciphers," 255.
Gilded Chair, The, 33-34, 40, 81, 94-101, 107, 119-120, 139, 231, 246.
"Girl from Galacia, The," 148-149, 249.
"Girl in the Picture, The," 167, 170, 172, 250.
"Girl in the Villa, The," 150, 249.
"Girl with the Ruby, The," 166, 249.
"God of the Hills, The," 142, 251.
"Going Through the Bank," 254.
"Goth, The," 105-106.
"Government by Magic," 207, 253.
"Governor's Machine, The," 77.
"Grazier, The," 78-79.
"Great Cipher, The," 53, 162-163, 250.
"Great Legend, The," 43, 148, 152, 249.
"Great Symbol, The," See: "Symbol, The"
"Great Terror, The," 254.
"Guardian, The," 225, 251.

"Guilty Man, The," 225-226, 251.
"Haunted Door, The," 162, 164, 248.
"Heir at Law, The," 225, 251.
"Hidden Law, The," 131-132, 248.
"Hole in the Glass, The," 219-220, 250.
"Hole in the Mahogany Panel, The," 157, 249.
"House by the Loch, The," 160-161, 250.
"House of the Dead Man, The," 128-129, 247.
"Humanizing the Law," 208, 253.
"Immorality of Chance, The," 205, 253.
"Immortal Millions, The," 205-206, 253.
"Inspiration, The," 167, 170, 171-172, 250.
"Interrupted Exile, The," 82-83, 247.
"Intriguer, The," 84-85, 247.
"Invisible Army, The," 254.
"Invisible Client, The," 224, 251.
"John W. Davis," 54, 160, 214, 255.
"Jury and the Judges, The," 209, 253.
"Justice and the Justice," 205, 253.
"Keeping Out of Court," 208-209, 253.
"Last Adventure, The," 158, 250.
"Last Check, The," 83, 247.
"Laughing Woman, The," 250.
"Laughter of Allah, The," 43, 148, 152, 248.
"Layman and the Law, The," 202, 252.
"Leading Case, The," 227, 251.
"Lesson of the Roosevelt Trial, The," 206-207, 253.
"Life Tenant, The," 83, 247.
"Locked Bag, The," 105-106, 247.
"Lord Winton's Adventure," 150, 152, 249.
"Lost Lady, The," 156, 250.
"Madame Versay," 82, 246.
"Man from America, The," See: "Cambered Foot, The"
Man Hunters, The, 42, 56, 195, 203, 211, 212-213, 246.
"Man Hunters, The: American Instances," 254.
"Man Hunters, The: German Detective Methods," 254.
"Man Hunters, The: Italian Criminal Orders," 254.
"Man Hunters, The: Scotland Yard," 212, 254.
"Man Hunters, The: The Austrian University System," 254.
"Man Hunters, The: The Detective Department of Paris," 212, 254.
"Man Hunters, The: The Dragnet," 254.
"Man Hunters, The: The Swiss Method of Preserving Evidence," 254.
"Man in the Green Hat, The," 156-157, 248.
Man of Last Resort, The, or, The Clients of Randolph Mason, 23, 75-80, 246.
"Man Who Threatened the World, The," See: "Menace, The"
"Man with Steel Fingers, The," 165, 250.

"Mark on the Window, The," 226, 251.
"Marriage Contract, The," 85-86, 216, 247.
"Men of the Jimmy, The," 74.
"Menace, The," 170, 173, 250.
"Metal Box, The," 223-224, 252.
"Miller of Ostend, The," 43, 59, 149, 152, 248.
"Miracle, The," 251.
"Missing Link, The," 216.
"Mobilizing the Whole Nation," 214, 254.
Monsieur Jonquelle, Prefect of Police of Paris, 37-38, 53, 161-166, 246.
"Mottled Butterfly, The," 165-166, 250.
Mountain School-Teacher, The, 45-47, 59-60, 100, 175-186, 233, 246.
"Mountain School-Teacher, The," (serial publication) 45, 47, 250.
"Mrs. Van Bartan," 77-78.
"Mute Voices, The," 226-227, 251.
"My Friend at Bridge," 81-82, 246.
"Mysteries of the Law: Fact and Fiction," 198, 252.
"Mysteries of the Law: The Bit of Lint," 252.
"Mysteries of the Law: The Bit of Paper," 252.
"Mysteries of the Law: The Blue Stain," 252.
"Mysteries of the Law: The Inner Voice," 252.
"Mysteries of the Law: The Nicks in the Knife Blade," 198, 252.
"Mysteries of the Law: The Will in the Teapot," 198-199, 252.
"Mysterious Stranger Defense, The," 170, 171, 250.
"Mystery at Hillhouse, The," 142-144, 251.
Mystery at the Blue Villa, The, 43, 145-152, 246.
"Mystery at the Blue Villa, The," (story title) 147, 249.
"Mystery at the Mill, The," 216, 228, 251.
"Mystery of Chance, The," 140.
"Mystery Story, The," 39, 41, 113, 114-115, 156, 211, 253.
"Naboth's Vineyard," 133-134, 199, 249.
Nameless Thing, The, 36, 101-108, 125, 146, 150, 159, 231-232, 246.
"Nameless Thing, The," (story title) 104, 247.
"New Administration, The," 147-148, 248.
"No Defense," 105, 247.
"Nick Carter, Realist," 51-52, 213, 254.
" 'Old Rounder, The,' " 254.
"Once in Jeopardy," 78.
"Other Mary, The," 216, 251.
"Our Continental Policy," 209-210, 253.
"Pacifist, The," 149, 249.
"Pennsylvania Pirate, The," 83-84, 247.
"Phantom Woman, The," 220, 250.
"Plan of Malcolm Van Staak, The," 215, 246.
"Plan of the Other Wise Man, The," 252.
"Pressure, The," 105, 248.

"Problem of the Five Marks, The," 164-165, 250.
"Protecting America from Espionage," 254.
"Pumpkin Coach, The," 159, 249.
Randolph Mason: the Clients, See: *Man of Last Resort, The*
Randolph Mason, Corrector of Destinies, See: *Corrector of Destinies, The*
Randolph Mason: the Strange Schemes, See: *Strange Schemes of Randolph Mason, The*
"Recall of Judical Decisions," 203-204, 253.
"Reforms in Legal Procedure," 202, 253.
Revolt of the Birds, The, 57-58, 186-194, 217-218, 233, 246.
"Revolt of the Birds, The," (serial publication) 251.
"Reward, The," 44, 45, 155, 167, 250.
"Riddle, The," 132, 248.
"Ruined Eye, The," 162, 163-164, 248.
"Rule Against Carper, The," 79.
"Rule-Ridden Game, The," 212, 254.
"Satire of the Sea, A," 160, 249.
"Science and the Forger," 203, 253.
"Secret Ciphers," 254.
"Shall We Burn the Court House?" 197, 252.
"Sheriff of Gullmore, The," 74-75.
Silent Witness, The, 59, 75, 216, 222-228, 246.
Sleuth of St. James's Square, The, 44-45, 152-161, 162, 246.
"Sleuth of the Stars, The," 149, 248.
"Some Girl," See: "Girl from Galacia, The"
"Sport of Fortune, The," 104-105, 160, 247.
"Spread Rails, The" 158-159, 248.
"Spy Methods in Europe," 254.
"Spy Stories," 254.
"Statement of Nathaniel Copeland, One Time a Circuit Judge of the Virginias, The," 252.
"Stolen Life, The," 148, 151, 248.
"Stolen Treasure, The," 220-221, 251.
Strange Schemes of Randolph Mason, The, 23, 31, 32, 64-75, 80, 246.
"Straw Man, The," 122, 138, 249.
"Study of Footprints, The: The Bare Foot," 254.
"Study of Footprints, The: The Shod Foot," 254.
"Sunburned Lady, The," 151, 250.
"Survivor, The," 224-225, 251.
"Symbol, The," 170, 173-174, 251.
"Test Case, A," 215, 246.
"Tenth Commandment, The," 41-42, 129-130, 248.
"Thief, The," 105, 248.
"Thing on the Hearth, The," 154-155, 250.
"Treasure Hunter, The," 136, 248.
"Trial by Jury," 210-211, 253.

"Triangular Hypothesis, The," 164, 250.
"Trivial Incident, The," 35, 103-104, 247.
"Twilight Adventure, A," 131, 248.
"Two Plungers of Manhattan," 72-73.
Uncle Abner, Master of Mysteries, 36-37, 38, 42-43, 100, 109-144, 146, 161-162, 186, 199, 201, 205, 211, 216, 221-222, 222-223, 232, 246.
"Unknown Disciple, The," 250.
"Vanished Man, The," 226, 251.
"Ventures of Mr. Clayvarden, The," 215, 246.
"Virgin of the Mountain, The," 84, 247.
"Wage-earners, The," 150-151, 249.
Walker of the Secret Service, 55, 155, 166-174, 198, 246.
"What is the Monroe Doctrine?" 209, 253.
"White Patch, The," 227-228, 252.
"Witch of the Lecca, The," 149, 249.
"Witness in the Metal Box, The," See: "Metal Box, The"
"Witness of the Earth, The," See: "Wrong Sign, The"
"Woman on the Terrace, The," 164, 250.
"Woodford's Partner," 73.
"Wrong Hand, The," 128-129, 247.
"Wrong Sign, The," 157, 249.
"Yellow Flower, The," 159-160, 250.